BABY SURPRISE IN COSTA RICA

SOPHIE PEMBROKE

OFF-LIMITS FLING WITH THE BILLIONAIRE

SUZANNE MERCHANT

MILLS & BOON

First published in Great Britain 2023
by Mills & Boon, an imprint of HarperCollins*Publishers* Ltd,
1 London Bridge Street, London, SE1 9GF

www.harpercollins.co.uk

HarperCollins*Publishers*, Macken House, 39/40 Mayor Street Upper, Dublin 1, D01 C9W8, Ireland

Baby Surprise in Costa Rica © 2023 Sophie Pembroke

Off-Limits Fling with the Billionaire © 2023 Suzanne Merchant

ISBN: 978-0-263-30642-2

04/23

BABY SURPRISE IN COSTA RICA

SOPHIE PEMBROKE

MILLS & BOON

To everyone who needs a holiday right now…

CHAPTER ONE

JENNY BOUCHARD STEPPED out of the four-by-four that had delivered her from the airport and felt the heat—and the fear—hit her as the air-conditioned bubble of denial the car had provided so far fell away.

I'm really doing this.

I must be losing my mind.

Around her, the Costa Rican jungle seemed alive with sounds—the breeze through the trees making the leaves whisper, the chirping of insects and the calls of unfamiliar birds echoing. If she closed her eyes, she might still be on the plane, or even back in her LA apartment, listening to her rainforest playlist as she tried to sleep.

But she didn't close her eyes. Instead, she scanned her surroundings for the place she'd travelled thousands of miles to visit—and the man she'd come here to find.

'This does *not* look right,' she murmured to herself as she turned slowly, searching for signs of the luxury treehouse resort she'd expected to be there.

Nothing.

Why was she even surprised? It wasn't as if she didn't already know that men were all promises and no delivery. Except he hadn't promised *her* a luxury treehouse resort—he'd promised his investors. And in her experience men tended to be far more loyal to money than to women.

Jenny pulled her light, sleeveless blouse away from her already sticky skin and considered her options. Just like she'd been doing for the last month or more—ever since the third pregnancy test returned the same answer as the first two: *pregnant.*

First off, she needed more information. She turned back to the airport transfer car to ask the driver if he was *sure* this was the right place, but the four-by-four was already pulling away, back onto the dusty road out of there, towards the city. Eyes widening, she chased it for a few steps, but the driver never looked back, or even checked his mirrors.

At least he'd left her suitcase behind, leaning neatly against the nearest tree. She peered at the trunk, then strained her neck to stare up at the leaf canopy, trying to figure out what sort of tree it was. She'd done some research on this area of Costa Rica, this particular stretch of tropical rainforest that ran along the Caribbean coast, learning about the biodiversity of the area, the transport options, the cuisine—she didn't like to travel unprepared.

Except, it seemed, for the fact that the luxurious treehouse resort she'd come to visit didn't exist.

The website had been stunning—full of promises of a remote retreat getaway location, with yoga and mindfulness sessions, trips to nearby waterfalls or zip lines through the rainforest, local restaurants down by the beachfront, snorkelling, rainforest safaris…

And luxury treehouse accommodation. That had been

a definite—a place to stay. She wouldn't have come otherwise.

Of course she hadn't been able to actually book a room on the website. But she hadn't thought she'd need to.

Josh and Winter had said that Liam was down in Costa Rica, at his latest resort property, and shown her the website. And she knew, from the time she'd spent in Iceland with Liam at his *last* new resort, that he always reserved a suite of rooms for his personal use. So she'd figured she'd stay with him—especially since, generous as she was, Winter didn't pay her enough in her role as PA to afford Liam's resort prices anyway.

But now there was no sign of Liam. And no sign of the treehouses.

This is what people do. They let you down.

How had she forgotten that, even for a moment?

Perhaps she could blame pregnancy brain.

She pulled her cell phone from her pocket and was just trying to decide who she could call when she heard a laugh from further down the track that led deeper into the rainforest. A familiar laugh, rising above the bird cries and the insects and the buzz of humidity that filled her ears. A laugh she'd last heard low in her ear as Liam teased her to the brink in his private hot spring lagoon...

Maybe she wasn't in the wrong place after all.

Grabbing her suitcase, Jenny set off further down the track, looking for any sign of the structures and promises the website had given her. She didn't spot anything to reassure her—no *Welcome to Paradise* signs or a nice, friendly reception hut or anything. But she heard more voices—shouts and calls and laughs—so she pushed on anyway.

One last turn and she entered a clearing in the trees, abuzz with activity. Building materials—mostly wood of varying sorts, from what she could tell, and ropes—were neatly piled around the space, and a group of men had gathered at the far side of the clearing, all too focused on something going on in a large, sturdy tree to notice her.

'Okay, let's do this!' She recognised Liam's voice as his words rang out, but she still couldn't see him. 'On three!'

The countdown echoed through the trees and suddenly a smaller group pulled on a rope Jenny hadn't spotted, and something flew up from the ground towards the tree canopy. She jumped back, even though she was already a safe distance away, a smile stretching her lips as she realised what it was.

A bridge, made of rope and slats of wood, leading from one treetop to another. She squinted up into the canopy again and saw the base of a treehouse in the first tree, obviously still a work in progress.

The website hadn't lied, then. It had just been a little…premature.

This place was going to be amazing, she realised with delight. Totally different to the Ice House Hotel in Iceland, but spectacular in its own way. She could see why Liam was apparently so excited about it.

'Secure!' Liam yelled. He must be up in the tree, Jenny realised. 'Coming down!'

And suddenly all the fear that had been mounting in

her gut since she'd landed in Costa Rica came back with a vengeance.

Not finding Liam here in the rainforest would have been bad, sure. But right now she wasn't convinced that finding him was going to be any better.

Gripping the handle of her suitcase tightly with sweaty palms, she forced herself to focus. She was here to do a job and get out. A courtesy visit, that was all this was. She knew Liam—well, no, that was a lie. But she knew enough to know that he wasn't looking for a family, or anything resembling a relationship right now. Of course, she hadn't been either. That much they'd made clear to each other before they began their…rendezvous in Iceland.

She was under no impression that her news was going to be welcomed. But that didn't mean she wasn't under a moral obligation to share it.

She needed to tell Liam about the baby, so that she could plan her future and move on. Until she'd told him, everything was in flux. Uncertain. And Jenny hated not knowing, not being in control of what happened next, more than anything.

She'd given up her power over her own future once before, trusted a man she thought loved her to take care of things, and it had almost ruined her life. She had absolutely no intention of doing it ever again.

Jenny thought of the small silk pouch at the bottom of the rucksack she'd used for hand luggage, and her grandmother's battered and worn Tarot cards inside it. Grandma had believed they could tell the path of a person's life if read correctly—something Jenny had never really bought into. They'd never been able to tell *her* future, or she'd have been better prepared for this eventuality, and the long series of personal disasters and failings that had led her here.

But she *did* believe Grandma when she'd told her the cards could explain her *present*. Because the pictures they held were all stories, and they could be read any way the dealer wanted. When she looked at the cards, she picked out the issues and the images that were already on her mind, and they helped her find clarity of thought.

That wasn't why she kept the cards, of course. She kept them because they were the only thing she had left of her Grandma, of a family that had loved her, once upon a time.

But it was why she'd pulled them out on the plane and shuffled them, feeling their worn edges soft under her fingers, and turned over the first three cards onto the fold-down table of the seat in front.

Past, present and future, Grandma would have said, but Jenny knew they were all here, right now. Hindsight, experience and fear might be better words. Hope, if she was feeling really optimistic.

Which she wasn't, currently.

The cards hadn't told her anything she didn't already know.

First, she'd pulled Judgement for the past. She'd drawn that one for Winter before they went to Iceland too, she remembered—told her it was the card of consequences and reckoning, but also of rebirth and metamorphosis.

That it asked a person if they were ready to face their past and move on to their future.

She let her hand rest against her stomach. It wasn't as if she had much say in whether she was ready or not, was it?

The last card, the future card, had been the Wheel of Fortune. A reminder of the unpredictability of life, and that everything changes. Again, not a new concept.

And between them both, in her present position, had been the Knight of Wands. The card her Grandma had whispered was the *naughtiest* card in the Tarot. Jenny hadn't understood why when she was younger. It was only when she matured that she realised how damn sexy it really was. The Knight of Wands was the card of undeniable chemistry, inexplicable attraction—of the pull of that one person you knew you should stay away from but just couldn't resist...

Basically, everything Liam had been for her since she'd met him in Iceland nearly three months ago.

And any moment now she'd be seeing him again.

As she watched, a figure swung his way down from the tree where the rope bridge had been secured, barely even using the ladder leaning against it to descend. She recognised his body before his face; with his shirt off, the planes of his back and then his chest as he turned were so familiar from those days in Iceland...if rather more tanned than she remembered. Sweat ran in rivulets through the dust that covered his body, and Jenny felt her mouth turn dry and knew it had nothing to do with the Costa Rican heat.

She swallowed and raised her gaze, taking in his dark

hair, dulled by sawdust, and his bright blue eyes—and the moment he spotted her standing across the clearing.

Here we go...

Liam Delaney stared across the clearing in the Costa Rican rainforest and tried to figure out if he was hallucinating. He'd been working hard, these past few weeks, and now it seemed like his dreaming self had taken over his waking one.

That, or Jenny Bouchard—the one-week fling he hadn't quite managed to get out of his head, or his dreams—had sought him out for a replay of their time together in Iceland.

He took in her blonde hair, caught up in a high ponytail that left her neck bare as it cascaded down her back, the sunglasses perched on her nose in place of her usual black-framed specs, and the sleeveless blouse and khaki shorts she wore with her trainers.

She looked real. And in his dreams she was usually wearing a lot less. Smiling more, too.

It was really her.

Liam brushed aside the questions from the crew about what was next. The day was getting away from them anyway, and they all deserved an early finish. The cheer that went up when he told them they were done for the day confirmed his hunch that they wouldn't mind.

He left them clearing up, ready for tomorrow, and crossed to where Jenny stood, watching him.

'You know, when Josh told me you were here getting your next resort hotel ready to open, I was kind of expecting the place to at least be built already,' she said, folding her arms over her chest as he got closer.

'I like to be hands-on from the very start.' He stopped in front of her, letting his gaze roam over the curve of her neck, the swell of her breasts under that thin blouse. All the places he'd only had his memory to remind him of until now.

'I remember.' Her voice lowered with the words, and Liam knew he wasn't imagining the flash of heat in her eyes.

It had been the same the day they'd met in Iceland. She'd somehow manoeuvred him into carrying her bags and showing her the suite she was sharing with Winter, and he'd known immediately that he was going to be doing whatever this woman wanted for the whole week she was staying at his hotel. The connection, the chemistry between them, had been instantaneous, and undeniable.

And when he'd met her gaze as he was leaving the room shortly after, he'd known from the unsettled expression on her face that she'd felt it too—and was as surprised by it as he was.

Now she'd surprised him again, showing up here unannounced. God, he hoped this wasn't some sort of 'can't live without you' desperation thing. They'd both been very clear about what their week in Iceland meant—a good time and nothing more.

He wasn't in the market for anything more.

His concern must have shown on his face, because Jenny gave him a sly smile and said, 'How worried are you right now that I'm here to pronounce undying love and propose to you?'

'Little bit,' he admitted, and she laughed.

It was that sound that put his mind at rest most of all. Jenny had the filthiest laugh of any woman he'd ever met, and he loved it. Loved the promise in it—as well as the memories it brought back.

She wouldn't laugh like that if she was there for anything more than a booty call. Would she?

'So, what brings you to my neck of the rainforest?' he asked, as casually as he could. 'I mean, if it's not your sudden inability to live without me?'

'I had a week off.' She shrugged, and Liam found himself suddenly distracted by the movement of that thin blouse over her breasts. 'And Josh mentioned your next project was somewhere hot for a change, so I thought... well. I'm betting you can imagine what I thought.'

He studied her face and saw that same warmth in her smile, that promise behind it, but there was something in her eyes that was less familiar. She was holding something back.

Was she really here to see him, or to avoid something else?

Not my problem.

He wasn't her boyfriend, or her brother—thank God. He was just a guy she'd known for a week and had a lot of fantastic sex with. Well, he'd thought it was fantastic, and if her showing up here was a sign of anything, surely it was that he was right about that?

Whatever her problems were, he couldn't fix them. But

he *could* give her a fun week off—and himself a well-deserved break at the same time. The crew could manage without him for a few days, he was sure.

And maybe a few more days with Jenny would be enough to get her out of his system at last, and stop him dreaming about her every bloody night. They just hadn't let their fling run its full course, that was all, before she'd had to leave to go back to LA with Winter and Josh. And even when they'd been together they'd been distracted, dealing with her boss and his best friend rekindling their long dead marriage—and helping out a little, behind the scenes.

But Winter and Josh weren't there now. It was just the two of them, in the middle of a rainforest. What kind of an idiot would he have to be to not take advantage of the situation she'd given him?

'Well, as you've noticed, the resort isn't actually completed yet—or open to the public,' he said. 'But lucky for you, there is *one* finished treehouse here for you to stay in, if you'd like.'

He leaned in closer and whispered the word in her ear. '*Mine.*'

CHAPTER TWO

LIAM'S PERSONAL TREEHOUSE was set a bit further back into the rainforest. Jenny assumed this was so that, even when the whole resort complex was complete, he'd still have some privacy—something she'd noticed in Iceland mattered a great deal to him.

Perhaps she should have considered that before descending on him in the middle of nowhere with no warning. But if she'd told him she was coming…he might have told her not to. And the news she had to share with him, well, it didn't feel like something she could do over the phone.

Or at all, right now. Her courage had faded the moment she saw that cautious smile on his lips and she'd realised he was worried she was there for *commitment*.

Which she wasn't. At least, not for herself.

As she trailed after him along the track towards his treehouse, Jenny tore her attention away from the muscles in his bare back, and his ass in those low-riding shorts, and forced herself to focus on what she was there to do.

Tell Liam that he was going to be a father and ask if he wanted to be involved at all in the child's life.

She was prepared for him to say no. Hell, she was expecting it. Liam had never given her any indication that he wanted anything more from her than a few nights of great sex—and that was all she had wanted too.

But it seemed the universe had other ideas. And now they had to deal with them.

The only question was how. She knew she had to give Liam a chance to be involved but, honestly, she was banking on his saying no. If he said no, she could set out to figure out her own future alone, and have it under her control.

Far better for him to say no now, and never meet their child, than to decide to bail later, once the kid was already attached.

Jenny knew how that felt. Her own family had abandoned her just when she needed them the most, because she didn't live up to their ideals of what a daughter should be. There was no way in hell she was putting her own child through that.

If Liam said yes, he wanted to be part of the kid's life, then changed his mind later...

'Here we are.' Liam paused at the foot of a broad, hefty-based tree. It took Jenny a moment to spot the staircase running around the outside of it, and for a second it looked like he'd placed his foot on a tree root and just intended to climb. 'It's perfectly safe, I assure you.'

'It's beautiful.' Jenny stepped back to take in the full effect, now she knew that it was there.

The spiralling stairs were made of wood, like everything else she'd seen so far, but the narrow banister that was in place to protect people walking up them was made from twisted tree roots and rope, intertwined with live foliage to give more cover. It was only when she tilted her head right back and looked up that she could see the base of a treehouse—a larger one than the structures being built in the clearing—stretching back between this tree and several others behind it.

If she hadn't been looking, she might have continued through the rainforest without ever realising this house was there, it was so well camouflaged by its surroundings.

Liam flashed her a smile—that one that made her legs feel just a little weak. 'Come on up.'

She gripped the tree root railing and followed him up the stairs that spiralled around the tree trunk, perfectly angled to avoid anyone hitting their head as they approached the platform that housed Liam's rainforest home.

Jenny had to admit to a certain amount of curiosity as to what sort of place he'd built here. The hotel in Iceland had been cutting-edge in style with see-through glass elevators and stairs, stark modern Scandi styling in the bedrooms and every luxury made available. From what she knew of his other retreat resorts—in the US and overseas—they also focused on luxury for their elite customers. But she couldn't quite see how that kind of luxury would translate to the middle of a Costa Rican rainforest.

Stepping into the treehouse from the wooden porch at the top of the platform, it was instantly clear that Liam had managed it, though.

Where the Iceland hotel had taken its inspiration from

the unique landscape, the grey skies and the snow, and the local culture, so too did the treehouse. But, instead of stark neutrals and glass, here the style and texture was far more natural.

The main room of the house, suspended between three huge trees, was an open-plan living-dining-kitchen space, with wooden walls, floor and roof. It should have been confining, or too much, but the mix of colours and grains to the wood somehow lifted it beyond that feeling she'd expected of standing inside a children's playhouse. Of course, the furnishings helped too.

Everything remained neutral, just as in Iceland, except here those neutrals were warm creams and browns and ochres, and used in squishy-looking sofas and textured rugs. The open shelving in the kitchen was stacked with what looked like local pottery and glassware, and any functional items—like a dishwasher and fridge—were hidden away behind pale wooden doors.

Then there was the view. Each of the walls was left open to a balcony that ran almost the full circumference of the living space, save where the stairs were. There were windows that could be closed, but Jenny wasn't sure why you ever would, when you could be so connected to the world outside.

Without a word, she slipped through the open doors onto the balcony and leaned against the twisted wooden railing, feeling the knots and grain of the wood under her skin. From up here in the tree canopy it felt as if she was part of the world of the birds and animals who inhabited the rainforest. The sound of their calls, their rustling in the leaves, surrounded her and she found herself more at peace than she'd been in weeks.

Since Iceland, really. Since she'd lain in bed with Liam Delaney, completely sated, after he'd comprehensively taken her mind off any worries she might ever have had.

She'd never had sex that stopped her brain functioning until she met Liam. That stopped her planning and thinking about the future.

'You like it then?' he asked from behind her now, and it took her a moment to remember that he was talking about the accommodation, not sex.

She turned to face him with a smile. 'It's gorgeous.'

Then she swallowed as she realised she could as easily be talking about him as the treehouse.

He was still topless, which didn't help, his skin part dull with dust and part sheened with sweat. The tan he'd acquired since relocating from Iceland to South America gave a new definition to his lightly muscled torso, and Jenny found it hard not to remember every moment she'd spent touching his skin with her hands, her mouth, every inch of her body.

And here inside there was no audience to make her feel bad about ogling. Liam certainly didn't seem to mind the attention, if the smile that spread across his face was any indication.

She twisted back around to stare out over the rainforest canopy rather than acknowledge his knowing smile. 'It feels like I'm really part of the rainforest up here.'

'That's what I was aiming for.' He moved to stand beside her, and she couldn't help but look at his muscled forearms against the wood, rather than the wonders of the natural world around her. 'And if you like feeling part of the scenery here, I should tell you that the rainforest shower in the bathroom is spectacular.'

He didn't look at her as he spoke, but Jenny grinned at the not-so-subtle undertones of his words all the same.

'Is that so? I look forward to trying it out, especially after a long day's travelling. But really, I think you need the shower more than me right now.'

Liam looked down at his dust and sweat-smeared torso. 'You may have a point. But then, we are all about conservation and eco-tourism around here. We should probably try to find a way to save water…'

She needed to tell him about the pregnancy tests. About the baby. About being a father.

But the moment she did…things would change, just like they had for her the moment she held that positive test in her hands. And she wasn't ready for that, not yet.

Was it so greedy of her to want just one more night—or afternoon, really—with Liam Delaney?

Perhaps. But she was taking it anyway.

Shifting to face him as she leaned against the railing, Jenny met his gaze head-on. 'Seems to me there's only one answer,' she said. 'We'll just have to share.'

Next time Liam built himself a new suite of rooms at his latest resort, a shower big enough for two was definitely going to be a priority.

Not that the rainforest shower he'd installed in the treehouse wet room was anything to sniff at. With the wide, square shower head above, and some miracle of water pressure, the warm water falling on them really did feel almost like rain. And honestly, with Jenny's bare body pressed up against him—wet and warm and willing—he wasn't really thinking all that much about the shower anyway.

Just that he wished he had slightly more room to do everything he wanted to do to her right now...

Jenny trailed a soapy washcloth over his shoulders, following it with her mouth as the soapsuds washed away, and he bit back a moan at the sensitive tingles in his skin as she reached the dip above his collarbone. God, he'd thought he'd remembered exactly how good she was at this, but it seemed even his dreams couldn't live up to the real thing.

Any concerns he'd had about why she'd hunted him down to Costa Rica had disappeared the moment she took up his hinted invitation to share a shower. *This* was why she'd come. Because they were bloody incredible together, and just the feel of her body against his was enough to put him right on the brink.

It had been weeks. Months, even. And as much as he appreciated the slow, teasing approach, she was going to have to save it for round two.

Liam grabbed her around the waist, spinning her against the tiles of the wet room and pressing her to them with his kiss against her mouth, before moving his way down her neck. 'This shower really isn't big enough for what I want to do to you.'

'I think we're probably clean enough by now, don't you?' she gasped back.

'One last check…' Dropping down to his knees, he kissed his way across her breasts, her stomach and down to her thighs, before surging up between her legs with his tongue.

'Oh!' He felt her thighs tense and relax under his hands. 'I suppose I can live with that.'

With a grin, Liam went to work, savouring every second as the rainforest shower from above ran rivulets down his back and face. Oh, he remembered this. How responsive she was. How perfectly she reacted to everything he tried. It didn't take long to bring her to the brink…and stop.

She slapped a hand lightly against his shoulder. 'That's it?'

'That's starters.' He slammed his hand against the button to switch off the water, then reached for a fluffy towel from the hook on the far side of the room. He didn't bother wrapping one around himself—the air was hot enough that he knew he'd dry in seconds. But he took a few moments to run the towel over Jenny's body, knowing how hypersensitive she'd be right now, how every touch would just remind her of what she was aching for.

Him. Inside her.

It was very important that she not forget that before they reached the bed.

'Enough,' she said, her voice raspy, and he dropped the towel to the floor. 'Bed. Now.'

'As you wish.'

Later, he'd take time to show off the views from the wide, wide window that spanned the whole width of the bedroom. To let her admire the size of the bed he'd had to build up here, build the room around almost, because there was no way to carry one so big up the stairs—the mattress had been a battle enough. Later, there'd be time for all sorts of things.

Right now, all Liam could think about was burying himself in her again.

She tugged him towards the bed and he took just a moment to admire her body, the familiar curves and dips, the softness of her pale skin. That gorgeous blonde hair hanging darkly wet over her shoulders, almost covering the breasts he'd forgotten were quite so full.

He knelt on the edge of the bed, half over her, as he reached across to the bedside drawer and pulled out a condom. Beneath him, Jenny tensed for a second, then relaxed, and he decided not to question it. If she was worried about who he'd been with since her, she needn't be. There hadn't been anyone, although he didn't like to think too much about why.

His dreams had been too full of her to want anyone else. Clearly that was something else to try and get out of his system this week.

Protection in place, he rested on his elbows above her, smiling down. 'I missed you, you know.'

Her return grin was impish. 'I missed this.' And then she was reaching out and guiding him inside her, and Liam knew that none of the rest of it mattered right now.

Live in the moment, that was his philosophy these days. And God, what a moment to live in.

From the moment he felt her around him, Liam knew there was no way this was going to take long. Neither of them had the patience to take it slow any longer, not this time. Still, he drew it out as best he could, until he felt her start to tighten around him with her orgasm, and his hips started to stutter and he couldn't hold off his pleasure a moment longer.

Collapsing half on top and half beside her with a grin, he waited for his heart to return to a normal tempo, and considered that, really, he might as well have waited to take the shower until afterwards, since he was clearly going to need another one now.

'I don't know what made you decide to come all the way down here,' he said, skimming a hand across her side and over her breasts. 'But I'm damn pleased you did.'

He brought his hand down a little to rest against her belly, and felt her tense under his hand. Frowning, he looked up to see tension in her face too—jaw tight, eyes wary.

He was missing something here. And he hated that.

'Jenny…'

She shook her head. 'Don't—' She broke off.

Oh, whatever this was, Liam was damn sure it wasn't going to be good. He pushed himself up to sit beside her, removing the condom before staring her straight in the eye.

He almost didn't want to ask. But not knowing would be worse, somehow.

'Why did you come to Costa Rica? The real reason, this time.'

She winced and looked away. Looked down. At her stomach.

His whole brain was screaming *no*. But she obviously couldn't hear it, because she kept talking.

'Because I'm pregnant.' She looked up and met his gaze again. 'And you're the father.'

CHAPTER THREE

SHE WAS WATCHING Liam unspool before her very eyes. Not that she blamed him; that wasn't *exactly* the way she'd prepared herself to share the news on the plane. And she definitely hadn't planned to be naked when she did it, but pregnancy hormones were a real thing. So was the stupid chemistry between them that had got them into this mess in the first place.

And now, here they were. Both naked. Him horrified, eyes wide and mouth open. Her guilty and regretful and, although she'd deny it if asked, a little disappointed.

She shouldn't be. She'd known, coming here, exactly how this was going to go. She'd practised the conversation in her head plenty of times, and felt pretty confident filling in Liam's lines for him.

I'm pregnant, she'd say. *And you're the father.*

You're sure? he'd reply, and it wouldn't really be a question, because Liam wasn't that sort of guy. He wasn't marriage and babies and happy-ever-after material, but that was okay because neither was she. But he wasn't someone who'd skip out on his responsibilities or try to deny them. And he wouldn't pressure her either. *What do you want to do?* he'd ask.

I want to keep it, she'd tell him, firmly. *And I'm happy to do that alone. I know this isn't what we agreed, or what either of us planned for. I'm not here to demand anything or blame anyone. I'm here as a courtesy, to let you know, so you can be involved if you want. Otherwise, I'll walk away and raise my child and never bother you again.*

She'd practised that part over and over in the mirror until she could say it without her voice wobbling. Going it alone was scary, no denying that. But she'd done it before—started her life over without anyone by her side. She could do it again, and this time with a baby too.

Doing it alone was better than trusting people who could let you down. *Would* let you down, in the end. She'd trusted a man she'd loved before. She'd trusted that her family would always love her no matter once.

She had no intention of making that mistake a third time.

So Liam would nod, consider. Maybe he'd ask for a little time to think, and she'd give him that graciously. But, eventually, she knew what would happen next.

I'm not cut out to be a father, he'd say eventually. *I can't be part of this.*

And then she'd know.

Sometimes when she pictured it he'd offer her money—a lump sum, or a regular allowance. Sometimes he'd even go as far as asking for updates, or to be told when the kid started asking questions about their father. Others, he washed his hands of the whole thing and signed away all parental rights. It depended on how optimistic she was feeling on the day.

The point was, however she pictured it, their conversation was always cordial. Businesslike, even.

And she was always, always wearing clothes.

Liam blinked, for the first time in an age, then rolled off the bed and stalked into the bathroom without a word—presumably to get rid of the condom and clean up. Maybe even get dressed.

Jenny would love to do the same, but since her clothes were *in* the bathroom, and her suitcase abandoned somewhere in the living space by all the very open windows, she didn't have that option. Unless…

With a quick glance towards the bathroom to check he wasn't coming back already, Jenny dived into the drawers beside the bed—noting in passing how they looked like they were carved directly into the tree trunk that she now realised served as part of one of the bedroom walls—and pulled out a clean white T-shirt and a pair of grey boxers. Dressing quickly in them, she felt more prepared to face whatever Liam had to say next.

When he emerged, he had a towel wrapped around his waist and his hair was damp again. He glanced briefly at the bed, and she saw a twitch at his jaw as he realised she'd stolen his clothes, but he didn't say anything. Instead, he crossed to the drawers himself and pulled out another set of the same and dressed in them, before turning again to face her.

The silence between them made her uncomfortable. From the moment they'd met in Iceland there hadn't been silence between them—just teasing and banter and light, inconsequential conversation.

But the conversation they needed to have now was anything but inconsequential.

She tried, desperately, to remember her well-rehearsed speech—but every word went out of her head when she saw the confusion and disappointment in his bright blue eyes.

'I meant to tell you before, well… I meant to tell you *first*,' she said. 'I guess I just got a little carried away in the moment.'

His harsh laughter told her what he thought of *that* understatement.

'We were careful,' he said, finally. 'In Iceland. We took precautions.'

Jenny nodded. 'We did.' It had been her first thought too. That this *couldn't* happen, because they'd been so damn careful to make sure it didn't. 'But no contraceptive is foolproof. You know that.'

'I do.' A sharp nod. 'Okay. I'm not going to bother asking if you're sure it's mine. I won't insult you like that. You wouldn't be here if it wasn't.'

She acknowledged that with a dip of her head. At least *one* part of this was going to plan. She hadn't completely misjudged him after all.

'And you're keeping it, I assume,' he went on. 'Or, again, why come all the way to the middle of nowhere to find me?'

'Yes.'

'So. What is it you want from me, exactly?' There was an edge in Liam's voice she didn't like, a coldness that transcended the heat of the rainforest. How ironic that their time together in Iceland had been filled with heat and passion, warmth and friendship. And now they were here in Costa Rica in the sweltering heat, Jenny felt like she needed a sweater to protect her from the ice in his eyes.

She took a breath and forced herself to focus on the words she'd practised. She'd had her one last tumble with Liam, and she was under no illusion that he'd ever want her that way again, not now. All she needed to do now was rip the sticking plaster off, get the answer she knew was coming, and then she could be on the next plane out of South America and get home to LA and her job and her life.

She'd have to figure out how to tell her boss that she'd accidentally got pregnant by Winter's husband's best friend, but that was a bridge for later.

First she had to cross this one.

'You're right; I'm keeping the baby. And I'm happy to do that alone. This wasn't what we agreed in Iceland, and it definitely wasn't what either of us planned for. But I'm not here to demand anything from you. I'm here as a courtesy, to let you know, so you can be involved if you want. Otherwise, I'll walk away and raise my child and never bother you again.'

There. She'd said it.

Now she just needed to remember to keep breathing while she waited for his answer.

Liam stared at her, his insides swirling and his mind a fog, as he tried to make sense of her words. Of everything that had happened since he'd spotted her across the clearing earlier that day.

I'll walk away and raise my child and never bother you again.

He should take that option, he knew it. Hand over a chunk of cash and opt out of the whole fatherhood thing. It was the easiest option. The sensible option. The safe option.

The one that wouldn't break his heart, or the hard-fought-for peace of mind he'd finally achieved.

This isn't what either of us planned.

Understatement. This was the exact opposite of everything he'd planned for his life, ever since that day five years ago where his whole world collapsed and he wasn't sure he'd ever crawl out of the hole it left behind.

The world knew about the accident; it had been in enough papers and magazines, photos splashed all across the internet. They knew Liam had been lucky to escape that car crash with his life. And they knew that his girl-friend, who'd been driving, hadn't been so lucky.

The world didn't know that she'd been pregnant at the time. That Liam hadn't just lost his love but his future in that moment.

They didn't know that it was his fault either.

Jenny couldn't know all that; even Josh didn't know the whole of it, and Liam trusted him enough not to have shared what he did know with anyone.

She'd know that he'd walked away from Hollywood after that, probably even have heard that he went off the rails for a while—like he hadn't been halfway there already. And she knew what he did next, of course—setting up retreat hotels for burnt-out and wayward creatives to find themselves again, along with a lot of high-paying tourists.

But she wouldn't, couldn't, know how the news of her pregnancy would blindside him. And if he got his way, she never would.

He marshalled his thoughts, trying to stop them spinning around in some variation of *why?* and *how?* and *what now?*

When he spoke, he managed to keep his voice even and calm, which he was pretty damn impressed with, personally. 'Let's not either of us do or say anything rash.'

Perching himself against the windowsill, he watched her curled up against the headboard, dressed in his boxers and T-shirt, and felt his unruly body reacting to the sight again. As if that wasn't what had got them into this mess to start with.

'If you only came here as a courtesy, to tell me the situation, what was…this?' He gestured between the two of them. If she'd hoped to use sex to manipulate him one way or the other, he would be very disappointed in how badly he'd misjudged her.

She pulled a face. 'I told you. I got—*we* got carried away. It wasn't like I intended to show up here and jump back into bed with you. It was just…old habits, I suppose.'

Old habits, with someone he'd only met for the first time less than three months ago. It should be laughable. But he took her point.

It wasn't like there'd been anything much to their relationship *outside* the bedroom, when they'd met.

There never was, for him.

He had rules now, since the accident. Liam Delaney's rules for living, ones he'd never share with another person, but that he followed rigidly. Because when he didn't, that was when his life fell apart again.

Some rules could be bent, maybe a little. Others could be updated as circumstances changed. As long as he knew the rules he was operating by, and reminded himself of them often, he could stay on the right path. Grounded, safe, and no danger to himself or anybody else.

The number one rule, though, that could never be changed. *That* was the rule that underpinned his entire existence in this *afterwards*. Life after the accident. If he let *that* rule slide…he didn't want to imagine what would happen then.

Rule number one: never care too deeply about anything or anyone that can be taken away from you.

It was the loss that had nearly killed him. The yawning emptiness that had filled his insides and drained away everything that made life worth living.

He wouldn't survive losing another thing he loved. So he wouldn't let himself love anything.

It was as simple as that.

And for five years that rule had been easy to follow. He was discreet in his relationships, and always upfront about what he was offering. It had taken a while for him to even think about getting back in the game, so it wasn't as if there had been that many women since, anyway.

Jenny had been an unexpected delight; his plans for that week in Iceland had all been about promoting his new hotel, and helping two of his best friends find closure on their failed marriage. And if he'd been hoping they might both see what idiots they'd been to walk away from the love they'd shared, well, he'd got lucky there.

He wasn't against love for everyone. Just him. He didn't have the strength to withstand it.

Meeting Jenny had been more than luck; it had felt like fate. With the Iceland hotel up and running, and the Costa Rica project stalled at the time, he'd been desperate for a distraction. And Jenny, with her blonde ponytail, knowing smile and a line in flirtatious banter that drove him wild, had been just what he needed.

The fact that her wants and desires for any liaison between them—fun, sex, friendship, and then say goodbye at the end of the week—had dovetailed exactly with his had only cemented his belief that their fling was meant to be.

And it had been perfect, right up to the friendly goodbye they'd said the moment she'd left. They'd both known that there was a good chance they'd see each other again—she worked for his best friends, after all—and maybe they'd pick up where they'd left off when they did. But there was no expectation, no obligation.

No risk.

Because while he liked Jenny, he didn't love her—he hadn't even opened himself up to the possibility of that, and besides, who really fell in love in a week? Not Liam Delaney, he knew that much.

He'd been safe.

Until now.

Because as much as he trusted himself not to fall in love with Jenny, or any other woman, a baby was a different matter.

He hadn't changed so much from the man he'd once been that he believed he was capable of not loving his own child.

And that was the biggest risk of all.

So what the hell was he supposed to do now?

CHAPTER FOUR

CLEARLY THIS HAD been a mistake. Coming to Costa Rica. Sleeping with Liam again. Hell, even letting him seduce her in Iceland. Or, well, seducing him, actually.

All of it. Every last minute had been a mistake.

But especially thinking, even for a moment, that he'd appreciate her coming all this way to tell him he was about to be a father.

Coming here for sex? Sure, he'd thank her for that. But doing the morally right thing and telling him about the baby?

From the look on his face, he wasn't in the slightest bit grateful for that.

She pushed off the bed and made a move towards the bathroom to look for her clothes. 'I should go. If I head straight back to the airport I think there's another flight back to LA tonight.' She had no idea if that was true or not, but right now she'd rather sleep in one of those plastic airport chairs and wait until morning than stay another moment in this ridiculously luxurious treehouse with *him*.

She'd expected him to let her down. She hadn't expected it to hurt.

'Wait.' He moved faster than she'd anticipated, blocking her path to the bathroom so fast she almost crashed into him. 'I'm not saying… I just… I need time to think.'

'Time to figure out how to say you don't want anything to do with this, you mean?' Because of course he didn't. And she was furious with herself for letting herself think, however briefly, that he might.

'No. Look.' He raked a hand through his dark hair, leaving it looking even messier than usual. 'You've had… how long to think about this?'

'A month,' she admitted. 'Maybe six weeks.'

'And you needed that time to get your head around things before you came to see me, right?'

She nodded. 'I guess.'

Reaching out, he encircled her wrists lightly with his fingers and looked directly into her eyes. 'I'm not asking for a month, Jenny. I just… I can't think straight right now. And I need to think straight if we're going to figure out what happens next.'

'That's fair, I suppose.' She shook her hands loose and stepped away, towards the warm breeze from the window. It was harder to think when he was touching her. Her body got in the way of her brain.

He wasn't throwing her out. Wasn't demanding he never see her or the baby ever again. He just needed a little time. She'd expected that, hadn't she?

And she could give him that, to a point. After all, babies came with their own timetable. If she was going to head back to LA and figure out her future, she needed to know where she stood with him. What his expectations were, if he had any.

She couldn't live with not knowing where she stood for very long.

'I can give you a week,' she said, finally. 'After that, I need to be back at work in LA. And I need the time before the baby comes to figure out what I do next.'

'A week.' Liam nodded. 'I can work with that.' He sounded confident, but then he always did. Looking closer, she could see the doubt in his eyes.

There was no room for uncertainty in this debate though, so Jenny spelled it out a little clearer. 'By that, I mean we have one week to figure out our future, and the future of our child.'

His eyebrows shot up. '*Our* future.'

Of course his brain went there. Jenny rolled her eyes. 'I'm not trying to trap you into marriage or anything here, Liam. I just mean that by the end of this week I need to know what the future looks like. If this kid is going to have two parents or one, for instance.'

'Right.' He looked uncomfortable at the reminder that he could still walk away, while she really couldn't. Or wouldn't.

'At the end of this week either we'll have a plan I can work with for co-parenting, one that lets me plan my future with some certainty, or I'll walk out of your life for ever, and you'll sign all parental rights over to me. Okay?'

She could tell from the muscle pulsing in his jaw that it *wasn't* okay, but he was going to have to get okay with it real quick. Because this was what she needed and, since she was the one carrying the kid, he was going to have to work with her on this.

'Is that all of your demands?' he asked tightly.

Jenny was about to nod when she thought of something else. Something that had already derailed her plans once and couldn't be allowed to again.

But she had a feeling he *really* wasn't going to like this condition.

'Not quite,' she said. 'While we figure this out…there can't be anything else between us.'

'Anything else? Like what?'

So much for hinting. 'Sex. We can't have sex again until we come to an agreement on the baby.'

He blinked once, really slowly, as if the concept made no sense to him at all. Maybe it didn't. She'd fallen into bed with him the moment she'd seen him again, after all. It was kind of a change of pace.

'No sex.' His mouth twisted, as if he'd just sucked on a lemon. 'Can I ask why?'

'It's too distracting,' she said shortly. She wasn't about to tell him everything that had happened the last time she'd let her libido override her brain. When she'd let her inexperience convince her that sex meant love, and that two bodies bumping together could only lead to fairy tale endings.

Instead, it had cost Jenny her job, her family, her reputation, her self-esteem—her future. Fighting her way back from that was her biggest achievement to date.

She wouldn't let the chemistry between her and Liam put her back where she'd started again.

Now, his lips curved up into a smile. 'Is that so?'

The man really didn't need his ego stroking any more,

but Jenny had a feeling he'd be testing this boundary all week if she wasn't very, very clear about her reasoning. Or as clear as she could be without confessing all her past mistakes.

'When we're touching each other, or kissing, or more… it's too much. I can't think straight.'

'Which explains why you failed to mention that you were pregnant until *after* we had sex today.'

'Just like I told you,' she snapped back. He was sounding far too pleased with himself for her liking.

'So you did.' His smile only grew. 'I had no idea that my sexuality was so…potent.'

'*Our* chemistry has been a distraction right from the start. For both of us.'

He acknowledged the point. 'True. It is…' He trailed off, apparently unable to find a word to accurately describe that strange connection that had snapped between them from the moment they'd met.

'It's distracting,' she finished for him, repeating her earlier word choice rather than picking any of the others that sprung to mind.

Overwhelming. Incredible. Mind-blowing.

'And neither of us can afford to be distracted when making a decision as important as this,' Liam said, surprising her. 'I can't say I'm not disappointed, but I take your point.'

'Good.'

He pushed away from the bathroom doorway, where he'd been leaning, and shifted to one side to allow her access to her clothes. She didn't move towards them though. Not yet.

'So, we're agreed,' she pressed. 'One week to make this decision. And no sex.'

'Until the decision is made,' Liam said. 'Yes, we're agreed.'

She nodded sharply, trying to look as businesslike as was possible when she was wearing the man's boxer shorts. 'Okay, then. I'll just...' She darted past him, into the bathroom, shutting the door quickly behind her.

Gathering her clothes up from the floor, she caught sight of herself in the mirror. Her hair had dried into messy waves, as if she'd spent the day at the beach, and her skin was pink and flushed—from the sex or the argument, she wasn't sure.

Either way, she looked like she'd just been...well, doing exactly what she *had* been doing, and the sight of it, and the memories it awoke, made her blood warm all over again.

One week. I've just got to keep my hands—and lips—off him for one week. For the sake of my future. And our baby.

She gave herself a stiff nod in the mirror and set the shower to cool before she stepped in to clean up again.

One week. She could do that.

Couldn't she?

Liam retreated to the living area when he heard the shower start. Obviously Jenny was taking a little time, and putting some space between them, before they had to figure out what happened next. He couldn't deny he was grateful for it.

At first, he'd been taken aback by her requirement for no sex until they'd resolved the issues between them. He'd even wondered if it was a threat or an attempt to seduce him into making the right decision—withholding sex unless he did.

Except Jenny hadn't given him a *right* decision that she wanted him to make. As long as he decided one way or the other, it seemed like she'd be happy. Should he be insulted that she didn't care if he wanted to be a father to his child? Or relieved that she was willing to walk away without a backwards look if he decided otherwise?

He wasn't sure. None of it made sense yet. Just the very idea that she was in the next room, carrying his baby, sent his brain into a tailspin. And she was right—adding sex back into the mix wasn't going to help that one bit.

He couldn't think straight when he was touching her either. When she kissed him, the rest of the world disappeared and he was focused only on her pleasure. Well, and his. He wasn't a saint—hell, nobody had ever claimed that about him.

And he had to keep his head on straight right now. All his rules were on the verge of being smashed and he had to figure out how to handle that.

He couldn't let himself get…distracted.

Even if, at the end of this week, he decided to take the risk of being in his child's life, of loving them even knowing he could lose them, that one risk would be all he could manage. Maybe more than he could manage.

He definitely couldn't risk falling for his child's mother too.

And he could, he knew that. Falling for Jenny would be easy—too easy. All it would take was being distracted by the chemistry between them and, before he knew it, his libido would have made choices for his heart that his brain wouldn't back.

She was gorgeous, they had fun together, and the sex was incredible. Yeah, the risk was there.

That was why he'd been so clear about the parameters of their little fling in Iceland from the start. He couldn't let himself sway on those now, even if the situation had changed beyond all recognition.

Jenny was right. There were two options on the table here, and only two.

One: co-parenting with a woman he liked and respected but did not and would not love.

Two: walking away and forgetting this had ever happened.

And right now he still wouldn't risk placing a bet on which side he'd come down on in the end.

It was a damn good job she'd given him a week.

Except…she'd be here. That whole week. Within arm's reach but untouchable.

And Liam already knew that was going to drive him mad.

He heard the click of the shower switching off, and forced himself into action. Somehow, he had to make this week feel perfectly normal. Friendly, even. Not something that was turning his whole world upside down.

He couldn't let on how torn up he was by all this, all the painful memories it dredged up. He'd done his talking in therapy. He'd practised mindfulness and meditation, done the yoga poses and the detoxes. He was living in the goddamn moment now and leaving his past in the past.

And as for the future…well, he'd see about that at the end of the week. It didn't help anybody to plan too far ahead. The universe, in his experience, liked nothing more than upsetting well made plans.

For now, Jenny had to be hungry. She'd been travelling all day, and he'd not even offered her a sandwich before dragging her into the bedroom, so the least he could do was get dinner going.

Or ask someone else to bring it to them, he decided, as a glance inside his fridge forced him to revisit his plans. Grabbing his phone, he fired off a quick email to the housekeeping service he employed, asking them to restock the treehouse with food for two for a week. Then he called his favourite restaurant in the nearest town and sweet-talked Valentina, who owned it, into sending her nephew up to the treehouse on his moped to deliver them some dinner. It wasn't the first time, and he was hoping he could make takeaways a regular offering once the resort was open. They weren't too far away from town to make it feasible.

He'd just hung up when Jenny appeared in the bedroom doorway, dressed in her own clothes again—which was a shame, as Liam had rather enjoyed seeing her in his, but probably for the best considering everything. She was towelling off her damp hair, and there was a tension in the lines of her body that Liam didn't like. It was unfamiliar, the opposite of the relaxation they'd found in each other's company every time they'd been together—until today.

But he knew it wouldn't be going away in a hurry, so he kept his mouth shut.

'I heard you talking to somebody,' she said softly.

'My favourite restaurant,' he replied. 'They're, uh, I asked them to send up some food. I figured you probably wouldn't want to go out tonight, after travelling?' The observation turned into a question as he realised he'd just assumed that would be the case, and not asked her.

But she nodded. 'Yeah. That sounds good. Thanks.'

Crossing the room, she grabbed her suitcase, then stopped. 'Um, I was going to put this away somewhere, but—'

But she didn't know where she was going to sleep. Because they couldn't share the bed any more, could they? And the treehouse only had one bedroom. Damn, he should've known that would come back to bite him eventually. He just hadn't envisioned a situation where someone would come to stay and not want their own space, their own treehouse. Where *he* wouldn't want them to have their own space, away from him.

Except there was no more space, not yet. None of the other treehouses had been finished, and wouldn't be this week. He could call around the hotels down by the beach, but April was the busy season in Costa Rica. Chances of finding her a decent room were slim. And besides, if she was hidden away over there, how would that help him make the decision he needed to make?

'Put it in the bedroom,' he said hurriedly. 'You can take the bed while you're here.'

'And where will you sleep?' Jenny asked.

Liam eyed the squishy sofa for a moment, pitying his poor back, before remembering. 'There's a hammock out on the deck. I used it before the bed was finished. I'll be fine in that for a few nights.'

'If you're sure,' she said, sounding uncertain. 'I could always—'

'Like I'm going to let the pregnant woman sleep in the hammock. Honestly, it's fine.'

'Great. Thanks. Then I'll…' She gestured towards the bedroom and headed off to put away her case.

'There should be some empty drawers under the window,' he called after her.

Maybe, if she took her time unpacking, they wouldn't have to make excruciatingly awkward conversation until the food arrived.

CHAPTER FIVE

NIGHT IN THE rainforest sounded different to night-time anywhere else she'd ever slept.

Not that Jenny was sleeping. That would involve her brain stopping whirring around all the worst-case scenarios it could think of—for this trip, this week, Liam, the baby, her entire future…

It would also require whatever bird was making a racket outside the treehouse going to sleep too. And the crickets, or whatever insect was chirping that way. And what she thought might be frogs.

Liam had warned her that the howler monkeys might wake her up early. Assuming she ever made it to sleep at all. At the moment, it was seeming unlikely.

The worst of it was knowing that he was just outside, lying in that stupid hammock on the deck that surrounded the treehouse, hopefully with some sort of protection against bugs or he'd be miserable in the morning. She had the screened windows, plus the insect repellent body lotion she'd bought before travelling, *and* a net over the bed. What did he have?

Was he out there right now getting eaten alive by mosquitos? Should she check?

She got one foot out of the bed before she caught herself and stopped. Liam had been out here for weeks. His on-site knowledge of the risks had to be more complete than her internet research back in LA. He'd be fine.

And if she went out there now, in the middle of the night, he might get ideas.

Because she sure as hell was having some.

Jenny sighed, turned over, and tried to get more comfortable in the wide, soft, perfectly comfortable and luxurious bed.

Okay, fine. It wasn't the bed. Or the insects and rainforest noises.

It was the scent of Liam on the bedsheets that was keeping her awake.

The reminder of what they'd done there that afternoon. Of what they could do again, if she hadn't put her stupid 'no sex until we make a decision' rule in place.

Giving up on sleep, she sat up in the bed, reached to turn on the light—then stopped. She didn't want to advertise that she was still awake to Liam or to the bugs.

Because it *wasn't* a stupid rule, not really. It was a necessary one.

Jenny had let herself be led around by her libido before, when she was younger and stupider, and she wasn't about to make that mistake again. She wasn't sure how much more she could stand to lose if this all went to hell.

It was just the hormones, anyway. Pregnancy hormones were notorious for making women more sexually charged than normal, weren't they? Although personally sex had been the furthest thing from her mind until she'd seen Liam again.

And then when she had...

Jenny swallowed and reached for her water bottle— only to find it empty. Great. Well, at least she had an excuse to get up. And maybe a small wander around the treehouse would help her settle back to sleep again afterwards. Perhaps there might even be some leftovers of the delicious food Liam had ordered for their dinner. She couldn't help but feel that her enjoyment of the meal had been somewhat thwarted by the tension that filled the room as they ate.

She padded through to the main living area of the treehouse, easing the bedroom door open as silently as she could, and propping it open with the doorstop to avoid it banging closed again. Using her phone as a torch, she refilled her water bottle, then turned to the fridge, where they'd stacked the leftovers. The light from inside the fridge was far brighter than her phone, so she placed it on the counter as she surveyed the takeaway containers.

'Is everything all right?'

Jenny jumped at the sound of Liam's voice behind her, so violently she almost hit her head on the top of the fridge. While she waited for her heart rate to return to something approaching normal, she turned to find him standing on the other side of the kitchen counter.

At least he wasn't topless this time; instead he was wearing a loose cotton top and pyjama bottoms—presumably as a deterrent to the bugs, or in respect for anybody passing through this part of the rainforest, since she knew from personal experience that he usually slept naked.

'I just wanted to get some water.' She motioned towards the now filled water bottle on the counter.

In the light of the fridge door, she saw him raise an eyebrow. Dammit. She should have shut the fridge, except then she wouldn't have been able to see him at all, and that would have been even more alarming.

'And I thought I'd check on the leftovers from dinner,' she admitted.

'Of course. How are they doing?' he asked with a grin. 'Coping okay with fridge life?'

'They look a little forlorn, to be honest.' She returned his smile. 'Like they're not quite fulfilling their life's purpose.'

'Well, we should probably see what we can do about that then, shouldn't we?'

Jenny nodded sagely. 'We should. You get the plates and cutlery. I'll get the food out.'

By unspoken agreement, they left most of the lights dimmed, only turning on one of the lamps in the sitting area for enough light to eat by. She carried the takeout containers over to the low coffee table and they sat on cushions on the floor, safely separated by the heavy wood of the table, as they ate.

It was nice, she realised, halfway through a mouthful of cold empanada. This was the sort of companionship they'd had in Iceland, in between bouts in the bedroom. She'd worried they'd lost it completely, after she'd broken the news about the baby.

But it seemed it was still there. Even if it might only come out under the cover of darkness—and takeout food.

Maybe this was what they needed this week for, more than anything. To find a way to be friends. If Liam decided he wanted to be a part of this, they'd need to be friends—or at least friendly and civil—to co-parent successfully, wouldn't they? That was what the book she'd read on the plane in preparation had said, anyway.

She watched him across the table, darkly handsome in the half light, and felt that familiar heat curl in her belly just at the sight of him. Was it her imagination, or did his eyes darken too? While it was reassuring to know that she wasn't the only one struggling with this issue, it didn't make it any easier to resist either.

He smiled, and her insides flipped again.

Oh, this week was going to be *unbearable.*

This tension between them was going to be the death of him, Liam was certain. It seemed like they could only exist as strangers or lovers, and finding any middle ground was impossible.

But they were going to have to, if they were to even entertain this co-parenting possibility.

Maybe that was what they needed this week for most of all—a way to figure out how to *be* together without, well, being together.

Or stripping those light, loose cotton pyjamas from her shoulders and exposing all that bare skin he'd had his hands and mouth on so very recently…

Focus, Liam.

Right. Coexisting without sex. That was the plan here.

He tore his gaze away from her own heated one, ignoring the want he saw there. He knew how she felt. But he also knew what she'd said, and there was nothing to do but respect that.

He cast around the room, looking for something—anything—to start a non-sexual conversation about, and finding it harder than he'd imagined. His treehouse retreat wasn't exactly designed as a love nest—more a private escape. But he'd filled it with the textures and items he loved, and everything—from the soft sofas he wanted to lower her onto with his kisses to the solid wood table he couldn't help but imagine laying her on as he took her—made him think of sex.

Maybe it wasn't the treehouse. Maybe it was just him. Or her.

Luckily, Jenny took the conversational thread in hand.

'This food is amazing. Thanks for getting it. I couldn't have faced going out tonight—and if we had, we wouldn't have had leftovers.'

'And the leftovers are the best bit,' Liam replied.

She beamed at him and reached for another helping of the rice with chicken and beans. 'Exactly! I think I'm still making up for not wanting to eat much in the first trimester due to nausea.' She took another empanada and placed it on the edge of her already full plate.

But Liam had frozen, his fork halfway to his mouth. When she gave him a funny look across the coffee table he forced himself to complete the movement. Fork to mouth. Open mouth. Chew food. Swallow. Each step needed a conscious thought—and none of them did any-thing to distract him from the other thought ricocheting around his head.

'What?' Jenny asked after a long moment. 'You don't want to hear about morning sickness?'

'No!' Liam said hurriedly. He didn't like that resigned tone in her voice. The feeling that he was living down to all her worst expectations of how he was going to react to her news.

He was pretty sure he'd done that already. No need to make it worse.

'Then what?' She raised her eyebrows quizzically at him. 'You looked like I'd just started talking about our sex life in front of your parents.'

Her comparison surprised a laugh out of him, not least because in that instant he could absolutely imagine her sitting at that old farmhouse kitchen table back home in England, telling his mostly deaf father all about that time with the ice cubes and the hot chocolate, while Dad nod-ded along sagely without hearing a word.

'What *now?*' she asked with a laugh. 'Your face went really weird that time.'

He told her, and she laughed even harder—then so-bered up suddenly. 'I guess that's something else we'll need to consider. What you want to tell people—your family and such.'

'One step at a time,' Liam replied, mentally shuffling back from the reminder of his parents, and the fact he hadn't called them in almost a month. The news that he was going to be a father—if that was what he chose to do, at the end of the week—wasn't something that could be shared by phone, anyway. His mother would never forgive him if he wasn't there to be hugged the moment he told her. Jenny too, for that matter. Would she come to England with him to tell them? Or would that be beyond the constraints of their co-parenting agreement?

Too much. Too fast. Too deep.

He picked up another forkful of food and returned to intense focus on chewing and swallowing. Far safer than trying to picture a future that might never happen.

'So, what was it that freaked you out?' Jenny asked. 'If it wasn't the morning sickness thing. What did I say?'

'It was just…the first time you really spoke about the fact that our baby is inside you right now, and it felt… real.' Not a possible future, but something that was happening right now, in this room with him.

He knew intellectually, of course, that babies didn't just spring forth fully grown without any preparation. He knew that Jenny was pregnant. He just hadn't really imagined that the child could already be affecting the world it wasn't even part of yet, that was all.

Jenny gave him a small understanding smile. 'I think I get what you mean. I mean, I'm not even showing yet, but I can definitely feel the changes in my body. But no one else can. It's like…it almost didn't feel real because nobody else knew, and then I'd feel a wave of nausea, or my boobs would hurt, and I'd know it *was* real. Just still secret.'

Liam frowned. '*No one* else knew? You haven't told *anybody* but me? Not even Winter?'

'Just you.' She met his gaze with her own clear, honest one. 'I figured you had a right to know first.'

It was a perfectly natural decision. But somehow Liam doubted that was the real reason she'd made it.

He could understand not telling Winter, because her boss had her own issues with pregnancy that made it complicated. But not telling *anyone* else?

Liam couldn't help wondering if that was because she didn't have anyone else to tell.

What about her family? He thought again about his own. Were her family still around? What was her relationship with them? This was all stuff he was going to need to know eventually, if he went ahead with this.

His carefully curated small circle of people that mattered would have to grow, one way or another.

'Besides,' Jenny went on, nibbling on the edge of an empanada, 'they say not to tell people until after the twelve-week scan. Just in case.'

Just in case. He knew what that meant. He'd never spent a lot of time around babies or pregnant women—certainly not in the last five years—but that rule he remembered.

Julie had never made it to her twelve-week scan. She'd lost her life, and the baby's, in the accident, two weeks before they had it scheduled.

But before that she'd been adamant they not tell people too. Just in case.

Besides, I like having a secret that's just ours, she'd whispered to him late at night, when the horizon was already a little fuzzy from the beer and whisky he'd consumed before, during and after their dinner. Julie's eyes were clear, though—she'd stopped drinking the moment she saw that positive test. Smoking too.

She'd done everything right. Which was how he knew her death, their baby's death, was his fault.

Liam shook away the memory. 'And when is the twelve-week scan?' His chest felt tight just asking the question. If she said two weeks' time…but wait, if the baby had been conceived in Iceland… He tried to do the maths in his head, but the weeks had merged into one a bit since he'd arrived in Costa Rica. And wasn't there something about the dating going from *before* the sex? He was sure he remembered something about that, if only because it made no sense at all.

'Oh.' Jenny looked down at her almost empty plate. 'Um… Actually, I already had it. Before I came. I wanted to be sure…'

She trailed off, but he knew what she meant. She'd wanted to be sure the baby was okay. That the pregnancy was real, and viable. That this was really happening. She'd wanted to be sure before she'd told him, because otherwise what was the point in seeking him out at all?

Not that he'd been under any illusion that she'd have come all this way if it hadn't been for the baby, but still the thought stung anyway.

Was it that if she'd miscarried, or the scan had shown something bad, he might never have known he'd lost out on being a father again? He forced himself to focus on what he was feeling—something every retreat he'd ever been on had assured him was important, and something he avoided doing unless absolutely necessary.

It seemed necessary now.

No, he realised. He wasn't angry, or even annoyed or frustrated at her revelation.

He was…disappointed. A little sad that he'd missed out on that moment again—sharing that moment with her.

And, more than anything, he felt guilty that she'd had to do that alone. That she hadn't wanted to ask him—or anyone else—to be there with her.

He was starting to get the impression that, despite her bubbly nature, her confidence and her obviously good relationship with her boss, Jenny didn't have a lot of people in her life that she could trust.

He didn't know yet if he was capable of being one. But he couldn't dismiss the feeling that he *wanted* to be.

Liam swallowed, keeping the emotion down inside where it belonged.

'Are there…did you get pictures?'

Jenny beamed at his question. 'I did. Do you want to see?'

He nodded, and tried to ignore the sensation of falling deeper into something he wasn't sure he had the strength to climb out of again.

CHAPTER SIX

JENNY WAS SURPRISED by how well she slept after her midnight feast with Liam—at least, after she'd taken her indigestion medication, anyway. Pregnancy was just hell on the digestive system. Still, she woke up feeling more relaxed and refreshed than she had in weeks—something she assigned to having finally shared the giant secret that had consumed her life ever since she'd peed on that stick.

He'd seemed surprised that she hadn't told anyone else. But really, who was she going to tell?

Winter would be the obvious person, she supposed. More friend than boss after so many years, the A-list actress and director was definitely the person Jenny spent the most time with these days.

But Winter had experienced her own pregnancy issues, and they'd left scars. Jenny hadn't wanted to burden her with the knowledge. Add in the fact that she was so recently reunited with her ex-husband, Josh, and Winter had enough going on in her life without worrying about Jenny's too.

The fact that Josh was Liam's best friend, and that the two of them would definitely have Opinions about his knocking her up, might have played into that decision.

And apart from Winter…there really wasn't anyone else she *would* tell. Her job took her all over the world, gave her opportunities and experiences she'd never have had otherwise, and it fulfilled her in ways she'd never expected when Winter first hired her. But it didn't leave a lot of downtime for making friends who'd be excited to hear her news.

As for her family…well. She'd just have to hope that Liam's family would be excited enough for both of them, because she had no intention of even letting hers know what had happened.

Since her grandma had passed away, Jenny found it easier to believe that she simply didn't *have* a family any more. They'd made it clear that was what they wanted, anyway.

She'd always believed, growing up, that family were the people who loved you, looked after you and supported you even when the rest of the world turned against you. She knew now, though, that had been the naïve understanding of a child.

She'd made one mistake—she'd fallen in love with the wrong man—and her whole life had unravelled. And instead of being there to help her rebuild, to tell her that she was still loved, that there was no mistake she could make that would ever change that…

Her family had asked her to leave. Told her that she was a disgrace. That her actions were ruining their lives.

Grandma had been the only one who'd felt different, but she'd died just a few months later.

And since then… Well. Jenny knew now that family

didn't mean love any more than sex did. And neither of them were something you could trust enough to build a future on.

No, she wasn't going to tell her family. She wouldn't give them the chance to turn away from her child the way they'd turned away from her.

So, Liam was it, at least for now. Once she knew what level of involvement he wanted, and how they were going to make things work, *then* she could talk to Winter and start figuring things out. She was under no illusion that life would be able to remain the same once she had a baby. But she hoped in that future she would be able to hold onto the things she loved most about her life.

Maybe she could build an even better one than the one she'd been living for the last few years. With or without Liam's help.

She heard the screen door of the treehouse open, and realised Liam must be awake too. Time to get up.

She showered quickly and dressed in a T-shirt and a pair of shorts that were suddenly beginning to get a little tight around the waist, as if her body felt that now the secret was out it could start changing in earnest. Or maybe she was just bloated after her midnight feast. Her body was a mystery to her.

As she entered the living area, Liam looked up from where he sat at the kitchen bar and smiled, before nodding to the coffee pot. Then he turned back to whatever he was reading on his tablet.

Jenny weighed up the option of the coffee. She could tell by the aroma that it was thick and strong and dark, and it made her mouth water. But her doctor had been adamant that she was only allowed a certain amount of caffeine a day during her pregnancy, and she was pretty sure that one cup from Liam's pot would take her over her limit immediately.

Would she regret it later if she drank the coffee now? Trying to predict the future was a difficult and often fruitless task, but she didn't need Grandma's Tarot cards to tell her that, come her usual after lunch slump, she'd regret having used up her caffeine allowance so early.

Instead, she rifled around in the cupboards and found some fruit teas and made herself a cup of that instead, only glancing wistfully at the coffee pot a few times.

Liam pulled out pastries and fruit and breads for breakfast, and they ate in companionable silence—him engrossed in whatever he was reading and she watching him. They'd never had breakfast together, she realised, not really. Most nights they'd spent together in Iceland she'd crept back to the suite she was sharing with Winter, so her absence wouldn't be noted and commented on endlessly in the morning.

She wasn't completely surprised to discover that Liam wasn't much of a morning person.

'Sorry,' he said, after draining his second cup of coffee—not that she was bitterly counting or anything—and putting aside his tablet. 'I'm not much for conversation before my second cup of the day.'

'I noticed,' she said with a smile. 'So, now you're fully conscious…any plans for the day?'

He nodded and reached for another slice of watermelon. 'Actually, yes. I had a thought last night. If we're going to make any of this work at all, we need to figure out a way to be friends. Starting with learning a little more about each other.'

Jenny felt her shoulder muscles stiffen automatically and worked to relax them. 'Getting to know each other' always led to the sort of awkward questions she didn't want to answer, in her experience. But on the other hand she had to admit she'd followed a similar train of thought the night before too.

They needed to get to know each other if they were even going to consider co-parenting. But that didn't have to mean opening up about her past, her family, or any of that, did it? All Liam really needed to know was who she was *now,* and the sort of mother she'd be to their child.

She didn't have to tell him anything she wasn't ready for him to know. And she definitely wasn't ready to confess all about her past. She knew how he'd look at her if he knew—either the same way people had at the time, when the story hit the papers and online, with disgust and disappointment. Or, if she was lucky, pity—for the naivety that had led her into that situation in the first place.

She'd had more than enough of both those reactions at the time, and she didn't want to see *either* of them on Liam's face.

But it *would* be good to learn a little more about the enigma that was Liam Delaney—especially if he was going to be part of her and her child's life. Which meant giving up some stuff of her own, she supposed.

As long as she got to control how much.

So she nodded. 'I suppose there's probably more to learn about you than what you like in bed and that you're kinda bad at mornings.' Dammit. She really hadn't meant to say that.

His answering smirk told her that his brain had gone to the same place hers had, and for a long moment he held her gaze trapped in his own, imagining all the things they weren't saying. Or doing.

Nope. No sex. That's the rule. If I can't have coffee, I sure as hell can't have sex with this man either. It's far more dangerous.

Liam broke first and looked away, gathering up his breakfast things and carrying them to the sink, and the moment was over.

'So. You had a plan?' She reached for her fruit tea and tried not to wince at the taste.

'I thought I'd show you around a bit. Take you down to the beach, have lunch at my favourite café, that sort of thing.'

He reached over to take her plate too and began stacking the dishwasher. She suspected he probably had a housekeeping service who'd have done that for him while they were out, so maybe it was just a displacement activity. She could appreciate the need for that. And it was kind of…nice to see him doing something so domestic. Something she could imagine a father doing.

Not that he was on board with that yet.

'That sounds lovely.' She had to admit, after all the drama of yesterday—not to mention the travel, and the midnight snack—she was a little drained today, despite sleeping well.

'And we can talk,' Liam added. She wasn't entirely sure if she just imagined the ominous tone in his voice.

'I'll go get ready.' Jenny hopped off her stool and headed for the bedroom, her mind already whirring.

If Liam wanted to Talk, she was going to make sure she had her own stack of awkward questions to pose for every one he asked her.

He might be right that the only way to make a decision about their future was to open up and understand each other. But that didn't mean it wasn't going to be utter torture getting there. And she sure as hell wouldn't be the only one going through that.

The beach closest to the resort was one of Liam's favourite places in the world—and Jenny seemed charmed by it too. He'd discovered it almost by accident when exploring the proposed resort site and known instantly that he was in the right place.

'What's this place called?' Jenny had her sandals in her hand as they walked along the pale white sand. Beside them, the waves sparkled bright blue in the sunshine. There were a few intrepid surfers out there but it was still early, and few people not staying very locally would have made their way down the twisty jungle path to reach this particular beach yet—not when there were so many others nearby to enjoy.

The rainforest curled around both edges of the sand, giving the cove a secluded, protected feeling. There were no large resorts built up to the edge of the sand here—only a small, ramshackle café at the far end, owned by the sister-in-law of Valentina, who ran the companion restaurant in town. It always looked like it was about to fall down, but the food was every bit as good as the more polished town restaurant—maybe even better. Not that he planned to tell Valentina that.

Liam liked to think that this beach would almost be a secret, just for people staying in his treehouses, and a few others in the know. A special, private place without the crowds or the noise of some of the larger, better-known beaches.

'I wasn't sure it even had a name for ages,' he admitted. 'But then I heard one of the locals call it Playa Escondida—which means Hidden Beach, I think. So that's what I call it too.'

'It suits it.' She paused on the sand, turning a slow circle to take in all the views. Liam smiled as he watched her, something in him just glad that she found the same magic in this place that he did.

He'd built retreat hotels all over the world, always seeking out special places where his guests could rest, recharge, and check out of the real world for a while until they were ready to face reality again. From the Californian desert to the volcanic landscape and geothermal pools of Iceland, he built places outside time.

He was proud of all his retreats, but he just knew that his Costa Rican treehouse resort was going to be the most special of all.

Even Jenny was falling for it, he could tell. He watched

her turn, her expression more relaxed than it had been since she'd arrived, her blonde hair glowing in the sunlight.

God, he wanted to kiss her. He wanted to wrap her up in his arms and kiss her here, barefoot on this beach, the waves shining behind them, like the end of one of those romcom movies he used to star in.

What the hell was wrong with him?

It's just lust, he reassured himself. After all, being told he couldn't have something had always made him want it more.

But he wouldn't give in to that desire, even if Jenny indicated for a moment that she wanted him to. She'd regret it later, he knew, and he wouldn't do that to her.

Not until they'd made a decision about the future, anyway.

Jenny stopped twirling suddenly and froze, staring across the beach to the closest point where it became jungle. Liam followed her gaze, and grinned when he realised what had caught her attention.

'Is that a sloth?' she asked, her voice filled with incredulity.

'It is.' The slow-moving creature loped unhurriedly across the rainforest floor, right beside the sand, before starting to shimmy up the next tree. 'You're lucky to see one down on the ground; they only come down from the trees about once a week. But if you look up when we're in the jungle, you'll likely see a whole lot more.'

'This place is amazing.' The sloth disappeared into the tree canopy, and Jenny turned to him with a blinding smile that made his whole body tighten in response. 'So, what wonders do you have for me next?'

They took their time exploring their way along the beach, watching the few surfers tackling the waves, and observing a small snorkelling lesson taking off from a boat. They didn't see any more sloths, but they heard macaws overhead, and what might have been a monkey scampering through the trees as they approached the café.

Liam knew they were supposed to be spending this time getting to know each other, but it was hard to pull the conversation from the wonders around them to their personal histories and issues—especially when so much of his concentration had to go into keeping his distance from her. It would be so easy to just reach out and touch the small of her back as he guided her along their path, or to grab her hand to show her something interesting. Or even to catch her in his arms when she lost her footing on the soft sand and hold her close against him...

No. Not doing that.

Instead, he attempted occasional questions about how she came to live in LA, or her family, her childhood, but each time Jenny deflected them with an observation about their surroundings.

He was beginning to wonder if she wanted to hide from her own past as much as he did his.

Eventually, however, they reached the end of the beach—and Isabela's café. 'Come on,' he said, when she looked dubiously at the structure. 'I promised you lunch.'

Isabela bustled over to greet them the moment the door banged shut. Inside, the beach café was cool and shady, and even Liam felt it a welcome relief from the April heat—Jenny sighed blissfully beside him, and he realised he probably should have got her out of the sun sooner.

They were shown to the best table, such as it was—a rickety wooden thing set for two, away from the long bar where one or two locals sat and eyed them suspiciously, and beside the open windows where they could watch the activity on the beach, and the waves washing in and out.

With Jenny's permission, he ordered for both of them, asking Isabela in Spanish to just bring them whatever was best today. He'd eaten there enough to trust her judgement.

Isabela's teenage son brought them iced water and then, when they declined beer, some fruit juice Liam's taste buds couldn't quite identify.

'So, in the interests of getting to know one another,' Liam said when they were alone again. 'Is this your first time in South America?'

The tension that had appeared in her expression at his first statement faded a little, and she nodded. 'Never been further south than Florida before. But then, Florida's a long way from Canada, where I grew up. And even further from…where is it, exactly, you're from?'

'England,' he replied succinctly. 'In case the accent wasn't a giveaway.'

She rolled her eyes. 'I know that much. *Where* in England?'

'Norfolk. But you could have found that much out from Wikipedia.'

She flashed him a smile. 'I do have a bit of an advantage there,' she admitted. 'Your whole life is laid out on the internet by intrepid fans.'

Had she looked him up? Probably. It was hard not to, when the information was just sitting there. He'd idly googled other actors just while watching them in a movie—it was unrealistic to believe that Jenny wouldn't have looked up the man who'd fathered her child.

Which meant she must already know the answers to the questions she was asking. So why ask them? Unless it was to stop him asking deeper, more personal ones of her.

There was something guarded in her eyes, something brittle in her smile, and he suddenly wondered what he *would* find if he ran an internet search for Jenny Bouchard. Because nobody could avoid their life being documented on the internet any more, could they? It was always all there if a person knew where to look.

He knew where to look. He could do a little research after she went to bed tonight and find out all there was to know about the secrets Jenny Bouchard was keeping, he was sure.

But he'd rather she trust him enough to tell him herself.

'What?' Jenny asked, and he realised he'd been staring at her for long moments.

Liam shook his head. 'Nothing. Look, here comes our food. I promise you you're going to love this.'

He could be patient. He had time. Well, he had a week.

She'd tell him her secrets before that week was out.

CHAPTER SEVEN

COSTA RICA WAS so much more beautiful and amazing than Jenny had imagined, but she still returned to the treehouse that night feeling like she'd dodged a bullet. After their—admittedly delicious—lunch of local fare served tapas style, she'd expected Liam to start up his promised questioning in earnest.

But he hadn't.

Instead, he'd stuck to the general getting-to-know-a-person questions that had no hidden traps. She'd expected, at the least, a bit of a quiz about her family in Canada, and why she'd left, but as if he had a second sense for the sort of questions that would make her clam up, he'd avoided any mention of family at all, after his first couple of attempts on the beach.

He'd kept asking questions, though, all through their trip back to the treehouse, the simple dinner he'd cooked for her from the magically stocked fridge, right up until she started yawning and he sent her to bed and retreated to his hammock.

So now he knew her favourite colour—green—her favourite movie, her teenage crush, the most insane thing she'd ever seen on a publicity tour with Winter, that she only liked salted popcorn, not sweet, and a dozen other meaningless facts—but he still had no idea why she hadn't spoken to her parents in over five years, or why she'd moved to LA and started working for Winter in the first place.

Which was a good thing, she reminded herself when she woke up still thinking about it the next morning. She didn't *want* to tell him those things.

But it did make her feel a little guilty.

She knew that she couldn't possibly expect to raise a child with a man she couldn't be honest with, one she couldn't trust with the basic details of her past. But trust…that was a sticky word for her these days. She'd trusted her family. She'd trusted Anthony.

And look where all that trust had got her.

But this situation was different. She wasn't expecting Liam to love her. The point remained, though. If they were going to do this together, she couldn't hide from the truth. She'd have to tell him everything eventually.

Just not yet.

Of course there was still the strong chance that he was going to walk away at the end of the week and then there'd never be any need to tell him…

Except that wasn't fair either. He needed all the information to be able to make the decision about his future in the first place. It was no less than she'd expect.

Whatever the outcome of this week, it had to be based on a foundation of honest truth. There couldn't be any room left for what-ifs and wrong decisions.

Not having all the information, or at least not the *true*

information, from Anthony was part of what had led her down that road to disaster last time. She expected the truth from Liam, which meant she had to give it in return.

She just might need a little time to build up to it.

He, on the other hand, didn't have that choice—of waiting to tell her his secrets in his own time.

Because *of course* she'd googled him to find out all she could about him, before she came down to Costa Rica to tell him he was going to be a father. Who wouldn't?

So she knew about his parents' farm in Norfolk, how it had been about to go under until he'd saved it with the fee from his first big Hollywood movie. She knew he was the youngest of the family, with three older sisters. She could list the films he'd made, the co-stars he'd dated. She'd read all the old reports about his wild child ways, seen the photos of him staggering out of nightclubs with a blonde on his arm.

She'd read the interviews he'd given during those years—and noticed that he hadn't given one in the last five years.

And she knew why.

Even before she'd met him in Iceland, she'd known that much. Everybody in LA did. She remembered it happening, her first full month in LA.

Liam and his actress girlfriend at the time, Julie Oswald, had been at a party at some director's house in the Hollywood Hills. It was a big deal, lots of stars there, and lots of alcohol and drugs, by all accounts.

When they'd left in the early hours Julie had been driving. And, according to the inquest, she'd accidentally driven them through a red light and been hit by a car coming the other way that hit the driver's side. Julie had been killed on impact and Liam…

Liam, on the other side of the car, had survived. With, it seemed, miraculously few injuries.

At least, not physical ones.

Winter and Josh, two of Liam's closest friends even back then, didn't talk about what had happened next—and Jenny hadn't known how to ask without sounding like she was prying, which she would have been, and inviting questions she didn't want to answer about why it mattered to her anyway.

She wondered, though, as she watched him over breakfast, about the non-visible injuries. The ones that had changed the very person he was from the inside out, because of what had happened.

Jenny knew about that sort of injury, even though she'd never been in an accident half as traumatic as the one Liam had lived through.

Maybe those were the secrets she still needed to hear from Liam before this week was up. Maybe those secrets would be worth sharing her own for.

Starting from a place of total honesty.

What a novel idea for a relationship.

Probably only a possibility because this *wasn't* a relationship. Nobody in a relationship ever told the whole truth, did they? Otherwise the US divorce rate would be even higher.

'So, what's the plan for today?' she asked as he drained the dregs of his second cup of coffee.

'I thought I'd take you further up the coast a way, to another retreat of sorts,' he said. 'A friend of mine runs a yoga studio there and has a pregnancy yoga class this morning.'

Jenny blinked. 'You're taking me to pregnancy yoga?' Wasn't that the sort of thing that besotted, doting husbands and boyfriends did? Not casual flings who weren't even sure they wanted to be part of their kid's life.

Liam gave an uncomfortable shrug. 'Honestly, I needed to go up there this week anyway. We're negotiating her bringing her studio in under my resort banner and running sessions here for guests. It just so happens that she has a pregnancy class today.'

'Right. Of course.' That made more sense. Basically, he was finding a way to keep his business running while she was here. She couldn't complain about that.

'We might see some more sloths or monkeys, though,' he added, and she couldn't help but smile at the idea.

Not least because if they were admiring the wildlife they wouldn't be baring their souls to each other.

The roads they travelled on were twisty, uneven and often barely worthy of the name, but Liam's four-by-four took the sharp corners and dips without much complaint. Jenny stared at his tanned, toned forearms, the muscles there cording as he turned the wheel, and couldn't help but remember how it felt to have those arms around her.

She looked away.

Not thinking about that. Not thinking about him that way.

That was easier said than done, though. Even as she

stared out of the window instead, memories of the dreams that had plagued her sleep filled her head instead.

Dreams where she wasn't alone in that big bed in the treehouse. Where Liam's body was curled behind her, his mouth at her neck, his hand at her breast, his hardness pressed up against her.

The way his hand drifted down her body. The way she parted her legs to let him in…

She cleared her throat and turned her attention back to the car. Maybe she should turn the air-con up a bit.

'You're a good driver,' she said after he navigated another particularly tricky section of road.

He shrugged but didn't answer. Too late, she realised that it might be a sensitive subject, given his history, even if he *hadn't* been driving the night of the accident.

They drove in silence for a few more minutes. Jenny went back to scanning the trees around her for wildlife, but couldn't spot any. She was about to start counting trees to distract her from the memories of her dreams when Liam spoke again.

'So, next question.'

'You didn't ask enough yesterday?'

'Not by half.' There was something in his voice, a steely hardness, that told her he was done going easy on her. Which meant she couldn't afford to go easy on him either.

If he wanted her secrets, he'd have to give up his own in return. That much she knew for certain.

'How did you come to work for Winter?' he asked.

She considered her answer. On the one hand, the full

story gave away every humiliating, soul-destroying detail of the worst six months of her life.

But it didn't have to. Not if she told it right.

She wasn't ready to tell him everything just yet. She would, she promised herself. But she needed to work up to it.

And in the meantime she could give him *something,* couldn't she?

'I wanted to be an actress,' she said, keeping her tone breezy and her gaze away from his. 'So I moved from Canada to LA, and started looking for work.' She shrugged, as if a little embarrassed not to have made it in the notoriously difficult industry. 'When that didn't happen, I figured working for a star was better than waiting tables. I joined a recruitment agency, and they got me the interview. I had good office experience, I'm proactive, and Winter and I hit it off when we met. It was as simple as that.'

She'd expected it to be harder, but Winter had been determined and wasn't into wasting time. She couldn't have known then, she mused, how much that one interview would change her life.

'And you like working for her?'

'Very much. She's more of a friend than an employer these days.'

'But you still haven't told her about the baby.' Liam glanced across at her for a brief moment, before returning his attention to the road. 'You'll have to, though. Especially if you want to keep working for her.'

'I do,' she said quickly. The last thing she needed was

Liam getting any ideas about her giving up her life and her dreams to follow him around the planet with a baby in tow. 'And we'll figure it out somehow. Once I know what *your* expectations are in all this.'

It didn't hurt to remind him that it wasn't her holding up the ability to make plans for the future here.

'Right. I'm sure you will.' She listened hard for any sarcasm in his voice, but she didn't find it.

'Your turn,' she said, already formulating her question in her mind. She didn't want to ask about the accident, not straight off. But there was something she'd always wanted to know… 'Do you think you'll ever go back to acting?'

'No.' His answer was fast, firm and didn't leave a lot of room for follow-up questions. But she asked one anyway.

'Why not?'

'There's nothing left there for me.'

She stared at the bleak expression on his face, the absolute certainty that anything about that part of his life was over, and knew that the papers and the internet only had half the story.

They said Liam Delaney had walked away from that car accident with only minor injuries.

But they were wrong.

'We're here,' Liam said as they took a final turn and suddenly a small wooden complex tucked in between the trees came into view. 'There's Selena, my yoga teacher friend.' He nodded towards the terrace, where a gorgeous dark-haired, tanned and toned woman in a loose shirt and tight shorts stood, smiling widely and waving.

Of course. Of course Liam's friend was gorgeous. She

probably glistened rather than perspired too, like all the yoga gurus on YouTube, while Jenny would be sweating like a pig in no time.

Good job they'd taken sex off the table, really.

Jenny seemed a little reticent when he dumped her on Selena with barely a hello and goodbye, apart from the warm welcome hug Selena always insisted on. He'd planned to stay and show Jenny round a bit, maybe even watch some of the yoga session. But after her questions in the car…he needed some space.

And luckily there was always the excuse of work, of conversations he needed to have to keep building up the new resort, to keep him busy and distracted.

Distraction was definitely what he needed today. As if Jenny in her tight yoga gear, showing off every curve he wasn't allowed to touch, wasn't enough, then there were the questions.

Do you think you'll ever go back to acting?

Not if they paid him. Which they would, of course. A lot. But it didn't matter.

He wasn't that person any more, and he never wanted to be him again.

That thought gave him pause, as he considered the only question that really mattered this week. What would the old Liam do about the baby? Maybe if he knew that, he could do the opposite. It was what he'd done in almost every other area of his life.

Old Liam had been excited about Julie's pregnancy. He'd been gung-ho about parenthood, proud of his ability to father a child and naively confident that everything would work out fine, one way or another.

If they'd lived…

He slumped against the railing outside the yoga studio as the realisation hit him.

If they'd lived, he'd have been a terrible father. He'd have handed off responsibility to Julie, or the nannies they'd inevitably hire. He'd have breezed in between shoots and parties to do the fun stuff, sure, but he wouldn't have been involved—not the way his own parents had been. He hadn't had that in him then, too caught up in his own success, his own demons, and the lifestyle both afforded him.

Liam wasn't proud of the man he'd been back then. After leaving home and finding such easy success…he'd grown selfish, entitled even. Focused on finding greater success—or notoriety.

The accident had stolen that life from him—taken so many things he'd never recover from the loss of—but it had given him something in return: a new perspective on his own existence.

He was a different man now, because of the accident, and what followed. Whatever the old him would have done, he could do different. Better.

But did that mean he should settle down and raise a child? That this was his second chance? Or that he *shouldn't* be excited about the baby at all? What was the opposite action to the one he'd have taken then?

Was it responsibly stepping away, giving Jenny financial support but not getting involved emotionally? Because while he'd changed beyond recognition, one thing hadn't.

He wasn't going to be able to stay still and be a doting dad, the way his own had been. Growing up on the farm, his dad had been busy, for sure—farming meant working a lot of hours, and many of them unsociable. But he'd been *there.* If Liam needed him, he'd only had to tag along into the fields after he'd finished his morning chores feeding and cleaning out various animals. His dad would let him follow along until Liam was ready to talk about whatever was on his mind, and then he'd listen. *Really* listen. He'd keep working, and that was good because it meant Liam wouldn't have to look him in the eye while he talked. But he heard every word, because at the end he'd offer Liam the advice he wanted, or the words he needed to hear.

Liam had never once felt worse about himself, or a situation, after talking to his father as a child. He wished he could say the same about the experience as an adult.

He knew what his dad would say. He'd put aside all his disappointment about Liam as a man—his wild past, the way he never came home, his behaviour on the rare occasions he had visited before the accident—and he'd be purely excited at the prospect of another grandchild. He and Mum would welcome Jenny into their family, their home, in a heartbeat.

And if Liam told him he was contemplating *not* being a part of the child's life… he'd never understand.

Which was why he couldn't tell him.

But it didn't take away the fundamental question. How

could he be the kind of father his own had been if he was travelling all over the world between his resorts, setting up new sites, and continuing to build the business he loved—the business that had saved him after the accident?

And if he couldn't be the kind of father his kid deserved—would the baby be better off without him anyway?

He didn't find any answers on his tour of the yoga studio grounds, but when he returned to collect Jenny an hour later he found her smiling and glowing from the exercise. Hopefully that meant it had been a good decision to bring her here.

'You enjoyed the class?' he asked as he approached Jenny and Selena.

Jenny nodded. 'Very much. It felt good to stretch my body and feel like it's still mine—even if I'm sharing it right now.'

Sharing it with his child. Liam couldn't help the slight feeling of pride and satisfaction that surged through him as his gaze dropped to her still flat belly.

'It's important to keep that connection with your body,' Selena said with a smile. 'You did great today. Come back any time.'

She hugged Jenny, who looked mildly awkward at the interaction, then stepped away.

'Did you want to try the hot springs before we head back to the treehouse?' Liam asked. 'They're wonderful after a workout.'

'Oh, um…' Jenny darted a glance at Selena, who winced.

'I'm afraid that the hot springs are not recommended for expectant mothers, Liam,' she said apologetically.

'Right. Of course. Sorry.' Should he have known that? Probably. How much else was he supposed to know about pregnancy that he didn't? And how much more about babies and children? *You don't know how much you don't know,* his father used to say. 'I guess we'll head back, then.'

He'd half hoped that Jenny would be too tired to ask more questions on the drive back. But when she did, they weren't the questions he'd expected.

'So, you and Selena,' she said as he drove away from the yoga studio and hot springs. 'Were you two ever a… well, couple, I guess? Or anything.'

He blinked, then concentrated on the road. 'Me and Selena? No. She's married to Gael, who runs the place with her. He's been helping me out a lot with plans for the resort, and I'm hoping to bring them both in on-site when we open.'

'Oh. Right.' She stared out of the window rather than look at him.

'Were you…jealous?'

'No!' Her response was fast and emphatic—but not entirely convincing.

'Are you sure?' he teased. 'I mean, I'd understand…'

She reached across to lightly hit his thigh, and he grabbed her hand, swallowing at the instant spark he always felt when they touched.

Maybe teasing wasn't a good idea. Not when neither of them was willing to follow up where it might lead.

God knew he wanted to, though. And the idea of Jenny being jealous… It might be juvenile, but he had to admit he didn't hate it. Keeping his hands off her was a challenge, and keeping his thoughts away from how good it could be if they gave in… that was proving impossible. It would be nice to know that she was struggling with the same thing.

'Not jealous.' She snatched her hand away and tucked it under her leg. Almost as if she didn't trust herself not to touch him again.

Liam smiled. 'Of course not.'

'We don't have that kind of relationship, and it's not like we've made any promises to each other—or intend to.'

'Right.' They'd both been clear on that from the start. Neither of them was looking for anything serious or long-term—even if it seemed to have found them anyway. They'd be tied for life now, because of the baby. *If* he chose to be involved.

If he didn't, he would never see her again. He'd have to make sure of that.

If he stepped back she wouldn't want him showing up in her life, just because he was friends with her boss.

'It was just… I realised it was another thing we'll need to deal with. Plan for, even. If we end up doing this parenting thing together.'

'What? Selena and Gael?'

'No. I mean…if we're co-parenting, we'll both have to deal with the other dating other people. Maybe even settling down and getting serious with them. We'd need to agree how that was going to work too.' She sighed. 'There's just…so much. If we do this, we're connected for the rest of our lives.'

'Yeah. I had the same realisation today too.' The weight of it all hung heavy around his neck, threatening to pull him back down.

But down to where? The dark place he'd been after Julie died?

He couldn't risk that. Not even for his child.

He'd worked too hard to find this level of acceptance of the world. To make peace with his past and work towards a new future.

And the idea of watching his child's mother—watching *Jenny*—fall in love with another man…that stirred up emotions he'd kept buried for a long time now. Ones he didn't want to feel again.

But what was the alternative? Stay away completely, of course. But if he wanted to be involved he had to accept that idea of the future. Because of course she'd fall in love with someone—and any man in his right mind would jump at the chance to fall for her.

Unless he was willing to be that man—

He broke off the thought and centred himself, focusing very hard on the road ahead. That wasn't him. He wasn't there yet—and he suspected he never would be.

Love led to loss. And he knew too well that his broken psyche couldn't take any more of that.

They drove the rest of the way home in silence, each lost in their own thoughts. But when they arrived Liam hurried around to the passenger door to help her out, then left his hand on her arm to stall her for a moment.

'What?' She looked up at him, eyes wide and wondering, and the only thing he wanted in the world was to kiss her. To kiss her and never stop.

He looked away and cleared his throat. 'I just… We'll figure it out, okay? Whatever we decide, we'll do it together, and we'll make it work together. Yeah?'

He could see her throat move as she swallowed, her gaze never leaving his. Were the same thoughts flooding her brain that had taken over his? The feeling that what tied them together was more than just the baby growing inside her?

He didn't have the courage to ask.

Finally she nodded. 'Yeah. Together.'

Then, with a tight smile, she brushed past him towards the treehouse stairs. Liam took a moment to steel himself against another evening playing house with a woman he longed to touch but couldn't, then followed.

CHAPTER EIGHT

JENNY BRAVELY RESISTED the coffee again at breakfast the next morning, but when Liam announced his plans to take her to a little coffee roastery café where they could roast their own beans before drinking the strong, heavenly brew, she broke.

'I need to take a meeting with the owner anyway about supplying the resort when we open, so I thought it would be perfect,' he said. 'I remember from Iceland how much you like your coffee.'

'You do realise that pregnant women are supposed to limit their caffeine intake,' she snapped, and regretted losing her temper as he blinked cluelessly at her. 'Have you not noticed that I haven't drunk more than a cup of coffee a day since I got here?'

'Um…actually…no.' He winced. 'Sorry. I knew about avoiding alcohol, but I didn't think…sorry.'

Jenny's shoulders slumped, and she sighed. 'That's okay. I mean, it's not as if you've spent a lot of time around pregnant women, I suppose.'

Liam looked away. 'No. No, I haven't.'

He looked so distraught at his screw-up that she felt sorry enough for him to let him off the hook. 'Look, you go take your meeting. I'm pretty tired today anyway. I'll hang out here, enjoy the rainforest. Take a nap. That sort of thing.'

'Are you sure?' he asked. 'I won't be long. But there's stuff in the fridge for lunch when you get hungry. And I'll take you out for dinner to make it up to you.'

'It's a deal,' she said with a smile.

She'd expected to feel relief when he was gone. The past few days in each other's constant company in a rather small treehouse had been kind of intense—not to mention the moment yesterday by the car when she'd been *sure* he was about to kiss her. It was all getting a bit much, and she'd actually felt a little lighter at the idea of a reprieve. Of not spending every moment reminding herself why she couldn't just reach over and touch him, kiss him. Couldn't give in to the chemistry that still simmered between them, all the damn time.

She needed just a couple of hours to be by herself with her thoughts and figure out how she felt about everything.

But strangely, the moment he was gone, she just found that she missed his company.

It made sense in a way, she reasoned as she took a long, not too hot shower. When Liam was around she wasn't alone in this pregnancy. She wasn't solely responsible for the life growing inside her.

But he wouldn't always be around. Even if he decided to be part of this, they weren't going to be doing it as a couple. Their conversation about other partners in the car had only made that clearer.

So sometimes she *would* be alone. She would have to

learn to do this by herself. Just like everything else in her life over the last five years.

I knew that. I came here knowing I'd probably be doing this on my own.

But somewhere between shower sex and pregnancy yoga she'd got used to having Liam around again. Used to watching him from the kitchen counter stool as he cooked them dinner, or waiting until he finished his second coffee of the day to start a conversation.

It was worse, in a way, than after Iceland. Then, it had all been about sex. Now she wasn't allowed to touch him, because of her own stupid rules, so she had more time to notice the smaller, everyday things about him.

None of them, however, made her want to touch him any less.

She still dreamt about kissing him, making love to him, every night. And when she'd met Selena the yoga instructor, in all her toned, tanned, centred beauty, she hadn't been able to stop the surge of jealousy that had powered through her.

These were all things she was going to have to get a handle on—either as a co-parent with Liam or because after this week she'd never see him again.

Suddenly, she was itching to know which it would be.

She'd promised him a week; she couldn't rush him now. But she hated her future feeling so uncertain.

Ever since Anthony had torn away the future she'd confidently believed was hers—one with a big white wedding with celebrity guests, and a life in relative comfort and pleasure, with love and affection from a husband she trusted over everything—she'd always refused to put her future in the hands of others. But now it seemed she had no choice. Until Liam made his decision, she couldn't plan anything at all.

And she was *itching* to plan.

Towelling herself off after her shower, she pulled on her comfiest shorts and T-shirt and dropped to sit on the bed.

There was no real way to tell the future, she knew that. But even a clue would help…

Rooting around in her rucksack, she pulled out the small silk bag that held her grandma's Tarot cards.

Maybe they couldn't give her the certainty she needed about what would happen next in her life, but perhaps they could help her get her swirling thoughts in order before Liam got home.

No, not home. Back to the treehouse. She *really* couldn't afford to start thinking of this place as home.

She grabbed herself a fruit tea from the kitchen, then added a water jug and glass from the fridge to the tray and took the whole lot out onto the balcony and placed it on the table. Then she took a seat, cross-legged in the wide wooden chair at the table, just across from the hammock where Liam had been sleeping since she'd arrived.

It only took a moment to lay out the cloth she used for her readings, but she spent a little longer shuffling the cards and thinking about her questions while she held them.

Her grandmother had always tried to teach her to read the cards properly, but Jenny hadn't been interested.

Then, by the time she was, she was busy and working and there was never enough time to get into it when she visited.

And then her world had fallen apart, and Grandma had sent the cards to her without a note.

Grandma had died a few months later, before Jenny had even managed to ask her why.

Cards shuffled, she set out her favourite simple spread—three cards representing her past, present and future. Then she squinted at them and tried to figure out what they meant.

'What are you doing?'

She jumped at Liam's voice behind her, knocking the pack of cards so they fanned out across the table.

'You have *got* to stop sneaking up on me,' she said, one hand clutched to her chest. 'It's bad for the baby.' *And my heart.*

'Sorry.' He slid into the chair opposite her. 'But really. What are you doing?'

'Reading Tarot cards.' She used to be embarrassed when people found out about her little habit, but she'd grown to be confident in it. What did it matter to her what others thought of her anyway? 'They were my grand-mother's.'

'And you believe they can tell the future?' She could hear the scepticism in his voice and, for a moment, wanted to play with him, to pretend that she did.

But honesty was going to be the most important thing between them going forward, and she didn't want to risk that, even for a joke.

'No, I don't,' she told him. 'But Grandma always used to do a reading for me when I visited, and somehow it always helped to get my thoughts in order. I still couldn't tell what was going to happen next, but I had a better handle on what I wanted, and what I'd do, if that makes any sense?'

Liam looked more intrigued than sceptical now. 'I think so. Can you show me?'

Jenny considered, watching him carefully for any sign that he was mocking her. She didn't find one.

It felt like a strangely personal thing to share—not because the cards had any spiritual meaning to her but because they'd come from her grandma. The only family member who hadn't completely abandoned her when her world had fallen apart.

But if Liam was going to be part of her life, even only as a friend and a co-parent, he deserved to know who she really was. And if she wanted his secrets she already knew she'd have to be willing to give up a few of her own.

Maybe the cards could help her do that, at least.

She nodded and said, 'Okay, then. I'll read one card for you. But I warn you, I'm not very good.'

Liam watched curiously as Jenny gathered up the scattered cards and patted them back into a pack between careful hands. She was such a practical, efficient sort of person, planning for the future rather than guessing at it, that he was surprised to discover this side to her.

He was also interested to hear about her grandmother. She'd not mentioned any other family and from the way she talked about her grandma, she wasn't around any longer. Did that mean she was all alone in the world now, apart from Winter? And the baby, of course.

And perhaps even him.

She handed the cards to him and straightened the silk cloth she'd covered the table with. She'd arrived with only a small suitcase and smaller backpack, so if she'd included these cards and their cloth in her minimalist packing they must be really important to her.

He felt as if he was finally seeing behind the curtain of Jenny Bouchard, and it was far more fascinating than any hokey attempts to tell his future.

'What do I do?' The cards felt worn and warm in his hands. *Well loved.* The thought came unbidden.

'Shuffle them,' she replied.

'Any particular way?' It felt disrespectful to fan the cards together as if he was playing poker with his buddies.

But Jenny shook her head. 'Whatever feels right to you.'

He shuffled the cards gingerly, somewhere between just cutting them and a half-hearted ripple. When he went to hand them back to Jenny, she shook her head.

'Put them down on the cloth,' she instructed, and he did so. 'Now, cut the pack wherever feels right.'

There was no particular feeling that led him to cutting it towards the bottom of the pack, but she seemed satisfied anyway.

'Now, take the top card and turn it over,' she said.

Liam did as he was told, and stared at a naked man

and woman, with a snake climbing a tree beside her. The Lovers, the card read. Adam and Eve in the Garden of Eden, he realised. Temptation in all its forms.

He looked up at Jenny, who sighed. 'Of course.'

'I guess I can pretty much make up the interpretation of this one myself,' he joked.

She squinted at the card, and he knew she was deciding how much to tell him.

'Yes and no,' she said finally. 'The Lovers is a card about relationships, sure. But more than that, it's about choices, really. I mean, you pick one path—or one partner—and you say goodbye to your option on the rest. It's about decisions to be made about relationships, about the sacrifice that might involve, and about temptation, of course. Of the heart and the flesh, I suppose. And…' She trailed off.

'And?' he prompted.

'Grandma always used to say this card was about the loss of innocence too. Because of the Garden of Eden symbolism, I suppose. She said it reminded us that there was no coming back from a bad decision once it was made.'

'Hmm.' Liam sat back in his chair. When he'd thought it was about sex, and wanting but not touching, it had seemed the perfect card for them. Now she'd explained it more fully, it seemed agonisingly even more correct. If he chose to walk away at the end of this week, to sign away his parental rights to his child, that was it. There was no coming back from that decision. 'I guess I see what you mean about the cards showing you your present more than your future.'

'Right?' She gave him a lopsided, almost ironic smile. 'It's because all they really are—the cards, I mean—are stories in pictures. They're symbols that remind us of tales we've heard or things we've seen. And we interpret them based on where we are in our lives.'

He frowned. 'How do you mean?'

'Well, if I hadn't shown up here this week and you'd seen that card, you wouldn't have been thinking about the decision you need to make about the baby. You'd have been thinking about… I don't know…whether it was time to meet someone new, or stay alone for ever.'

'Or whether to call that hot girl from Iceland next time I was in LA.'

She flashed him a grin at that, and he returned it for a moment before going back to staring at the card.

'Except if you weren't here I wouldn't be looking at a Tarot card at all. And now I am…'

He shook his head, unsure how to finish the sentence. But Jenny did it for him.

'We've only got a few days left.'

'Yeah.' Three more days and she'd be walking away— either for ever or ready for them to start some complicated time-share parenting agreement that neither of them knew how to do.

Why was she doing this? Suddenly he had to know. To understand why she was putting herself through this, this way.

'Why did you come here, really?' he asked.

She looked surprised at the question. 'You know why. Would you rather I hadn't? That I'd kept the baby a secret from you?'

Yes, a small part of his mind whispered. Because then he wouldn't have had to make decisions about a future he didn't trust.

But that wasn't the largest part of him. 'No,' he said, frustrated with himself for not being able to make sense of all this yet. 'I guess I just… You're young and beautiful and fun and clever and lovely. Why are you settling for a future of co-parenting with me, rather than out searching for your true love and happy ever after?' She worked for Winter. She had to know it was possible, that it could be out there for her somewhere. Why didn't she want it?

Jenny didn't answer, looking away as she tidied up the cards. There was a story here, one he'd sensed from the first moment he'd known about the baby. And he was damned if he wasn't going to get it out of her at last.

'Even in Iceland you were adamant that nothing between us could be anything more than a fling,' he remembered.

'So were you!' she shot back.

'Yeah, and I had good reasons.' He leant closer across the table until she looked up at him. 'I want to know what yours were.'

She held his gaze for a long moment, but he'd been doing this longer than her and she finally broke away.

'I had…a bad experience with love. I know what it can do and, honestly? Whatever the supposed wonders of true love, I'm not interested.'

'What happened?'

The pause that followed was long enough to make him wonder if she was busy coming up with a lie, but when she spoke the raw vulnerability and hesitation in her voice told him it was the truth.

'I was young. I got my first big break as an actress on a TV show, filming in Canada. I was starstruck.' She shrugged, and Liam felt a slightly sick feeling flowing through him as he filled in the blanks.

'You fell in love with a co-star.' It was too familiar a story. Working so closely together, away from the real world, it happened all the time—especially when people spent their days pretending to be in love with each other for the cameras. It was only a small step from that to making it happen in real life.

Sometimes it was the real thing, like Winter and Josh. Others…

She nodded. 'Anthony. He was married.'

Liam winced. 'It ended badly, I assume?'

'Of course it did.' She rippled the cards through her hands again, looking at them, not him. Liam suspected she hadn't needed the cards to tell her that would happen, but she'd put her faith in the power of love anyway.

She'd been young, she'd said. He thought she meant 'hopeful'.

'He told me his marriage was a sham,' she went on, not looking up. 'That it was all for the cameras anyway, and any love that had ever been between them had dried up years ago. He'd never cared about anything, anyone else enough to want to end it though…'

'Until he met you.' Disgust curled through him as he pictured it. Jenny, young and naive and enthusiastic, not even understanding the situation she was walking into.

He'd been in similar positions in his youth—older women who'd wanted to use him to make their husbands jealous, or for the shock value in the press. It had never been about him, just how he'd looked on their arm, or on camera.

It had stung, when he'd realised. But he'd never really fallen in love with any of them.

Jenny had.

'Yeah.' She placed the cards in a neat stack on the table and looked up at him at last. 'You can probably imagine what happened next. I thought we were going to ride off into the sunset together and live happily ever after and he—'

'Went back to his wife.'

'Yeah.' Her fingers twitched towards the cards, but she didn't pick them up again. 'And that should have been the end of it, right? Except he was famous. Not Winter and Josh or you famous, but he was famous enough. And so was she. So the papers got hold of it and for a month or more it was *everywhere.*'

Something clicked in Liam's brain. The first time he'd seen Jenny, on TV at a press conference Winter had given before she'd come to Iceland, he'd thought she looked familiar. But he hadn't been able to place where from, at the time.

Now, he knew. He'd seen her in countless grainy photos in newspapers and online, around six years ago. He hadn't paid them much attention then—it was just one more juicy scandal that the press got excited about for a month or two then forgot all about.

'What happened?' he asked, his voice steely. Whatever it was, he was sure he didn't want to hear it.

But he would, for her.

Whatever it was had scarred her, damaged her the way his accident had damaged him. He recognised that same weight of responsibility, of knowing that if either of them had made different choices, had lived their lives to a different code, they wouldn't be where they were now.

Losing Julie, and the baby, it had broken him for good. But maybe there was a way back for Jenny, a way he could help her find, even.

So when she paused he added, 'Tell me, Jenny.'

CHAPTER NINE

SHE DIDN'T WANT to tell him.

Having an affair with a married man—whatever lies he'd told her about his wife and the state of his marriage, however many times he'd promised he'd divorce his wife and marry her—remained the most shameful thing she'd ever done in her life.

But losing him, realising his lies, wasn't what had completely destroyed her belief in love. Obliterated her faith in people, and her ability to trust.

It was the next part that was the hardest to tell.

'When they saw it in the papers…my parents were horrified,' she said. 'My whole family, really. They'd always believed that going into acting would be my downfall and, right then, well, it seemed like they were right.'

It had been her dream, acting. When she'd got her big break she'd honestly felt like all her hard work was paying off, her dreams were coming true.

But then it had emerged that she'd only been cast because the star—who had a phenomenal amount of sway on the show—had wanted to sleep with her, according to an anonymous source on set. Viewers started commenting on posts with the most vitriolic hate for her, her morals and, worst of all, her acting skills.

And her family…

'They believed everything that people were saying about me.' The words came out as a whisper. 'Every awful thing—every lie, and every truth, without ever trying to discern between the two.'

And a lot of it *had* been lies. The affair, such as it was, had been a small, low-key romance, compared to what she'd seen between celebrities since, while working for Winter. There hadn't been expensive presents or exotic trips away. She hadn't been flaunted on the red carpet or caught in seedy circumstances by the paparazzi.

There'd been flirting on set, and stolen moments together. Whispered promises and kisses that spoke of more. There'd been two afternoons in a nearby hotel, but never overnight. And that had been all.

Until he'd insisted on taking her out for dinner one night, and they'd been photographed kissing by a news photographer at another table, and that was it.

'The worst part was, I discovered later that he'd called that photographer himself, to make sure he was there to take the photo of us.' All along, she'd been nothing but a publicity ploy. She'd been in love. He'd been… Well. Using her was the nicest way she could finish that sentence.

Liam wasn't as polite, swearing under his breath as he took in the implications of her words.

'Anyway. I got fired from the show, of course—at his behest, I imagine.' It still hurt—a deep-down ache that would never go away, she suspected—that someone had taken her dream away from her so easily, without any thought for her at all. Worse still was the feeling that she might not have deserved it in the first place.

'And your family?' Liam's question was low, urgent, and she knew he'd homed in on the part of this story that pained her most of all, even after so long.

'They disowned me.' It wasn't the whole story—that involved lots of tense conversations with her mother, her father leaving the room whenever she entered it, and the heartbreaking realisation that her family were happier when she wasn't around, even after the newspapers had moved on and there wasn't a man with a camera camped in the bushes outside their house every morning. But it was how it felt, and where it ended. 'All except my grandmother, but she lived with my parents and didn't get much say on what went on in the house. And she died just a few months later, anyway.'

'And you were alone.' There was something else in his voice this time. Not just pity, or even anger on her behalf. An understanding she hadn't expected to find from him.

Except he'd been left alone too, hadn't he? After the accident. She might not know the details, but she knew that much from things Winter and Josh had said.

He'd been alone ever since.

'I wasn't alone for long, though,' she said. She didn't want him feeling sorry for her, even if this was something they could bond over. 'I moved to LA, started over. And instead of endless rounds of auditions where people looked at me like they sort of recognised me, then smirked when they figured out where from, I got the job working for Winter instead. And it was the best thing that could have ever happened to me.'

'You don't miss acting?'

It was a question she'd asked herself, often, over the past five years. Her dream job had been taken away from her, and she hated the idea that she'd given up on it since then. But...when she looked back at her time working as an actress, she knew that the biggest appeal had been her on-set romance. She'd always felt as if she'd just been told what to do, shuffled around and fed lines to say. And maybe that was different for other actors—she knew that Josh and Winter loved becoming other people on film. But for her it didn't feel that way.

She hadn't been surprised when Winter had decided to try directing either. The idea of having control over something sounded far more appealing than just doing what she was told.

And working for Winter... If her boss had been anybody else, then maybe being a personal assistant would have felt much the same as acting had—as if she was being told what to do all the time. But it wasn't like that with Winter.

Winter trusted her. She gave her space and autonomy and responsibility. Once Jenny had proven she was up to the job, Winter let her do it however she saw fit. She was in charge of their itineraries, organising travel and accommodation, gatekeeping people who wanted access to Winter's time. But she was also a respected advisor; Winter talked to her about projects before deciding whether to take them on, and she listened to her thoughts and opinions too. They were a team, even now she was back together with Josh, and Jenny found she enjoyed that far more than she'd ever liked acting.

'I really don't,' she answered finally. 'I thought I would but... I've found something else. Something that suits me far better. I like working for Winter—no, I love it. I'm good at it, I'm well paid for it and I enjoy it. Why would I want to do anything else?'

He gave her a wry smile. 'You're lucky to have figured that out—to find what you love and make it a career. Too many people never do.'

Was he talking about himself? Jenny remembered how fast he'd shut her down when she'd asked him about acting in the car yesterday. But now she'd spilled all her secrets...maybe he'd be ready to share some of his?

Or not. Liam Delaney didn't seem like the sort to share easily.

She took a deep breath and asked anyway.

He knew the question was coming from the look on her face—as if she was steeling herself against a knockback.

'What about you? You said there was nothing left for you in acting. But do you miss it, all the same?'

Did he *miss* it? He could barely even remember it.

Liam looked away, staring out over the balcony into the rainforest, letting the sounds of nature around him fill the silence.

He didn't want to answer her question, but he knew he owed her some reciprocal sharing. She'd spilled her secrets, helped him understand why she wasn't searching for a happily ever after to go with the baby he'd accidentally gifted her. And he *did* understand. Trust, once lost, was the hardest thing to regain.

She'd lost faith in love, in family, in people in general—of course she wasn't going to be looking to take another chance on love.

But he'd lost faith in himself. And he didn't know how to explain that to her.

'I don't *miss* it, exactly,' he said, searching for the right words. 'It's more like it was a part of my life I barely recognise any longer.' He sure as hell didn't recognise the person he'd been back then—and he didn't want to.

'So you really won't ever go back to it?'

The wistfulness in her question surprised him. 'Why? You a fan?'

'Isn't everybody?' She raised her eyebrows at him across the table. 'You were kind of a star.'

'And that was the problem.' He didn't want to tell her. But he owed her some sort of explanation for his lifestyle choices—as the mother of his child, if nothing else. He sighed and groped for the right words. 'I liked being a star far more than I enjoyed acting. I liked the attention, the parties. The drink and the drugs. The chance to live the wild, uninhibited life I thought I was entitled to.' God, how he hated to think of the man he'd been back then.

Jenny stayed silent, waiting for him to continue, which he appreciated. Getting this out was hard enough. Dealing with questions about it would be impossible.

'I was an idiot. Worse. I was all those bad words you

can't say on screen if you want a family-friendly rating. And I couldn't even see it.' He reached for the jug of water with slices of citrus fruits in that sat at the centre of the table and poured himself a glass. 'Other people tried to tell me—Josh, especially. But I couldn't hear them over my own ego. I was living the kind of life I thought film stars were *supposed* to live. And then I met Julie.'

She'd been an actress too, of course. He was a film star; who else was he supposed to date? She'd been blonde and beautiful and waif-thin for the cameras—and she'd liked to party as much as he had. He'd thought he'd loved her, believed it through the fog of alcohol and partying, but some days he wondered whether they'd just fallen down into the same hole together and that was the only thing that kept them as a couple.

'I remember seeing photos of the two of you together,' Jenny said softly. 'You were a beautiful couple.'

There was something behind her words, an emotion it took him a moment to get hold of. When he realised what it was, he almost laughed.

Not jealousy, he thought. Pity. Which he could understand, but he really didn't deserve.

Liam had made a practice, over the last five years, of being brutally honest with himself at all times. It was the only way he'd found to keep himself on a path that didn't lead to self-destruction. The moment he let himself believe that one drink, one party, one slip-up wouldn't ruin him, he'd be done for. He knew that about himself.

He was an absolutist—an all-or-nothing kind of person. It was just better for everyone around him if he stuck with nothing.

But brutal honesty had saved him. And the more time he spent with Jenny, thinking about a future he'd been avoiding for half a decade, the more he realised that brutal honesty was the only thing that was going to get them through this too.

'I loved Julie,' he said bluntly. 'But if you're thinking the reason I won't open myself up to a relationship again is because I'm still in love with a ghost, you're wrong. I'm not the same man who loved Julie, and if she hadn't died it wouldn't have lasted between us.'

'Why not?'

'Because I'd have screwed it up. Because I *was* a screw-up, and I only got my head on straight because of the accident.' How long could he have continued down the path of self-destruction he'd been on, otherwise? He shuddered to think. And he knew it would never have ended well, for anybody.

'When you left Hollywood.'

'Yeah.' He had to tell her the rest of it, he knew that. But how?

'And you're a success now,' Jenny went on, not looking up at him. 'You turned your life around, you straightened yourself out, and you build these incredible retreat hotels for people who need to escape from the real world for a while, because that's what you needed after the accident, right?'

'Yeah,' Liam said again. 'That's right.'

She lifted her chin and met his gaze. 'You've done all

that, Liam. But what's next? I mean, you say you're not still hung-up on your dead ex-girlfriend, but you're not moving on either, are you? And trust me, I understand not wanting to risk falling in love again. But we have the chance of a different sort of future now, and I guess I'm wondering what's holding you back from taking it.'

It was a fair question—one that anyone else would have asked long before now. But Jenny had given him the space he needed to work through his initial emotions about her announcement. And their week was running out.

He needed to face up to exactly what was standing in the way of his future—any future. And Jenny had a right to know what it was.

'Julie was pregnant when she died.' Rip the sticking plaster off, get the horrors out of his head and onto the table between them. Jenny's gasp barely penetrated his fog of memories. 'Ten weeks. We were over the moon, in the naïve way you are when everything still feels like an adventure. That's why she was driving—I was off my head, celebrating the news, even though we'd known for a few weeks, and she was the sober one for a change, try- ing to do the right thing for the baby.'

She'd wanted to go home, he remembered. She'd been tired, a little nauseous, and grumpy as all hell because she couldn't drink and he could. She'd wanted to go home and he'd asked her to stay. Told her she was no fun, that being parents didn't have to change them. That they still deserved to live their lives, not mortgage their happiness to the kid. That if that was what she wanted him to do, she should leave now.

She hadn't left. She'd stayed, and waited to drive his drunk arse home from the party. But she'd been tired—exhausted. And she'd missed a red light he'd been too drunk to even see, and the other car had come from seemingly nowhere.

And in a moment that dream of a perfect, easy life had disappeared.

'I'm… God, Liam. I'm so sorry.' Reaching across the table, she grabbed his hand and squeezed. 'I had no idea.'

'Her family managed to keep it out of the papers, thank God. I was in no state to do it. I was in no state to do much of anything, really.' Even his memories of that time were hazy, which he could only assume was for the best. 'Eventually, I dragged myself to some rehab centre in the middle of the desert and… Well. Sorted myself out. Learned some coping strategies and so on. But I knew I could never go back to the life I'd had before—and I didn't even want to.'

'I'm not surprised,' Jenny murmured. 'I know a little about how that feels.'

She did, Liam realised as he thought back over their stories. Their experiences had been very different, of course, but the bones of them… They'd both made mistakes and paid for them. They'd both lost, and they'd both found a way to keep on living. To put the past behind them and find a new present to exist in.

But now the future had come calling. For both of them.

'I think you do. And I hope that means you'll understand when I say this.' Liam turned his hand over under her palm, clasping her fingers in his own. 'If I could fall in love again then this, with you and the baby, could be a second chance for me—some sort of redemption, even. But I can't. Love is not in my cards, because I know—the same way you do—how it leads to loss and pain, and I know I couldn't survive that twice. It almost killed me last time and…to my shame, I'm not strong enough to risk that again. So if we do this, if we decide to co-parent this child, that is all we can ever be. Friends, perhaps, if we're lucky. But I need you to know I'll never be able to give you anything more.'

If he'd seen doubt in her face, if he'd thought for a moment she was hoping for more—chasing a fairy tale ending he couldn't provide—he'd have walked away right then and there.

But instead he saw reflected back in her eyes the very same emotions that filled his own heart.

Resignation, tinged with sadness perhaps, but solid and firm all the same. Liam felt his shoulders drop as he relaxed.

They were two broken people making their way in a world that wanted them to be whole again but couldn't tell them how to get there.

This chance at a future was the best either of them was likely to get, he realised as the last of his reservations about the situation began to crumble.

Maybe this *was* his second chance, after all.

CHAPTER TEN

'WE'RE NOT TAKING the four-by-four today?' Jenny asked, confused, as Liam handed the car keys to one of his employees.

'Not today.' Liam turned to pick up a small backpack stocked, Jenny knew, with water, bug-repellent, sunscreen and snacks. 'Today, we're doing something different. There are no roads where I want to take you, so today, we're exploring on foot.'

Their mode of transport wasn't the only thing about today that was different, Jenny reflected as she shouldered her own backpack and followed him out of the main clearing where the temporary office for his new retreat was based, and down an almost hidden path through the thickening rainforest.

After their soul-baring conversation the night before, the air between them felt lighter, in lots of ways. They'd put their secrets out there and found they had more in common than they'd imagined. Liam wasn't avoiding relationships and love because of a permanently broken heart, but for the same reasons she was.

Because love couldn't be trusted to stay. One way or

another, love broke everyone—whether it was now or in fifty years, if you were one of the lucky ones.

Liam and Jenny already knew they weren't the lucky ones.

But at least they were on the same page. Love wasn't going to be a factor in whatever followed next and, with their secrets shared, neither of them had to worry any longer that the other would be expecting more than they could give. That helped Jenny relax about the situation.

Of course she was still pregnant by an ex-movie star she wasn't in a relationship with, and now she knew about his ex-girlfriend's pregnancy…well, it made it a lot easier to understand why Liam might be pulling back from the situation.

Still, she had a good feeling about things as they headed off into the rainforest for the short hike Liam had promised would astound and amaze her. After quite a few days in the rainforest, and after visiting—if not experiencing—the hot springs and the beach and staying in the most incredible treehouse she could imagine, she was intrigued to find out what else there was to see that could be *more* amazing.

Around her, the rainforest canopy closed overhead, darkening their path. She couldn't see another soul ahead on the trail, or behind them, but she knew the greenery that surrounded them was teeming with life. With every step, she heard the buzz and hum of insects; birds called out overhead and the trees rustled with the movement of hidden creatures.

Liam came to a sudden stop in front of her—so sudden

that, as he turned towards her, she found herself pressed up against his glistening skin.

'Look,' he breathed under his breath, indicating towards the trees with the smallest motion, obviously trying to avoid drawing the attention of whatever he'd spotted.

Hyperaware that his body was closer to hers than it had been since the day she'd arrived, Jenny tried to concentrate on what he was showing her. She sucked in a breath as she spotted it.

There, sprawled out over the branch of a tree just above their heads off the path, was a furry black body with oversized hands and feet, a black tail curled around the branch behind him.

'A howler monkey,' Liam breathed. 'You've probably heard them in the mornings, but we're lucky to spot one here.'

'Is it sleeping?' It looked like it had settled in for a siesta, the way Jenny wanted to most afternoons since she'd got pregnant.

'Probably. They sleep a lot. And when they're not sleeping—'

He broke off as the monkey shifted. Jenny held her breath as they waited to see if he'd wake up...

In one swift movement, the howler monkey leapt up onto the branch on all fours, raised his head and howled.

Jenny couldn't help but laugh with delight, and beside her Liam did the same—even as the monkey scampered off through the trees, leaping from branch to branch.

'I wonder what else we'll see,' Liam said as they set off again.

The trail was only wide enough for one of them to pass at a time and, since Liam was the one who ostensibly knew where he was going, it made sense for Jenny to follow behind.

If she also appreciated the fact that it meant she got to admire his ass in his shorts, or the width of his shoulders under his backpack, well, she was keeping that to herself.

Because there was another fact last night had brought to life—one she couldn't quite shake, even if it receded slightly as they stopped to admire a sloth lolling under a tree branch, or macaws and toucans flying overhead.

They were getting closer to making a decision about whether they were going to parent this child together. Soon, she'd be leaving Costa Rica—and perhaps Liam—behind.

And they'd only sworn to keep their hands off each other until they made a firm decision about the future.

She'd worked so hard to put thoughts of Liam and her together out of her head, but it wasn't exactly easy. Their entire relationship before she'd come to Costa Rica was based only on sex. Learning more about who he was as a man—the lengths he'd gone to in order to overcome his past flaws, for instance—didn't exactly make her want him any less.

The heat she felt every time his gaze caught hers or his hand brushed against her side, or even if he *smiled* at her, wasn't helping either. And she had a sneaking suspicion he felt the same.

They'd agreed no sex until they'd made a decision. And they'd agreed they'd make a decision before she left Costa Rica at the end of the week.

They *hadn't* said they couldn't make the decision sooner and enjoy whatever time they had left together any way they pleased…

'Ah, here we go,' Liam said up ahead, and Jenny shook away her inappropriate thoughts to focus on whatever wonder of the natural world he'd found to show her this time.

Except this time it wasn't the natural world at all.

'Oh!' The path opened up into a clearing not unlike the one they'd started in, except this one was finished. There were no luxury treehouses as such, but there were a few cabins on stilts, and Jenny could see that they grew in numbers as the site got closer to the beach, just visible through the rainforest.

'Is that the beach we visited the other day?' She didn't remember seeing any cabins, but then she'd been a little distracted that day.

Liam shook his head. 'The next one along.'

'I didn't realise how far we'd walked.' Too busy staring at his ass.

He gave her a smirk and a warm look, as if he knew exactly what she was thinking. 'This resort is…not my competition, because we're after a different market of traveller. This place is for families, for a start, whereas mine is geared up for couples or solo travellers. But I thought you'd like to get a look at what it might look like when it's finished.'

Jenny turned slowly round to take in the sights. The main entrance to the resort was via a slightly garish arch on the road that ran parallel to the beach and led into this clearing where the main office sat. On a whim, she crossed to an oversized poster board next to it, filled with information about local attractions. Pictures of local wildlife bordered information about snorkelling lessons, diving trips and even a giant zip wire through the rainforest.

Her eyes widened at that. Heights weren't always her favourite, but she did love the rush of a zip wire—and moving through the rainforest from above, like the macaws and other birds did, had to be even more spectacular than sitting on the treehouse balcony.

A hand looped loosely around her wrist and Liam turned her away from the board. 'Whatever you're thinking, no. We're not done with our hike yet.' His gaze flicked towards the board for a moment and she thought she felt his grip tighten just slightly, not enough to hurt, before releasing again. 'And none of those things looks remotely safe for the baby.'

The diving trips probably had restrictions, and she could understand why the fast-moving beach buggies you could hire might make him nervous. But... 'Not even the zip wire?'

She wasn't imagining it; he definitely shuddered at that idea. 'Definitely not the zip wire. Come on. We'll get a drink and something to eat at the café here, then continue our hike.'

Jenny followed him as he moved towards another cabin on stilts, set out with pretty tables out front, but her mind stayed on his reaction to the activities board.

Safe for the baby.

For someone who was holding back, who three days ago hadn't known she couldn't drink too much coffee or go in the hot springs…she had a feeling that Liam was coming around. Had made a decision, even, about what happened next. And that gave her an extra bounce in her step as she followed him.

Because if he'd decided…well, then their self-imposed restrictions could come to an end.

And she couldn't quite stop herself smiling at that idea.

He shouldn't have made her walk in front of him.

The logic had been sound in his head. After they'd finished at the café, the trail he wanted to follow only went one way, so there was no need for him to lead the way to avoid getting lost. And he didn't want her first view of their destination to be blocked by his body—he wanted her to get the full impact the moment they arrived.

But that meant he was spending the whole hike staring at her legs in those shorts, and at the shorts themselves and the curvaceous rear end that they only just covered.

He forced his eyes higher, but even that just led him to her long blonde ponytail, fixed high on her head and bobbing with every step. Memories flooded his brain—memories of running his fingers through that hair, of seeing it splayed out on his pillow under her, or hanging down around her face as she rode him…

Liam blinked, swallowed, and forced himself to scan the trees for more howler monkeys. He needed the distraction.

While the question of what to do next hung between them it had been…well, not easy, but at least *possible* to keep Jenny at arm's length. But after last night's conversation Liam knew what he needed to do, even if he hadn't shared his decision with her just yet.

He wanted to give himself time to sit with his choice, make sure he was certain, before he did that. And even once he told her, there'd still be lots to sort out—money, for starters, and conversations about that always seemed to drag on, in his experience.

Deciding wasn't the end of anything.

Except the deal that they'd made, to keep their hands off each other until they had made up their minds on what happened next.

How far would she take that? he wondered idly, as the path beneath his feet twisted through the lush green vegetation. The air around them felt damp and humid, and he knew his shirt was sticking to his back under his rucksack.

Would she want all the 'i's dotted and the 't's crossed before she'd allow any closeness between them again? Or if he made the wrong choice—or even the right one— would she call time on anything physical between them anyway?

It was the not knowing that was driving him out of his mind. Not knowing if he'd ever get to touch her that way again. To kiss her. To hold her. To watch her fall apart in his arms from all the pleasure he could give her…

Up ahead, Jenny gasped as she turned the last bend— loud enough to send a bird fleeing from the nearest tree.

Liam smiled. They were there.

'Oh, my…that's the most beautiful thing I've ever seen!'

Liam scooted alongside her, as close as he could get, given the narrowness of the trail, and took in the awe and wonder on her face. Then he turned to look at the mighty waterfall he'd brought her to see. From a cliff face high above, water cascaded down over the rocks, crashing over outcrops and sending up foam as it hit the river at the bottom. Even from a distance, the roar of the water filled the air.

Around it, the verdant rainforest seemed to blossom even more generously, with brightly coloured blooms and the ever-present sound of life, thriving in the trees and foliage. The canopy opened up enough to show an oval of bright blue sky overhead, letting in rays of sunlight that caught the water droplets at all angles, sending rainbows scattering around them.

Jenny was right; it was beautiful.

Just not as beautiful as her face as she gazed at it.

She turned at last and beamed up at him. 'Thank you for bringing me here.'

'I wanted you to see it,' he admitted, around the lump in his throat. 'Before you leave.'

The reference to her impending departure didn't even seem to register with her. 'Can we get closer?'

Closer meant the slippery wet rocks at the bottom of the waterfall—or worse, standing in the current itself. Liam had been here plenty of times before, and seen many other tourists enjoying the site, but this was different. This was Jenny, who was carrying his child, and suddenly all he could see was the dangers inherent in the place he'd brought her to.

And he'd thought talking her out of the zip wire was the worst of it.

She bounced on the balls of her feet like a child, and Liam gave in. 'Come on, then. But be careful on the rocks.' He took her hand and together they picked their way through the undergrowth, until they reached the waterfall itself.

His heart remained in his mouth the whole time she scampered around the flat rocks that covered the base of the falls, and he stayed on high alert, ready to catch her at the first sign of her feet slipping. But Jenny was sure-footed and stayed firmly upright. Still, he was relieved when at last she stepped back onto dry land, with him right behind her.

The sun overhead was starting to sink down behind the high trees surrounding them, a glorious golden glow still filling the clearing around the waterfall. They'd been lucky to have it to themselves for the afternoon, but he suspected some sunset-seekers might join them soon enough, and he wanted them both safely back in his treehouse before the rainforest grew too dark. He had torches in his bag, but he'd rather not need to use them.

'Ready to head back?'

'Hmm?' Jenny remained staring at the waterfall, and in the moment Liam couldn't help but give in to just a little of the romanticism of it all. Or maybe just the temptation that was Jenny Bouchard herself.

He stepped up behind her, his arms wrapping easily around her waist as her backpack lay on the grass by her feet. She tensed for only a second before relaxing into his embrace, resting her head against his chest.

And just for a moment Liam had the strangest sensation of everything in the world being right.

Then she turned in his arms, looked up at him, and he saw the familiar heat in her eyes, and knew that everything could be a hell of a lot better if they just made a choice and gave up that stupid no sex rule.

'Liam…' Her tongue darted out to swipe over her lips, and he felt his blood warm and his body harden in response. Damn it, if such a tiny movement could affect him this way, if she actually kissed him he might have to take her on the spot. Which could possibly traumatise any approaching tourists for life, and maybe get them arrested.

'We should get back,' he said, his voice betraying him and coming out low and raspy. 'To the treehouse, I mean. Before it gets dark.'

'I know. I just…' She broke off, and he saw the helplessness in her eyes.

At least it wasn't just him. If the physical connection between them hadn't affected her the same way, he wasn't sure how he'd have lived with it.

It wouldn't last for ever, he was sure. A child—that was a for ever commitment, and one he'd made without even intending to. But he could keep that separate from this…thing with Jenny, couldn't he?

Because, whatever happened between them in the future, he knew he had to have her again.

CHAPTER ELEVEN

THEY WERE STANDING close enough that Jenny could feel the heat of his breath, the warmth of his skin—and if she pressed in just a little closer she'd know for sure whether their proximity was affecting him as much as it was her.

She wanted to. She wanted, needed, to feel him hard against her again.

But first they had decisions to make. And probably the middle of a popular tourist destination in a rainforest wasn't the place to do that.

Or was it? They hadn't seen anyone else all day. Maybe the only people who'd see them were the howler monkeys…

Focus, Jenny.

Decisions. She needed to know what Liam had decided before they could go any further. That was the key obstacle to just seducing him here in the middle of the rainforest.

They could figure out the details later, but he had to decide if he was in or out. Until she knew that…her whole future was still in flux. And she wasn't going to make that worse by giving in to their mutual lust.

A small part of her brain whispered that once he'd got what he wanted from her, what reason would he have to make a firm decision at all? She couldn't risk it.

'I want to kiss you so much right now.' Liam's hand clenched against her hip, and a muscle in his jaw twitched with the apparent restraint he was forcing on himself.

God, she loved that. Loved that this man—who'd spent years turning himself from an impulsive, careless star into a controlled businessman—wanted her so much his whole body was rebelling.

She couldn't resist. Not completely. She pressed a little closer and felt that familiar hard ridge behind his shorts, and knew he was every bit as out of control as she was when it came to the chemistry between them.

But chemistry wasn't love, or trust. It wasn't certainty or safety.

Even if it was a hell of a lot of fun.

Liam's eyes fluttered closed and, with her brain fighting her body, Jenny stepped away. Not far, just enough that they weren't actually touching any more.

Touching seemed unfair, given what she was about to say next.

'We promised each other we wouldn't let our libidos interfere with the decision we had to make.' And he understood now why that mattered so much to her, she hoped. Now he knew the kind of trouble her heart and her body—not to mention an overdeveloped sense of romance—had got her into before.

It was a point of pride to Jenny that she never made the same mistake twice.

'Then I think we need to make a decision pretty damn quick, don't you?' Liam's voice was strained. 'Because, honestly, I think my libido is tired of waiting on my brain.'

She couldn't help but laugh at that, and the small smile he gave her told her that her amusement had been his aim all along. But he also had a good point.

'Are you ready to do that? To make a decision about being a father or not?' In an instant, all laughter disappeared between them.

Because this was important. It wasn't just their future—or the possibility of slaking the need for another night together. This was about their *child's* future, and Jenny trusted him to take that every bit as seriously as she did.

Even that amazed her, now she thought about it. She trusted him to do this right—even if that meant walking away. Other than Winter, she couldn't think of another person in the world she trusted as much these days.

'I think I am, yeah,' he said softly. 'No, not think. I know. I'm ready.'

There was a steely certainty behind his words, reassuring her that this wasn't a man just saying whatever she needed to hear to get her into bed. In fact, she knew there was a good chance she *wasn't* going to like whatever he had to say at all.

But she'd respect it. She'd try to understand it. Because she understood *him* a lot better now—and the enormity of what she was asking him to do.

Liam Delaney had lost everything and blamed himself for it. He'd pieced himself back together from a darker place than she'd ever been, and held himself there through sheer force of will, and a distance from anything that could lead him down that dark path again.

She was under no illusion that she wasn't asking him to risk it again, for their child.

Only he knew if he was ready for that, and she'd have to respect whatever conclusion he came to.

Some people aren't ready, or cut out to be parents, she reminded herself, thinking briefly of her own family.

She'd rather her baby have one loving parent than two parents whose love was conditional on them never making mistakes, or only being the person they thought they should be.

She'd rather he never be involved at all than walk away when their kid needed him. When they loved and trusted him.

She knew how that destroyed a person. Made them feel like they'd never been worth that love in the first place.

Nobody was going to do that to her baby.

'So—' she started, then cut herself off as the sound of voices reached them from the trail they'd arrived by.

Apparently, their peace and solitude in this magical place was over. She took another step back, out of his personal space, and reached for her backpack as a cover for the disappointment she felt.

'Let's have this conversation back at the treehouse.' Liam's voice was still low and husky, and she felt it humming through her body. 'I think we're going to want some privacy for it. And after it.'

The promise in his words seemed to thicken her blood, until she could feel it pulsing through all her most sensitive parts.

After.

As much as she wanted to hear his decision, she had to admit that *after* was never going to be far from her mind… She needed to make sure she didn't let it take over. Her brain had to stay in charge here, not her body. A little distance and time from feeling him pressed up against her might help with that.

Time, distance and possibly a cold shower.

She hoisted her backpack up onto her shoulders again. 'Then let's get moving.'

The hike back to the treehouse helped Liam gain control of his body and mind at least a little before they talked— helped by the fact he insisted on leading the way, so he wasn't staring at Jenny's long, toned legs all the way home. But even as he shut the door behind them, and Jenny announced she needed a shower before they talked, he could still feel the tension.

They were going to sort this, one way or another, to-night.

With that in mind, he prepared by calling out for food, pouring them both a non-alcoholic drink and making sure the living space looked as cosy and friendly as it was pos-sible for a luxury treehouse in a rainforest to look, before taking his own turn in the shower.

As the cool water battered against his sweat-salted skin, he ran over his decision in his mind one last time, determined to ensure he was making the right one.

Then he switched off the water and let the sudden si-lence lull him into calm as he towelled off and dressed, ready to face Jenny again.

'Food's here,' she said softly as he padded back into the living area. Dressed in a soft, loose T-shirt over shorts that clung to her every curve, she sat cross-legged on the sofa, a plate of the same local food they'd eaten the first night balanced on her lap. Her damp hair was piled up on the top of her head, with just a few tendrils clinging to her neck and hanging against her cheeks. Skin scrubbed clean, her face glowed a healthy pink, but her eyes were wary.

What had *she* been thinking about in the shower? What was she expecting from him now? And was he about to live up—or down—to expectations?

Behind it all, the heat between them still lingered. He felt it in her gaze as she watched him fix his own plate and take a seat in the armchair opposite her. It wouldn't do to be too close for this conversation, he knew.

They ate in silence for long minutes, neither risking looking at the other too long. But, as much as he'd ordered to replenish them after their hike, he couldn't draw the meal out for ever.

'So.' Jenny swallowed her last mouthful of food and looked up at him. 'You've made a decision?'

He nodded. 'Yeah. I have.' He forked some extra rice and beans onto his plate, then into his mouth, to buy him a little time before saying anything more. He had to get this right, and that meant not jumping in with both feet the way he always did. No, the way he *used* to.

He wasn't that man any more. And that was the only reason he could make this decision at all.

'Care to share?' From the look on her face, Jenny was wise to his tactics.

He didn't rush, though.

'You know now, I think, how much of a shock your news was to me. And why my first reaction was, quite honestly, terror,' he said.

'Because of Julie. And the baby you lost.' Her words were quiet, gentle, but she wasn't shying away from what he'd told her or couching his tragedy in careful euphemisms. Good. They needed to be clear and honest about this. It was the only way it was going to work.

'I'm still scared,' he admitted. 'I'd made the decision that a family wasn't in the cards for me, and you coming here has turned the life I was living, the life I expected to have, upside down.'

'It wasn't exactly planned on my part either, you realise.' There was a touch of annoyance in her voice.

'I know. I wasn't...' He took a breath and started again. 'What I'm trying to say is, it took me a little time to get accustomed to the idea. The thought of being a father.' He'd never be the kind of father his own had been, Liam knew. But he also knew he had to try.

'And now you've got used to it? What are you going to do?'

That was the only question that mattered, wasn't it?

'I want to be a part of the baby's life. I want to try... to be a good father.' He scanned her face for a reaction, but she kept her expression completely neutral—perhaps sensing that he wasn't finished yet. 'But I can't offer you any more. I can't give you love or for ever. I'm not going to marry you just because I got you pregnant—' He held up a hand when she started to interject. 'And I know you wouldn't want that anyway.'

'Damn straight,' she muttered. 'I *never* asked for that from you. I never would.'

'I know,' Liam replied. That wasn't the sort of woman she was. It was one of the things he liked most about her. And one of the reasons why he felt reasonably confident about the next part of his decision. 'But I *do* want us to be friends. Not just co-parents handing the baby over at the door without speaking. I know that before this week we never really explored anything outside of the physical connection between us. But over the last few days... I like to think we've become friends.'

She gave him a small smile. 'So do I.'

'And I'd like to keep that,' he went on. 'I want us to parent our child together as friends and work together to give him or her the future they deserve.'

The smile grew. 'I can live with that.'

'Good.' For a long moment he held her gaze, basking in the warmth of that smile, and everything felt possible.

For a moment.

Then she jerked her head away, looking down at her hands. 'But what about...' She took a deep breath, then forced the words out. 'What happened at the waterfall... that's going to keep happening between us, isn't it? I mean, if we're around each other a lot...what do we do about the chemistry between us?'

It was a fair question, Liam knew—and one he'd given a lot of thought to over the past twenty-four hours. He wasn't sure how long his proposed answer would hold, but it was the only one he had for now.

'It seems to me that the physical connection we have… it's too strong to just ignore it. And it's so damn good that trying would seem a waste. Don't you think?'

A flash of heat in her eyes told him she agreed. 'So what do you suggest?'

Liam stood and moved around the table to sit beside her on the sofa. 'I think that, as long as we've got our ground rules straight, there's nothing wrong with being friends—and co-parents—with benefits, for as long as this chemistry lasts. Is there?'

Jenny stared at him as he sat beside her, the corner of his lips turned up in a one-sided half-smile, the same heat she'd seen by the waterfall still smouldering behind his eyes. Looking away, she reached for her water glass and tried to think.

She could say no, and she knew he'd accept it and walk away. He wouldn't push her or ask for any more than she was willing to give.

And he'd been very clear about what *he* could give.

Not love. Not for ever. Not the clichéd Hollywood happy-ever-after.

But that wasn't what she'd asked for anyway.

And what he could give…

Friendship. Respect. Someone to take on this crazy parenting journey with, so she wouldn't be alone in it.

Co-parents, that made sense. The relief that had trickled through her as his words sank in was proof that, even if she hadn't known it, even if she'd told herself over and over that she was happy doing this alone, his answer was the one she'd been hoping for all along.

And friends, she liked that too. Far better to be a team, and one working happily alongside each other. She *liked* Liam—not just his body, or the way he made her feel in bed. She liked him as a person, and that had been…not exactly a surprise, because she wasn't in the habit of falling into bed with people she didn't like. But the extent to which she enjoyed his company, felt comfortable talking to him, sharing things with him, she hadn't expected that when she'd arrived.

So. Friends who co-parented. That she was on board with.

But the benefits part…

For as long as this chemistry lasts.

That was the key part of his offer, wasn't it? He wasn't *expecting* it to last—and neither was she, really. Which meant she would have to guard her heart against believing it was anything more than lust between them. And she had to prepare for the day it was over too.

The end of their physical relationship would be another certainty to build into her model of the future—and she'd have to hope it would be mutual and amicable when it came.

Could she do that? Live waiting for that other shoe to drop?

And could she trust her heart not to fall too far, too fast, beyond what she knew he could give?

She studied his face again as he waited for her answer, never rushing her, or pushing. Just giving her the time and space to make her decision. He'd even shifted a little on the sofa to make sure there was clear space between them—not that it made any difference. She could remember the feel of his body against hers even if there was an ocean between them.

The heat they shared wasn't going away in a hurry, so they'd have to deal with it as co-parents anyway. And yes, any purely physical arrangement wouldn't last between them, for logistical reasons or whatever, and she'd have to prepare for that. It was an added complication, for sure.

But the idea of never having Liam again…she couldn't bear that.

Really, he was offering her the best of all possible worlds here, wasn't he? A baby, a supportive friend to raise it with, her independence and freedom to shape her own future *and* great sex. Who could ask for anything more?

But she was going to be a mother. Which meant putting her child first.

'If our physical relationship ever interferes with our ability to parent our child together—'

'We end it,' Liam interrupted. 'In a heartbeat.'

His quick certainty reassured her. 'Agreed.'

And in that case what was there, really, holding her back?

She took a last sip of water, placed her glass on the table and turned to fall into his kiss.

CHAPTER TWELVE

TWO DAYS LATER Liam's body still hummed with pleasure as he stepped out of the shower and saw Jenny still dozing in the bed they'd barely left since they'd agreed on their new arrangement. God, he was tempted to climb back in and claim some more.

Except he had to, at some point, check in on the resort. He'd left everything he could in the hands of his employees this week—even more so over the last forty-eight hours—but he was the boss, and the buck stopped with him. So he'd go down to work.

And then he'd get back up here as fast as possible to slip between those sheets with Jenny again.

Pulling on shorts and a T-shirt, he bent down to place a kiss on Jenny's cheek, but she stirred and met his lips with her own instead.

'You're going?' Her voice was fuzzy with sleep, her golden hair spread across his pillow, and it made him wonder if the guys couldn't manage on their own for just one more day…

'I just need to check in.' He brushed a lock of hair away from her eyes. 'I'll be back.'

'You're sure you have to go?' Her hands, warm from

the covers, slid up his thighs as she kissed him again, and he felt his resistance melting away.

He shifted on the edge of the bed until he was practically lying over her, as Jenny's hands disappeared under his T-shirt, caressing the skin of his back, her nails scratching lightly across his shoulders in the way that drove him insane.

Kissing his way down her neck, he tried to explain. 'The guys have been alone on site for three days now. Who knows what sort of chaos they've got into?'

'How much worse could another half an hour make it?'

'Half an hour?' he asked. 'Is that all you want from me?'

She pulled back and gave him a promising grin. 'For starters. When you come back again… I might have other requirements.'

How was he supposed to resist that?

He let her strip the T-shirt from his torso altogether and shucked his shorts as he slid back between the covers with her again. The guys could wait another half an hour…

In the end it was more like an hour, not least because he had to shower again afterwards. Still, Liam reckoned he could get a couple of solid hours work in before the need to see Jenny again, to touch her again, became too overpowering.

'Okay, I'm really going this time.'

This time, she didn't try to stop him leaving.

Yawning, Jenny sat up, resting her back against the smoothed tree trunk that formed the headboard of the bed. 'Mmm… 'kay. Should I come too?'

He shook his head. 'Stay here. Eat some breakfast. Take a shower. Relax. I won't be long.'

'I should pack too,' she said, before yawning again. 'My flight's tomorrow.'

Something tugged inside his chest at the reminder, but he ignored it. The world was small these days. She might leave, but she could come back—or he'd go to her. They had an arrangement, after all. And, in less than six months, a child that would tie them together for the rest of their lives.

It was funny how that idea—which had been so terrifying to him a week ago—was almost a reassurance now.

He kissed her again and headed for the door, while she waved sleepily after him—lying down again before he'd even left the room, which made him smile. He'd worn her out.

He kind of liked that.

He'd expected to be plagued by thoughts of Jenny naked in bed, waiting for him, as he climbed down the twisting tree root stairs and headed for the main complex area. But, instead, different thoughts flew into his head, squawking like the macaws overhead, and every bit as insistent as the howler monkeys that still woke him every morning.

It was her comment about packing that had done it, he decided.

Of course she had to go. She had a job to get back to— as did he, since it was clear he wasn't going to give this project his full attention as long as she was here tempting him away.

It was just that the week had passed so quickly. He'd thought there would be more time to, well, talk. And admittedly spending the last two days in bed had cut into that time dramatically, but still.

They *had* talked, he supposed. About lots of things. Even beyond their past traumas and reasoning for avoiding love and happy ever afters.

In the darkness of their bedroom last night, for instance, they'd whispered all sorts of secret ideas of who they hoped their child would be—what elements of each of them he or she would take, physical and personality-wise.

'Mostly, I just want them to be themselves,' Jenny had murmured eventually, as sleep started to claim her.

'So do I,' he'd whispered back, as he'd kissed the crown of her head and watched her fall asleep.

So yes. They'd talked.

But it was only now he was faced with the idea of her leaving that he realised quite how much they *hadn't* talked about.

It had been so easy to just exist in the bubble of their bedroom, making the most of their time together. But at some point they were going to have to deal with the more complicated questions.

Like where they'd each live. How much time they'd spend together. Whether the baby would move between their homes, or if he'd go stay with them whenever he was in LA. How parenthood would work around both their jobs. Would they need a nanny? He assumed so. How did that even work?

Suddenly, joking about ridiculous names, or whether the child would have his eyes, didn't seem quite so comprehensive as planning for the future went.

I hate planning for the future.

Because it never went the way he expected it to, anyway, so what was the point?

But a child…a family…that was going to take some planning. And Liam didn't have the faintest idea where to start.

There's time for all that.

Once Jenny had headed home to LA they could talk about it—by phone or email. It would be easier, he was sure, when they weren't able to get led astray by the temptation of their bodies.

Everything would be fine, he assured himself again as he spotted his site manager crossing the clearing towards him, clipboard in hand.

For now, he just needed to focus on his work, and worry about his family later. Compartmentalisation was what had got him this far—putting his past behind him, saving the future for when it happened and focusing on the here and now.

And the here and now looked like it had its own problems to solve, from the frown on his site manager's face.

Jenny woke up again a while later, still alone, and lay for a long moment staring at the wooden branches of the treehouse ceiling. After two days, more or less, of constant Liam, the silence around her felt deafening. Her body felt abandoned without his fingers trailing over her skin.

Even her voice, when she tried it in the empty room, was husky, as if there was no point in using it if he wasn't there to hear.

'Right,' she told herself, sternly and aloud. 'That's quite enough of that.'

She forced herself up and out of bed and headed for the shower, making mental lists as she went. She didn't have time to moon over a man—even one as spectacular in bed as Liam. She had work to do, and a future to fix.

Her job as Winter's PA had trained her to plan the work, work the plan—and expect changes. As such, Jenny never made only one plan—she always had a backup at the ready.

When she'd arrived in Costa Rica, her plan had been to tell Liam about the baby, then head out if he wanted nothing to do with her and spend a few days holed up in a hotel in the city, taking long thinking walks and deciding exactly how she wanted her solo parenting future to look, and figuring out what she needed to do to make it happen, before she went back to LA and told her boss.

Obviously, that plan had changed. Plan B had been giving Liam the time he needed to figure out *his* next move and using the time to get to know each other. *That* plan, at least, had gone as it was supposed to.

But, distracted by Liam, she'd failed to figure out exactly what happened next. And with her flight leaving tomorrow, she needed to get onto that. Fast.

She couldn't go back to LA and tell Winter about the baby without at least the semblance of a plan. She needed to know, as a minimum, if she was going to be able to keep on working in the job she loved.

What if he expects me to move to Costa Rica? Or wherever his next project is?

She shook her head. Liam knew she wasn't the sort of woman to follow a man around the globe. He'd work with her on this.

But she still needed to figure out exactly what she wanted their co-parenting future to look like before they could discuss it.

Showered and dressed, she settled back into the chair on the balcony, Tarot cards, notebook and pen on the table in front of her. Crossing her legs under her, she closed her eyes for a moment and let the sounds of the rainforest soothe her tangled mind. The breeze in the leaves. The birds overhead. The insects chirping and buzzing around the flowers. Something larger moving through the branches of a nearby tree—maybe a monkey, or even a sloth.

She opened her eyes and smiled at the beauty and wonder of her surroundings, her heart already calmed.

Then she reached for the cards.

What do I want from my future? she asked them silently, holding the worn and battered cards in her hands. For a moment, she could almost feel that her grandma was there, watching over her shoulder as she shuffled them.

But when she drew her first card she couldn't make sense of what it tried to tell her. She squinted at the image of the Four of Wands. Usually that meant a celebration—

even a wedding. Just what they'd each promised they weren't looking for.

Unless maybe he just didn't want to marry *her*. No. Jenny shook the thought away. Liam wasn't looking for commitment or marriage and neither was she.

But what if he met someone new and that changed?

She turned the card face down on the table and reminded herself that Tarot cards couldn't really tell the future. All they could do was give her clues to interpret her own state of mind.

And she did *not* want a big wedding and a happy family and everything that card represented.

She turned over the next card and sighed as the lovers stared back at her.

This wasn't helping.

Shoving the cards back into their bag, she opened her notebook instead and started to write—just a stream of consciousness of everything she was worrying about. What did she want from Liam, and their co-parenting arrangement? What sort of a mother did she want to be? What mattered to her most, and where was she willing to bend?

The words came easily now she was focused on what mattered, and she wrote until her hand ached. Pages and pages of thoughts and fears and ideas and hopes and dreams. Not about marriage or happy ever afters, but about a fulfilling, energising life and relationship with her child.

Finally, she put down her pen and smiled out into the darkening trees.

Wait. Darkening?

She'd grabbed a light lunch from the fridge earlier, but now it must be approaching dinnertime. And Liam still wasn't back.

Packing up her things, she stowed them back in the treehouse and headed out to see where he'd got to—and what he wanted to do about dinner. They'd talked about going out, but there was always the chance they'd just end up with takeaway in bed again...

She skipped down the stairs that spiralled around the tree and headed back towards what would, eventually, be the centre of Liam's latest retreat resort. It was easy enough to track him down; his site manager, who she'd been introduced to earlier in the week, was frowning at a clipboard as he pointed her absently in the direction of one of the treehouses currently under construction.

Jenny crossed to where he'd indicated and stared up at the large tree that formed the centre of the structure. She could wait until he came down, she supposed. Or else—

She spotted the ladder leading up to the next tree, and the temporary rope bridge leading across to the treehouse, providing access until the staircase was built.

Maybe she could just go and surprise him...

Liam had lost track of time, debating the latest issue in the current treehouse build—something that had taken a lot of explaining by the team who actually knew what they were doing because, while he was a very successful businessman, and had plenty of experience of working on traditional structures, building hotel rooms in trees had consistently thrown up far more problems than he'd ever imagined were possible.

Still, after a long afternoon's discussion, and some phone consultations with the experts, they finally had an answer to the issue that had been thwarting them all day. Which meant he could head back to *his* treehouse and take Jenny for dinner. Finally.

He clapped his lead builder on the back and took his leave, turning towards the opening that would eventually be a door. The stairs up to the treehouse were still to be built, but the temporary rope bridge they'd put up the day Jenny arrived led across to the linked platform they were using as a base while they were building.

But before he could take a first step onto it he realised there was already someone else crossing towards him.

'Jenny!' He smiled at first at the sight of her—and she looked up and beamed back. But the way she was gripping onto the rope that served as a handrail, and the paleness of her complexion, didn't look quite right. Frowning, he stepped forward, reaching out towards her as the bridge swayed under his weight. 'What's the matter? Is everything okay?'

'I'm fine,' she said, shaking her head to dismiss his concerns. Except, as she did so, the bridge swung a little more from side to side. And Jenny turned paler, her knuckles white as she held the rope on either side of her.

'Are you sure?' He moved closer, just as she took another step.

And then it felt as if the clock slowed—just enough to

give him ample time to register every awful moment of each second that passed.

Jenny's foot slipped against the wooden plank of the bridge; damp from a brief shower of rain not long before, it had little grip under the soles of her sandals. Her foot, then her leg slid off the edge of the rough and ready bridge, through the gaps in the ropes that covered the sides, even as she gripped tight to the handrail.

And in that instant all Liam could see was history repeating itself.

He'd done it again. He'd brought a woman to danger and disaster, all because she'd followed him to this place. Because he hadn't been careful enough when they were in Iceland. Because he couldn't resist her. Because he hadn't just sent her away the moment she'd arrived—told her that he could only be bad for her, and for the baby, and they'd be better off without him.

Because he'd dared to think for a moment that he could have this—be a father, even with the caveats he'd put in place—Jenny was in danger.

It was such a long way down…

Her scream cut through the humid air of the rainforest and, without realising he'd even moved, Liam found he'd crossed the metres between them and hauled her up into his arms, huddling them both in the centre of the godforsaken rope bridge, desperately trying to keep her safe.

His heart hammered against his ribcage, his breathing harsh and uneven in the muffled silence of his blood pounding in his ears.

'I'm okay. Liam. Liam!' Jenny pulled at his hands and

he loosened his grip a little but didn't let go. 'I'm okay, really. I just slipped!'

'You almost fell.' In his mind's eye, that was all he could see. Jenny, sliding out from under the inadequate ropes of the bridge, dropping the too long distance to the ground. Screaming for him to help.

If he hadn't reached her…

'But I didn't,' she said softly. 'The ropes would have saved me. Liam. Let go. Come on, I want to get down from here.' She shuddered a little. 'I never did really like bridges. Especially ones that move.'

Neither did he any more. And he wanted her down from there more than anything. Moving was risky, but it had to be better than staying up there and taking the chance of her slipping again.

So, with a deep breath, he started moving, his jaw clenched tight. He kept a tight grip on her arm all the way back across the planks of the bridge, and down the finished staircase of the next tree, only releasing her when they both had their feet on solid ground again.

'Are you okay?' she asked, her forehead creased with concern.

'I should be asking you that.' His voice was shaking, he realised. As if *he* were the one who'd almost fallen.

Almost died.

Because she would have. No doubt. She said the ropes would have saved her, but what if they hadn't? What if one snapped? She'd have fallen. And from that height, onto the hard, tree root covered floor of the rainforest… She'd have broken every bone in her body. And the baby…

They'd both have died. He'd have lost them both.

He'd have lost everything. Again.

God, he wanted a drink. Except that wouldn't help—it never had before. He was past that.

But he was also past putting himself in situations where his whole existence could be torn away from him in an instant.

Or he had been. Until Jenny came to Costa Rica and turned his life upside down.

'I'm fine,' she said now, taking his chin in her hand and forcing him to look at her. 'Look, I'm fine.'

'We should get you to the hospital. Have you checked out. The baby—'

'Is also fine,' she said, although how she could possibly know he had no idea. 'I didn't fall, Liam. You caught me. I barely even bruised myself. Come on. If you're done here, we can go back to the treehouse, decide where we want to go for dinner. Okay? I promise. Everything is fine.'

This time, he thought as he let her lead him back towards the treehouse he had claimed as his own. Everything was fine *this time.*

But what about next time?

CHAPTER THIRTEEN

LIAM WAS FREAKING OUT.

It wasn't as if she didn't understand a little bit. He'd been faced with the pregnant mother of his child being caught in an accident again—of course he was going to be a bit shaken. But this time, as she'd pointed out to him on the walk home, it was in no way his fault and, most importantly, she was absolutely fine. In fact, he'd saved her—although she maintained she'd have found her footing again even if he hadn't caught her up in his arms. She'd still had a good handle on the ropes, after all. And besides, the net of ropes that covered the side of the bridge would have caught her otherwise. Probably.

It was just a slip. She was fine.

Now she just had to convince him.

Which she intended to do over dinner, given the chance. She'd left him to shower and taken the opportunity to change into the dressiest item of clothing she'd brought with her—a halterneck jumpsuit that did marvellous things for her currently enhanced cleavage. If he planned on driving them down to that restaurant by the beach, she might even risk wearing her heeled sandals with it.

He was longer in the shower than usual, so she took her time over her hair and make-up too. When she took a last glance in the mirror, even she had to admit she cleaned up pretty nicely.

It was their last night together in Costa Rica, and she intended to make the most of it.

First, a nice dinner. Some flirtation and teasing to take his mind off that afternoon then, maybe, they'd be able to talk about some of the details of their co-parenting arrangement that she'd spent the day working out in her notebook.

Once they'd got all that straight, they could head back home to bed and *really* make the most of her last night. After all, she didn't know how long it would be before he could make it over to LA again.

Knowing that he would make it at some point helped, though. They would be a team. And then there were all those benefits they'd been enjoying over the last couple of days…

Finally, everything seemed to be falling into place—against all the odds.

Before this week, she'd steeled herself against hoping too hard for anything. She'd prepared herself for going it alone because she knew that she couldn't trust anyone else to make the future she wanted for herself.

But now… Liam wasn't responsible for giving her the future she pictured; she still held tight control over that. But he was involved. A partner, even. And that made all the difference.

Jenny smiled at herself in the mirror just as Liam

opened the bathroom door. She enjoyed the stunned look on his reflection for a moment, until she realised that he wasn't dressed for dinner. He was back in a T-shirt and shorts and, as the look on his face faded to confusion, apparently not planning to change.

'We talked about going out for dinner tonight?' she said, turning to face him.

'Yeah, right. We did.' He ran the towel over his head one last time, then tossed it behind him into the bathroom. 'I guess… I thought after this afternoon you'd want a quiet last night.'

She blinked at him. 'Liam, I told you. I'm fine. I didn't even get hurt.'

'But the shock…that can't be good for the baby, right?' He didn't meet her gaze.

There was something very wrong here.

'What's going on?' she asked bluntly. They'd never messed each other around before, and she didn't intend to start now.

Honesty and clarity. That was how they'd got this far. And now she needed some more of both.

He looked away. 'Nothing. I'm just…concerned for you.'

'That's not all.' Concern would be holding her, touching her, *looking* at her to check she was okay. This was something else entirely.

Oh, God, she realised suddenly. *He's changed his mind.*

She dropped to sit on the edge of the bed as the knowledge sank in. She didn't need him to meet her gaze. Didn't even need to hear the words—although she fully intended to make him say them, to make this real, to make him acknowledge what he was doing.

But the facts of it were clear even in the silence. She could feel it, seeping into her bones, infecting her heart.

Just when she'd managed to trust enough to believe that they could do this, to put herself out there again to let someone else into her future, even if only as a friend and co-parent, he was about to turn the tables on her again. Just like Anthony had done when she'd thought they were going to get married. Just like her parents had when she'd let them down.

Her gut told her the truth, and she was a hell of a lot better at listening to it these days.

Liam wanted out.

The old her would have just watched him go. She'd have believed this was her fault, that she should have done things differently. And maybe she'd still have those thoughts later, once she was alone again.

But right now...right now she was going to make him explain to her exactly why he was doing this.

She needed honesty and clarity. One last time.

The self-loathing that had settled over him like an oil on the walk back to the treehouse hadn't washed off in the shower. Just the knowledge of what he was about to do made him feel unclean—and he knew that feeling wouldn't fade in a hurry.

Still, better to be a bastard now than let Jenny and the baby come to depend on him and *then* run.

Better to leave now and have them stay safe and sound away from him.

He couldn't be the man she needed. They needed.

He could only bring them pain, or danger, or both.

His actions had caused the death of the first woman he loved, and his unborn child. And maybe Jenny was right and she was fine after today's near miss, but that wasn't the point.

The point was, he lived a life incompatible with nice, safe, normal family life. With love and happy ever afters. With stability and ease.

She deserved that. So did their child.

What had he been thinking? Imagining that he could be what she needed?

Liam had pieced himself back together with parcel tape and string after the accident. Every day he followed the rules that kept him nominally healthy and sane.

He didn't drink. He didn't lose control. He didn't care too much.

He focused on what he could give to others from a distance—on building his business, on sending money home to the family farm from it, on giving people who needed it the safe space to regroup and recover.

He could send anonymous free breaks at his resorts to people he read about in the papers or on the internet who looked like they needed someone to give them a chance to put their lives back together. But he could never get close to those people or have them even know of his existence.

Because that way led to friendship, closeness, affection.

Even Josh and Winter, or his own family, he had to

keep at arm's length, not letting them in too close, or too far. Because if he did…he'd lose them. He'd put them at risk—and himself, too. Because one more loss could be the thing that tipped him back over that edge he'd teetered on for so long.

He'd almost lost Jenny and the baby today on that bridge.

It had nearly stopped his heart, but it had also reminded him of the most unbreakable of all his rules, forged in the aftermath of the accident, when he'd just been trying to find a way to keep on living.

Don't care about anything so much that you couldn't survive losing it.

How had he ever deluded himself that Jenny and the baby would be any different?

Because you wanted her in your bed, not your heart, he reminded himself.

For all they'd promised to make their decisions without their libidos getting in the way, he hadn't, not really.

He hadn't been able to resist her, so he'd given her what he thought she wanted.

But he couldn't give her love. Or safety or security. Or a future that even remotely resembled the one she deserved.

Would she believe him, if he told her that? Would she understand, and accept it?

He hoped so. But he couldn't take that chance.

Which meant he had to lie.

'Liam.' Jenny looked up at him seriously from where she sat on the edge of his bed. The same place he'd left her lying naked that morning, waiting for him to come back.

He wished he'd known then that would be the last time he'd ever see her that way.

'Tell me what's going on,' she pressed.

He took a breath. 'I can't do this.'

She didn't crumple; that wasn't her way. Her back remained straight and strong, her face gave nothing away. Only the tiniest dimming of the light in her eyes gave any indication that she'd heard him at all.

'Can't do what, exactly? I need specifics.' The ice in her voice was unfamiliar; everything between them had always been so warm. Full of humour and affection and fun and attraction.

Not now.

'My site manager needed a meeting today; that's why I was gone so long.' Start with a truth, weave in the lie. 'There are some problems on the site here in Costa Rica, and the build is going to take longer than planned. Which means I'm going to need to spend more time here—and then I'll be straight off to my next project.'

'Next project?'

'There's a new site come up—perfect for my style of retreat resort. But I have to move quick if I don't want to miss the opportunity.' This bit was all lie. Oh, he'd had the odd meeting about possible sites, but he wasn't committing to anything yet. In fact, he'd planned not to, for a while. To get this place running, then spend some time with Jenny in LA, or wherever.

'Which means?' She knew. He could tell she already knew. But she was going to make him say it. Own it.

He couldn't blame her for that.

'I'm not going to have the time or the energy to be involved with the baby in the way we'd discussed.' Not that they really *had* discussed how it was all going to work. But his imagination had filled in the gaps in their conversations nicely, and he couldn't deny the slight wrench in his chest as he gave it all up. 'Really, I don't think it would be fair to you or them to be so unavailable and uninvolved, just swooping in when I had the chance then disappearing again.'

'So you're doing this for us, then,' Jenny said flatly.

He ignored her inference and ploughed on. He couldn't let her try to talk him out of this or point out the flaws in his arguments.

This wasn't about logic. This was about a gut feeling. And every instinct he had was screaming at him to get out before he ended up in another situation that tore him apart and broke him for good this time.

'I think it's best if I'm, well, a silent partner of sorts,' he said. 'I'll support you financially, of course. But I don't want to be a part of the baby's life.'

'Or mine.'

God, it hurt to say it. 'No.'

What she hated the most, Jenny realised as she stared at him, was that she was *surprised* by this turnabout.

She shouldn't be. Everything she knew about men and relationships should have told her this was where it would end. Didn't it always?

He'd got what he wanted from her—had her back in his bed for forty-eight hours. And apparently that was enough. Why on earth would he want to saddle himself with her and a baby now?

Love always lets you down.

She knew that.

But she'd thought because this *wasn't* love, because they'd agreed it *couldn't* be love, that she'd be safe. That she could have this small sliver of happiness and support and not suffer for it.

How wrong could she be? Because having this rug pulled out from under her was already worse than realising how badly she'd been used last time around.

At least she didn't have to tell her family that she was going to be an unwed working single mother through choice, because they'd already disowned her for her last transgression.

And this one wasn't a transgression. It wasn't a mistake. It was her child and her life and her future and she would make the best possible life for the two of them that she could and damn everybody else.

Even Liam Delaney.

Especially Liam Delaney.

She just should have known better—that was the only reason she felt like crying. Because she'd wasted this week imagining a life that was never going to exist. Because she'd let herself believe in him, in them. Because she'd grown used to the idea of them being a team in this. That she wouldn't be alone.

She *wouldn't* be alone, though.

She'd have her baby. Her friends.

She'd be fine.

She just wished she'd remembered the brutal truths she'd learned about love and sex the last time around. Then she could have protected herself against this. That was all.

Liam was still talking—rambling on about transferring money to her accounts, about making sure her health insurance was good enough, about a house he owned somewhere in LA—but she wasn't interested in any of it. The details could wait—hell, they'd waited this long, hadn't they?

All she needed right now was to get out of here with her head held high and her dignity intact.

'That all sounds good,' she said calmly. 'But we can sort out the details when I'm back in LA and can talk to my lawyer. I'm assuming you'll want this agreement to be properly contracted and so on. Especially on the parental rights issue.' He'd agreed to sign them away if he wasn't involved, and she was going to hold him to that.

Liam blinked, looking slightly blindsided by her agreement. 'Right. Yeah, I guess we should.'

She nodded. 'Fine. I'll set up an appointment—we can do it by video call—and get it all sorted.'

'You're...okay with this?' His voice was cautious—as if he couldn't believe he was lucky enough to get away with this without a woman wailing and screaming at him. Begging him to stay. To love her.

Maybe that was what he was used to in his relationships—women who expected more than he was able to give and blamed him for his inability. But Jenny had known from the start that he couldn't do this, and yet she'd let herself hope anyway.

That was on her.

And there was no way in hell she was going to let him see that she was disappointed.

'Of course,' she said curtly. 'Honestly, I was pretty surprised when you said you wanted to try. I know this wasn't what you had planned for your future. Like I told you that first day, I was expecting to come here, tell you what was going on, then turn around again and leave to get on with it on my own.' She forced a smile. 'Looks like I was right about you all along.'

'I guess you were.' He returned her smile with his own uncertain one.

He didn't even realise she was lying. God, he was probably *relieved* she'd taken it so well.

And if Jenny got her way he'd never, ever know that she felt like she was dying inside right now.

CHAPTER FOURTEEN

HE FELT AS if he had whiplash. How had they got here? He knew it was his doing, but suddenly the situation seemed totally out of his hands as Jenny stood up and crossed the room to her suitcase.

'You know, I was thinking, now we've got the basics sorted, I might as well head back to the airport tonight, don't you think?' Her voice was calm and rational, everything he didn't feel right now. 'I can get a room at the hotel there and be ready for my flight tomorrow in plenty of time. I just need to pack up—do you think you could arrange a car for me? I've got the number of the airport transfer service who brought me here...'

He shook his head when she offered the card. 'I'll get one of my guys to take you.' That would be safer than an unknown driver on this difficult road.

And before he knew it he was outside, trailing down the staircase to find someone to drive her to the airport.

He didn't even consider taking her himself. She'd have suggested it if she wanted that. And besides, he didn't fully trust himself behind the wheel right now. His hands were still shaking.

He needed to centre himself. To do all those exercises he'd learned on his first retreat then avoided using unless strictly necessary. Most of the time he could keep himself under control through sheer willpower. But when things got bad he fell back on the tools that had saved him the first time.

The fact he needed to use them now was surely a sign that leaving Jenny to get on with her own life was the right decision. No one else had affected him this badly since the accident.

Of course, he hadn't let anyone else as close.

That had been his biggest mistake, he decided. If he hadn't let her in, it wouldn't hurt so much to push her away.

Better now than later, he reminded himself. *Better away but safe than hurt or dead.*

By the time he made it back to the treehouse with the news that the car was ready when she was, Jenny was waiting for him by the front door, her fingers gripping the handle of her small suitcase, her backpack slung over her shoulder. She'd changed out of the outfit she'd been wearing earlier, into more comfortable travelling clothes, and her hair was pulled back in a simple ponytail, her face scrubbed clean of the make-up she'd applied before.

Just looking at her made Liam regret again the loss of that last night dinner, or a final night with her in his arms. But if he'd let himself have that…would he still have been able to let her go tomorrow?

He wasn't sure.

This is for the best.

'The car is waiting by the entrance,' he said, his voice husky. 'My site manager's driving you. He needed to head back to the city tonight anyway. He's ready when you are.'

Jenny stepped forward, her case trundling behind her. 'I'm ready now.' She reached up and pressed a kiss to his cheek. 'Thank you for a lovely week. I'm glad we had those last couple of nights together before I had to go. But from here on, I think we can manage most things over email and the phone, don't you?'

Liam forced a smile. 'Of course.' She understood what he'd meant, by stepping away—or else this was what she wanted too. From the way she'd taken it, he was starting to believe that must be the case.

They'd had their fun, their second chance at a fling, and now they needed to get on with their real lives. What was wrong with that?

'And now I'll get out of your hair!' She laughed, but there was something in it that sounded just a little bit brittle. Forced even.

Or perhaps he was just projecting his own emotions onto her.

Because as much as this was his choice, as much as he knew this was the right decision—the only one he could have made, in the end—it still felt like his heart had cracked inside his chest.

The hotel was dark and the lobby empty except for a young girl on the reception desk when Jenny arrived.

She'd booked a room on her phone in the car, so check-in was quick and easy. In no time she was up in her small, no-frills room, listening to planes still taking off and landing not far from her window.

She placed her suitcase on the floor, dropped her backpack beside it and sat on the edge of the bed. It was comfy, at least, but she knew she wouldn't sleep.

If she slept, she might dream of Liam. And she couldn't risk that.

She had plans to make. Everything she'd worked out sitting on the balcony of the treehouse earlier that day—and, *God*, how was it still the same day?—that was all out-of-date now. She'd been imagining her future with Liam in it, as a partner if nothing more.

Although, she had to admit, in her head, he'd been a lover too. A co-parent, friend *and* lover.

Wait.

With a groan, she fell backwards onto the mattress and threw her arm over her eyes.

Of course he'd pulled away—she could hardly blame him. Co-parenting friend he slept with? Yeah, that sounded an awful lot like what they'd both promised the other they weren't asking or looking for.

It sounded like a marriage. Like commitment.

Like trusting the other to always be around and not screw things up.

And they both knew that neither of them was up to that. He couldn't give it and she couldn't trust it.

She knew from bitter experience that other people's weaknesses always led to betrayal and disappointment.

It was absolutely for the best that she was out of this situation now and could focus on building the future *she* wanted.

Forcing herself to concentrate on what came next rather than what she'd left behind in the rainforest, Jenny got to her feet and fished her notebook and pen out of her backpack. After a moment, she reached back in and pulled out her grandma's Tarot cards too.

Maybe that was why she hadn't been able to get a good reading from them earlier. Because she'd been refusing to see what was right in front of her—that she was angling to build a life exactly like the one she'd said she didn't want. No wonder the Four of Wands had been taunting her—what she and Liam had planned had been a marriage in all but name. One with a built-in expiry date to boot.

But now she was seeing more clearly, right?

She used the kettle in the room to make herself a cup of herbal tea, then settled into the chair by the tiny table in the window at the end of her bed. From there, the wide glass windows looked out over the airport, and she watched the lights of the arriving and departing planes rise and fall against the night sky for a long moment, centring her thoughts.

Then she opened her notebook and started to read.

It was all there in her own handwriting. Everything she'd hoped and dreamed for with Liam, and their child. The dream life she'd thought, so briefly, that she wanted.

She'd been here before, though. That life wasn't the one she'd been handed.

So she needed to make the most of the life she did have. Turning to a fresh page, she started a new list.

Things to do next:
  1) Tell Winter about the baby.

That would be hard; her boss would be happy for her, she was sure, but there was history there too that would complicate Winter's emotions. And that was before they even started on the logistics of making her job work as a solo parent.

  2) Find a lawyer.

She'd never really needed one before, but if she and Liam were going to come to an arrangement over how this worked, she'd need one. She didn't want Liam's money, although heaven knew he had enough of it to spare by all accounts. She'd happily work to look after her own child and, one way or another, she had faith she'd make it work—after all, she was lucky enough to have a Hollywood A-lister as her employer, so she was already in a better position than many women.

But she did want *certainty*. If Liam said he didn't want to be part of the baby's life, fine. She could accept that. But she didn't want him changing his mind in five years' time and confusing the hell out of their kid without her permission.

A lawyer would help her figure out what ground rules they needed to set, and what was a fair contribution, if

Liam felt he wanted to make one—even if she suspected he'd only be doing it to assuage his own parental guilt.

3)...

What next? There were a million things to do before the baby arrived, she was sure, but until she'd done the first two it was hard to get moving on the other stuff. So much depended on the decisions they made about her job and Liam's remote involvement.

So maybe she just started there. Got the basics in place before moving any further.

Fine.

She nodded to herself and checked the time. Middle of the night in Costa Rica, but fortunately Winter was staying in a completely different time zone right now, and middle of the night for Jenny was already halfway into tomorrow for her boss in London.

As she held her phone in her hand, she ran through exactly what she needed to say.

Winter, I need to tell you something important. While we were in Iceland I had a fling with Liam Delaney and now I'm pregnant. I've told him, and we've decided together that it's best if he's not involved in the baby's life, or mine, although he says he wants to contribute financially. When we're both back in LA, can we sit down and figure out how we can make this work with my job? I love working for you, and I don't want to leave, but I accept we might need to consider some changes to make it all work.

That sounded sensible and put-together, right? As if she and Liam had approached this as adults—not falling into bed before she'd even been able to tell him about the baby, spending the better part of a week getting to actually know each other before falling *back* into bed, then parting ways when they realised that neither of them was actually capable of a functional relationship.

Winter would have questions, though. She could already hear her boss's voice in her head.

Jenny, are you in love with Liam?

That, at least, was easy enough to answer, she thought as she dialled Winter's number.

Of course not. We had a lot of fun together, and I like and respect him as a person, but a relationship between us just isn't in the cards. Of course I'm not in love with him.

How could she be when she'd just said goodbye to him for the last time?

Yes, she felt abandoned, again. Lonely, again. As if she'd fallen into exactly the same trap that love and family had set for her last time. She'd had her future and her support ripped away from her, the exact same way she had when Anthony had gone back to his wife and her family had disowned her.

She *hurt,* that much she could admit.

But that was understandable, wasn't it? Under the circumstances.

That was all. It didn't mean anything more.

The phone started to ring.

Falling in love with Liam Delaney would be absurd.

Ridiculous. Making *exactly* the same mistakes all over again. She was better than that. She'd learned from her past errors. She'd protected her heart this time, so even if it hurt it wouldn't break her.

Still ringing.

Just because they had amazing sex. And because she could talk to him, in a way she never really did to anyone else. And because he cared about her and wanted her to be happy and safe. And they had the same ideals for their child—to be happy and themselves above all else. And because they laughed at baby names together, and because she could picture their whole lives together and it made everything brighter and better just having him there.

'Jenny?' Winter answered the phone at last. 'Is everything okay? I thought you were on holiday. Isn't it the middle of the night for you?'

Just because the idea of living her life without him, raising their child without him, made her shiver with the loss.

'Jenny?' Winter asked, sounding concerned. 'What's happened?'

There were tears running down her face, Jenny realised as she answered. How long had she been crying?

'I fell in love with Liam Delaney,' she said through her sobs.

CHAPTER FIFTEEN

THE IMPORTANT THING, Liam knew, was to get back into his routine. He needed the familiar cadence of his days, the purpose of doing things that mattered to him, to get back on track after the disruption of Jenny's visit.

Ever since the accident, routine and purpose had been what kept him moving forward at a reasonable pace, living in the present rather than looking back, or panicking about what the future might hold. That was what he needed now. To be in the present.

So, in the present of the following morning, he got up at his usual early hour, even though he hadn't really slept. He did his usual exercise routine on the balcony, listening to the sounds of the rainforest around him and letting them centre him. He breakfasted on fruit and toast and drank his two cups of coffee while reading the news on his tablet, just like always.

Then he looked up, expecting Jenny to be there waiting to ask him about their plans for the day, and had to pretend his heart didn't sink a little when he remembered she wasn't there.

That she wouldn't ever be there again. Because he'd sent her away.

It's for the best, he reminded himself, and went to shower and get on with his usual daily routine.

On site days, it was easy enough to keep busy and push Jenny and the baby out of his head. The evenings were a little harder, but he'd found ways to distract himself. He had practice with this, after all. He knew how to compartmentalise.

And if his staff found him grumpy and more difficult to work with than usual they didn't say anything—although the looks of concern they shot his way tended to say more than their mouths did, anyway.

Josh had called a few times in the days since Jenny left Costa Rica, which he assumed meant she'd told Winter everything. He couldn't know for sure, since he hadn't picked up the phone, or listened to the voicemail messages. The texts he'd received also went unread for now. He knew himself, knew how he handled trauma. He needed space between himself and the event, and *then* he'd deal with it, and other people.

Trauma. Strange that he was equating the amicable decision not to be in a relationship of any sort with Jenny with the sort of life-destroying trauma he'd been through in the past. It *wasn't* the same, of course it wasn't. But the echoes and reverberations of loss always seemed to call back to that moment. Reminders could be just as hurtful as smaller, fresh traumas. Or something. He couldn't remember what the counsellor who'd told him that had said, word for word, but he did know what worked for him.

And for now it was avoidance.

His site manager looked genuinely relieved when, after

almost a week of such avoidance, he had to go up into the rainforest to visit a few potential suppliers. First up was the hot springs yoga sanctuary, where Selena greeted him with a warm smile—and a gently rounded belly.

'Liam! No Jenny with you today? I wanted to compare bumps...' She threw her arms around him for a sideways hug, and he felt the hard pressure of her pregnant stomach against his side.

'She had to go back to LA.' He stepped away as quickly as he could without being insulting. 'Congratulations! You didn't have that last time I visited, did you?'

She laughed. 'Last time, I was wearing a loose shirt. Did you not notice? I just looked podgy. But it seems to have popped out this week, so now I'm showing it off!'

'Well, congratulations. To you and Gael.'

'You already said that.' Selena peered at him with concern. 'Is everything all right? When does Jenny get back from LA?'

'She's not coming back.' Better to face it head-on, get the truth out there so everyone else could move on as well as he had. 'We don't have that kind of a relationship any longer.'

'But her baby—'

'Will be her baby. Now, are you ready to talk about schedules?'

Selena nodded cautiously at his abrupt change of subject but, as he'd hoped, followed his lead. After an hour or so of discussion, they had a working plan for yoga classes at the new retreat—and Selena had suggestions for someone who could cover her classes when she had the baby.

'I think this will all work out fine.' Liam got to his feet and held out a hand for Selena to shake. But instead she gripped it in both of hers and pulled him close. On tiptoes, she whispered in his ear, 'You know it's okay for you to be happy, Liam. You just have to choose it.'

'I'll see you next month,' was all he said in reply.

Back in the four-by-four, he stared out of the windscreen with his hands on the steering wheel for a long few minutes before starting the engine and heading off to his next appointment, though.

Thankfully, he thought as he pulled in to the coffee roasting café, this was a place Jenny had never visited with him. There'd be no memories of her beaming at him in the sunshine here, and no well-meaning but nosy friends to ask questions about her. That would help.

He slammed the car door behind him, drawing rather more attention from the customers sitting outside the café than he'd intended, and headed inside to find Raúl, the boss.

'Liam! Come try this new blend.' Raúl beckoned him over towards the counter. Out back, through the window, Liam could see visitors roasting their own coffee beans to try. Jenny would have enjoyed that, if she hadn't been pregnant. If she'd come back after the baby—

He forced a stop to that train of thought. She wasn't coming back here. Not ever. And that was good.

The new coffee was delicious, and Liam enjoyed a catch-up with Raúl on how business was going. He liked to work with local businesses wherever he set up a retreat, and he was pleased to think that his resort would help Raúl and his family keep their business going.

'Papá!' A small boy came darting out from behind the counter, latching onto Raúl's legs where he sat on the high stool beside Liam.

'Santiago, this is my friend Liam,' Raúl said gently. 'Would you like to say hello?'

The boy peered out around his father's legs, took in Liam in a head-to-toe look, then shook his head.

Raúl laughed, and even Liam managed to crack a smile. 'Well, okay then. I think Mamá is looking for you anyway,' he added, glancing over Liam's shoulder.

Liam looked around and saw Raúl's wife, Maria, bustling towards them. Her dark hair fell in waves over her shoulders, her lush lips were curved in a smile and her eyes danced. But the thing Liam noticed most was the way her pregnant belly entered the room a good few seconds before the rest of her.

Is everybody pregnant suddenly?

Logically, he knew that Maria must have been pregnant the last time he'd seen her, probably a month or two ago, as she'd been away visiting family when he last came to the café. But it hadn't registered with him then, or he hadn't considered the information important enough to remember.

But now…now every child, baby or pregnant woman was a reminder of the life he'd sent away.

Maria led Santiago back into the rooms behind the bar, where he was supposed to be eating lunch, apparently. Raúl kissed his wife on the lips before she went, his hand lingering on her pregnant belly. Liam looked away.

'Only another few weeks and there'll be four of us, not three,' Raúl mused as they left. 'It's going to be chaos.'

Liam laughed, but only because he could tell from his friend's tone that he was looking forward to that chaos. Embracing it, even.

'Congratulations, if I haven't said it already.' Liam raised his coffee cup in a toast.

'Thank you. We're so excited!'

'I can tell.' Even if he couldn't understand. How could Raúl embrace such uncertainty? There were so many things that could go wrong every moment. Loving his wife and his children the way he did…what if he lost them?

Having had his own heart crushed by that loss, Liam knew the bravery it took to risk that. And while he admired his friend for being able to do it, he wasn't sure he'd ever understand how he could be *happy* about it.

'Don't you worry about them?' Liam blurted out the question without thinking first, and was surprised by the knowing look his friend gave him in return.

'Every moment,' Raúl admitted, his expression suddenly sober. 'Loving Maria, and Santiago, and the new little one…it's as if my heart resides outside of my body, with them. So yes, I worry.'

'But you risk it anyway,' Liam said. 'Why?'

'I love them.' Raúl shrugged. 'So how can I not? Besides, I know how much poorer my life would be without them.'

'You'd still have your business. Your work.'

'But what would it mean, without them? This is why we

do it, isn't it?' Raúl said with a wide smile. 'The ones we love—family, friends, our people—are what give meaning to the work, don't you think? And everything else, of course!'

A tour group arrived at the door and Raúl slipped from his stool to go greet them, leaving Liam alone with his thoughts. Which was just as well, as it seemed, all of a sudden, he had far too many of them.

It was good to be back at work, Jenny told herself as she surveyed the hustle and bustle of the film set. Surrounded by people and action, kept busy and active, all of it distracted her from what had happened in Costa Rica.

Which didn't mean she was ignoring the future. Quite the opposite.

Winter had been brilliant. From the moment Jenny confessed all, her boss had been her biggest cheerleader. She and Josh had hurried back to LA to meet her flight, and together the three of them had figured everything out.

In a matter of days Jenny had a lawyer who specialised in custody agreements, recommendations for three of the best day cares in the city, plus two excellent nannies to interview, and a request had gone out to head-hunters to find her an assistant.

'You already do the work of about three people,' Winter had pointed out. 'If we get someone else in to take the admin stuff off your desk, you can focus on the things that no one else could do—like really managing my and Josh's careers.'

Jenny had blinked. 'That sounds like a promotion.'

Shrugging, Winter had grinned. 'I'd better give you a pay rise then, hadn't I?'

So now she had a plan, and Jenny was finally starting to relax again about the future. Unfortunately, when she wasn't kept busy by work, that just gave her more time to think about the things her plan *didn't* include.

Like grandparents. Or a father.

Not thinking about Liam.

That was a rule she'd imposed on herself—and she'd asked Winter and Josh not to talk about him either, at least for the first little while. Her hormones were crazy enough with the pregnancy, and she really didn't need anything else setting her off when she was trying to be professional.

She suspected that Josh had tried to contact Liam, though, after Winter told him what was going on. Josh could be kind of protective that way sometimes, she'd learned. But if he'd spoken to his friend he hadn't told her what Liam had to say.

What else *was* there to say, anyway? Jenny was pretty sure they'd covered it all in their businesslike farewell.

She was on her own raising their child, and she'd probably never see him again. Just get the occasional guilt cheque to cover expenses.

And she was fine with that. Really.

Apart from the thing where she was madly in love with him and her heart hurt every day thinking about how she'd given up and walked away.

But what was done was done, and she had too much pride to try and convince a guy to change for her. She'd done that last time, and look where she'd ended up. She wasn't getting on her knees to beg a man to stay ever, ever again.

Liam had been honest about what he could offer, and it had never included love. So what right did she have to ask for it?

With a sigh, she forced herself to focus on the activity going on around her. Josh and Winter were starring in their first movie together since their reconciliation, and it was kind of a big deal—not to mention a last-minute one. Josh had already been slated to star as the romantic hero of the piece when the actress originally cast opposite him had to drop out. Getting Winter in for the role had been a no-brainer for anyone who followed Hollywood gossip and had an inkling of an idea how big it would be for them to appear on screen together again.

But it did mean a lot of press interest, and requests for interviews and so on. While the movie of course had its own publicity team, and Winter hired professionals herself as needed, she liked Jenny to go through the requests personally and pick the ones she thought were the best fit for the brand Winter was trying to project.

Also, the ones with interviewers that wouldn't drive Winter crazy. Jenny had a sprawling spreadsheet of every journalist who'd ever spoken to Winter, every photographer who'd taken her photo, and notes on the results. She noticed there were one or two requests she could throw out immediately, according to the second sheet of 'publications and websites I will never work with again' she and Winter had put together based on their coverage of her and Josh's split five years ago.

She was just starting to get into a groove, coming up with a list of possibilities to go through with her boss later, when a hush on the other side of the set caught her attention. She looked up, frowning, as the initial silence shifted into a buzz of chatter and excitement.

What the hell was going on over there?

Placing her notes on the table in front of her, Jenny stood up to get a better view of what was causing the furore. And as she did she spotted a familiar dark head breaking through the crowd gathered behind the cameras.

Liam.

CHAPTER SIXTEEN

LIAM BRACED HIMSELF as he stepped through the doors onto a film set for the first time in five years, knowing the busyness and the noise and the lights and cameras were a full world away from the life he'd been living in the rainforest of late. Not to mention the memories that just being back on set would throw at him.

He sucked in a deep breath and reminded himself why he was there. His purpose today mattered more than his past anyway.

This was about his future.

Getting in had been easy enough—a quick call to a suspicious Josh, whose fears he'd allayed as best he could with a few assurances and a promise to explain everything *after* he'd spoken to Jenny—and he was in.

Dealing with the stares, the whispers and the attention was quite another thing.

He could feel everyone's eyes on him as he thrust his hands into his pockets and walked as nonchalantly as he could across the studio. He'd been an actor once. He could at least *act* as if none of this was bothering him even if, in truth, his heart was jackhammering so hard at what was to come he suspected they could use it as a sound effect.

Then he spotted Jenny, frowning towards the crowd, eyes probably narrowed behind her black-framed specs. Her hair was up in a familiar high ponytail, a few blonde strands framing her face, and she had a pen shoved behind her ear. There was no obvious outward sign of her pregnancy, but Liam noted—after Selena's comments— that she was wearing a looser, more flowing top than she usually favoured.

He paused for a moment and looked at her, letting the truth of what had brought him back to LA really sink in.

It was that pause that was his downfall, though, because before he could start moving again towards Jenny, someone grabbed his arm in a vicelike grip and began dragging him back towards the doors.

'Winter!' He tried to free his arm from her biting fingernails, but without any luck. 'What are you doing?'

'Stopping you from making things worse.' She shoved him outside the doors to the studio set they were filming in. He could see the trailers the stars used between shoots off to the side, but he didn't imagine he was going to be invited in to Winter's for a cup of tea. 'Did Josh know you were coming here?'

'Um…' Liam winced and tried to decide whether dropping his friend in it would make things worse or better.

'He did, didn't he?' Winter's hands balled up into fists. 'Oh, I'm going to *kill* him!'

'Please don't,' Liam said. 'Jenny and I went to a lot of trouble to get you two back together in Iceland. Killing him would ruin that effort rather.'

'*You* got us together? You insufferably arrogant man.'

Winter took a step closer, rage burning in her eyes. 'As if you know the first thing about love. If you did—' She broke off and Liam waited, curious to see if she'd finish the thought.

When she didn't, he murmured, 'Maybe I'm learning.'

Her eyes grew wide and she stopped short of shoving him against the wall. 'Liam,' she said, her voice suddenly softer. 'Why are you here?'

'I'd rather talk to Jenny about that before you, if that's quite all right.'

'Then we'd better get this over with, hadn't we?' said a voice from behind him, and every muscle in his body tensed—especially his heart.

Jenny.

'Do you want me to stay?' Winter asked in a loud whisper as Jenny moved towards her.

Jenny shook her head. 'I can handle this.'

At least she hoped she could. Just seeing him again, breathing the same air, watching him move, was sending her mind and body into overdrive.

Hormones. Just blame the hormones.

Except it wasn't just the pregnancy hormones, she knew, because this had happened in Iceland too—long before she was willing to accept what it might mean.

When Liam Delaney was in the room she couldn't look anywhere else. Couldn't *think* about anyone else.

Which, of course, was exactly why he had to leave.

Fast.

Winter stepped away, but only as far as the studio entrance, keeping the curious crowd of onlookers at bay by shutting the large doors in their faces, which Jenny appreciated. They were probably holding up filming since their female lead was out here playing bouncer, but right now she didn't care.

She had some things she needed to say to Liam Delaney, and then he would leave again and she could go cry for an allotted ten minutes then get back to work.

That was her plan for the immediate future, and she intended to follow it to the letter.

'Liam, if you're here to change your mind, to renegotiate our agreement about the baby, you're wasting your time,' she said firmly. 'I won't be messed around like this. You showing up every time you feel guilty isn't going to help anybody—not me, not you, and certainly not the baby.'

'I know—' he started, but she cut him off. This was her time to talk.

'You wanted out of this situation, and I gave you that. No fuss, no demands—nothing. I gave you everything you wanted, and now it's your turn to give me something.' She drew a deep breath. 'Since you're in town anyway, I want you to meet with my lawyer and sign over all parental rights to me, like we agreed. That way I can be sure about what my future holds.'

'Nobody knows that for certain, Jenny.' His voice reverberated through her, as if her body was reacting to the memory of all the secret things he'd whispered to her over their nights together. She forced herself to ignore it. 'Trust me. I know. I spent the past five years trying to make my life as safe from change or disaster as possible. And then you showed up and blew that all away in less than a week.'

'Well, I'm very sorry if contraceptive failure has ruined your life, Liam, but—'

'That's not what I meant.' Why was he smiling? Shouldn't he be angry with her? Or guilty or sad or something—anything other than smiling gently at her.

She couldn't take his smile. Not today.

'Then say what you *do* mean and leave. Please.' She needed to get out of here. Away from him.

She needed to get back to work and focus on the future she was building for herself and her baby. A future without Liam Delaney in it.

He stepped closer and reached out to take her hand—but she yanked it back out of his reach. If he touched her... She needed to keep distance.

'I can't give you a perfect vision of the future, Jenny,' he said softly. 'But if you'll give me ten minutes, I'll give you all the certainty I have.'

There was something in his eyes. A seriousness blended with hope that made her nod without even thinking about it.

Oh, this could be a huge mistake. But somehow, Jenny couldn't stop herself from making it.

'You can use my trailer,' Winter called from the doors, giving up the pretence that she hadn't been listening in all along.

Jenny swallowed and attempted to mentally prepare herself. 'Come on, then.'

* * *

Liam knew this was his last chance—his only chance—to put this right. If she sent him away after this…well, he'd have to accept that. to sign over parental rights and let her build the future she wanted. Without him in it.

God, he hoped she didn't send him away.

Jenny shut the trailer door behind them and leant against it, even as she gestured for him to take a seat. Preserving her escape route, he assumed. In case she didn't like what he'd come here to say.

'So talk,' she said. 'Why are you really in LA?'

'Because I realised, after you were gone, it was already too late.'

'*What* was too late?' she asked, frustration colouring her voice. 'Liam, I don't understand.'

He gathered his thoughts as fast as he could, wishing he could remember all the clever things he'd decided to say on the plane. But they'd all rushed out of his head the moment he'd seen her again.

'I pushed you away because I was trying to protect my heart,' he said finally. 'After I lost Julie and the baby… I thought I'd lost everything. It took so damn long to piece myself back together again, and I thought the only way to keep me that way, to avoid ever being torn apart like that again, was to make sure I never fell in love again. To never care about anything or anyone that could be taken away from me.'

'I can understand that,' she said softly. 'I think I did something similar, for a long time.'

He looked up sharply, meeting her gaze, wondering

if something had changed since they'd said goodbye. If their time apart had made her realise some of the same things he had. If maybe, just maybe, she was ready to give this—give him, them—a chance.

'But I realised it was too late,' he said. 'When you slipped on the bridge… I think I knew then, but I was too scared to face it. So *terrified* of losing you and the baby that I—'

'Sent me away.'

'Yes. Because I thought, somehow, that if I wasn't in your life you'd be safer. And that if you weren't in mine I could go back to living the same safe, emotionless life I'd been living for the last five years.'

Jenny pushed away from the door and took a step closer. 'So what changed?'

'I did,' he replied. 'When you were gone…that same life I'd lived before didn't feel safe any longer. It just felt empty. I missed you, and I missed the future we'd talked about and…' His eyes burned with unshed tears as Jenny moved closer again, perching on the small table in front of him and taking his hand in hers. 'I realised that living in this world, knowing that you and our child were out there, but not being part of your lives, not loving you, cherishing you, celebrating you the way you both deserved…that would be far worse than any other existence I could imagine.'

Jenny blinked at him. 'You love me?'

'With all my heart. You and our baby.'

She looked away, and he squeezed her hand to let her know he wasn't done yet. 'I can't tell you what the future will bring, and I can't make promises about it because I know too well that the future can change in the blink of an eye. But I can make promises about my heart, because that belongs to you and to our child.'

He swallowed and forced himself to say the scariest line he'd ever had to say which, given how many horror movies he'd starred in, was really something.

'So if you still want me, I am all in. Not just as co-parents, but as a family. Because I'm going to let myself love you both as much and as long as the world allows.'

His words were both barbs and salve for her battered heart.

Barbs because, just when she'd thought she had her future planned out, he'd thrown it all into disarray again. He'd brought uncertainty back into her life just when she'd been certain, and when she needed that certainty more than anything. Or so she'd thought.

Because that salve…he loved her. And she loved him too. Loved him so much her heart ached with it, and hearing he felt the same soothed that pain.

He was right; he couldn't make promises about the future. Nobody could. And just like him she'd worked so hard to stop history repeating itself that she'd run away from him at the first sign that things wouldn't work out. She'd put up all those walls she'd only just begun to let down after finding her place in LA.

After finding him in Iceland.

Being with Liam in Iceland, even in a purely physical relationship, had started her on the path to opening herself up again, she realised now. To realising that she could have pleasure, and fun—even happiness, on her own terms.

Spending time with him in Costa Rica, though…that was when she'd seen the whole of him, his heart and soul for the first time.

That was when she'd fallen in love.

'You're right,' she said, her voice husky in the stillness of the trailer. 'You can't promise me anything about the future. No one can—not even Grandma's Tarot cards. The future will always be uncertain. It will always be a risk.'

'Jenny—' he started, but she shook her head to stop him. She wasn't done yet.

'But what being back here in LA without you has taught me is…you are worth taking the chance. The life we could build together with our child, however that ends up looking, that's not a risk. It's *everything*. Everything that matters to me. And I want to see where we end up.'

Maybe she could stand a few surprises if she had Liam at her side. If she knew what she was battling through the uncertainties for—her love, and her family.

'Do you mean…' He trailed off, as if afraid to say what he was hoping for.

Standing up, Jenny tugged on his hand until he was standing facing her, then smiled at him.

'I mean… I know you're scared of the future. So am I. And we've both been given good reasons to be cautious about love and everything that it brings. But…maybe it's time we were scared *together*. What do you think?'

Liam returned her smile with a warm grin of his own.

'I think that if we can face the future hand in hand, we can face anything. Together.'

As he kissed her, Jenny heard a muffled whoop of joy from outside the trailer and realised that Winter had probably been listening in the whole time. Hell, she was probably planning the wedding already.

But then Liam deepened the kiss, and she forgot to think about anybody, or anything, outside the wonderful future she was going to build with the man she loved by her side.

EPILOGUE

THERE WAS A howler monkey somewhere near, calling from the trees. Liam smiled at the sound of it, even as his best man startled and looked around, trying to find the culprit.

'What was that?' Josh asked, looking alarmed.

'Howler monkey,' Liam said. 'Nothing to worry about.'

'Right.' Josh continued to nervously watch his surroundings. Liam supposed that, for a farm boy from middle America, used to wide open plains and crops, the dense foliage and amazing animals of the Costa Rican rainforest must be a bit of a change of pace.

The treehouses that formed the backbone of his retreat resort were all built now, solid wooden staircases that wound around the trunks leading to luxury spaces in the canopy where a person could think, reflect and reconnect with the natural world.

Today, the balconies were hung with bunting and ribbons and the clearing at the centre filled not with tourists but with his and Jenny's friends, and even his family.

But no Jenny. Not yet.

'Did you ever imagine you'd end up here?'

'In the rainforest? No.' Liam craned his neck, searching for his bride.

'I didn't mean…well, I suppose I did, a bit,' Josh said. 'Costa Rica is pretty incredible. But no, what I *meant* was…when I got my second chance with Winter, it was more than I ever believed I deserved or was even possible. And for you…you were always so adamant that you didn't want this—marriage, a family, all of that. Did you ever really imagine you'd end up here?'

And then, from between the trees, Winter appeared in a bright red sundress, and the crowd began to settle. From somewhere, music started to play and Liam felt his heart speed up as he watched the gap in the trees until…

Jenny. She stepped out, her white halterneck dress glowing in the sunlight as it hugged her curves before flaring out into a skirt that ended halfway down her calves. Her blonde hair was pinned up off her neck, her lips painted a rosy red, and she beamed at him as she made her way down the gap their guests had left for an aisle, Winter following behind.

Instead of a bouquet, she held their daughter on her hip, her head raised and her gaze inquisitive as it always was. Liam watched them draw closer, his heart full to bursting, before he remembered that his best man had asked him a question.

One that deserved an answer.

'I never thought for a moment I could be so lucky,' he said as Jenny passed the baby to Winter and took the last couple of steps alone to join him in front of the celebrant. 'But then, the future always does have a way of surprising us, doesn't it?'

* * * * *

OFF-LIMITS
FLING WITH THE
BILLIONAIRE

SUZANNE MERCHANT

MILLS & BOON

With thanks to Sue and Geoff,
on the Roseland Peninsula, for the years of friendship
and warm hospitality which continue to nurture
my love affair with Cornwall.

CHAPTER ONE

'CASS? CASS, where are you? There's a man in the garden, and he's... What are you doing?'

Cassandra gripped the ladder and balanced the broken piece of plaster cornice across the top of it. She shuffled her feet until she could perch on the second step from the top. If she ducked her head, she could see a slice of the view.

The sea sparkled, blue and silver. Above it, clouds raced across the pale spring sky. It was her favourite view in the world. It could soothe fears, calm tempers and bring her that sense of home that she treasured above all else.

Except soon it wouldn't be her view any more. The realisation that this was probably the last time she'd see it hit her like a physical blow that threatened to expel the air from her lungs and stop her heart in mid-beat.

She twisted her head, dragging her eyes away, and looked down at Tess, her PA, instead.

'Last-minute repairs,' she said through gritted teeth. 'This bit fell off again last night.'

'Perhaps you should come down...'

Cassandra wished she'd been more honest with the staff of the Cornish Hideaway Hotel. She'd told them she'd been forced to sell, but she knew she'd been too upbeat when she'd described her plan to persuade the new owner, whoever that might be, to retain the staff.

Tess clutched a chipped mug of coffee in one hand and bit into the flaky Danish pastry she held in the other. She looked up at Cass again and her eyes widened in surprise.

'Cass? You look…different.'

For a horrible moment Cass thought Tess was going to choke on that mouthful of pastry, adding manslaughter to her own personal list of crimes. Deception, and deliberately ignoring hard facts when they were staring you in the face were two of the others she could think of.

But Tess gulped and swallowed a mouthful of coffee.

Cass squirmed.

'How did you get your hair to do that? And are you wearing make-up?'

Cass put a hand on the neat knot at the back of her head, checking it was still intact. She'd secured it with proper hairpins and half a can of hairspray, but its defiance of gravity still seemed miraculous. She shrugged.

'Hairspray actually does what it says on the tin. I think it's really wallpaper glue in a spray-on formula.'

'You look pale. Have you had any breakfast?'

'It's the make-up. And I didn't sleep that well last night.'

She had hardly slept for a week. Not since the lawyers had said she had no option but to accept the offer she'd received for the Cornish Hideaway Hotel. It wasn't high enough to clear the debts but, as they'd pointed out, with each day she delayed those debts would continue to mount.

And then, early this morning, they'd let her know about a new possible buyer. She'd breathed a sigh of relief, not because she hoped for more money—there was scant hope of that—but because it meant she could delay her decision by another twenty-four hours, at least.

'Why,' asked Tess, brushing flakes of pastry off her shirt

and onto the floor, 'have you put your hair up and put on make-up?'

'There's someone else coming to look at the Hideaway. He's booked in to stay the night. I need to look business-like. I'm going to change…'

'That must be who I saw, and I don't think you have time to change, but you can probably sneak a coffee in, if you're quick. *He* was talking to George in the garden. He's *divine*-looking.' She rolled her eyes. 'Who is he?'

'The CEO of a company called Marine Developments. That's all I know.'

'I think George was bending his ear about never having enough time to grow his vegetables because of all the running repairs he has to carry out on the building, but he looked really interested even though he was probably bored…'

Cassandra shook her head. The mere thought of coffee—of *anything*—made her stomach heave.

She straightened her knees and inched around again, wishing she'd changed before tackling this job. Wishing she hadn't seen the broken cornice at all, wishing… Wishes were a waste of time and energy. And anyway, they never came true.

'I must get this done,' she muttered. If only Tess could stop talking to her, just for a minute, and let her concentrate.

She yanked the claw hammer from the waistband of her jeans and propped the ancient piece of moulded cornice in place. Squinting, she aimed a vicious blow at the rusty nail protruding from one end of it.

'Oh, Cass, he's…'

'Ow! *Crap!*' The hammer clattered to the floor and the cornice flew through the air. Cass sucked her injured fingers and squeezed her eyes shut, instantly losing her balance. She swayed, lost her footing and slithered down the ladder, into the arms of the man she had vowed she never wanted to see again.

'Merde!' His voice was deep, with the hint of a Gallic accent. 'What the *hell* are you doing?'

Cass stared up into grey eyes, stormy with annoyance, and the memory swamped her. The firm yet gentle grip of his hands on her upper arms felt oddly familiar, even after so many years. And his eyes held the same steeliness, except anger had replaced the concern they'd held back then. For one insane moment the essence of his strength almost overwhelmed her, and she thought how easy it would be to surrender to it; to lay her head on his broad chest and let someone else take the strain.

She dismissed that madness, placed her hands instead of her cheek on his chest and pushed herself away from him. He let go of her arms, massaged his shoulder and nudged the offending piece of cornice out of his way with the toe of a polished leather shoe.

He would have had to duck through the door, she thought, even though it was one of the newer doorways, built to an almost twenty-first-century height. He ran a hand through his windswept dark hair and glanced around the room, and then his gaze returned to her face.

Cass stepped backwards until she felt the ladder behind her. She raised her chin a fraction and took a deep breath, hoping the hammering her heart had set up in her chest would steady. But as long as those implacable eyes held hers, she knew she had a snowball's chance...

The suit he wore screamed 'bespoke', or, more likely, *fait sur mesure*. The words were probably stitched into the lining. Beneath the jacket and crisp white cotton shirt his body looked—*felt*—hard and toned. As rock-solid, she was willing to bet, as the business deals he and his father struck.

In the fourteen years since their last, brief meeting he had been transformed from a twenty-something diffident young man, obscured by his father's shadow, to a thirty-something

fully-fledged, independent powerhouse. She'd hoped—
prayed—that the sale of the Hideaway would escape the notice of the formidable Chevalier clan. How naïve was that?

He stopped rubbing his shoulder and extended his right
hand. His fingers were long and bronzed, the nails squared
off and expertly manicured.

He had no right to be early; to catch her unprepared. The
business suit she'd brought down from London last week was
useless , hanging behind the door of her attic bedroom. And
right now she could have done with the extra inches a pair of
heels would have given her.

'Miss Greenwood.' All trace of annoyance had been wiped
from his eyes and his voice. His tone was even. 'Shall we start
again and renew our acquaintance in a more civilised way?'

His gaze drilled into her and she knew she had to return
it or betray her confusion. Mesmerised by the sheer force of
his confidence, Cass put out her hand. He flexed his cool fingers around hers and she wished her palm wasn't damp with
anxiety. He'd notice, of course. He wouldn't miss a thing. Her
hand was trapped, just like the rest of her, but if she hoped to
save any of her self-respect, she needed to break the contact
between them.

His presence and his utter self-assurance were intimidating.
From the arrogant tilt of his head as he surveyed her study, to
his faintly dismissive expression, it was obvious that Matheo
Chevalier did not doubt himself. He might as well have spoken the words out loud. He was about to gain control of what
he and his family had wanted for so long.

She opened her mouth, but he spoke first.

'We met once before.' Her hand was still in his. 'I came
here with my father, but you probably don't remember. You
must have been…about sixteen?'

Cass remembered. It wasn't a time she'd ever been able

to forget. She remembered the sense of desperation that had gripped them then. She and her father, crushed by grief, struggling to come to terms with the changed order of things. Despite all the treatments the doctors had tried, all the money her father had spent on futile attempts to halt it, the disease had claimed her mother's life with cruel speed.

Cass had felt as if she'd been cast adrift on an alien sea with no familiar landmarks to navigate by, dreading the next blow but not knowing from which direction it would come. She'd clung to her father; he'd always known what to do. He'd been the rock on which she and her mother had depended. His solidarity had been unquestionable.

But she'd quickly discovered he was no longer the father she recognised. He'd become unreachable, engulfed in grief so intense that he seemed to have to expend all of his energy on keeping it locked inside him. Cass became afraid to talk to him, afraid of what might happen if he allowed any of it to escape.

Within a few weeks the next blow had materialised in the form of the rich, successful hotelier Charles Chevalier. He'd wanted to buy the hotel, pointing out that he was willing to pay over the odds for what was, by rights, his property anyway. Joe Greenwood would be able to settle his debts, he had said, contempt in his tone, as if he was doing them a favour, trying to force them to part with the home they loved.

Matheo Chevalier had retreated from the argument that had erupted between the two older men. After his weeks of silence, Cass had felt an odd sense of relief that her father could still string a coherent sentence together. But then she'd listened, shocked, as, in language more colourful than anything she'd ever heard, he'd declared he'd sell his soul to the devil before he sold the Hideaway to a lying, cheating Chevalier.

Fast forward fourteen years, and here was the son, hiding behind a different company, about to try again.

She pulled her hand from Matheo Chevalier's, memory stoking her anger. He might be smooth-talking, but he was his father's son, and she wasn't going to forget it.

He'd tried to be kind to her during the few frightening, confusing days of their visit. He'd asked about her mother, and she'd attempted to describe the dark, bottomless pit of sorrow that yawned inside her. He'd lost his mother, too, he'd said, when he was ten, and then he'd been sent away to boarding school, where he hadn't been allowed to be sad.

They'd walked on the beach, climbed on the rocks, and talked. It had been cathartic for Cass. She had told him of her fear of the future, of how she sometimes thought she heard her mother's voice and how her father had become a stranger who had decreed that nothing in the hotel could be changed. Nothing at all.

And if he was his father's son, she was her father's daughter. Old grievances ran deep.

'I remember you.' Her voice surprised her with its firmness, considering how wobbly she felt. She remembered how she'd reacted when he'd first tried to talk to her, the mix of fear and betrayal of loyalty to her father. 'But I remember your father better.'

'And I remember yours,' he responded, drily. 'I'm unlikely ever to forget his opinions of my family, or his lack of restraint in expressing them.'

'My father never believed in mincing his words, and he had scant regard for moral weakness.'

'Which he considered my father to have in spades.'

'And your grandfather, too.'

His laugh was low. 'You've changed in the past fourteen

years. I remember you as something of a wild child. And fragile.'

His eyes travelled over her, and she hoped he saw that the wild child had been well and truly banished. Any latent wildness had disappeared for good that day a year ago, when her father had died, shockingly and suddenly, leaving her with nothing but the almost unbearable responsibility of saving the hotel and preserving the livelihoods of its faithful staff.

As for fragility, she'd shed that, too. What didn't kill you made you stronger, and she had survived. The years of coping with her father's descent into depression, forcing herself to leave him to go to college, forging a career for herself in the competitive world of interior design and surviving the break-up of a controlling relationship had transformed her into a stronger woman than she'd have believed possible back when she'd first met Matheo Chevalier.

If she'd seemed wild, it had been wild with grief, perhaps, or maybe fear at what the future could possibly hold without her mother to keep her safe.

'You've changed too. You were the only person I'd really spoken to in weeks, and you seemed to understand.' She shook her head. 'But it seems you've assumed the family mantle with enviable ease. And you have a new company name. Did you mean to take me by surprise? To catch me out?'

His eyes darkened, slate hard, and his mouth, which had softened as he studied her, compressed into a straight line.

'Yes,' he said. 'I have changed. And Marine Developments is a company that was set up two years ago. It's not exactly new.'

'Your father, I remember, has always got what he wanted. He's played a long waiting game.' She shrugged. 'But I'm afraid you may be too late. I'm about to accept an offer.' Suddenly the too-low bid seemed attractive, if it meant not selling to the Chevaliers, but she knew her lawyer would not share that view.

'Naturally you are free to sell to any of the other bidders.'

Cass was not free at all. She'd be pressured into taking the highest offer, and quickly, and she was sure he knew that. The knowledge would be giving both him and his father enormous satisfaction.

'But your position is very weak. It would be sensible to go for a straightforward sale to the highest bidder.'

Cass didn't want to be sensible. She wanted to keep her home, and the staff, some of whom had known her all of her life, around her, so that all the memories of her parents and her childhood would not be obliterated by the plans of a mega-successful property developer.

'Selling at all is a betrayal of my father's wishes. I will never compound that by selling to the Chevaliers.'

Matheo Chevalier slipped a leather bag off his shoulder and put it on the desk as if he already owned it. He turned and strolled over to the window. 'My interest in the Hideaway has nothing at all to do with my father.'

'You expect me to believe that?' Disbelief coloured her voice. 'Your grandfather and then your father used every means available, some definitely unscrupulous, to try to get control of the Hideaway. Don't tell me this has nothing to do with the past.'

Cass looked past him, towards the sea. White caps had appeared, foaming on the crests of the waves as they rolled into the cove below. The wind must have changed direction, she thought absently. She tried to focus on what he was saying, through the fog of despair that engulfed her at the thought of finally leaving this place, with its ever-changing weather but never-changing comfort of home.

She'd spent the whole of the past year trying everything

possible to keep the hotel going, but when the accountants had presented her with the bald financial facts she'd been forced to accept that selling was unavoidable. At least this way she'd be able to pay most of the outstanding bills. And if she used the full powers of her persuasion with the new owners, some of the staff might keep their jobs.

'I would like to have found a way...' She hated the defeat she could hear in her own voice.

She brushed a cobweb from her jumper and glanced down at her faded jeans and scuffed trainers. How could she expect anyone to take her seriously, dressed like this?

From the corner of her eye she caught a movement, and she swung her gaze back into the room. Tess, whose presence she'd completely forgotten, was sidling silently towards the door, her eyes huge with surprise.

'Tess, wait...' she called out, desperate to offer an explanation, though she didn't have the faintest idea how to phrase it. The long-standing feud between theGreenwoods and the Chevaliers was the stuff of legend at the Hideaway, along with the myth of the treasure, reportedly to have been smuggled out of France by the Chevalier ancestors, on the run from the Revolution and a date with Madame La Guillotine. Now the identity of the latest prospective new owner was going to get out in the worst possible way. She had no reason to believe Tess would be discreet. She'd be bursting to tell everyone what she'd heard.

'Tess!'

Matheo's voice, like a blade sheathed in velvet, carved through the silence and Tess, who had ignored Cass's plea, froze.

'Tess,' he repeated, a fraction more softly. 'Could you organise some coffee for us, please? There are points I need to discuss with Miss Greenwood.'

Cassandra watched as Tess struggled to respond. She looked like a mouse caught in the mesmerising stare of a cat. Then she ducked her head and swallowed.

'Coffee. Yes…of course.' She backed towards the door. 'Mr Chevalier, sir.'

His laser gaze flicked back to Cassandra, but she thought the corners of his lips twitched. Her skin pricked and she shivered.

'Are you cold? The heating in here doesn't seem to be on. It's only April, after all.'

'Yes, but it's been spring in Cornwall for a month. Officially. It was declared four weeks ago.'

It may have been spring, but there was no denying the cold. The truth was she'd turned off the radiators in all the private areas of the building months ago, trying to save on the fuel bill. 'Put on a vest, and another jumper' she'd advised anyone who complained about the cold and damp. As long as the guests were warm, everyone else could make do.

His eyebrows arched. 'Does spring come to Cornwall before anywhere else in the country?'

'Spring is declared in Cornwall when a champion magnolia in each of seven different Cornish gardens has fifty or more blooms fully open. That happened on the third of March.'

'Is the garden of the Hideaway one of the seven?'

'Well, no… People don't come here particularly to see the garden. It's grown a little wild.'

'Is "wild" a creative word for "neglected"? Like the building?'

'It's an old building. Ancient. There's always something needing to be fixed. It keeps our gardener, George, very busy…'

'Trying to stop the place from falling down and landing up on the beach.' He nodded towards the cove below. 'I had a conversation with George on my way in,' he continued. 'He said he'd like to grow enough vegetables and fruit in summer to supply the kitchen but much of his time is spent patching things up rather than on productive gardening.'

Cass wished George hadn't been quite so candid but what he'd said was true. And he would have been no match for the sort of intense questioning Matheo Chevalier would have directed at him. She'd defy anyone caught in the beam of those eyes not to tell all, immediately. She tried a different tack.

'George has been here a long time and he knows the building better than anyone now that my fa—' She breathed in and out again. 'Anyway, he knows every corner of the building, and all its weak spots. He can fix anything...'

He turned to face her fully, and his broad-shouldered frame blocked a significant amount of light from the window. 'This whole operation is a collection of weak spots held together by old habits and sentimentality, by the look of it,' he continued. 'George would be better employed doing what he says he does best and growing vegetables for the restaurant.' He pushed a hand through his hair. 'These days, everyone wants to know where their food was grown and how many air miles it took to get it onto their plates. Serving fresh, organic produce grown in the garden with zero carbon footprint would be a powerful marketing tool.'

'I know that.'

She'd thought about it, of course she had, but the constant round of necessary repairs had taken up most of George's time and there was no money to pay anyone else to do the work.

'You haven't acted on something you know would obviously improve business,' Matheo said bluntly. 'Anyone who works for me gets fired for that sort of lapse.'

'Well, luckily I don't work for you,' she snapped.

'This hotel is dowdy, run-down, unexciting—the list is end-less, and I don't expect to be impressed by the staff, either.'

Cass felt anger swelling in her chest. This man knew noth-ing of what it was like to hold your breath at the end of every month while you tried to balance the books, or how putting on an extra jumper in the winter might keep your body warmer but your fingers were still sometimes too cold to hit the right buttons on the keyboard. He'd had it easy all his life. All he'd had to do was follow in his father's arrogant footsteps.

'There are good people here. People who've been loyal and faithful to the hotel and to my family for years. They don't de-serve to be discarded without a chance to prove themselves. Some of them know no other life, and—'

'What I need are people who know what they're doing and who have the initiative to get on with the job.'

'They all know what they're doing. Some of them have been here so long they could do their jobs blindfolded...'

Too late, Cass realised she'd played straight into his hands.

'Yes, that's what I thought. The first thing this place needs is some new ideas and a fresh approach.'

Matheo Chevalier moved from the window and gestured to the desk. 'Shall we sit down, or would you prefer to stand by the window? It's slightly warmer there, in the sun.'

'The sun will be gone in a few minutes.'

'How do you know what the sun will do?'

If Cass hadn't known she couldn't possibly be right, she would have thought a hint of curiosity had crept into his voice.

'Because the wind has changed. Earlier today the sea was flat calm and a particular shade of blue, but now there are white caps on the swells and a weather front on the horizon. When it hits land, it'll rain and we won't see the sun again until tomorrow.'

And, she thought, I'll have to sleep on the sofa in the staff sitting room again. Her little attic room had a leak in the roof which even George had been unable to mend, and the rain would drip relentlessly onto her narrow childhood bed.

He looked out at the sea, his gaze narrowed. 'I suppose if you've spent your entire life in a place you get to be able to predict the weather. I've never had that…' He stopped and Cass wondered if his frown was one of regret or simply of incomprehension.

He pulled up a second chair and Cassandra watched as he removed his jacket and slung it over the back of what had been her chair until he'd decided to use it. He inserted a forefinger into the knot of his tie, pulling it loose and undoing the top button of his shirt, exposing the smooth golden skin in the hollow where his neck joined his shoulder, and the protuberance of his collar bone.

Then he removed a pair of heavy gold cufflinks and rolled up his sleeves. He crossed his arms, resting his muscled forearms on the desk.

'Mademoiselle Greenwood? Will you sit down?' A corner of his mouth lifted as he regarded her. 'There are a few things I'd like to discuss with you before finalising my bid.' He glanced towards the door. 'Will the coffee arrive soon, do you think?'

Cass lowered herself onto the edge of the chair beside him.

'I usually go and get what I need. So shall I…?'

She began to rise again but he shook his head, just firmly enough to show who was in charge.

He looked up as a soft tap sounded at the door.

'Ah. And here it is.'

Cass sat down again. How did he do that? Even Tess had listened to him.

'Thank you, Tess. The coffee smells excellent. Could you put it on the desk, please?'

Tess carried a tray across the room, her bottom lip caught in her teeth. She placed it on the desk and backed away.

'Um… I brought sandwiches. It's almost lunchtime and I know Cass hasn't had br—'

Cass shot Tess a look and she closed her mouth.

'Thank you. And please will you inform the restaurant I'll be dining there tonight, and I hope Mademoiselle Greenwood will join me?'

'Oh, but Cass and I go to our yoga class on Mondays. Cass, aren't you…?'

'That'll be all, Tess, thank you,' he said.

'Yes, Mr Chevalier, of course.' Tess almost ran from the room.

Dinner with him in the restaurant was quite possibly the worst idea Cass had ever heard. And anyway, she was busy. The yoga class shone like a beacon of hope at the end of what was becoming a difficult day.

'Thank you, Mr Chevalier, but I won't be able to join you for dinner. I'm busy this evening.'

'Could you skip yoga tonight?'

'But may I suggest you make a reservation at a restaurant in town instead?' she carried on, ignoring him. 'I don't think the Hideaway serves the sort of food people…um…like you prefer to eat.'

The crease between his brows deepened.

'What sort of food do "people like me" prefer?'

Cass felt herself flushing. She had the feeling he was hiding amusement behind that frown.

'I think you know what I mean. Our menu consists of plain, old-fashioned dishes of the meat and two veg variety. It's what our loyal guests expect. People who've been coming here year after year don't like change.'

'Ah. And can I expect jelly and custard for pudding?'

'It might be spotted dick this evening.'

Two could play at this game.

'Good,' he countered smoothly. 'It'll be like being back at my English boarding school.' His mouth curved and she noticed the hint of a dimple in his cheek. 'It'll remind me how happy I was to be expelled. But I presume your…yoga class… won't last all evening?'

His tone rated yoga somewhere on a level with English boarding schools. Cass thought if she had to dine with him, she might stab him with a steak knife.

'Can you talk me through some figures?' He pulled a slim laptop from the case on the desk and flipped it open. 'I'm hoping you'll be able to clarify a couple of things. Then they might make less depressing reading than the accounts for the last financial year your lawyer provided.'

That, thought Cass, was highly unlikely.

CHAPTER TWO

QUITE QUICKLY, he found the figures could depress him deeply. For the first time, Matheo Chevalier questioned his interest in this failing hotel. What was driving his desire for it? Was his need for revenge really worth it? Instead of feeling excited by the prospect of acquiring what generations of his family had craved, he felt weighed down by the possibility.

He searched in vain for a single positive thing to focus on. What the hell had Joe Greenwood been thinking of over the past fourteen years? Whatever it was, it had had nothing to do with running a profitable hotel and everything to do with preserving some sort of time capsule. Then he pushed himself away from the desk, allowed himself to be irritated by the squeaking wheel on the elderly chair, and swivelled towards Cassandra. She sat, chin sunk into her palm, staring out at the teeming rain. Her gaze was unfocused, and he wondered what her life had been like, living with a father who had evidently paid no attention to the world around him, and probably not to his daughter either, at a time when she would have desperately needed security and comfort.

She'd lost her mother and then her father and she was about to lose her home. None of it made him feel good. He considered what it must be like to feel the loss of family so deeply and realised he had no idea. His memories of his mother consisted of acute sadness and then lonely isolation in his English boarding school. He tried to take a mental step back, to make this less personal, but for some reason totally unfamiliar to him it was difficult. The room was colder than ever and he allowed himself to blame that for his feeling of uncertainty and irritation.

'Does that fireplace work?' He looked at the impressive carved chimney breast then frowned at the smoke-black stain on the wall above it. 'If it does, why don't we light a fire?'

Cass got to her feet and walked over to the Victorian iron radiator under the window. Bending down, she did something to the valve and a loud gurgling sound rumbled from the pipes.

'Since I will shortly no longer have responsibility for the heating bills, I've turned it onto maximum. We'll be warm as toast in a few minutes.'

He had trouble believing what he was hearing. 'Are all the radiators in the hotel turned off?'

Cass shook her head. 'Only the ones in the private areas. We've always made sure our guests are warm and dry. But the cost of heating increases constantly, and the system is antiquated. I knew we wouldn't be able to afford the oil for much longer.'

'Is that "we" as in you and your father?'

She laughed. 'No. My father had all the radiators on and the heating going full blast for most of the year. Being cold or damp just increased his misery, and Cornwall can be both of those, even in summer.'

'Was it only after he died that you began to put cost-saving measures into place?'

'It was only after he died that I had anything at all to do with running the hotel.'

Matheo tried to hide his surprise. He'd assumed she'd always been here, a part of this ramshackle arrangement of rooms that called itself a hotel. It was worse than he'd thought possible.

'What were you doing before?'

'I was working. In London.'

He found he wanted to know exactly what it was she'd been doing in London. What had become of the wild teenager he remembered? The one with the long, long dark hair and deep blue eyes, running away down the beach when he had attempted to talk to her. He recalled how, after their first, brief encounter, she had scrambled over the rocks and vanished.

It was as if when the next wave came in and washed her footprints from the sand it had washed her away too. That wayward teenager in the gypsy skirt and seashell necklace had been erased. In her place stood this serious, defensive young woman, with her wild hair severely tamed. And an air of only just hanging on to her emotions.

An utterly foreign sensation unfurled somewhere behind his breastbone. It took him a moment to identify it as regret. She was hurting and he and his family were partly to blame. He wished he could change that.

Matheo massaged the base of his skull. He blinked, trying to blot out the thought, but instead found himself focusing on the disturbing image that had burned itself onto his retinas— the image of Cassandra's endless legs, in faded blue jeans, as she had bent over the valve of the radiator. He groaned inwardly. This was not the time or the place to entertain regrets or to lust after a pair of legs, but the punch of desire which the sight of them had dealt to his stomach was real. He needed to get out of here and go for a five-mile run to kill these inappropriate and massively misplaced thoughts.

He tried to focus on all the negatives he'd uncovered in the past couple of hours, but there were too many. At least the attempt took his mind off the slim woman who stood looking out of the window, ignoring him.

'What are you thinking about?' he asked, his curiosity surprising him.

'I'm thinking,' she replied calmly, leaning against the radiator, 'that you're right.'

'What about?' He frowned, trying to second-guess her. 'The staff?'

She lifted her chin and shook her head. 'No. I was thinking that my position *is* impossibly weak. I'll be pressured into accepting the highest offer, even if it's not what I want to do. The idea of selling to you is almost unbearable, but if you—'

Matheo, against his expectations, had to admit to being intrigued. An inner strength seemed to enable Cassandra to hold herself together. And what other woman he'd ever met could predict the weather by looking at the sky or know that the arrival of spring depended on the whim of a flowering tree and not on the solid evidence of the calendar?

'I'll offer enough to enable you to clear your debts,' he interrupted. 'That way you can walk away...'

'But that's just it,' she said, softly. 'I don't want to walk away. I want to do my best to ensure that the members of staff—at least those who want to stay—are given a chance.'

He turned to face her fully. The quick rise and fall of her chest under her jumper belied her steady voice.

'I'll agree to consider any offer you make for the Hideaway if you'll agree to certain things. Two things, actually.'

'What two things?'

'Firstly, that you'll give the staff members the opportunity to prove themselves. They don't deserve to be thrown out without a chance.'

'And the second?' He noticed the beat of the pulse at her throat quicken.

'That you allow me to have a say in the renovations.'

He propped his chin on a fist and watched her. Her expression was impassive, but he'd already noticed the physical signs of stress.

'I don't think either of those things are going to happen, Miss Greenwood.'

'Then I don't think I'm going to sell to you, Mr Chevalier.' Defiance flashed in her eyes.

'You need my money, and I don't need you or your staff, so you don't have any bargaining power. A deal must be mutually beneficial to both parties. That's how it works.'

'I can refuse to sell to you.'

'You can, but I don't think you will. Think of the alternative. The burden of debt, the threat of bankruptcy. And your lawyers will put you under pressure.'

'You're assuming the employees are no good.'

'There's no room in business for sentiment. Every single member of staff, from the doorman to the manager, needs to have pride in their position and be prepared to give one hundred and ten per cent all the time.'

'You're jumping to negative conclusions when you know nothing about them.'

'Maybe, but I think I'm justified. It doesn't look as if anything has changed here for fifty years, from the décor to the housekeeper, and probably the mattresses.'

'As I said, our loyal guests don't appreciate change.'

'And the average age of your typical loyal guest is?'

She hesitated. 'I don't know. Most of them are elderly.'

'You *should* know. What's going to happen when they're unable to holiday here any longer? You need to attract a younger, hipper, *wealthier* guest, and to do that a lot is going to have to change.'

There was a pause, and when she answered defeat coloured her voice.

'Yes, I've realised that.'

'And why are you worried about the staff when you won't be here anylonger?'

He wished he could take those words back. *Of course* she worried about the staff. He was fast learning she was that kind of person, and it made this whole process of acquisition difficult when it had never been difficult before.

She stared at him. 'Forgive me for saying so, Mr Chevalier, but that is a silly question. I *care* about them, that's why, but perhaps you don't know what it's like to feel personally responsible for other people's livelihoods and wellbeing. Mrs Brown, the housekeeper, cared for my mother when she was ill. George searched for me when I ran away, after she died. The chef has baked me a birthday cake every year I've been here, and he's done the same for countless others.'

She stopped, and he saw she was breathing fast. There was a flush on her cheeks and her eyes were bright with what looked suspiciously like tears.

'Do you need any more reasons?' she finished.

'Are there any? And I'm sorry if I've upset you.' He felt appalled at the raw emotion in her expression and her voice, and desperate to stop it. Losing control of a situation, especially one of his own making, was a new experience for him and one which he disliked. He wondered how it had happened after a few short hours in Cassandra's company.

She brushed the edge of a finger under her eyes.

'It's too late for tears. I just wish you wouldn't judge people without any evidence. Money may fix many things, but it can't mend relationships or buy simple human kindness. Perhaps one day you'll discover that for yourself.'

Matheo stood up, trying to regain control. How had this happened? What should have been a day spent familiarising himself with the business so he could fine-tune his bid had turned into an emotional roller-coaster ride. He'd always hated roller coasters. The sense of being out of control, of not know-ing what would hit you next, was unbearable. His stomach swooped and with a jolt of alarm he realised that Cassandra Greenwood, whose legs had already proved to be dangerously distracting, was altogether much too beautiful. Her violet eyes shimmered like amethysts in her pale face. Her dark hair, so severely styled, had rebelled, and a few wayward tendrils had worked their way out of the knot to curl against the creamy skin of her neck.

He pressed his palms onto the desktop and hauled his at-tention back to the conversation they'd been having.

'I asked, Mademoiselle Greenwood,' he said, the effort it took making his voice tight, 'if there were any more reasons why you think the members of your team should be kept on. *Are* there?'

He watched her struggle to keep calm. Her fingers gripped the iron radiator on either side of her hips, and her chest rose and fell erratically, but she looked at him without flinching, her violet gaze direct and challenging.

'I've…given them the impression that they may have a few months' trial under the new ownership.' She pushed a lock of hair off her face with a hand which trembled slightly. 'But I should have realised that was just a dream born of desperation. Anyway, by now Tess will have told them—*all* of them—who you are, and although they will never believe I'd sell to you they'll know their jobs are lost if I do.' She pressed her hands together. 'The Chevalier name is mud at this hotel.'

She glanced out of the window, and he followed her gaze, but there was nothing to see but grey clouds scudding over a grey sea, and rain coming down in sheets. He was no longer cold, though he wasn't sure if his warmth was as a result of the radiator, which had creaked into life, or of the charged at-mosphere in the room.

'I've told them any new owner will hopefully put money into the hotel, to fix all the things that need fixing, get new equipment for the kitchen, rebuild the quay and restore the boat so we can offer sailing trips again... The list of what we haven't been able to afford is endless.'

Matheo ground the heels of his hands into his eye sockets and rubbed. Then he dropped his hands and walked across the room towards her. She straightened.

'I don't think you've been thinking logically.'

'I was thinking that I could soften the blow if I could tell them they still had a chance of keeping their jobs. I thought I might be able to influence any new owner's plans for the building, so that some of its character could be preserved.' She lifted her shoulders in a gesture of resignation.

'If you and your father had run the place properly you wouldn't be in this position now. If I make the offer I've mentioned it will be in excess of the value of what is barely a going concern, but if I buy it, by the end of the year the Hideaway will be one of the most desirable boutique hotels in the country. I cannot run it as a charity for the sake of the workforce.'

'My father believed the people were as important—no, more important—than the profit. He was caring and humane and money meant nothing to him.'

'Unfortunately, money becomes very important when you don't have enough of it. If you'd paid more attention to the business before your father died you might have realised just what sort of state his affairs were in. What were you doing in London? You should have been here.' The look she sent him made him feel suddenly a little unsure of his ground. 'I mean, then perhaps you'd have realised what was happening.'

'I was building the company in which I'm a partner.' She paused and he tried to hide his surprise, recalibrate his opinion of her. 'But,' she continued, 'if the Hideaway is such a disaster, I suggest you reconsider. Or is the opportunity to get hold of it just too tempting to resist? Is revenge really that sweet?'

'It has nothing at all to do with the revenge you imply and everything to do with spotting a business that can be turned around and made profitable,' he retorted, trying to regain the advantage. Cassandra, in her navy fisherman's jumper and worn denims, looked nothing like a businesswoman. He couldn't even hazard a guess at what sort of company she was building. 'It can be done with any business. I happen to do it with property, mainly hotels.'

'Credit me with a little more intelligence and insight than that. I clearly remember your father doing his utmost to buy the Hideaway from my father fourteen years ago, when he thought he'd caught him at a low ebb. What sort of person descends on a man broken by grief, and tries to force him to sell his home and livelihood?'

'If your father had sold then…'

'That's not the point.' She lifted her chin. 'The sort of man who would do that is the sort who was hell-bent on revenge, because his family had never been able to accept that the hotel belonged to *us*. My father denied yours that triumph, and I'd love to deny it to you.' She pushed her hands into her pockets, and he thought they were shaking.

He moved away from her and returned to stand behind the desk. 'Revenge would, indeed, be sweet, but not necessarily for the reasons you think.'

'I don't know what that means. Now, if you'll excuse me, I need to speak to the staff.'

Cassandra turned and walked towards the door, her back ramrod straight and her head high. It was all Matheo could do to stop himself from reaching out a restraining hand to stop her. She might look vulnerable in unguarded moments, but she had an enviable core of steel, which would take her a long way if she chose to head in the right direction. She was the sort of person he liked to hire—personable, approachable, and with a titanium-strength self-belief. He dismissed the thought, only for it to be replaced by the far more disturbing one of how it would feel to hold that delicate face between his hands and... He wouldn't begin to go there. He couldn't, not now. He was exhausted, not thinking straight. When last had he had a long enough night's sleep? He didn't know. He'd have to get out for some fresh air. But then he thought of something he wanted to know.

'Mademoiselle Greenwood?'

She stopped in the doorway, keeping her back to him.

'What is your company?'

She turned, her narrow shoulders lifted.

'It's called FuturePlan. We remodel and repurpose hotels and buildings like this one.' She shrugged. 'Which is why I suggested I could be involved in this project. We're a small company, so our overheads are lower, which would keep the cost down...'

He held up a hand.

'Hang on. Let me get this right.' He folded his arms across his chest. 'You're suggesting that I employ you to work on the renovation of this hotel? To keep costs down?' He shook his head. 'Are you familiar with any of the Chevalier work?'

Cassandra took two steps back into the room.

'Of course I am. Your hotels are famous. They're huge and modern; stunning pieces of architecture and insane levels of luxury. But you haven't done anything like this before, have you? The Hideaway is unique and iconic in its own way, and I know it better than anyone. We have ideas, Nick and I—good ideas—about how it could be.'

'Nick?'

'He's my partner in FuturePlan. The chief architect. I head up the interior-design team.'

'And you have ideas which haven't been put into practice?'

'No, they haven't,' she answered, shaking her head. 'There's been no money. And anyway, my father refused...' Her eyes dropped to the floor. 'My father didn't want anything to change.' She took a deep breath, and her eyes met his again. 'My idea was that we could do the remodelling, using my knowledge of the building and the local area, if the new owners would give the staff the chance to prove themselves.' She turned and walked back to the door.

This time Matheo did not try to stop her. The room felt darker after she'd left. He checked the light bulbs in the ancient fittings before deciding it was the leaden clouds outside that had stolen the light.

He still needed to resolve some discrepancies in the figures with her, but if necessary he'd employ his forensic accountant to unravel the mystery. But he needed to move quickly. He thought it very likely that she'd sell to anyone but him if she could.

If asked to guess what Cassandra Greenwood did for a living, he would never have got it right. He tried to avoid making assumptions in life—they could so often trip you up—but he realised he'd come to the possible purchase of the Hideaway with very little idea of what actually lay behind its ancient stone walls. Cassandra's offer was bold, and he admired that, but he had no intention of agreeing to it. Why would he risk employing a small, unknown company when he could choose whoever he wanted to do the work?

He returned to the window and took in the vista. A grey sea heaved under an angry grey sky and grey rain blurred the boundary between them. There was no room in his life for doubts or regrets, which was fortunate, he thought, as otherwise he'd be entertaining a whole room full of them right now. But he wasn't letting them in. There was no reason why this hotel couldn't become a great success story, just like his others. Okay, it was different from the sort of project he normally took on but that didn't mean it would be more difficult. The lawyers working on behalf of Cassandra Greenwood would talk her round, make her see financial sense, and she'd accept his offer.

He knew that the regret which nagged at him had nothing at all to do with buying the hotel and everything to do with the person from whom he planned to buy it. He usually dealt with faceless names on a contract. But he'd been tricked by his memories into coming here in person and it had been a huge mistake. The dark-haired girl with the amethyst eyes had danced on the edge of his consciousness for fourteen years and the temptation to discover what had happened to her had overridden his legendary cool reason and calculated good sense.

He sat down in the squeaky chair and returned his attention to the computer screen. He'd go through the figures one more time, but he knew there was something wrong. He'd picked it up straight away, but he just couldn't work out how it was happening.

He stretched his arms and folded them behind his head and found his eyes straying to the window again. If this was his office, the first thing he'd do was turn the desk around so that his back was to the view and he could see exactly who was coming through the door. The whole layout of the room, he realised, was a microcosm of the rest of the place. It was casual to the point of being chaotic. The sagging sofa looked suspiciously as if a large dog had been sleeping on it for years and the threadbare Persian rug needed a good shake-out—or possibly throw-out. There was a row of shells on the window ledge and a row of cards on the dusty bookshelf.

Curious, he went over and peered at them. They were thank-you cards, a few dating back years, some with the same scrawled signatures at the end of effusive messages of gratitude for days and weeks spent at the Hideaway. Cassandra had said they had loyal guests who returned time and time again, and here was the proof.

He shut down the computer, dropped his phone into his trouser pocket and picked up his jacket. He needed to get out of here.

Cass didn't want to see anyone and the chances were good that she wouldn't. Their few guests would be dozing in the sitting room, replete with their afternoon cream tea, and the kitchen staff would be preparing dinner. There ought to be someone at the reception desk, but with luck...

She started up the stairs and met Tess coming down. She was in her purple leggings and pink top.

'Cass! I've been waiting for you. Aren't we going to yoga?'

'Oh, Tess, I don't think I'm in the right frame of mind for yoga now.'

'He made you cry! Oh, Cass, I hate him. I want to slap him. I—'

'No! I haven't been crying.'

Cass put a hand to her face and found it was wet with tears.

'Well, if I have it's because I'm so frustrated.' She sniffed. 'He...he just wouldn't listen to me.'

Tess nodded vigorously. 'He's *way* too sure of himself. And *way* too smooth to be cool.' Then her expression changed, her eyes taking on a faraway look. 'But he was nice about the coffee. And his voice...' She put a hand on Cass's arm. 'I'm sorry, Cass. But you won't sell the Hideaway to him, will you?'

Cass scrubbed a hand over her face, knowing she'd be smudging her make-up. This morning, when she'd put it on, felt like a lifetime away. She dropped her eyes and studied her feet. 'I'm so sorry about what's happened, Tess. This is all exactly what my dad would not have wanted, but I just don't know. And I'm tired of the struggle.' She shook her head. 'He says he'll pay enough to clear all the debts, and that's very tempting, but then I think of my dad and I'm determined I'll never sell to a Chevalier…'

Tess squeezed her shoulder. 'Maybe yoga is just what you need, Cass. Space to recharge and reset?'

'Space to cry, and I can't afford that. You go. Maybe I'll see you later.'

She pushed past Tess and took the stairs to the attic two at a time.

CHAPTER THREE

MATHEO'S FEET POUNDED the beach, his arms and legs pumping. The sand was a little soft for running, but that was good. He needed a tough workout, requiring mental and physical effort, if there was any hope of clearing his head. His plans for the Hideaway had been sharp and clear-sighted, but Cassandra's suggestion of a deal had blurred them, casting doubt on his usually straightforward thinking. He was properly warm, for what felt like the first time in hours, but the sweat trickling off him was immediately sluiced away by the driving rain. His chest heaved as he sucked in deep, fast breaths but he pushed himself harder.

The waves of the full tide heaved themselves out of the sea and crashed against the foot of the rough cliffs at the end of the beach and he stopped, frustration bubbling through him. His planned route along the water's edge was blocked. He could turn back and retrace his steps or attempt the run up the overgrown path which snaked through the tumbled rocks towards the clifftop.

But as his eyes followed the line of the track upwards, he froze. A figure stood silhouetted against the racing grey clouds, perilously close to the edge. Dark hair streamed behind her in the wind, and as he watched she turned abruptly and disappeared.

He launched himself into a sprint towards the foot of the cliff.

The climb was challenging and by the time he scrambled onto the top, grabbing at tussocks of wet grass to heave himself up, it felt as if his lungs were on fire. He got to his feet, vaulted over a low gate and continued, without breaking his stride, along the side of a stone church.

His pace picked up again on the level ground and he turned the corner of the building at full speed. Then he slithered to an abrupt stop as he saw Cassandra coming towards him.

'Mademoiselle Greenwood.' His chest heaved as he filled his burning lungs with the cool, damp air. 'Are you alright?'

'Were you following me?' she asked, stopping and wiping the rain off her face with a sleeve.

'No. I was out for a run.' He glanced backwards, the way he'd come. 'On the beach, and I saw you...'

His breath began to steady and he shook his hair out of his eyes and studied her. It was impossible to tell whether her face was wet with tears or rain.

He looked away, over her head, and realised she'd been standing in a small graveyard. The ground sloped away towards the cliff edge but from the beach it had looked as if she'd been about to launch herself over the edge.

His knee-jerk reaction had almost made him look like an idiot. He never acted on impulse. He'd learned that lesson long ago, watching his father's calculated actions. He weighed up every situation, every deal, with the utmost care, the coolest head, before making a considered response.

'You startled me. Hardly anyone else ever comes here.'

'I'm...sorry.' The apology sounded like a foreign word to him. 'I...thought maybe you needed help. The wind is fierce. It's slippery underfoot...'

'Thank you.' She nodded. 'But I'm fine.'

'I thought you'd be talking to the staff.'

She glanced behind her, towards the gravestones. 'I had to do this first. It'll be dark by the time I've finished the staff meetings.'

She stepped around him and he turned to watch her as she walked away.

She clicked the gate closed behind her, and then broke into a jog.

When she'd been swallowed up in the gloom Matheo turned and walked into the teeth of the wind, which roared off the sea and over the clifftop, flattening the grass and the clumps of daffodils which grew among the headstones.

He soon found her parents' names and stood looking down at the neatly tended mounds. He tried to put himself in Cassandra's shoes, wondering how she felt, but it was impossible. The desperately sad look he'd seen in her sparkling eyes was beyond his experience.

Then he swept his dripping hair out of his eyes and turned back, viciously crushing the stirring of something—pity?—which threatened to undermine his resolution. If he allowed pity to inform his decisions he'd be running a charity, not a mega-billions company.

The descent of the cliff path was even more difficult than the ascent had been, but he tackled it at full speed, despite the dangers posed by the slippery surface and loose pebbles. He wasn't finished yet—he still had more energy to expend today than most people had in a week. Besides, he needed to snuff out a treacherous little glow that threatened to ignite in his belly.

Cass didn't slow to a walk until she was sure she'd put a good distance between herself and Matheo Chevalier. What had that been about? Why would Matheo Chevalier, the latest in a long line of Chevaliers to want to crush her family, rush to her aid? They'd shown nothing but contempt and disdain for the Greenwoods for generations and she couldn't believe Matheo was any different. Not if he was his father's son.

Her mind flashed back to earlier in the day when she'd tumbled into his arms at the foot of the ladder. What strange power did he wield over her senses that he could make her want to let him protect her? The feeling went against all the principles by which she lived her independent life.

Was it simply because it was so long since she'd had any physical contact with a man? She tried not to think about Jason. She felt too vulnerable and stressed to allow those memories any breathing space, but as usual that meant they were able to slide in and grab her attention. They'd met when she'd started her first job as an assistant in the interiors department of a large company. She'd been flattered that a member of the accounts department had noticed her and had taken the trouble to lavish care and attention on her. With hindsight she realised she'd been an easy target. He'd recognised her vulnerability, but he hadn't been interested in discovering its roots. He'd exploited it to indulge his need to dominate and control. At the time it had been a relief to allow someone else to look after her, after the years of caring for her mother in her illness and then her father in his depression. But then, bit by bit, he'd become possessive, demanding to know where she was at all times, and beginning to dictate all kinds of limitations on her life. He'd wanted her to move in with him and she'd been afraid of his fury when she'd refused.

When she discovered he'd put a tracker on her phone she'd known she had to end it.

It had been tough. It would have been so much easier just to give in to his demands. At first she'd missed the security the relationship had given her, after the chaotic life she'd been forced to live after her mother's death, but she'd not been prepared to pay the price he seemed to feel she owed him for it. She'd called on the strength she'd gained through the difficult years and used every ounce of it. Now she felt confident she'd never again put herself at the mercy of anyone else, because she'd grown strong enough to lead the life she wanted on her own terms. She just wasn't always strong enough to block the memories of how he'd treated her.

She'd met Nick and together they'd formed FuturePlan. A few years later, with a combination of a lot of talent and a little luck, they'd completed three small but prestigious projects and had just signed a deal which, if successful, would raise their profile massively.

She'd travelled extensively in search of the best of everything for the striking interiors she designed. Her professional self-confidence in her taste, her instinctive eye for the unusual had strengthened with each challenge, but on a personal level the experience with Jason had left her anxious and wary, with issues involving trust and honesty.

Her father had been destroyed by the loss of his soulmate. She herself had almost been crushed by a man who said he loved her but only if she stuck to the rules he made.

Love, she'd decided, was a brutal, dangerous game.

And then her father had died.

Matheo Chevalier was a businessman, just like his father, with a ruthless approach and a lack of sensitivity to the needs of others which would make Genghis Khan look like a philanthropist. She needed to remember *that*.

Her father had despised his father, her grandfather his grandfather. And she should despise them all.

If she'd been tired before, Cassandra reflected, she was beyond exhaustion by ten o'clock. The emotional strain of the day was catching up with her, fast. She had to stop before she collapsed, and, feeling as she did, that was a scarily real possibility.

The meetings with the staff had been horrible, even though most of them had suspected what was coming. The ancient enmity between the Chevalier and Greenwood clans was well-known, and as soon as Tess, round-eyed and bursting with an air of conspiracy, had announced the name of the latest man bidding to be the new owner, any hopes of a reprieve had been dashed.

The kitchen was dark and eerily quiet, but through the fog of fatigue she managed to find one of the standby ready meals she kept in the freezer. She slammed the door of the elderly microwave and cranked the dial. It whirred, clicked and pinged. Then she carried the container to the staff sitting room, curled up on the sofa and began to eat, staring out at the darkness and listening to the steady beat of the rain. She felt unable to comprehend how this could be her last night under the roof of the creaking old building that had been home for her entire life.

Matheo had stared at the columns of figures on the screen until his eyes ached. His frustration was in danger of tipping over into anger. When had he ever not understood a spreadsheet? Never, was the answer. Never, until now. The figures simply didn't work.

He stood up and massaged his temples with his fingertips. He wished he were on St Celeste, where he controlled everything that happened, from one warm day to the next.

His discreet, quiet staff on the Mediterranean island were the few people he trusted implicitly these days. The sense of peace and security that enveloped him each time he returned was addictive and he'd become increasingly reluctant to leave. Most of his business could be conducted remotely and he bitterly regretted ignoring his better judgement and coming to see the Hideaway for himself. It had been unnecessary and he was paying the price.

Emotion had intruded on what should have been a straightforward business deal. The two did not mix and he should have known to stay away. Perhaps he should reconsider, let the past go and get on with his life. But he recognised that his pride was a huge stumbling block.

He ran a hand over his jaw, rough at this late hour. The kitchen would be closed, but perhaps he'd be able to find some coffee somewhere. He regretted leaving the restaurant before the grim-faced waiter had brought him a pot earlier, but he couldn't wait to get away. The meal had been mediocre, the atmosphere depressing, with just two other tables occupied by couples he could only assume had been coming here so long they were practically a part of the furnishings.

And the furnishings were another thing. Dusty, faded, and so dated someone kinder might have dubbed them 'vintage'.

The entire hotel appeared to be deserted, the quiet broken only by the soft creaks of the ancient inn as it settled for the night. In the distance he could hear the thunder of the surf on the shore and the rain still rattled in fierce gusts against the mullioned windows. Remembering the layout from the plans of the building he'd studied, he made his way towards the kitchen. Dim wall lamps provided low-level lighting in the passages, but the public rooms were in darkness. Then he spotted a faint bar of light glowing beneath a door.

Cassandra Greenwood slept, curled up, on a sofa under the window. Her cheek rested on one hand while the fingers of the other held a fork, which in turn lay in the plastic tray of some sort of half-eaten meal. Her dark hair rippled in glossy waves over the cushions.

Matheo stopped, his breath catching in his chest. An inner voice exhorted him not to break the spell. He thought he'd never seen anyone look more beautiful, or more tired, even in sleep, in his life. She still wore the jeans and cable-knit sweater in which he'd seen her last, and he frowned. The clothes must be damp and cold, even though she'd worn a rain jacket. With infinite care, he stepped forward, picked up a plaid rug which was draped over the back of the sofa, and dropped it over her.

She shot upright, sending the remains of the food flying onto the floor and the fork clattering into a corner.

'Mademoiselle Greenwood, what are you doing here? Haven't you got a bed to sleep in?' He spoke quietly, as if still afraid to wake her.

'That's the second time today you've scared me.' She shook her head and pushed her fingers through her hair. 'And no... I mean...yes, but it's wet.'

'I didn't mean... *Wet?* Why is it wet?'

'There's a leak in the roof above it.'

'Well, why haven't you had it fixed? What about George? Why hasn't he done it?'

'It only leaks when the wind blows in a certain direction.' She glanced towards the window. 'The rain gets in under the lead. And George has tried but he's always too busy mending the bits that matter.'

'And you having no bed to sleep in doesn't matter?'

'No, not really. This may be an old sofa but it's comfortable.' She gathered her hair behind her head and twisted it in her hands, then she let it fall and stretched up her arms, before folding them across her chest.

'I apologise for startling you.' He may have startled her twice, but he had apologised twice, too. This was unfamiliar territory. 'I was hoping to find some coffee.' He shrugged. 'I don't suppose there is a hope in hell of anyone answering if I ring the bell at the front desk?'

'Absolutely no hope at all.' Her smile was slight, but even so a dimple faintly indented her cheek. 'You're getting the hang of things. Everyone either went home or went to bed hours ago. If you want coffee, you'll have to make it yourself.' She leaned back against the sofa cushions, wriggling her shoulders. 'There's a tin in that cupboard.'

'And I suppose it'll be instant, yes?'

A slight twitch at the corner of her mouth made him feel she found the situation amusing. Then she nodded, once.

Matheo frowned. 'The coffee Tess provided was very good. It wasn't instant.' He wondered whether to give up and return to the infuriating spreadsheet. But giving up wasn't his style. He looked around and saw a kettle, a sink and a fridge. 'Would you like a cup, always assuming I can find it?'

'There are camomile teabags in the cupboard. I'll have a mug of that, thanks.' She stifled a yawn. 'Then I might have a chance of getting back to sleep before I have to wake up again.'

Matheo opened the cupboard above the kettle. A shiny glass and chrome cafetière stood on the shelf, alongside a tin of instant coffee and a motley collection of mugs. Several of the mugs had slogans on them—*Drama Queen*, said one, and *Don't Tell Me to Keep Calm* another. *I'd Rather be Somewhere Else*, stated a third. He hesitated, wondering about what sort of message he wanted to send, and then he grabbed the nearest two and placed them rather too firmly on the work surface.

When had he ever considered what message a mug might send? When had he ever *cared*? Something about Cassandra's presence was messing with his mind and playing games with his body, sending inappropriate and frankly unacceptable messages on route marches all over it.

In the fridge he found a packet of French coffee, next to the milk.

Her voice came from behind him and he could hear the smile in it.

'Sorry. Your expectations were obviously so low it felt like a pity to disappoint you. I'd still like the camomile, though.'

Matheo kept his back to her and took a moment to absorb the fact that she was laughing at him. It wasn't something he tolerated and it hadn't happened for a very long time. He waited to feel annoyed. But then he realised that instead of the anger he should have felt, the idea of her smiling, at anything, made everything feel a little better.

He made the coffee and tea and carried the mugs over to the sofa. Cassandra sat cross-legged on the cushions. She took the mug of tea in both hands and wrapped her fingers around its warmth, inhaling the sweet aroma.

Matheo continued to stand.

'Sit down, if you like.' She waved her mug at a pair of faded armchairs.

He drew in a deep, unsteady breath and then sipped from the mug. *I'd Rather be Somewhere Else*, it announced to him. Too right. *Anywhere* else, to be precise. He saw that Cass's mug said *Angel*, with an irritating little halo above the 'A'. Perhaps it said *Devil* on the other side.

He was pleased she hadn't suggested he share the sofa with her. She intrigued him and her nearness made his blood pound in his veins and his thought processes feel alien, his reactions unpredictable.

He needed to sort out this confusion. He needed to get himself under control.

He sat down on one of the chairs, leaning forward and propping his elbows on his knees. 'I think I'll have to get my forensic accountant to solve the financial complications I've come across. But if you don't mind company, I'll see if you can shed any light on the problem first.'

Cass sipped from her mug, staring down at the floor. He

followed her gaze and saw the spilled food she'd knocked from the sofa.

'I didn't realise you were getting a takeaway.'

'It was a ready meal from the freezer.'

'Why didn't you change? You shouldn't sleep in damp clothes.'

Matheo had returned from his run and taken a hot shower. At least there had been hot water and the shower, once it had got going, had worked.

'Most of my things are packed, ready to leave. I hadn't planned to go out and get soaked.'

She put her mug on the floor and stretched again and Matheo dragged his eyes away from the strip of ivory skin at her midriff, and the tantalising glimpse of the small indentation of her navel.

'You'd been to visit your parents' graves.'

'Yes.'

'I'm sorry.'

Her eyelids flew up and her gaze was startled, surprise briefly masking pain.

'That's what I said to them, with good reason. But why are *you* sorry? You think you're about to achieve what generations of your family have failed at. You should be…expectantly triumphant.'

Matheo closed his eyes and pinched the bridge of his nose, wondering how to express compassion. When he opened them again, he saw she was watching him, waiting for his answer.

He nodded. 'Yes, but I'm sorry…' He searched for the words. 'I'm sorry for your pain. For your loss. Of everything.' He wasn't at all sure where the sentiments had come from but expressing them made him feel a little less conflicted. 'And I'm sorry your relatives left you with this mess. If your father had paid any attention at all to running this hotel properly, you and I wouldn't be having this conversation.'

'I'm not at all sure about that. Your family has been hell-bent on getting the Hideaway back ever since your great-grandfather lost it to mine.' She tipped her head up to study the ceiling and later Matheo thought that was the moment when the fight went out of her. He felt a sense of unreasonable panic, anxious to see her spirit return, to spar with him. He felt as if he'd crushed something beautiful and delicate and couldn't see any way to repair it.

'We were fine,' she continued, her voice quiet, 'until my mother died, but my dad just let things slide after that. He'd mortgaged the place to pay for her treatment and there was never going to be any way he could pay that back.' She shrugged. 'He'd started gambling to try and make the money we needed. I didn't know anything about that until after he died…'

Like his grandfather, he thought, but he clamped his mouth shut before the hurtful words could escape.

'Perhaps,' he said carefully, instead, 'gambling was a family weakness?'

He saw her fingers tighten around the angel-devil mug, the fine bones of her knuckles gleaming beneath the skin. 'My great-grandfather won the Hideaway from yours in a perfectly fair game of cards. That your ancestor was so arrogant and reckless with his property was something I've never understood.'

'My father says the game wasn't fair.'

'From my sixteen-year-old point of view, your father seemed arrogant. Perhaps that's your family weakness?'

'You're entitled to your opinion, obviously. It doesn't change the fact that your father—'

'Please stop talking about my father.' Her voice was brittle with strain. 'He didn't plan to die and leave me with this mess. Don't you think I wouldn't rather have him back—have them *both* back—have things like they were before, like they were meant to be—than any of this?' She made a sweeping gesture with one arm, encompassing the room, but its intensity implied the whole property. 'Don't you think I might wish he'd sold the hotel years ago, even to your family, if it would have given him a few extra years of peace? I wasn't here for him. I never even got to say goodbye...' She rubbed a hand across her face.

Matheo's voice was low when he spoke again. 'You went to say goodbye to your parents this afternoon. You could hate your father for leaving you with all this. But you don't.'

'No. And I can never make up for not being here. I can never make it better.'

'Do you want to talk about it?'

Talking about emotions was not something Matheo did. Not ever, if he could help it. But something about the way her eyes gleamed and the resolute way she straightened her shoulders made him say it. The little flame, which he now acknowledged was sympathy, flickered in his gut. He let it burn.

Cassandra stared at her fingers, knotted around the mug. 'I always thought there'd be time. I knew my father was depressed. He'd been on medication for years, but I thought he was healthy enough. I imagined that one day I'd be able to have a proper conversation with him again. After my mother died, he changed overnight. He became obsessive about keeping everything exactly as it had always been, as if she might come back and expect to find it just as she'd left it.' She glanced up at him and half smiled. 'When you and your father turned up, the only time he'd spoken to me in weeks was to yell at me.'

'*Why?* What had you done?'

'I'd put on one of Mum's cardigans. I wasn't cold. I was just desperate to find a connection to her, to feel her presence, somehow. He told me never to touch anything of hers again. And I didn't, until after he died.'

'That's—extreme behaviour. You didn't deserve that.'

She shrugged. 'Maybe not. But it was his way of coping and I had to respect that. I had to force myself to go away to college, but I knew the staff would continue to run the hotel and look after him. They did, but there was nobody to authorise repairs or introduce new ideas. Things began to crumble. It's ironic that Nick and I were renovating boutique hotels successfully but were never allowed to touch this one.' She smiled. 'Don't you think?'

He nodded. 'Yes. But now?'

'It was only after he died that I discovered the true state of affairs. I took a year off from FuturePlan and came down here to try to put things right, although I've continued to go up to London when I can to keep up with what's happening. It was naïve, stupid, even. It was never going to work. FuturePlan is doing well—very well—but the cash flow doesn't allow us to put funds into this. I must sell it to pay off the debts.' She pulled up her knees and hugged them. 'It's a pity. We have such a great vision of how it should be.'

Matheo was way out of his comfort zone. He didn't want to hear any of this, but he'd encouraged her to talk and he now searched for a response. But before he could come up with one, she spoke again.

'So I've learned never to put things off. Never to think there'll always be another chance. There usually won't be.'

'Where were you? When he died, I mean,' Matheo asked on impulse. Her answer wouldn't matter to him, but he felt he had to say something and the dimness of the room made it easier to talk.

Cass swallowed hard.

'In India, on an ashram. I was on a buying trip for a project and I'd taken a few days' holiday at the end of it.'

Matheo nodded. 'So you feel guilty? If you hadn't taken a holiday in India but come home to Cornwall instead...'

'Exactly. It probably wouldn't have made any difference. He would still have had the heart attack. But at least I would have been here.'

'What are you going to do now? Where are you going?' He put his empty mug on the floor and leaned back in the saggy chair.

'I need to get back to work. Nick has been incredibly generous giving me so much time, but there's a lot on. It's the end of an era for me but I know it's timely. In a way, the struggle over the past year has been good. It's been exhausting and dispiriting but it's allowed me to accept, gradually, that the hotel has to change. The debts, over which I've had nightmares for months, need to be addressed. It's time for me to move on and allow the Hideaway to move on, too. It can be reinvented for the future.'

'Do the debts include payments owing to the staff?'

He kept his eyes locked on her face. Its openness seemed to display her every emotion. He knew he was probing, just as he knew the staff were all paid up to date.

'The staff are all paid. I don't owe them anything.'

But his infallible business sense and intuition, which had helped propel him to where he was, suddenly shifted up a gear. He was sure that very close to the surface lay the solution to the imbalance in the figures he'd found.

The grip of her arms around her knees tightened and she stared at the floor, avoiding his eyes.

'I know,' he responded. He felt like a stalking predator, and he experienced a sudden distaste for the role. 'That's what I need to ask my accountant to explain. Every other part of the business is in debt up to the hilt, but you've continued to pay the staff, every month, on time.' He paused. 'Where has the money come from?'

Cassandra raised her head and returned his stare. 'I don't owe you any explanations.' Her whole body radiated defiance.

Not many people faced Matheo down when he was determined to get something they were unwilling to give but his lack of success with Cassandra was entirely his fault, he thought. Her mouth, with its full lower lip, was a major distraction and prevented him from focusing his full attention on what was important. He dragged his eyes away from her face and stood up.

She uncurled her legs and, in a fluid movement, rose from the sofa. Her baggy sweater did not disguise her slender build and he thought again about how her outward appearance of fragility masked an iron will and tough determination.

He took in the tremor of her bottom lip, slightly swollen from where she'd caught it in her teeth, and the tell-tale glitter of tears on her lids. She blinked them back and bit her lip again and a wary defiance replaced sadness in her eyes.

Nothing was going to make any of this okay and he hated the feeling that gave him.

She turned away from him, tucking her hands into her armpits. 'Please... I need to get some sleep.'

From the door Matheo glanced over his shoulder. Despite her attempt at bravado there was a vulnerability about her that tugged uncomfortably at an unfamiliar part of him.

And then he thought of something which might make things just a bit more okay.

'If you sell to me,' he said, 'I'll consider your proposal.'

Cassandra stared at the door as it clicked closed behind him. Had he really just said that? She shook her head, bewilderment whirling through her. She took two steps backwards and sat down, flinging herself against the back of the sofa and pressing her fingers to her cheeks.

Any hope of a good night's sleep had just been shattered. Did he expect her to feel happy, or grateful? Because she felt neither.

She pulled the tartan rug off the floor and wrapped it around her shoulders as cold began to seep through her, but it wasn't the sort of cold that a threadbare blanket could fix.

She felt trapped and threatened. If she accepted his offer, could she even trust him to stick to his word and consider the proposal she'd put to him, or would he walk away once he had possession of the Hideaway? Her stomach clenched at the thought. If he was anything like his father, his word would mean nothing. She'd trusted the last man who'd promised her something, before realising that when Jason said he loved her his love came with conditions; conditions she had been unable to fulfil.

Here was another man in a position of power, telling her she might be able to have something—something which was in his power to give or to withhold—if she did as he demanded. If she refused, she'd have to accept a lower offer, and probably be declared bankrupt. How would that affect her position at FuturePlan? And she'd relinquish all control over what would become of her loyal and beloved friends who made up the staff of the hotel.

But if she accepted? Would he follow through? And if he did, there was no guarantee that he'd sign FuturePlan to the project. He'd only said he'd *consider* it.

Panic bloomed in her chest, squeezing her ribs and making it hard to breathe. Her heart pumped uncomfortably fast. She'd promised herself—*vowed*—that never again would she allow anyone to dictate to her. She reminded herself that Matheo could only have power over her if she allowed it. But she hadn't ever imagined what else might be at stake; the other lives which could be affected by a decision she would make.

She eased herself down onto the cushions, pulling the rug over herself, and stared at the ceiling. The sofa, which had always been comfortable before, now felt as if several bricks had been stuffed into it. In her head she heard Jason's voice, telling her she'd only ever amount to anything if she did as he said, behaved as he demanded.

Never again.

Matheo Chevalier wasn't Jason, but he was just as dangerous. He'd put her in an intolerable position. Her self-confidence, which she'd built with such care, now felt fragile and unstable. The idea of trusting him was terrifying. The thought of betraying her father's wishes was heartbreaking.

She had to talk to Nick.

CHAPTER FOUR

PEARLY GREY LIGHT was seeping across the sky when Cassandra finally dropped into a restless sleep, her exhausted brain churning on a useless treadmill of unanswered questions So when her phone alarm buzzed she struggled through layers of fatigue, her head aching and her eyes heavy. She pulled herself upright on the sofa. The clouds and rain had vanished, blown away by the gale, and the sea lay quiet beneath an opalescent sky, waiting for the touch of the sun to give it a rose-tinted colour wash.

Suddenly she needed to see the sun rise over the beach in the cove below the hotel, one last time. She stood, tugging at her crumpled clothes and raking her fingers through her hair. Then she twisted it up on top of her head and, searching her pockets, found a pencil to spear the untidy knot in place.

The door behind her opened and she swung round, all her senses on high alert, but it was not Matheo Chevalier who stood there, fresh from haunting her dreams. It was Tess, looking wild-eyed and anxious.

'Cass! I went to your room but you weren't there, just the bucket on the bed and your suitcase on the floor. Are you okay?' She clapped a hand to her forehead. 'Sorry, stupid question. How could you be okay?'

Cassandra felt a rush of affection for her friend.

'No, you're right, I'm not okay, but I should be asking you that question, Tess. How are you?'

'Oh, Cass, I'll be fine. But you…'

'I'm going down to the beach.' She saw the look on Tess's face. 'But,' she added, 'I need to do this on my own.'

'Seriously, Cass, you look awful. When did you last actually *sleep*?'

'Thanks, Tess. You make me feel like a million dollars.' She smiled, her face feeling stiff and awkward. 'As for sleep, what's that?'

'Let me come with you to the beach, Cass. I won't talk, honest. I'll be really quiet. I just don't think you…'

Cassandra held up a hand.

'I appreciate your concern, Tess, but I want to do this by myself. And I'll be fine. You don't need to worry about finding my clothes in a neat pile at the high-water mark and a one-way set of footprints in the sand.'

'Are you sure, Cass? Please…'

'Quite sure, but thanks anyway. You're a brilliant friend. Now, I need to go, or the sun will rise without me there.'

The beach above the high-tide mark had dried after the rain, and a thin, crisp layer crusted its surface. Cass removed her boots, rolled up her jeans, then dug her toes into the cool sand. It tickled her feet and made her smile again. She spread her arms wide and turned in a circle, before heading down to where little ripples washed onto the shore, leaving a delicate tracery of foam behind them as they receded. The water was icy cold and she gasped as it swirled around her ankles. The air felt clean and rinsed after the rain and she took several deep breaths of it, wishing she could store it up for some time in the future when she knew she'd miss the taste and smell of the sea. She stooped to pick up a delicate shell, which gleamed with its own mother-of-pearl rainbow on the sand. When she straightened up, Matheo Chevalier was standing in front of her.

He was dressed for running, but bare-footed this time. Under his T-shirt his chest rose and fell in deep, even breaths, as if he'd finished his warm-up and was ready to tackle a marathon.

'You were right. About the weather, that is.' He glanced at the horizon, where the burnished rim of the sun had just begun to reveal itself. 'We're going to see the sun this morning, despite the rain last night.'

Cass's stomach tightened as his eyes locked onto hers. Her mouth dried. She tried to think of something to say but no words could get past her constricted throat. She wanted to drag her eyes away, but he kept her gaze in his steady stare, as if he held an invisible thread connecting them and was increasing its tension with every ticking second.

'Did you get any sleep in the end?' His words washed over her. She had to make a conscious effort to stop listening to the sound of his voice and concentrate on what he was saying.

'Not really,' she finally managed as her brain creaked into action. 'Your parting shot kept me awake.'

She was shocked by his sudden appearance. He must have been watching her, when she'd thought she was alone. A little lick of anger flared in her stomach. All she wanted was solitude, this one last time, on her beach. Only it might be his beach soon.

He nodded. 'I'm sorry about that. It was ill-timed, but I realised I might not see you again. Have you reached a decision?'

'No. I want to watch the sunrise.' She filled her lungs with the cold, crystal-clear air again. 'On my own.'

He inclined his dark head with the utmost gravity.

'Of course, Mademoiselle Greenwood. I apologise for intruding.'

He extended his right hand, and the thread tightened again, pulling her hand into his. His grip was cool and firm, hinting at a strength that filled her once more with that unnamed and uncomfortable longing. She felt the hard pad of his thumb move against the inside of her wrist, and her tummy hollowed. His free hand came up and rested on her shoulder, just where the curve of her neck began. She knew that beneath his thumb he could feel the hectic beat of the pulse at the base of her throat.

'I wish you *bon voyage*. I look forward to hearing your decision.'

As that thread tugged her closer to him, she could see the roughness of his unshaven chin, the cleft that was almost, but not quite, a dimple in his cheek. But mostly she could see the strong, straight line of his mouth. Her world had shrunk to this very small space and everything else receded into the irrelevant distance.

She thought he was going to kiss her and there didn't seem to be anything she could do to stop him. She didn't think she wanted to. Her blood thrummed in her ears as her lips parted in anticipation of the touch of his mouth. He smelled fresh and clean, and he exuded an energy that she desperately wanted to share. She wanted to press her face into his chest and just breathe his essence into her soul.

His lips, feather-light, brushed her cheek, and then he drew back. Her lids fluttered up and she saw he was frowning down at her, strong brows drawn together. A small sound escaped from her throat and a silver flame fleetingly lit his dark eyes.

She wanted to freeze the moment and stay in it for ever, so she wouldn't have to make impossible decisions. But she had to stop it. If even contemplating selling the Hideaway to him wasn't betrayal enough, wanting to kiss him would stamp a seal on her treachery that would stay with her for eternity.

But before she could push him away his hands closed around

her upper arms. She felt dizzy and confused for a moment and then the world stopped spinning in crazy circles and snapped back into brutal focus.

What was she doing, standing ankle-deep in freezing water, wanting to kiss her worst enemy? She pulled away and stepped backwards, but he kept a light hold of her.

'I thought you were going.' The chill of the water had spread through her whole body.

'I will go just as soon as I'm sure you aren't going to fall over into the sea.'

'Why would I do that? I'm perfectly fine.' She shivered violently.

He lifted one shoulder, a wealth of expression in the spare movement, and then dropped his hands.

'You're sure you're all right?'

He moved away, out of the water, raking a hand through his hair. Then, nodding courteously, he turned and jogged off down the beach, picking up speed as he disappeared behind the rocks that curved around the side of the cove.

The smooth, controlled rhythm of his running was at shocking odds with Cassandra's jangling nerves. Her jaw began to ache with the effort of suppressing the bouts of shivering that kept attacking her. She would not, ever, acknowledge a need for Matheo Chevalier.

Her fingers strayed to her cheek, but she snatched her hand away and buried it in her pocket. Her limbs felt heavy, but she told herself it was the result of extreme tiredness. It was nothing to do with the adrenalin rush that had hijacked her mind and body and almost run away with them.

Had he been taunting her? Reinforcing his power over her, letting her know he'd soon have everything he wanted from her, if she needed the renovation project badly enough? She kicked uselessly at a little wave that washed around her feet and saw the pale shell she'd picked up earlier lying on the sand in the shallow water. It must have fallen from her fingers when she… Stopping her thoughts right there, she bent and retrieved it, turning it over in her fingers. Its perfect beauty soothed her a little and she tucked it into her pocket.

Let me remember the beauty, she thought, *not the pain and loss.*

She turned and walked out of the water, onto the sand, which now gleamed in the early morning sun. Shoulders hunched, she hurried to collect her boots, and then made for the rocky path that climbed up to the hotel lawns. The granite building loomed above her, dominating the landscape as it had done for centuries, the ancient slates of the roof shining like pewter.

Hoping to avoid seeing anyone, she hurried up the back stairs to her room to pack her few remaining things, forcing her mind into coping mode.

But later, when she'd said her tearful goodbyes, as the taxi pulled out onto the narrow lane, she was compelled to look back one last time. So in the future, if anyone asked her, she'd be able to say yes, she knew exactly how it felt when your heart broke in two.

Matheo jogged down the beach towards the rocks. He found his rhythm within a few strides and picked up speed. The rocks were his goal right now. Once past them he would try to clear his head, to think straight, when he knew she could no longer see him if she was watching. He needed to keep up his steady pace just in case she was. It seemed to take for ever, but eventually he knew he was hidden from her view. Even then, however, he didn't stop because if he did he'd turn and go back to her.

And then what? He slammed his mind shut. He didn't dare think about that.

His simple farewell kiss on her cheek had turned into something weightier, freighted with emotions he didn't want to explore.

Her scent, of rain and salt spray, lingered in his nostrils. And had that been a pencil skewered in her hair? A *pencil*? He'd been seconds from pulling it out, so that he could feel the mass of shiny dark waves, tumble through his fingers like liquid ebony.

Matheo ran to a stop, bent forward and braced his hands on his knees, breathing fast and sweating hard. He remembered the wild girl he'd encountered on this very beach fourteen years ago, and his heart twisted. She'd been sad and vulnerable, and his father had been determined to wrench her home from her; his father, who always got what he wanted, whatever it took, whatever damage he did. But, and Matheo experienced a bleak dart of satisfaction, his father would not get the Hideaway.

No, *he* would be the one to take Cassandra's home from her. It felt as if the dart had pierced his heart and the satisfaction withered and died. He'd tear what she loved best from her, just as his father had tried to do. But then he'd never see her again and eventually these feelings of regret and sympathy would fizzle out. He would not allow them to weaken him, make him vulnerable.

He straightened, swearing under his breath, then he plunged into the sea, gasping as the icy cold water hit his overheated skin. He ploughed on, deeper, and then dived into a wave, surfacing beyond it and striking out through the surf, hammering home his determination with every powerful stroke.

CHAPTER FIVE

CASS STOOD WITH her back to the room, gazing at the view of the city spread out beneath her. Behind her, Nick, her business partner, shuffled papers on the table.

'So that's the story, Nick,' she said, after a pause. 'If I sell to Matheo Chevalier, I'll be betraying all my father's principles and wishes. But potentially I, or rather *we*...' she turned to face him '...will have a shot at getting the contract to renovate the Hideaway, and the staff might be given a chance to keep their jobs.'

'And if you don't?' Nick picked up a pencil and rolled it between the palms of his hands. Cass knew it was one of his stress-busting techniques. 'What then?'

'Then I accept a lower offer. I can still try to negotiate but the company behind that bid is not known for its flexible approach or its imagination.' Cass pressed her fingers into her temples. 'And I'll be left with unpaid debts.'

'Has Matheo Chevalier even made an offer? Because until he does...' Nick placed the pencil on the table and spun it in an arc with the tip of a finger.

'It came in ten minutes ago. It's very generous and it would clear all the outstanding bills.' She bit her lip. 'My lawyer was at pains to point that out.'

'Cass, I don't share your personal history with either the hotel or the Chevaliers so I can try to give you a balanced opinion. And from where I'm standing there seems to be no contest. The only question I have is, can you trust him to follow through on his promise to consider your proposal?'

Cass sat down at the table and propped her chin in her hands. 'I wouldn't trust his father, but I… I think Matheo is different. The lawyers have already emailed me a draft contract. It includes his undertaking to consider my proposal.'

'You know,' Nick said, carefully, 'that the project you were working on before your father died was completed last week?'

Cass nodded. 'I'm sorry I had to pull out of it. Really bad timing, but I'd been off the project for a year anyway, so…'

'You were responsible for the interior design, Cass. It all went ahead just as you planned it, and it's stunning. It's getting five-star reviews and it's been nominated for two awards. None of that would have happened without your input. It's a great shame you weren't able to see it through to completion.'

'Thanks, Nick. You're very generous, but what's that got to do with the predicament I find myself in today?'

'Looking at the situation objectively, it just might help you to make a decision. We're riding a wave of success at the moment. Other projects are progressing, but winning a contract from Matheo Chevalier would ensure our current high profile is maintained. He'd be the most important client we've ever handled. It wouldn't be a big contract for him, but if he likes what we do there'd be more work from him in the future. He's building a formidable chain of hotels.'

He crossed the room to stand next to Cass's chair. She folded her arms and stared out of the window. She felt as if every fibre in her body was stretched to breaking point, and even though Nick was obviously doing his best to appear relaxed, she could feel the tension radiating off him.

'Also,' he continued, 'renovating the Hideaway is what you and I have talked about doing ever since we started the company, isn't it? The way things are, this is the only chance you're going to get to do it, if we land the contract.'

Cass nodded. 'I know. It's just that this way I feel as if I'm being forced into it. You know how I am about coercion.' She smiled. 'Legacy of Jason, but I don't need to tell you that.'

'This is not coercion, Cass. Not by me, and not by Matheo Chevalier. It makes sound business sense to accept an offer that will clear your debts and potentially give you the two things you hope for from the sale. I can try to understand how incredibly difficult it must feel for you, given the history between your families, but I don't think your father would have wanted to see you bankrupted for the sake of an argument that goes back generations and for which there is never going to be a satisfactory outcome.'

Nick left her side and walked around the table to the window. Tense muscles stretched across his back.

'What you're saying,' she said quietly, 'is that it's a no-brainer. I should accept the offer.'

He didn't speak for a full minute, and then he shrugged. 'Yes,' he said. 'That is what I'm saying.'

Cass dropped her head into her hands and inhaled a deep breath. 'Thank you, Nick. I know you're right. I just needed to talk it through with someone, to get it all straight in my head.'

Cass walked towards the lift, fixing her gaze straight ahead, and when the doors swished apart she was relieved to find it empty. Her first goal was to get out into the anonymous London streets and find a lethally strong cup of coffee. Her second was to avoid talking to anyone else on the way.

With Nick's moral support she'd accepted Matheo Chevalier's offer for the Hideaway and now she was struggling to feel anything at all. She'd imagined this moment many times over the past few weeks, when she knew selling was inevitable, and she'd wondered how she'd feel. Devastated? Crushed? *Unburdened?* She felt none of those.

There was an emptiness inside her where anxiety and stress had lodged for so long, and she supposed it would eventually shrink to nothing or fill with something else. Would she eventually feel guilt for betraying her family or simply relief that her nightmare of a year had ended?

As the lift dropped towards the ground floor she grimaced at her image in its mirrored walls. All colour had leached from her face. The eyes that stared back at her were dark and troubled. But she squared her shoulders and issued a quiet challenge to her reflection. She may have once been fragile, but she reminded herself she'd had to learn to be tough to get to where she was now.

She'd taken the rest of the day off, to organise her flat and her wardrobe. Both had suffered from her long absences in Cornwall and were in urgent need of refreshing. Then tomorrow she'd be back at her desk, putting together FuturePlan's bid for the renovation of the Hideaway.

She would put out of her mind the way Matheo had made her feel when he'd kissed her goodbye in the sea. It had been nothing more than a simple farewell kiss, and anything more she'd read into their encounter had been the result of her stress, anxiety and lack of sleep.

She and Nick would gather a team which would throw everything at their bid. She owed it to the staff and to her parents to make a success of it. She may have lost the hotel to their worst enemy but, if Matheo would allow it, she could give it back some sparkle and shine to take it on the next stage of its journey.

Matheo Chevalier slowed his pace as he neared the end of the beach. *His* beach. On *his* island. It was a still spring morning with a freshness to the breeze that would take any heat out of the day later. Ripples of water caressed the pristine sand and further out the Mediterranean reflected the blue of the sky. Even the few wisps of white cloud were echoed by the froth of foam, dancing on the surface of the sea.

He gazed out at the perfection of the view but didn't see it. His thoughts had kept him awake for a large part of the night and he was frustrated and annoyed by that. On St Celeste he usually slept undisturbed, the quiet he found on the island providing him with the peace he craved. He knew it was said that he was becoming a recluse, but he didn't care. This was where he wanted to be, preferably alone, except for his loyal staff.

He'd grappled with the problem for hours, but as he waded into the sea to cool off after his run he decided what to do. As soon as he'd finished his swim he'd go to his office and send the email that would sort things out.

Since Wednesday last week, when he'd left Cornwall and flown in his private jet from Bristol to Nice, via a one-night stopover in London, his inbox had been cluttered with news and messages about the new hotel in the Western Isles of Scotland, called the Sandpiper. He'd heard of it over the past couple of years but never paid much attention. Now he wondered why.

It was stunning. He'd studied the pictures for hours, intrigued by the melding of ancient buildings and modern structures and the eclecticism of the interiors, where classic antique pieces of furniture sat beside new, modern designs, looking as if they were made to occupy the same space as each other. Natural light poured in through wide windows, but log fires warmed richly furnished nooks, where heavy curtains would keep the icy winter winds at bay. The attention to detail in the renovated building, the new extension and the layered interiors was astounding.

It had taken him no more than a few minutes to decide that this was how he wanted the Hideaway to be. He'd made up his mind and he was not known for changing it. He was anxious to get the project started.

Cassandra Greenwood had accepted his offer. He'd have been astonished if she'd refused it but he hadn't been sure of her. She was a businesswoman who could see the advantages in his bid, but at the same time the unresolved trauma of the loss of her parents and her home could have adversely affected her judgement. He admired her attachment to her roots and her reluctance to sever herself from them. He wished his feelings about his past were less conflicted. He seemed to have been trying to escape it for most of his life. But he was pleased Cassandra Greenwood had made the sensible decision.

Now he wondered if he'd been hasty in agreeing to consider her proposal if she sold to him. She'd probably have accepted his offer in the end, anyway. Her lawyer would have put her under pressure to do so, and Matheo could have saved himself a lot of trouble and several sleep-deprived nights.

Had he been right to allow his pity for Cassandra to affect the deal he'd done? Now that he'd bought the Hideaway, he should follow through with his promise. He'd had it written into the contract, but he could probably get out of it, if necessary. But it wouldn't be difficult to give the members of staff who wished it a chance to stay on. He could delegate that and need have no more to do with it.

The renovations were a different matter. He'd decided he wanted the team who were responsible for the Sandpiper and he'd make sure he got it. He felt a rare frisson of excitement run through him at the thought of what they would be able to do with the Hideaway. But he'd promised he'd consider a proposal from Cassandra and… Nick? Was that her partner's name?

While coming to his conclusion he'd tried to be objective. He acknowledged the strange pull that seemed to draw him and Cassandra to each other but he rationalised it away. It was all down to their shared history; to the way they'd connected fourteen years ago, when he'd provided the listening ear she so desperately needed, having lost her mother to cancer and her father to all-consuming grief. The attraction she held for him must go back to that. It couldn't be anything else.

On his one-night stop-over in London, he'd driven up to the North London cemetery where he knew his mother was buried and searched for her grave. It had obviously lain untended since the day she'd been buried. He'd scratched the moss from the headstone with a fingernail and pulled up some of the brambles encroaching on it. Later, back in the suite he kept at Claridge's, he'd gone online to find a gardening contractor and engaged them to care for the site and make sure there were fresh flowers placed on it every week. Then he'd considered repeating the exercise, this time in Cornwall, for the graves of Cassandra's parents. But he decided against it. It would be high-handed and she wouldn't like that.

He walked out of the sea and back along the beach, enjoying the feel of the sun on his back, drying off the droplets of water, leaving behind a faint, sparkling trace of salt on his skin. He'd told Cassandra that if she sold to him he'd consider her proposal, and he intended to keep his side of the deal. He'd ask them to prepare a proposal and he'd arrange for them to travel to St Celeste to present it to him.

But he'd be completely honest and up-front about it. He'd tell them he'd already decided on another company.

Having made the decision, Matheo felt happier. He owned the Hideaway, at last, and he'd finish up with a spectacular boutique hotel in a matchless location. The deal had been a challenging one because he'd thought Cassandra might sell to someone else at any moment. But he'd kept his cool and eventually thrown her the bait he was sure she'd take. And she had.

What could possibly go wrong?

CHAPTER SIX

AFTER THE STABLE comfort of the big jet which had brought her to Nice in the South of France, the helicopter felt small and lightweight. Cass clutched the slim case containing her laptop to her chest and thought about the fact that she was about to meet Matheo Chevalier again. Would he be different on his own private turf? Less demanding? More...*forgiving*?

She wished, very much, that Nick had been able to accompany her. But he was tied up in pitching for another project and she was on her own.

It had only been a few days after the sale had gone through that Cass's lawyer had let her know that Matheo was honouring his side of the agreement and anticipating a pitch from FuturePlan. He'd given them an almost impossible deadline—he was obviously anxious to get the project underway.

At least the insane hours they'd had to work had taken Cass's mind off the sense of bereavement that had hit her two days after she'd accepted the offer. It was as if the loss of the hotel had been a catalyst for facing all the other losses she'd suffered. She'd pushed through the pain, working eighteen-hour days, refusing to dwell on the past. She thought their proposal was brilliant and she was prepared to push Matheo Chevalier to the brink to get him to accept it.

What she'd do if he turned it down she didn't know, because she hadn't allowed herself to think about that. Her vision for the refurbished Hideaway was so strong it filled her imagination to the exclusion of all else.

She felt tired, and anxious about what the next few hours would bring, but she was fired up with enough determination to get through almost anything.

The uniformed driver who'd met her would not have looked out of place on the bridge of a ship. He'd driven her a short distance across the airport to where a line of private jets and two helicopters were parked, and deposited her, with reserved deference, at the foot of a set of steps that led into one of them. The taciturn pilot had handed her a pair of ear defenders and they'd been airborne much too quickly. Now they were rapidly descending, even though all she could see in every direction was the deep blue of the sea. The craft dipped alarmingly as they changed direction and skimmed just above the glittering water. There was a flash of white sand, followed by dusty green vegetation, and then she could see a landing pad rushing up to meet them. The skids touched down with a gentle bump and the rap of the rotor blades slowed to a lazy slap and then stopped altogether.

Cassandra exhaled. The door opened to a waft of warm air, faintly scented with lavender, and she was invited to step out.

An electric buggy waited at the foot of the steps, her carry-on bag already on board. The driver greeted her with a half-salute. The vehicle buzzed along a winding path, bordered with lavender bushes, and stopped at a small timber bridge. The structure beyond it was so well designed and situated it was almost invisible in the surrounding trees.

'Your suite, *mademoiselle*. We hope it is to your satisfaction.'

Cass nodded. 'Thank you.' The sapphire sky and the twenty-four-carat sunlight were a dazzling combination. A light breeze fanned her damp skin, taking the edge off the midday warmth.

The murmur of the sea was a soothing background to the tumble of crystal-clear water flowing over pebbles in the stream beneath the bridge in front of her. London felt a million miles away. Cornwall might as well have been on another planet.

Cass followed the driver as he wheeled her luggage across the bridge. He shouldered open the timber door and ushered her inside. He lifted her bag onto a wooden rack and made a sweeping gesture. '*Bienvenue à* l'Isle de St Celeste, *mademoiselle*. I trust you will find all your needs met. You will be collected in an hour.' He backed out, pulling the door closed behind him.

As Cass's eyes adjusted to the dim interior, she made out the marble gleam of a bathroom, cleverly designed with glass walls facing an internal courtyard where delicate ferns grew. At first glance she thought the living space had no walls, but then she saw they consisted almost entirely of bifold glass doors, which stood open. The space led onto a timbered deck where two sun loungers stood in the shade of the overhanging trees. A wide bed, swathed in misty netting, dominated the room and a cream linen sofa and a pale wooden desk completed the furnishings.

Wooden steps led from the deck onto bright sand, which sloped away to meet the aquamarine of the sea. Millions of diamonds appeared to dance and sparkle on the surface of the water.

Cassandra wanted to sprint across the beach into the sea and push the thoughts of her impending meeting with Matheo Chevalier to the back of her mind. She longed to feel the soft silk of the water caressing her skin and soothing her overactive mind. But there was no time for relaxing. He'd emailed a tightly timed schedule and their first discussion would be in under an hour. What a pity this piece of paradise would not be hers to enjoy for little longer than one night.

She contented herself with slipping out of her shoes and stepping down the steps to bury her feet in the warm sand, wriggling her toes and feeling the arches of her feet tickle. Then she turned her back on the seductive beach and retreated indoors to change. The persona she intended to present to Matheo Chevalier was very different from the one he'd seen in Cornwall.

The double doors to the conference room were closed but the member of staff who had escorted Cass through the remarkable building pulled one open. She had wanted to stop every few steps to appreciate some other new element of the design of it. Now she hesitated on the threshold, her courage suddenly faltering. A clutch of panic sent her heartbeat into overdrive and brought a sweat to her palms, causing the strap of her laptop bag to slide through her fingers.

The two-week deadline they'd been given for this pitch meant she'd used the long hours of work to bury the realisation that she'd been forced to sell her heritage to the highest bidder. She'd found it almost impossible to acknowledge the identity of that bidder, even to herself. Her ancestors, all of whom had vowed never to let the Chevaliers get their hands on the Hideaway, would not have believed what she'd done, whatever her reasons.

Now she was about to see Matheo Chevalier again, face to face, for the first time since she'd accepted his offer. He'd known she'd had no option. She'd been backed into a corner with no way out apart from doing as he demanded, and she'd sworn no man would ever dominate her like that again.

Would he gloat? Rub in the fact that she'd been the one to lose the fight that had endured for generations?

He could try, but if she was about to see him again he was about to meet her true self for the very first time. Those few days at the Hideaway had come at the end of a long year of physical and mental stress. She'd been crushed by the realisation she'd have to sell and then by the arrival of Matheo Chevalier, with his money, power and position of unassailable strength. She reminded herself that he could only humiliate her if she allowed him to. She had a successful business and a great future. And perhaps her pitch this afternoon would allow her to leave her mark on the Hideaway, even if it was no longer her home.

She straightened her spine, lifted her chin, and, taking a firm grip on her laptop bag, stepped into a lofty room filled with light.

A polished wooden conference table, contoured to suit the curved glass walls of the space, occupied the middle of the room. Sleek wooden chairs, upholstered in cream leather, were arranged around it. A screen dominated one wall, and views of the sea, through floor-to-ceiling glass, another. A huge seascape hung on the wall opposite the windows, reflecting, rather than competing with, the Mediterranean, which filled the view.

It was one of the few spaces she'd ever entered that took her breath away.

She looked around, trying to take in the details without looking awestruck. The combination of perfect, low-key fittings, superb craftsmanship and sheer quality of furnishings added up to an atmosphere of absolute but understated luxury. She knew how difficult it was to achieve that look. And what it cost.

Her attention was drawn to the far end of the room as another pair of double doors swung open. Cass watched Matheo Chevalier walk through them.

He was dressed in light-coloured chinos and a pale blue linen shirt, the rolled-up sleeves exposing his strong, bronzed forearms. He looked more relaxed, more accessible, than he had in the dark suit and tie in Cornwall. Even so, she instantly remembered how his presence dominated a room; how he *possessed* the space around him; even a space like this. His thick, dark hair looked damp, as if he'd just stepped out of a shower. Easy confidence radiated from every toned muscle of his body. She'd seen him own his own power and relish using it and she thought she was about to see it again.

In spite of the talking-to she'd given herself, the breath left Cass's lungs and refused to come back. Her tongue stuck to the dry roof of her mouth and her heart, brought under control a minute ago, began to hammer again. Surely everyone else in the room could hear it. Matheo Chevalier had been followed in by two other members of his staff, and one of them was busy repositioning a chair at the head of the table.

She dragged her eyes upwards from where they were fixed on Matheo's long-fingered hands, but her stubborn mind instantly returned to the memory of how they had circled her upper arms, steadying her so that she wouldn't overbalance into the sea.

His intense grey eyes did a quick sweep of the room as he walked towards her. She managed to suck a gulp of air into her screaming lungs and relax the vice-like grip she had on her bag. For a split second her brain said she was going to be okay.

Then his eyes landed on her.

She wanted to see the moment when he registered the difference between the Cassandra who stood before him today and the one with whom he'd sparred in Cornwall.

He missed a beat, but only one.

Was it surprise that darkened his eyes to that impenetrable slate? His gaze drilled into her and she struggled to hold her nerve. He stopped in front of her.

Close up, she could see he'd obliterated whatever emotion he'd experienced on recognising her and his eyes now held an expression of calm welcome. A muscle flicking in his jaw was the only indication that he might be processing anything else.

He may have been wrong-footed for a nanosecond, but he was evidently supremely practised at not showing his feelings. She extended her right hand towards him.

'Monsieur Chevalier. It's a pleasure to meet you again.'

He took her hand and kept his eyes riveted on hers. And then he spoke, his French accent more pronounced than she remembered.

'Mademoiselle Greenwood. Welcome to St Celeste.'

Matheo Chevalier stared at the woman in front of him. His brain, so analytical, so quick, was having trouble computing this. Was he hallucinating?

His world had rocked crazily on its axis in the split second it had taken for his eyes to see her and his brain to recognise her. Something had slammed into the rock-solid plane of his stomach with the force of a tank, threatening to knock the air from his lungs, and the impact, real or imagined, almost stopped him in his tracks. It was only his relentless practice of self-control, his rigid refusal to ever show his feelings, that prevented him from exclaiming in surprise. He breathed in through his nose, and out again, and kept on walking towards her.

Perhaps she'd disappear as he got nearer, like a mirage in a shimmering haze of heat. The memory of her that had played on the edges of his imagination since he'd dropped a light kiss on her cheek, standing ankle-deep in icy water, bore no resemblance to this.

He stopped close to her, but she remained as solid and real as anything else in the room. Only now everything had retreated to the blurred periphery of his vision and she was all that remained in sharp focus. He could smell her scent and he wondered how it could still take him back to a cold early morning on a Cornish beach. She was offering to shake his hand and he wanted to reach out to touch her to make sure she was real, but he hesitated. Holding on to his sanity seemed hard enough, without feeling her warm, satin skin under his fingers, or even the glossy beauty of her hair.

He hauled his eyes from her face and looked at that hair. It was swept up in a neat chignon, smooth and tamed, and held in place by a clasp decorated with a pale gold seashell.

What's happened to the pencil?

The question hammered uselessly in his brain.

His eyes flicked back to her face and he thought he glimpsed uncertainty there, as though she'd like to put some distance between them. Then his gaze swept on, taking in her cream linen jacket, sculpted to accentuate her slender waist, and the hint of ivory lace edging a camisole, just visible in the V between the lapels. The narrow skirt was short enough to make a man wonder how much further those legs went, and her feet, last seen in scruffy trainers, looked perfectly at home in a pair of nude killer heels. They revealed the pearly gleam of polish on her toenails.

He'd told himself her faded jeans and fisherman's sweater couldn't hide her slender figure. That was true, but what they'd hidden were her subtle curves.

He shook her hand and unclenched his jaw, noting that Cassandra Greenwood looked calm and self-possessed. Adrenalin pumped round his body. He hadn't felt this…*confused*…for a very long time. Not since his father… But this was no time to let that memory rise to the surface of his brain. He didn't dare allow it any oxygen. Now was not the time for the coruscating anger that always accompanied it.

He folded his arms across his chest and wrapped his hands around his biceps in case they shook. Then he rocked back on his heels. He allowed his gaze to travel from Cass's toes, up her legs, over her torso, to her face. She had caught her bottom lip, glistening with a hint of tinted gloss, in her teeth, the only sign that she wasn't completely relaxed. He frowned and released his hands enough to tap his fingers in a pent-up rhythm against the muscles of his upper arms. He rolled his shoulders.

'Shall we begin?'

The air of the room hummed with tension. Cass wondered if he welcomed everyone pitching for his business in this brusque manner or if he especially wanted to unsettle her. She swallowed, her brain racing to decide how to respond to him. She'd expected a warmer reception, perhaps a preliminary chat. But if this was how he wanted the meeting to be, she'd roll with it.

She slid her laptop from its case and opened it, finding a socket set into the light wooden floor to plug it in. They'd printed a glossy brochure filled with computer-generated images of how their vision of the Hideaway would look and she slid a copy across the table to Matheo. At last his eyes left her face to look at the pages as he flicked through them. Then he dropped the book onto the table and indicated the two men at his side.

'Tim and Ben, two of my assistants. They'll help you to set up.' He settled into the chair at the head of the table and rested his forearms on its polished surface, his hands loosely linked.

Within a few minutes her computer had been connected to the St Celeste wireless network and the FuturePlan logo flashed up on the screen, faint in the bright daylight. This, thought Cass, was hopeless. They wouldn't be able to see anything of her presentation. There were no blinds or curtains at the vast windows so there appeared to be no way of darkening the room. She opened her mouth to speak but Matheo held up a hand.

'Before you begin, I need to tell you that I have already

identified the company I intend to use for the renovations of the Hideaway Hotel.'

Cass stared at him, shocked. Then suddenly she thought she understood what was going on.

'There is no point to my presentation, then. This trip, in fact the past two weeks, have all been a waste of time. All you're doing is paying lip service to the contract. Is that all you ever intended to do?'

If he was surprised at her directness, he gave no sign. She remembered telling Nick that she thought they could trust Matheo. She'd been wrong.

'The relevant word in the contract is "consider". I said I would *consider* your proposal.' His voice was even, steady. 'As you probably know, I've fulfilled my obligations to the members of staff at the Hideaway. I said I would also consider allowing you to be involved in the renovations. I do not break promises. But I think it is only fair, and honest, to tell you that I have decided on the company I plan to employ to do the work.'

The instructions FuturePlan had received had been precise. The presentation would take place on St Celeste at three o'clock in the afternoon and the company's representative would stay the night on the island and take the first flight from Nice back to London the following morning. Perhaps, thought Cass, since there'll be no need for any post-presentation discussion, I might even make the last flight out this evening.

But she refused to be rushed. She and the team in London had spent long days and nights putting this together. She'd rehearsed it endlessly, up until the flight had touched down in Nice, going over answers to possible questions, making sure she had all the facts and figures in her head. She had no notes or prompts. She owed it to Nick and the rest of her colleagues at FuturePlan to give it her best shot. Even if Matheo Chevalier wasn't interested in their proposal, she was going to make sure he was impressed with their pitch, she thought, irritation at his high-handed manner shivering through her. She might never see him again after today, but she was determined he'd remember her.

In the years ahead, when FuturePlan was famous and their projects seen as some of the best, most sustainable and eco-friendly in the world, he'd wonder why he hadn't signed them.

She was about to switch her attention to Ben or Tim, to ask if there was any way they could darken the room, when Matheo inclined his head.

'The impact of your presentation, Mlle Greenwood, depends on you.'

'But if you've already made up your mind…'

'I have.' His eyes, flint-grey, held hers. 'So, change it.'

He nodded to Ben, who raised his hand to a panel of buttons set into the wall near the door. The window was transformed into darkened glass and the only remaining illumination in the room came from a few hidden low-energy lights at floor level.

Cassandra closed her eyes briefly, confident that any show of frustration or anxiety on her part would be hidden in the dark. She inhaled and exhaled deeply and quietly and pressed her hands together in her lap before moving her fingers to the touchpad of her laptop. She tried to relax her jaw and throat.

'Well, then,' she said, 'prepare to be amazed.'

CHAPTER SEVEN

AFTER THE FINAL image of the presentation had faded from the screen there was silence in the conference room. Cassandra let it grow. Then she clicked off her computer.

'Thank you,' she said into the quiet.

She heard Ben push his chair back and within seconds the darkness retreated from the windows and natural light poured in again. The sea glittered in the afternoon sun.

Ben placed a glass and a jug of water at her elbow. Ice clinked as she poured it and took several swallows. Her mouth and throat felt parched. She closed her computer and returned it to its case, before deliberately turning her head to look at Matheo.

He had relaxed back in his chair, his arms folded, and his narrowed gaze appeared to be trained on the horizon. If his expression hadn't been thoughtful, Cassandra would have decided he hadn't taken any notice of her presentation. Then, as if he felt her eyes on him, he turned.

'Even if I haven't changed your mind,' she said, 'I hope I've at least made an impression.'

The straight line of his mouth lifted on one side; the side where the almost-dimple indented his cheek. He nodded, leaning forward.

'Yes, you have.'

Cassandra felt her cheeks grow a little warm under his scrutiny. She gripped her hands together and dipped her head.

'Good. I'm glad. At least I'll be able to return to London and report that you "considered" our ideas.' She lifted the glass at her elbow and sipped at the water again, then glanced at her watch. 'And I think if I hurry, and your helicopter is available, I might be able to catch an evening flight home. There is little point in staying if we have nothing further to discuss.' She pulled the laptop bag off the table and slipped the strap over her shoulder, not wanting to look hurried, but desperate to leave.

'The arrangement was that you would stay the night on St Celeste.'

'Yes, I know, but under the circumstances…'

'Under the circumstances, there are questions I'd like to ask you. I found several points in your presentation intriguing. Obviously, you know the Hideaway better than anyone and you've put that knowledge to impressive use in this scheme.' He turned to study the view again. 'With a few alterations to the old building you imply you could bring in much more natural light, but not compromise the timeless quality of the interiors. Here, the light is an integral part of the building. It's an element in its own right. You can't deny its importance.'

'It's the quality of the light that's different. In Cornwall, it's clear but never harsh. That's why schools of painting were established at Newlyn and St Ives, and the work of artists who lived there is unmistakeable for the expression of natural light on their canvasses. The same is true of the Mediterranean, but it's a…*different*…light.' She took a breath. 'You can let Cornish light into ancient interiors and it will enhance them. Mediterranean light sits better with big, modern spaces, like this conference room.'

He nodded. 'Yes. None of the images appear over-lit or harsh.' His gaze, when he returned it to her, was thoughtful, softer. 'But neither does this room. I'd be interested to know more about how you develop your ideas.'

Cassandra's teeth fastened on her bottom lip as she considered his words. Was there a possibility she might have swayed him in their favour? She needed to pursue this line of discussion now, while the images and her descriptions were fresh in his memory and the impression she'd made still endured.

'I'm happy to answer any questions you may have. Now would be a good time as I could return to any sections of the presentation you'd like to see again.' She slipped the strap of the laptop bag off her shoulder and began to unzip the case.

His smile, when he unleashed its full wattage, was devastating. It reached his eyes, making them crinkle slightly at the corners, and confirmed that the indentation in his cheek was a proper dimple.

'I admire your enthusiasm and determination. But I have a conference call in,' he glanced at his watch, 'twenty minutes, and I need to prepare for it.' He pushed back his chair and stood up. 'However, I'd be pleased if you'd join me for dinner at eight, on the terrace, when we can continue this discussion. I hope you won't turn me down a second time.'

Cassandra's heart sank a little. She felt she had the advantage of immediacy and that could well be lost over the next few hours, especially if his conference call was with the company he'd already chosen. However, she couldn't report back to Nick that Matheo Chevalier had wanted to discuss their proposal further, but she'd opted to return home instead. And over dinner she might be able to ask him which company he'd chosen for the project. It was always useful to know the competition.

She pinned on a smile and nodded.

'The last time you asked me to dinner was not a good day. I might enjoy it more this time. As long as there is not spotted dick on the menu.'

His lips twitched. 'I can guarantee it. I can also guarantee that you'll be blown away by the view.'

The last time he'd asked her to dinner it had felt like a command; one which she could not obey.

This time it felt like an invitation.

CHAPTER EIGHT

DISAPPOINTMENT, HOT AND BITTER, hit Cass as soon as she closed the door behind her. She'd insisted she could find her own way back, and she had, hurrying along the gravel paths as quickly as her heels would let her, her bag banging at her hip. As long as she kept going she could hold her emotions in check, but in the dim privacy of her suite she let them engulf her.

When had Matheo decided which company to hire? Had he known all along? He said he did not break promises, that he needed to be honest with her. But if he'd let FuturePlan do all that work, if he'd been playing her like a fish on a line for his own entertainment, that was dishonest in its own way.

She dumped her bag on the floor and flung herself onto the bed, staring at the pale wooden ceiling, each joint perfectly dovetailed, each plank honed to a butter-smooth shine. Just another man, she thought. Just another man who couldn't be trusted.

Her phone buzzed with a message from Nick, consisting of a single question mark. She wanted to keep the disappointment to herself, not to spread it through the office in London, but she knew Nick and the rest of the team would be waiting, anxiously, for news. She sent him a brief reply, saying she'd see him tomorrow, with a more detailed explanation. She imagined their despondency; how the optimism that had kept them going would drain away and exhaustion would take over. She hoped they'd believe she'd done her best in a no-win situation.

Since she'd slipped down that ladder into Matheo Chevalier's arms she'd felt like a puppet with him tugging her strings. Now she felt as if the strings had been cut, along with any possible further link to her beloved Hideaway. All that lay ahead was a return to work. It was work that she loved, and she knew she'd quickly become absorbed by new projects, but she'd been so full of hope, for so many reasons, for this one.

Things that seemed too good to be true usually were, she thought, and she should have known that. Perhaps someone without her connection to the Hideaway would have seen at once that Matheo Chevalier had never intended to let Future-Plan anywhere near the project. Having made the leap and sold to him, she'd been blinded by the possibility.

She thought about the evening ahead—making conversation, answering his questions, doing her best to sway his thinking while knowing it was a hopeless task—and she wished she was on her way home.

She rolled over onto her tummy and propped her chin in her hands, looking out at the white sandy beach and the ripples washing ashore from the blue, blue sea, and suddenly she knew the one thing that would make her feel better was the beach. All of her life it had been her playground, the place where she relaxed or where she went for solitude or solace.

She slid off the bed, kicked off her sandals and rummaged through her bag to find the bikini she'd stuffed in as an afterthought. She hadn't anticipated having time for a swim, but now it seemed like a necessity. It would lift her spirits.

She yanked the clip from her hair and peeled off the linen jacket and skirt.

Minutes later, she was running over the warm sand to dive into the crystalline water.

It was cold and she gasped when she surfaced, then she rolled onto her back and floated, arms and legs spread, like a starfish. She closed her eyes and relished the sensation of the warm sun on her face and the water rocking her tired body. When she finally emerged, she sat on the sand for a few minutes to dry off, and then made her way back to the wooden steps to her terrace.

The powerful shower sent a cascade of hot water pouring over her head and body, leaving her skin tingling. She wrapped herself in one of the soft bathrobes that hung behind the door and wondered what to do next. There were still three hours to wait before she'd have dinner with Matheo.

The lack of activity on her phone spoke silently of the massive disappointment she knew Nick must be experiencing. She was trapped in a frustrating web of luxury from which she longed to escape.

It was warm in the quiet dimness, and the hours of travel and accumulated short nights were taking their toll. The vast bed beckoned to her emotionally drained and physically exhausted body.

It was as comfortable as it looked. White linen sheets slid smoothly over her skin as she shed the bathrobe and slipped between them, surrendering to their soft caress. She might never again have the chance to be lulled to sleep by the sound of the Mediterranean Sea washing onto the sand, or the breeze whispering in the Stone pines.

Matheo finished his unsatisfactory conference call and switched off his computer. Perhaps he was tired. Perhaps he just wasn't interested enough in what the other guy had to say. Whatever it was, he'd found it difficult to concentrate and had had to ask him to repeat himself several times. Tim had sent at least one concerned glance in his direction, and after that had listened carefully, ready to prompt him when necessary. Now he was pretending to busy himself on his own laptop, as if he was reluctant to leave him, Matheo, on his own.

That irritated him further. He needed time and space to himself to try to resolve what was bothering him. But first he needed to work out exactly what that was.

Cassandra's presentation had been flawless. There seemed to be nothing it hadn't addressed, in as much detail as was necessary. She herself had been fluent, with strings of facts and figures at her fingertips. That she'd used no props, apart from the images on the screen, had impressed him.

Something about it, though, was catching at the periphery of his brain, but it was something he was finding impossible to pull into focus.

He didn't think it was the startling discrepancy between the exhausted and stressed Cassandra Greenwood he'd met in Cornwall and the cool, elegant woman who had waited in his conference room, ready to astonish him.

She had astonished him, on every level.

He'd been dragged back to that early morning, the smell of rain, the tang of salt, and the feeling of that tug, pulling him towards her. The memory of it was what had taken him back to the Hideaway in the first place, when he could have conducted the deal from the safety and comfort of this very desk. He'd tried to deny it, pushing it to the back of his mind, but he couldn't forget how the fleeting whisper of her cheek beneath his lips had driven him to run himself to a standstill. Only when he'd swum too far out to sea and then had to use all of his mental and physical strength to get back to the shore had he been able to shift her from front and centre of his mind, and then his respite was brief.

He wanted to sit across the table from her and see if he could unravel whatever it was that bothered him. His pulse had quickened when she'd suggested she might leave, needing to find a reason to persuade her to stay.

He told Tim he was going to the gym, but he found no relief from his thoughts on the treadmill or lifting weights. He showered and changed, then retrieved the FuturePlan brochure from the conference room and took it out onto his private terrace, but he couldn't figure out why he found the designs and ideas so beguiling. Irritation made him feel unsettled. He wasn't familiar with the feeling of being unable to solve a problem. There was still an hour to go before dinner. As his impatience grew, he flipped to the front of the brochure and began paging through it again.

Cass struggled up through layers of sleep and forced her eyes open. She lay still for a moment, her limbs heavy with lethargy, then she reached out for the light switch. It wasn't where it should have been. Instead, her hand encountered something soft and gauzy, which seemed to go on and on, in every direction. She shot bolt upright, panic clawing at her, and saw that, outside, dusk was rapidly dissolving into dark. Her brain creaked into action and the memories of the past few hours began to shuffle themselves into some sort of order. The soft murmuring of waves on the sand was not the Atlantic Ocean in unusually subdued mood. It was the warm Mediterranean. And that noise was not George hammering slates onto the roof that had blown off in a storm, it was someone knocking on her door.

She pushed her way through the mosquito netting and fumbled for the bathrobe she knew she'd discarded somewhere amongst the bedclothes.

'Just a minute,' she called, pulling it around her and trying to tie the belt.

The fog of sleep clouded her head. She couldn't think

straight. She found a light switch and flicked it on in time to see the door handle turn and to remember that she hadn't locked it.

Matheo's deep, measured voice snapped her into full, wary awareness. Instinctively, she pulled the robe more tightly around her naked body.

'Mademoiselle Greenwood, were you asleep?'

Grave and seductive, his tone lent an intimacy to the words that caused her stomach to clench.

She tried to breathe, to banish any trace of anxiety or panic from her voice.

'Yes.' Was that the best she could do? Her voice was faint and breathy in her own ears, betraying the confusion and vulnerability she was trying to hide.

'It's past siesta time.'

'What time is it?'

'It's eight o'clock. In the evening.'

'*Eight?* I've been asleep for *hours*. I could've been almost home by now.'

He laughed.

'You could have. But you're having dinner with me, remember?'

'I was exhausted. I'd been travelling…' She stopped, remembering that she didn't need to justify herself to him.

'Forgive me for disturbing you, but you must be hungry.'

'I'm…sorry. I only planned a quick nap. If you'd rather cancel, that's fine…'

'Not at all. May I come in?' Without waiting for an answer, he stepped inside and closed the door behind him. 'The kitchen staff are waiting to serve dinner.'

Cassandra backed away, clutching at the neck of her bathrobe. 'I'm sorry,' she repeated, completely thrown off balance by his presence and her state of undress.

He strolled through the room, towards the terrace. 'I'll wait while you dress.' He nodded towards the bathroom.

She stood irresolute, not moving. 'I'm not sure...'

He glanced at his watch. 'Five minutes?'

He turned his back and stood staring out into the dark. Beyond him Cass could make out the pale glimmer of the sand and the shining black sheet that was the sea. In spite of his relaxed manner there was rigid tension across his wide shoulders. She wondered why.

She looked at the clothes in her cabin bag. When she'd packed, dinner *a deux* with Matheo Chevalier had not been on her agenda. She pulled out a rolled-up silk kaftan and a pair of loose linen cropped trousers and retreated to the bathroom.

Minutes later she surveyed herself in the mirrored wall. The lilac silk accentuated her eyes. She hoped it drew attention away from the dark circles under them. The dab of concealer that she'd applied had not done the job. She seemed to have lost her lipstick but found some gloss, which would have to do. Her hair was damp, but she twisted it up into a knot and fixed it with the shell clip she'd used earlier.

She closed her eyes and took a deep breath, exhaling slowly and mindfully, as a knock sounded on the bathroom door.

'Five minutes. Time's up.'

She'd probably keep him waiting another ten minutes. Matheo had folded his arms and leaned against the doorframe, so his guard was down when the bathroom door opened and Cass stepped out into the soft light of the hallway. The air left his lungs, and he struggled against an unfamiliar constriction in his chest when he tried to fill them again. He straightened, although he thought he might need the support of the door behind him if the effects of this adrenalin rush didn't ebb soon.

The diaphanous silk top she wore shimmered as she moved

towards him, and the way it clung confirmed the memories he had of her body beneath it. Her direct gaze and fiercely determined air didn't quite mask the wariness shadowing her huge eyes. Her hair, which had been so tamed and smoothed earlier, had returned to its wilder state. A few tendrils had escaped from the knot held by the shell clip, and they curled against the creamy skin at the vulnerable-looking nape of her neck.

He thrust a hand through his hair. 'Shall we go?'

He turned the door handle, and she stepped outside, brushing against him. At the hint of her touch the unfamiliar tightness in his body, in which every muscle and sinew seemed to be under stress, wound itself up a couple more notches. He told himself it was because he needed to solve the problem that had plagued him ever since her presentation earlier this afternoon.

The sweet perfume of lavender and rosemary scented the warm night air. Tiny hidden solar lights glowed along the route of the winding pathway, although the glitter from the millions of stars in the velvet sky would have provided light enough. Cass looked up and marvelled at the jewelled depths of black space above her, wishing she could forget the disappointment of the afternoon and simply enjoy the place. She followed Matheo as he led the way towards the soft glow that shone from the island's main house.

Steps led up to huge glass doors set in wooden frames, though once through them it was difficult to tell if she was inside at all. The marble floor gleamed in the light of hundreds of lamps hanging from the trees and shrubs that grew in the atrium, their tops disappearing into the gloom above. Cass stopped to look around her. The clever use of natural materials and the spare, uncluttered design lent the space an otherworldliness. She felt she should tiptoe in her sequinned pumps to avoid disturbing anything.

Matheo strode towards the upward curve of a glass staircase, which seemed to float in the soaring space above them,
among the palm trees. He waited for her at the bottom, and
then looked down at her footwear.

'Slight design fault. Glass steps can be a little slippery.'

'You could have the edges of the treads sandblasted. It
would provide grip and would hardly be noticeable, amongst
all this...beauty.'

'Thank you. I'm glad you like it. And that's a good idea.
I'll remember it.'

He placed his hand under her elbow and guided her up the
stairs. As they reached the top she eased her arm free again,
and then almost wished she hadn't as the impact of the location hit her.

'Oh...wow...'

The bifold doors on the landing stood open and a polished
wooden floor spread out onto a terrace bounded by a glass balustrade. The uninterrupted, three-hundred-and-sixty-degree
view was jaw-droppingly, breathtakingly incredible.

White sand glimmered in the starlight, lit by lights hidden in
the shrubs and plants on the fringes of the beach below them.
Ripples, glowing with phosphorescence, crumbled their foam
onto the wet shore and then sucked back with a soft sigh. A
balmy breeze hissed through the leaves of the pines and the
marble-black sea shifted restlessly, the only break in the horizon a smudge of light beginning to spill over its lip as the
moon inched its way into the spangled sky.

In the other direction, the lights of the coast blinked and
shimmered in the distance.

Cass stood rooted to the spot, trying to absorb the beauty
and at the same time catalogue all the design features that gave
the space such a feeling of wholeness and of fitting so exactly
with the surroundings.

'Would *mademoiselle* care to be seated?'

A waiter hovered at her elbow. He led the way towards Matheo, who stood at a table near the edge of the terrace.

Candles in glass lanterns flickered all around them. She sank onto soft cushions, still gazing around wide-eyed in every direction, trying to commit the details of the scene to memory. She wanted to take photographs, but it was Matheo's private space and he was a very private man.

Matheo took his place opposite her, his appraising gaze fixed on her face.

'What do you think?'

'It's one of the most beautiful places I've ever seen.'

'And your professional opinion?'

She looked around, finding it difficult to be objective and analytical.

'It's exquisitely designed and decorated. It blends seamlessly with the surrounding landscape and there is not a single jarring note. The use of timber and glass is inspirational.' She lifted her shoulders. 'Why are you employing another company for the Hideaway? Just use whoever did this.'

'With such a location,' his outstretched arm encompassed the bay below them, 'the brief was simple: the building must not argue with what's here already. As far as possible, it needs to disappear. Sites like this are rare. They merit special attention.'

He reached out and poured water into a tumbler in front of her, ice clinking against crystal.

'With a site like the Hideaway,' he continued, 'you could knock the building down and...'

'No, you couldn't.' She spoke too quickly, so stopped and took a sip of water. 'I mean because it's listed,' she finished.

His cheek creased as a corner of his straight mouth lifted and she felt a flush stain her cheeks.

'I'm aware of that. I was going to say you could knock it

down and build something dramatic and modern, but it would argue with the landscape. The Hideaway has been there for hundreds of years, and it's evolved over time, just as the landscape has. Why try to make a bold new statement when the existing one speaks loudly enough for itself?'

Cassandra tried to absorb this. His words mirrored her opinion exactly but hearing them from him disconcerted her. Unexpectedly and against her will she felt the solid rock of her dislike of all he stood for shift.

'But all your hotels—all the dozens of them across the world—are in a similar mould.' She wrapped both her hands around her glass of water and met his gaze. 'I know from experience a certain type of customer values that. Some people don't like to be challenged by their surroundings. Familiarity gives them security. The Hideaway will be different.'

'That is true, but while my hotels might all be similar, each one is individually designed and styled to make the most of the site and to appeal to the projected guest profile. After all, why check into a hotel in Gstaad that feels the same as one in Singapore?'

The waiter appeared; white linen was swathed around a bottle beaded with condensation.

'White wine, *mademoiselle*?'

She nodded and watched the pale liquid splash into her glass and then into Matheo's.

He lifted one powerful shoulder. 'My global brand delivers the emotional security guests like, with touches of individuality. Wherever you are in the world, the standards are equally high. Guests can relax knowing their expectations will be met, but unique features will always reflect the surroundings, link them to the landscape.' He nodded his thanks to the waiter. 'However, the Hideaway is a new departure for me. Something more individual and…intimate.'

He raised his glass and tilted it towards her. 'Mademoiselle Greenwood.'

Cassandra sipped at the wine, eyes on his lean fingers where they gripped the stem of his glass. She tried to focus on what he was saying.

'Your ideas for the Hideaway intrigue me. I've been pondering them for the past few hours.'

Cassandra took a deep breath, placing her wine glass carefully on the table.

'Are you saying I managed to change your mind?'

He shook his head, crumbling her hopes.

'No. I'm wondering where they originated. Have they evolved over time, through all the years you've lived there? Or have you studied other projects, other designers, and taken inspiration from them?'

Cassandra took time to think about her answer, wanting it to be as accurate and truthful as possible.

'They've mostly come,' she said slowly, 'from my own very personal experience of living there. But I wouldn't have had those ideas if I hadn't studied interior design and worked with architects on other projects. It's difficult to separate the two elements. It's just something that…happens. And when it feels right, it usually is.' She could see he was listening intently. 'Could I ask *you* a question?'

A bowl of chilled soup had appeared in front of her. She took a piece of bread from the basket on the table and began to pull it to bits.

He leaned forward, interest sparking in his eyes. 'Of course. But that bread is meant to be eaten, Cassandra, not shredded.'

Listening to the slightly accented syllables of her name rolling off his tongue made her pause. The sound stirred a memory of running down a beach, his voice on the wind…

'Does our proposal resemble, at all, what you imagine the

Hideaway could look like? And how similar is it to the one by the company you've chosen?'

He nodded. 'Yes, and no. Yes, I imagine the Hideaway being very like the proposal you presented. And no, because I don't yet have one from the company I…think… I've chosen.'

'Well, then, how do you know you'll like their work? Who are they?'

Matheo looked away, over her shoulder towards the sea. 'I've become aware of a new hotel, which has opened to great acclaim. The pictures on the internet are incredible. Somehow, they reflect exactly the vision I have for the Hideaway. I haven't read enough yet to discover who was behind the project—it's been a busy time—but it only took me a few moments to decide I want to hire them.'

'Were those few minutes quite recent? Or have you known all along you weren't going to hire FuturePlan? Were you simply fulfilling the terms of the contract?' She sipped at a spoonful of the iced gazpacho.

'While that is irrelevant, it was nevertheless a few days ago.'

'It is not irrelevant to us. Our team put huge amounts of time and energy into getting the bid ready in the tight timeframe you gave us.' Her voice dropped. 'And I made a decision to trust you.'

'It is irrelevant because whatever had happened, I would have considered your proposal. I had made you a promise and I never break promises. Not ever.'

'I'm not sure that makes me feel any better, but I appreciate your honesty.' Cassandra tipped her head back. 'But what if,' she continued, gazing at the millions of stars, 'what if they don't want the project? What then?'

He looked at her, his dark brows pulled together. 'They'll want the project. Everyone wants my business.'

It sounded arrogant but Cassandra knew he was right. His

name, wealth and influence packed a huge punch. Everyone wanted a part of it. Of *him*. And she was no exception.

'Well, assuming you're right, what's drawn you to them?'

'An element of originality, based firmly in traditional principles. It's hard to define. The best I can do is to ask you to apply your ideas for the Hideaway to a different project and see what you'd come up with. It's…' He shook his head. 'It's difficult.'

With those words, something fell into place in Cassandra's brain. She almost heard the click. She swallowed the bread she'd been chewing and put down her spoon on her plate. Gripping her hands in her lap, she scrunched the linen napkin into a tight ball. Her pulse quickened, so much that she thought Matheo might see it jumping at the base of her throat. She tried to control her breathing as it threatened to become shallow and unsteady.

'What,' she asked quietly, holding his gaze, 'is this project called?'

'You might have heard of it,' he said. 'It's in the Western Isles of Scotland. It's called the Sandpiper.'

CHAPTER NINE

MATHEO WATCHED CASSANDRA'S eyes widen. He'd never worry about drowning in the sea again. Those eyes would do for him right here at the table. A faint flush spread across the skin of her cheeks and then the colour drained away, leaving her pale. Her lips parted and then her teeth nipped on the bottom, fuller one.

'Mr Chevalier… Matheo…'

'Is something wrong? Are you ill?'

She shook her head and reached for the tumbler of water. He noticed that her hand shook slightly. He tried to think what had upset her. She'd asked the name of the hotel in Scotland.

'No. I'm not ill, thank you. Just…surprised. You see, that hotel…the Sandpiper…is the most recent project FuturePlan has completed. Those designs were done by Nick. The interiors are mine.'

A combination of shock and astonishment hit him. His first reaction was to deny that she could be right, but he stamped on that at once. Cassandra wouldn't make up something like this. What would be the point? And she couldn't be wrong. Unless there was another hotel of the same name. It seemed highly unlikely.

He sat back, keeping his reaction under control, hidden, behind a frown.

'Are you sure you're not confusing it with another hotel?

And if you've been at the Hideaway for a year, how could those designs be yours? You haven't been closely involved with the project, obviously.'

Her laugh sounded a little unsure, but her eyes now glowed with excitement.

'There is absolutely no doubt. The hotel opened last week. It's true I wasn't involved with it for the time I was in Cornwall, but the designs were all completed before I took time out at the Hideaway. They're mine. You would have seen echoes of them in the presentation this afternoon. It's my style you recognised.'

The puzzle that had been snagging at his brain all evening suddenly resolved itself. The colours, the ancient stonework buildings, the clever uses of timber and glass, while unique, bore a similarity of style, which he now saw clearly.

He felt confused. Where did he go from here? It was obvious that Cassandra and the team at FuturePlan, when they heard about this revelation, would expect the contract to be theirs. It was the only honest way to proceed. He examined his feelings and had to admit to himself that the reservation he felt stemmed from the idea of having to work with Cassandra.

She was no longer that damaged girl he'd met years ago, or the woman with fierce determination in her blue eyes who had fought to keep her home and then fought to have a say in its future. He'd come up with a fair way to ensure she sold to him and he'd fulfilled his side of the bargain.

The Cassandra who had turned up in his conference room this afternoon was a different person altogether. Professional, polished and supremely well-prepared to push him into a decision in her favour, she'd impressed him more than he'd ever expected possible. He'd thought before that she was the sort of person he liked to hire, and those thoughts were coming back to bite him now.

Because he wasn't at all sure he could work with her. Her presence unsettled him, testing all the self-protective barriers he'd put in place. Her eyes would find a weak spot, her laugh another. Before he knew it, he'd allow that thread to tug her closer, and then it would snap...

But he saw, very quickly, that there was no way out of this. No honest, honourable way.

St Celeste was where he felt protected, safe. He trusted his staff and nobody came to the island without his knowledge. If, he thought, his brain running ahead of itself, he asked that Cassandra stay here to work with him on the scheme, he'd feel happier about giving the contract to FuturePlan. That way he could control their interaction and keep himself informed of what was happening. If he felt his defences wavering, he could send her back to London at a moment's notice on some pretext.

It would only be for a few days, while they established the basics of what he wanted. After that it could all be done remotely.

Cassandra was watching him, her eyes bright with excitement. This meant so much more to her than just another job. He'd be giving her the opportunity she'd craved. Perhaps winning the contract for FuturePlan would compensate, in a small way, for her loss of the Hideaway. He'd wanted to make it all feel better for her and now it looked as if he could.

'Obviously,' he said, eventually, 'this puts everything in a completely different light.' The waiter placed plates of perfectly braised chicken in front of them, with an accompanying bowl of bright steamed vegetables. 'If what you say is... accurate... I see no reason why the contract shouldn't go to FuturePlan. I'd need to see your presentation again, to clear up a few points...'

'That's no problem. Perhaps tomorrow morning, before I leave?'

Matheo decided to put off the issue of her leaving until he could discuss it with her and her partner at the same time. Now he raised his glass. 'To the future of the Hideaway, Cassandra.'

She tilted her glass towards him, giving him the full benefit of her smile. 'My father always said if your family got their hands on it, they'd obliterate the hotel and build some hideous modern construction in its place, so it's a relief to know our ideas for its future are similar.'

Matheo dipped his head, the hard planes of his face emphasised by the shadow that fell across them. His mouth compressed.

'Your father had a low opinion of my family. The feeling was mutual.'

'We both know that. Selling to you was one of the most difficult decisions I've ever had to make, despite the deal you offered.' She spooned vegetables onto her plate. 'But now I think it was the right one. I spent a year trying to save it, but I slowly came to accept that the only way to really salvage it was to sell it, hopefully to a sympathetic buyer. I never expected it to be a Chevalier.'

'But you know we've wanted it for decades.'

'Oh, I know you wanted it. I just didn't expect you to be sympathetic to my wishes for it. I thought you and your father would want to remove all trace of us.'

'My father possibly would.'

'Are you going to be able to persuade him?' A shadow clouded her eyes. 'I've just realised working with you will mean working with him. I don't know if I can do that.'

He saw the knuckles of her hands turn white with tension as she gripped her knife and fork.

'As I've said before, my father has nothing at all to do with my purchase of the Hideaway. Marine Developments is my own company. He has no part in it.'

'I chose not to believe you. You seemed to be so like your father, although when we first met you weren't. Not at all. What's happened?'

'Let's just say our methods made us incompatible business partners, which means you won't have to work with him. He'll be angry when he learns I've bought the Hideaway, but that's my problem, not yours.'

He sat back and took a mouthful of wine.

The risen moon now painted a silver path towards the shore, and Cassandra wondered what the little cove below the Hideaway looked like tonight. Was the moon visible or was it, as more often than not, obscured by clouds scudding across the deep Cornish sky?

'As the people who had the original disagreement have long-since died, I don't understand how you can find buying it satisfying, or why it should bother you father.'

'My father never gives up until he gets what he wants, so, yes, he will be angry. As for my motives, revenge, they say, is a dish best served cold.' He dropped his gaze, wrapping his fingers around his wine glass.

Cassandra felt a cold fist close around her heart. 'Are you saying this is revenge against your *father*? I thought…'

'It's a personal matter. I don't care to discuss it.' His tone was sharp.

Cassandra bit her lip. 'It's just…family is so important…it seems such a waste…'

'Every family is different. Mine is…dysfunctional. That seems like a good word to describe it.'

'Another thing that's said—' Cass dragged her eyes away from his fingers and fixed them on his face '—is that the best revenge is to live your best life. That's what I plan to do.'

Matheo raised an arm and gestured towards the sea, the island, the beach. 'Perhaps this is my best life?'

'It's hard to imagine a better one. But isn't it sometimes lonely amid all this…perfection?'

Matheo leaned back in his chair and folded his arms across his chest.

'Never. But since you're here, invading my privacy—' he smiled '—and FuturePlan is going to be working for me, there is something I'd like to ask you.'

'I think I've told you everything there is to know about the Hideaway.'

'Perhaps not quite everything. This afternoon I received the report I'd requested from my forensic accountant.' She was aware of how closely he was watching her. 'He's good—very good—at what he does. But he has been unable to solve the mystery of how the staff of the Hideaway were being paid. And I wonder if you would care to shed any light on it.'

Cass caught her bottom lip in her teeth and looked down at her hands. She wondered what he knew. Was he trying to trick her in some way, to see if she'd tell the truth? And what use could the information possibly be to him? He owned the Hideaway now, including any remaining debts, but there were no debts on the staff payroll.

'Why does it matter? It makes no difference now.'

'You're right. It doesn't. But I don't like mysteries and I'm curious to discover the answer, if you'll share it . You must know it.'

If she didn't tell him the truth now, he'd find out some other way. She sighed out a breath.

'It's nothing sinister. Like your relationship with your father it's a personal matter, which I've chosen never to discuss, but I don't see that it matters now.' She looked at the uneaten food on her plate and felt her appetite fade. Remembering how she'd struggled to keep everything afloat, to ultimately lose control of it, made her feel sad. Although the outcome was a good one for the hotel, the staff and even for herself, she suddenly felt tired. The rush of excitement associated with getting the contract had drained away. She longed to slip into that comfortable bed and give herself up to sleep, and the quickest way there was to tell Matheo what he wanted to know. 'A trust fund was set up for me by my grandfather. He was a mining magnate and I was his only grandchild. I gained access to it when I was twenty-five.' She tucked an escaped tendril of hair behind an ear. 'I invested some of it in the partnership with Nick when we started FuturePlan. I planned to sell my flat in Camden and buy a house with a garden. Luckily, I hadn't got round to doing that, as I've been able to use it to pay the staff wages for the past year. They were due paid holidays, too, and some hadn't always been paid in the past, so I made up the arrears. But it's almost all gone. So maybe you coming along when you did was my lucky break, after all.' She smiled. 'Did you ever dream that one day you'd be cast in the role of the good guy?'

She held Matheo's stare. Then he shook his head slightly and seemed to make up his mind.

'I consider that,' he said, 'to be an incredibly kind and generous thing to do, but also a perfect example of throwing good money after bad.'

'You're probably right, at least about the good money part. And considering the state of the finances I inherited with the Hideaway, I accept your point. But perhaps you've never needed a job, or been responsible for another soul, whether it is your elderly mother or your cat.'

She was right, of course. He had no idea at all. No one else had ever relied on him and he'd never had to fight for anything. Except once, and he'd lost that battle in the most humiliating way. He dragged his mind back to the present and the calm resignation of her expression.

'All I was doing,' she went on, smoothing out the white linen napkin she'd scrunched up in her fists, 'was trying to ensure people kept their jobs for as long as possible. I tried to encourage them to look for other opportunities, but no one wanted to listen. They seemed to think if we all tried hard enough things would work out.'

'I spoke to some of the staff after you left. I was trying to get an idea of how they'd react to my plans if you accepted my offer.'

'Which you were confident I would.'

He nodded. 'Yes. Fairly confident. Anyway, they all hold you in extraordinarily high regard, you know. They're fiercely loyal to you.

That kind of loyalty and affection is rare. And enviable.'

Cassandra took a deep, deep breath.

'Thank you.'

Matheo rested his folded arms on the table. He leaned towards her.

'George was especially robust in his praise of you.'

'George? I thought he resented all the repairs I asked him to do, when he'd rather have been growing vegetables.'

'He told me you'd encouraged him to concentrate on growing crops for the kitchen, but he felt the demands of the old building were more important. Your leaky bedroom was of great concern to him.'

'He kept me going sometimes, when I was ready to give up.'

'As soon as you accepted my offer I had Pierre, the interim manager, sort out the staff issues. I can forward his report to you. But in the meantime, I can tell you that George will spend the time during the renovations establishing a vegetable and fruit garden that will hopefully provide for many of the hotel kitchen needs.'

'That's such good news. ' She smiled at him. 'I never

thought I'd be grateful to you for anything you did at the Hideaway.'

Cass lifted her eyes from her plate of food to look at him. There was a silver gleam of triumph in his eyes and she knew she'd misjudged him. In fact, she'd misjudged him long before he'd set foot in the Hideaway. But history had dictated what he'd be like, and until now history had been deadly accurate.

She took another mouthful of wine and noticed that her glass had been filled again. Suddenly, she felt light-headed and dizzy, and put the glass down.

'Are you all right?'

She shook her head. 'I just haven't eaten properly today.'

He indicated her plate. 'Well, this is better than anything you'd have got in the economy cabin of the red-eye flight back to London you wanted to catch. I fly the chef from a Michelin-starred restaurant on the Riviera over, when necessary.'

'Of course you do.'

He laughed. 'Ask him, if you don't believe me. He loves to discuss his dishes with guests. And if your plate returns to the kitchen untouched, he'll be out here to discover why.'

Cass took a mouthful of food. The knot of anxiety which had been a permanent fixture in her tummy for weeks had loosened.

'This will make up for the apology for a snack I'll be served on the flight home tomorrow,' she said.

Matheo stood at the glass balustrade on the edge of the terrace. It had been past midnight by the time they'd finished their meal and Cassandra had declined coffee.

He'd watched anxiety fade from her features and a new strength and positivity flow into her as she'd realised the renovation contract would go to FuturePlan and absorbed his information about the staff of the Hideaway. It had given him inexplicable pleasure. He examined the feeling and savoured it. Was this how it felt to be responsible for someone's happiness and to be able to make things better?

They were two professionals with similar ideas about a project close to both their hearts, for different reasons. He was glad he'd bought the failing hotel, even if his motivation had been flawed.

He pushed himself upright and decided to draft an email to Nick and Cassandra, setting out his requirements for the next few days.

Sleep, always elusive for him, felt impossible tonight.

CHAPTER TEN

MATHEO LOOKED UP to see Cassandra striding across the terrace towards him. She wore a cream linen shift and chic sunglasses, and her leather satchel swung from one shoulder. He flipped his laptop closed and stood up.

The morning breeze had whipped up frothy white tops to the waves and it snapped at the edges of the broad umbrella which shaded the table. It briefly flattened her dress against her body, teasing a tendril from the glossy ebony braid of her hair.

'Good morning.' She dumped the bag next to a chair and sat down, pulling out her laptop. 'Why didn't you discuss it with me first?'

Matheo frowned and decided the flush on her cheeks and her sparkling eyes were not the result of sunshine and the sea breeze. She was angry.

'I sent the email to both of you.'

'Yes, but you sent it at some unearthly hour of the morning. Nick is an insanely early riser and the first thing I knew about it was my phone buzzing in my ear and Nick saying it was a good idea for me to stay on here for a few days, because it's what you want.' She stared at him, her eyes flashing. 'I didn't know what he was talking about. I felt like a total idiot.'

The loose lock of her hair brushed across her face and she swiped at it with a hand that trembled.

'I'm sorry. I didn't mean that to happen.' He sat down opposite her and removed his sunglasses, dropping them into the top pocket of his shirt. 'I often work late and I needed to get the points down in the email while they were fresh in my head. If anything, I thought you'd read it first.'

'You must have already had the idea when we were having dinner. You could have mentioned it then.'

He nodded. 'I did think of it last night, but you were tired and I thought you might not be in the frame of mind to consider my suggestion.'

'Mr Chevalier. Matheo.' She replaced her shades. 'If we are going to work together you will have to agree to treat me as an equal, to Nick and to yourself. Nick and I are partners. You are our client. Please don't make allowances for me that you would not make for anyone else.' It sounded as if she was forcing the tremor out of her voice by sheer willpower.

'I apologise.' Matheo picked up the cafetière of fresh coffee. 'I should have discussed it with you first, or at least waited until this morning to send the email. It was a misjudgement on my part. Coffee?'

Cassandra sighed out a breath and her tense shoulders dropped. She surveyed the table.

'Yes, please. Mmm... Almond croissants are my absolute favourite and the coffee smells amazing.'

Matheo pinched the bridge of his nose, not convinced that her anger had subsided. 'Did you sleep well?'

She nodded. 'Yes, until Nick phoned. And, thanks to that wake-up call, I've already done some work.'

'*Work?*'

She pushed her sunglasses onto the top of her head, opening the computer. 'Do you have a problem with that? I had some newideas about the Hideaway after our discussion last night, and I thought I'd get them down while they were fresh in my mind, just in case you'd like to use them.' She clicked a couple of keys. 'Do you want to have a look?'

'Yes, I'd like to see them. Very much.' He ran a hand over the back of his head. 'But first, what did you say to Nick?' He felt tension wind up in his body. Her answer would shape not only the next few days but also the way the rest of the project would progress. If they could build an understanding from the beginning, face to face, running it remotely from St Celeste would be that much easier.

Cassandra adjusted the angle of her screen.

'I said "no". I'm annoyed that you just assumed I'd do as you want. I've only just returned to work after a traumatic year, which didn't end well. As you know.' There was pain in the look she flashed at him. 'I've spent two weeks working against a frankly unfair deadline. I have a life, both at work and at home, to be getting back to.'

'It would only be for a few days, but obviously if that isn't possible I'll understand.' Disappointment crept over him. He realised he'd done exactly what she accused him of. He'd assumed she'd stay, because he wanted her to, and his mind had already leapt ahead to the idea of sharing a few days with her. Apart from discussing the project, he was beginning to enjoy her company. If he got to know her a bit better, away from the emotional landscape of the Hideaway, if he found what made her tick, the whole project would run more smoothly.

Across the table, some of the tension seemed to drain out of Cassandra.

'I said "no", but then we discussed it more sensibly, when I'd woken up properly and actually read your email, and we've agreed I should stay until Friday. That gives us four days, which should be enough to start with.' She turned her head and looked out at the sea, breathing in deeply. 'It's a wonderful place to work, obviously, but...'

'But what?' Anxiety tugged at him. Why wouldn't she be happy to stay? Was it that she couldn't bear to be near to him, with their history of antagonism? He'd be able to empathise with that. He'd won the battle over the Hideaway but perhaps she wasn't ready to concede the war.

The thought that she might never be ready caused uneasiness to twist in his gut.

'It's so exquisite. The surroundings could be seriously distracting.'

Matheo relaxed into his chair and smiled.

'Thank you,' he said, pouring coffee into her cup, 'for agreeing to stay. I must learn not to fire off emails at three o'clock in the morning. After breakfast I'd like to go over your presentation again. The room will be dark. No distractions.'

Hours later, Cassandra settled down to work at a table on the terrace of her suite, but she found her mind wandering from the plans for the Hideaway. The restless sea kept pulling her gaze away from the notes in front of her, reflecting her equally restless thoughts.

The time spent with Matheo had flown by.

When Nick's call had dragged her from sleep early this morning, she'd been confused and then furious. Now she smiled at how Nick had talked her down from her panicked response. He'd had practice at it, over the years, especially in the early days of their partnership, when her break-up with Jason, and the reasons for it, had been raw. He'd prompted her to seek help from a therapist and just knowing he understood enough to make the suggestion had helped.

He'd suggested she read Matheo's email and reminded her that he was reclusive and perhaps not comfortable with unfamiliar people. Maybe this was how he liked to work.

She'd still been angry at Matheo's approach but finally

agreed to his plan, because, as Nick said, he was an important client and they needed to establish a good working relationship with him. She pointed out to Nick that working closely with him was difficult, since they were meant to despise each other. But she conceded she'd enjoyed his company at dinner, especially after she was able to drop the bombshell about the Sandpiper into his life.

Now she thought back over the morning and decided she'd set the ground rules at breakfast. Matheo didn't know about the unreasonable panic that consumed her when she felt she was being backed into a corner with no means of escape, but she hoped he'd remember to consult her about any decisions affecting her life in future.

He knew how much she resented his ownership of what had been her home. She knew he'd bought it in an act of revenge against his father. She would have preferred it if her family had remained his enemy, rather than his father. How awful it must be to be estranged from your only family member. It must make him very unhappy, she thought, although he hid it well. Internalising that sort of pain was not good for anyone, though.

To be that unhappy amidst the perfection of St Celeste must be brutal, as if nature was laughing at you.

But working with Matheo had been easy. They'd rerun her presentation and he'd stopped her with a question when he wanted more detail on something. He'd understood her explanations immediately, every time. In the darkness of the conference room, she'd been able to hear from the timbre of his voice whether he liked a suggestion, or not. Whether something interested him or didn't capture his imagination.

It felt as though they were uneasily in tune with one another, trying each other out, testing each other, in a quiet way.

She hadn't expected to find it so enjoyable, and she hadn't wanted it to end, so when they'd covered all the points relating to the Hideaway for the day and she had new ideas to work on she delayed returning to her suite by asking Matheo questions about the island.

He was passionate about his home, and keen to share that passion with her. He'd commissioned a young architect to design the buildings, with the idea of making them as eco-friendly as possible. Rainwater was harvested and stored in an underground cistern. Solar panels on the roofs generated electricity, which was stored in batteries in the basement. The gardens, planted with native species to withstand the hot summers and stormy winters, were irrigated by a natural spring, which rose in the centre of the island.

The timber for the soaring, curved shapes of the buildings was sourced from sustainable forests, and the glass was all recycled.

He admitted that the helicopter—and the private jet he also owned—were indulgent, but he often needed to travel at short notice. To compensate, in a small way, he made large donations to climate-change organisations each year.

Cassandra was awestruck by how he'd been able to translate his passion for protecting the environment into reality.

She felt herself adjusting her opinion of him, wondering how much more there was to discover about his ideas; about him. She could no longer think of him as simply the spoilt billionaire son of a billionaire father, forcing her to sell her home to him because of an age-old argument over a game of cards. With his considered opinions and concern for his surroundings, she wondered what had driven him to want to acquire the Hideaway in an act of revenge against his father. That behaviour felt out of character for the person who'd shown her a little more of himself through his enthusiasm for protecting this small island in the Mediterranean.

They'd eaten sandwiches at the conference table without

interrupting their discussion. He hoped to use as many environmentally friendly features as possible in the renovated Hideaway, he said. For Cassandra, who'd imagined the hotel being pulled to bits by a developer with profit the only goal, this was almost unbelievable.

While the hotels that had made him famous, and rich, were all big names, in big cities across the globe, he wanted to move to smaller, boutique establishments, where he could implement his innovative ideas. The Hideaway was the first in what he hoped would be a chain of similar hotels, each incorporating sound eco principles but maintaining their original identities.

Cassandra reflected that only twenty-four hours earlier she'd thought the project was lost. She stretched her arms above her head and then began to re-read her notes. Her head was bursting with ideas.

Matheo had a business meeting and dinner in Nice in the late afternoon. A meal would be served in her suite and he'd see her for breakfast the following morning.

It was one in the morning before Matheo landed back on St Celeste. He wondered if the noise of the helicopter had woken Cassandra and whether he should knock on her door and suggest a nightcap.

He quickly decided that was a bad idea. She didn't like things being sprung on her—he'd learned that, and he wondered what had triggered that response. He wouldn't pry. It might send her into a panic and drive her away. Because he'd made it clear she could leave when she wished. He hadn't suggested she could also stay longer.

He pulled off his jacket and tie in his bedroom and slid open the door to his private terrace. The meeting and charity dinner this evening had been unavoidable. As one of the trustees he'd needed to show up, but the hours had dragged and he'd found himself constantly thinking how much more enjoyable dinner last night, on the terrace with Cassandra, had been. Their day today had essentially been one long business meeting, but it hadn't felt like work. It had all been pure pleasure.

CHAPTER ELEVEN

MATHEO LOOKED AT the screen but his brain wouldn't engage with it. He pressed the heels of his hands into his eyes and looked again, but his mind would not cooperate.

Not while her pale forearm lay so close to his bronzed one on the table, and her slim fingers flew over the keyboard, pulling up a screenful of images of cool interiors, warm Persian rugs and deep sofas. Her fragrant scent, of lavender and lemon, sifted over him, and he inhaled it despite knowing it would only disconnect his brain even more.

She'd be leaving tomorrow, and he could hardly bear the thought.

He'd become comfortable working with her. Their intellectual understanding seemed to run deep and he felt they were seamlessly connected in their goals for the Hideaway project. Nick had emailed sketches and Cassandra had skilfully translated them into three-dimensional images on her computer.

They'd spent hours, earlier in the day, back in the darkened conference room, looking at them on the big screen, discussing the fall of light, the angle of a staircase, the necessity of each room having a view, whether of the sea, the garden or the wooded, rolling hills.

When he'd joked, two days ago, that there'd be no distractions in the darkened conference room, he'd been wrong.

He found her enthusiasm, her knowledge of her business,

her interest in his ideas, just her *presence,* were major distractions. She was natural and relaxed and seemed unaware that when her arm had brushed against his in the dark a charge raced across his skin, spreading an awareness of her closeness through his whole body. He'd held himself rigid, avoiding touching her again, but desperately wanting to see what would happen if he did.

They agreed on almost everything, but she wasn't afraid to argue a point with him when she felt strongly about it. It was refreshing, when so many of the people he dealt with simply acquiesced as a matter of course. Wealth brought comfort and privilege, but it meant he never knew for sure if people wanted to be with him for *who* he was or for *what* he was. It made it impossible to have a meaningful discussion, a frank exchange of ideas. He got what he wanted but at the cost of never knowing whether another solution might have been better.

Beneath the table their knees had been inches apart. If he'd moved his chair to the left, just a fraction, they'd touch. He'd wanted to, but he didn't. What if she recoiled, shocked? What if she didn't?

It had been a relief when he could get up and restore the room to its normal brightness. Continuing their discussion in the light would be much easier.

Except it wasn't.

In the shade of the umbrella on the terrace, he found himself fascinated by the dancing colours in her eyes as she described something with enthusiasm or puzzled over an element of design. They held a Zoom meeting with Nick in London, to clarify points of the contract, and he had to concentrate, hard, on speaking to him and not being distracted by Cassandra's pure profile, the curve of her neck where it joined her shoulder, the shadow at the V-neck of her dress.

Perhaps it would have been sensible to cut her stay short.

Probably he should never have suggested she stay at all. The rock on which he'd re-established himself two years ago felt unstable. He felt threatened by feelings he'd vowed he would never entertain again. If he allowed them to gain traction, he'd open himself to the possibility of pain and humiliation, all over again.

He believed in honesty and fairness, *integrity* above all else. But if Cassandra discovered the true man who lurked beneath the version he presented to the world, her beautiful eyes would fill with pity, and then derision.

He couldn't bear the thought of that, either.

She was fired up with a positivity he envied. Surely no-one could come within her orbit, in this mood, and not willingly be sucked into it. He angled the laptop away from his line of vision and rested his forearms on the table. The glass felt cool beneath his heated skin.

Surprise brought her thickly fringed eyes snapping up from the screen.

Matheo sucked in a breath and slid his gaze beyond her. The sea shone, blue and white, beneath the Mediterranean sky and the faint shape of a ship broke the perfect line of the horizon. When he looked at her again, she was watching him. He avoided eye contact and glanced down at the table.

'I think,' he said, quietly, 'that I—we—need a break. From all this. It's…a lot to absorb, in a short time.'

In the quiet that followed, Matheo was sharply aware of the distant mew of a seagull, wheeling over the waves, and the sad sighing of the breeze through the Stone pines that clothed the slopes of the island. These background sounds, he thought, would now remind him for ever of the time Cassandra Greenwood had invaded his personal space. It would always feel a little poorer, lonelier, for her absence.

He watched her chest rise on a deep breath. She shut down the computer and flipped the lid closed.

'A break?' Her brows contracted together. 'Are you saying you want me to leave? Because I'm leaving tomorrow. But if there's a flight, I could get it tonight, I could…'

'No. No, that's not what I'm saying. Unless you want to leave, of course… I wouldn't want to force you.'

'Force me to stay, or force me to leave?' He saw a flicker of uncertainty in her eyes, and in the way her teeth closed over her full lower lip.

'Neither, Cassandra. I know you don't like…that is, I know you like to make your own decisions, or at least discuss options.' He ran his hand over his jaw, wondering how he'd got into this discussion when all he'd wanted—*needed*—was the chance to try to get his reactions to her under control.

'How do you know that?' She picked up the pencil she'd been using earlier and tapped it on the glass tabletop. 'Has Nick said something?' Suspicion edged her voice.

'Nick? No, not at all. Besides, I promised you I wouldn't discuss anything that affects you, without your participation. Didn't I?'

She nodded. 'Yes. But that doesn't mean…'

'It means I wouldn't. I've told you before that I don't break promises.'

Cassandra folded her arms across her chest. He noticed the tips of her fingernails whiten with the pressure put on her upper arms. He remembered how his hands had circled them in that exact spot, and how fragile, yet strong, she'd felt.

Perhaps that was the essence of her. She was strong, forthright, determined, principled, but all those good traits hid a fragility which she was at pains to keep covered up.

'I want to believe you,' she said, 'but I don't find it easy.'

The breeze off the sea lifted the hem of her skirt and she smoothed it down, trapping it with both hands. A glossy lock of her hair, dark against the ivory skin of her cheek, whipped across her face and Matheo, without thinking, reached out and smoothed it away, tucking it behind her ear.

She tensed and moved away from him, and he dropped his hand.

'Has someone,' he asked gently, 'made it difficult for you to believe, in the past?'

She was silent for a beat. Then she nodded, once.

'Yes. He promised he'd... he said things would be better...if I did as he wanted, but...' She shook her head. 'I don't need... you don't need to know about it.'

'I think I'd like to, though. If you want to tell me.'

'It's over. I've dealt with it. But sometimes, when I'm feeling unsure about something, or unhappy, there're things I can't cope with. I panic if I feel trapped or threatened.'

'So the past year has been difficult for you. You were fighting a battle you must have known you couldn't win. You were on your own, with the weight of responsibility for the Hideaway staff on your shoulders. And then, when you'd made the most difficult decision of your life, possibly, I came along and forced you to make an even more difficult one. Is that about right?'

Cassandra nodded, biting her lip again, her eyes fixed on the sea below them.

'When my mother was ill, my father promised he'd make her better. He really believed he could do it if he tried hard enough. I don't think he was at all prepared when she died. I certainly wasn't. All I could think of was he'd promised, and the promise was broken.' She unfolded her arms and lifted the heavy skein of her hair off her neck, pulling the plait over her shoulder and twisting it in her hands. 'Then he seemed to pretend that she hadn't died at all. Everything had to be kept exactly as it was, as if he expected her to walk in the door at any moment. That was even more confusing.'

'I'm sure he didn't intend to make things worse for you. He was locked in grief from which he seemed to have no escape. I saw that for myself. Did he ever accept her loss, do you think?'

'No. I don't think he ever came close to acceptance. He was on medication for depression, but he needed more help than that. The only reason I managed to go away to college was because I knew the staff would care for him. They did, so you see why I owed them a debt. Then, in my first job, I met Jason. I was flattered by his attention. It was a relief to find someone who would care for me for a change. And he did, for a while.'

Matheo could see where this story was going and already felt angry. 'Only then you found his care came with a hefty price tag. Is that it?'

'Mmm. He was very good at withholding affection and approval unless I did as he demanded. I understand now that it was emotional blackmail and coercion, but when you're in the middle of something like that it's not easy to see, or accept, what it is.'

He clenched his fists and felt his jaw tighten, fury at the unknown man boiling through his veins. 'Bastard,' he grated.

Her quick glance was surprised. 'It's ok. I ended it. His fury when I refused to move in with him was off the scale and it made me afraid of him. Luckily, I got away. I had to change jobs because we worked for the same company, but that turned out to be a positive thing. I met Nick and we started Future-Plan, and...'

'And Nick?'

'Nick understands. He encouraged me to see a therapist. He knows what situations I find stressful and helps me to manage them positively, rather than by avoidance. Like staying here to work with you. I felt as if I had no control, that the decision had been made for me, by you, because it was what you wanted. Leaving would have been avoiding dealing with my reaction. Nick helped me to get it into proportion and to allow me to control my anxiety.'

Matheo drew in a long breath. He'd been avoiding his next question for days, because he was afraid of her answer, but he knew he had to ask it now.

'Are you and Nick…partners on any other level? Is that why he understands you so well?'

'No.' She looked up at him. 'It's strictly business and friendship between us. Nick is married. To Dan. He's a lawyer.'

Matheo released the breath he hadn't realised he'd been holding and breathed out his tension. He hadn't wanted to ask about her relationship with Nick because he didn't want it to look as if he cared.

It seemed that he cared, a lot.

Cassandra dropped her bag, stripped off the linen dress and pulled on her bikini and silk kaftan. Then she headed out onto the veranda, grateful for the shade and for the cool sea breeze, which stirred in the muslin curtains behind her.

She sat on the top step and looked across the beach to the sea. She should message Matheo now, before she could overthink this. She'd tell him she had to leave today.

But when she picked up her phone she remembered the expression in his eyes when he thought he was hiding it. He'd looked stricken when she'd suggested she could bring forward her departure and, in that instant, before he'd dropped his gaze, she'd glimpsed his loneliness.

They'd both lost people they'd loved. She had lost her parents and her home, and his mother had died and he was estranged from his father. The close, loving relationship she'd enjoyed with her parents meant she could not imagine the torment it must cause him, whatever the reasons behind it.

She'd navigated grief and despair with help from caring

friends and her therapist, but Matheo had retreated to this island, where, except for his attentive staff, he was alone. He seemed to have no support network.

But she couldn't allow sympathy to colour her judgement. She'd worked hard to shed the negative influences of her toxic relationship with Jason. She mostly felt comfortable with how she coped with the world.

She was in danger of jeopardising that.

Being near Matheo was becoming increasingly difficult. She reminded herself, repeatedly, that he was a Chevalier and therefore never to be trusted, but that thread, which had first tugged them towards each other fourteen years ago, still stretched between them, pulling at her each time they met. She was sure he felt it, too.

In the darkened conference room, she'd experienced a moment of madness when she longed for him to touch her, to make her feel cherished and special. To have him show he cared for her, just for a minute. She'd stood firmly on her own feet for so long, steering clear of any emotional involvement or physical contact with anyone else, and sometimes it became exhausting.

She'd shoved her treacherous feelings aside and leaned away from him, putting a few more inches of physical distance between them. He was the most important client they'd ever had. He was the billionaire every company hoped to attract. Somehow, she and Nick had caught a lucky star, and she felt as if she was about to destroy it.

Because anything apart from a strict business relationship between them would be a disaster, professionally and personally. Mixing business and pleasure never worked.

They'd signed the contract and so she had made up her mind to trust him on a professional level. Trusting him on a personal level, with her emotions, was a different thing altogether.

He bore a destructive grudge against his father, which he refused to discuss. How could she ever trust someone who wished their own father ill?

Never, was the answer. This was reckless physical desire, nothing more. It came from spending too much time together, in a romantic and exotic location, finding qualities in each other they'd each thought the other lacked, and discovering a shared passion for beauty and sustainability in the built and natural environment.

But none of these logical arguments could stop her from feeling herself light up each time she saw him. Neither could they take away the longing to experience the brush of his lips on her cheek again, or his steady hands on her arms, holding her upright in the cold sea.

All this meant she really should leave this evening, even if she had to spend the night at a hotel at Nice Airport. She'd be safe there, from Matheo and, most of all, from herself.

He'd suggested meeting again at five o'clock. She'd tell him then that she had to leave.

At a minute to five Cassandra came walking towards him where he waited at the foot of the steps. She stopped and he saw a flash of confusion cross her features before her gaze narrowed. Both her hands curled around the strap of her satchel.

'What's happening, Matheo?' Her eyes travelled over him. 'I thought we were having a meeting.'

He glanced down at his board shorts and bare feet. 'We're not having a meeting. We're having a picnic.'

CHAPTER TWELVE

ALLOWING HIM TO bring her to this secluded place had been all kinds of foolish. But he'd looked so relaxed—and *pleased*—when he'd announced the picnic she hadn't wanted to refuse. Most of all, she hadn't been able to say what she should have said. The faint lines of anxiety, an almost permanent fixture on the handsome planes of his face, had softened with his smile. Turning down the invitation to accompany him would have felt childish. Telling him she wanted to return to the main-land, to spend the night in an airport hotel, would have felt massively ungrateful.

But now she regretted the way she'd followed him through the trees to the jetty without a murmur.

At the end of the beach, smooth boulders tumbled haphaz-ardly into the turquoise water. The tide, slight as it was in the Mediterranean, must be coming in because the line of her foot-prints, pressed into the pristine sand, were already blurred by the push and pull of rippling water. Slanting sunlight feathered through the branches of the tall pines that fringed the cove.

The sleek silver and white boat bobbed in the shallow water, its anchor rope slack. They had skimmed over the glassy sea, the wind in their faces, until Matheo had throttled back the engine and spun the wheel, turning in to where this crescent of sand curved between two headlands. She could see he'd spread out a rug and carried a picnic basket ashore. She heard the muted pop of a champagne cork.

'What are we celebrating?' she called as she made her way back towards him.

He handed her a flute of fizz and gestured to their surroundings. 'Let's just settle for being here.' He took a mouthful of champagne. 'Do you like it?'

She nodded, sipping from her glass. 'It's...beautiful, yes. Remote.'

'It's my favourite place on the island. Probably in the world. It's where I find true peace and quiet.'

'And solitude?'

'That too.' His brows drew together. 'Do you have a favourite place?'

Cassandra bit her lip, unwilling to spoil the moment.

'Do you need to ask?'

His frown deepened. 'I'm sorry. That was a thoughtless question.'

'Yes, perhaps.' She shrugged. 'But over the past few days, working with you, it's begun to feel less...*raw*. It helps, knowing I have a say in how it's going to be and knowing how closely your ideas match my own. In an odd way it feels as if I'm preparing the Hideaway for the future, a new lease of life, rather than losing it.'

'I'm glad. That makes me feel less guilty for being the one to take your home from you.'

She sat down, her legs folded under her. 'I've been working all day...'

'You've been working all week. I decided it was time for a break.'

'*You* decided, huh?'

She saw the implication of her words register, and she smiled.

'I'm sorry. I should have checked with you first…are you teasing me?'

'Just a little. I'm happy to take a break. And I love picnics.'

'I also wanted to show you more of St Celeste. You can't leave tomorrow without seeing some of it.'

They ate tiny, juicy tomatoes dipped in humous, and spicy sliced salami. There was French bread to soak up fruity olive oil and salty olives stuffed with almonds. The chef had sliced ripe peaches into a dish of raspberry coulis, and as Cassandra licked peach juice off her fingers she rolled her eyes.

'Delicious.' She held out the bowl for him. 'Have some.'

Matheo removed his shades and his iron-dark eyes fixed on her mouth. Her heart lurched as he reached towards her, but he was offering her a paper napkin.

'You have juice on your chin.'

His voice was as smooth and dark as good chocolate. The brush of his fingers as she took the napkin sent a shiver rippling through her.

This was why she should have left.

Her defences against this pull between them, which grew tighter and more intense each time they met, were crumbling. It was wrong and unfaithful of her to feel this way. Matheo and his family stood for everything her father and her ancestors had fought against and loathed, and to betray them was unthinkable. And her determined belief in her own strength and resilience could be shattered.

She shuffled a little further away from him, out of his reach.

'Tell me more about the island. Has it belonged to your family for decades?'

Matheo drained his glass and tucked it into the basket. He rested his elbows on his bent knees and looked beyond Cassandra towards the sea. His eyes, hard as flint, had lost their smile.

'The island,' he said, 'does not belong to my family. It belongs to me. I bought it. I developed the buildings. I decide who visits.' His implacable gaze shifted and connected with hers. 'And the guestlist no longer includes my family. Not ever.'

The tension radiating from him made the air between them snap.

'Ah, so that's an awkward subject,' she ventured. 'You've mentioned the rift…'

She'd never heard a laugh more dry or devoid of humour. She wanted to reach out to him; to somehow dispel the anger and stress in his tense muscles, to soften his rigid mouth, bring that warm flame of emotion back into his eyes, but she felt afraid of what her touch might unleash. 'Matheo…'

He stopped her with a quick shake of his head. 'A rift.' He seemed to taste the word to try it out. 'That's a…tidy…word for the explosion that ripped my life apart.' He pulled a hand across his face.

Silence stretched between them, marked by the rhythmic wash and suck of the sea and the sudden, restless shushing of a sunset breeze in the trees.

She picked up the spoon with which she'd eaten the peaches and rubbed a thumb over the smooth silver handle. Its curve was a comforting shape.

'Do you want to tell me why you've gone to such insane lengths to settle a score with your father? Because I don't understand how…'

'Of course you don't understand.' His hands were bunched into fists, his knuckles gleaming white beneath the stretched skin. 'How could you?'

'I thought you'd bought the Hideaway on behalf of your father. I hope, now that you've thwarted his plans to own it, you feel better. Perhaps you'll be able to let go.'

He glanced across at her, shaking his head.

'I thought it would make me feel better too, but it hasn't. My father…betrayed me…and nothing I can do is going to repair the damage. There's nothing he can do, either. Not any more.'

'Do you want to tell me about it?'

'I've told you before, it's a personal matter. I do not discuss it.'

Cassandra's heart fell as she realised he was not going to break the silence that held his pain captive. His expression had closed down. The iron-cold remoteness of his eyes told her she was pushing against a wall which would never give way. She tried one last tactic.

'Is it,' she asked softly, 'about your mother?'

The breeze ruffled across the water and she shivered, wrapping her arms around herself.

'You're cold. We should head back.' He reached into the bag and pulled out a beach towel. 'I brought these in case we went for a swim.'

'Thank you. And I'm sorry I asked about your mother.'

He shook his head, flicking his hair off his forehead.

'That's okay. It's not about her, although, looking back, my father's treatment of her was enough to cause me to hate him. At the time I was too young to realise.'

Cassandra pulled the towel around her shoulders, tucking up her knees and feet. 'What happened, Matheo?'

'Her illness was kept quiet. I was shocked and completely unprepared for her death. Rather like you.'

'No.' Cassandra shook her head. 'I knew my mother was ill. I just believed she'd get better.'

'I was sent to boarding school the week after she died. Crying was considered babyish, and grief was seen as self-pity. I learned to bury my emotions and I learned to defend myself against the bullying. Eventually I was expelled, for breaking one nose too many.' He smiled. 'I considered that achievement to be the greatest of my school career. Obviously, I was sent to another school, but my reputation preceded me and I was left alone. I was a little disappointed. I had so much anger to get rid of.'

'So you've never had any help, dealing with the loss of your mother?'

'None. It was as if she simply hadn't existed. A few years ago, I managed to find out where she was buried but I'd never been able to face visiting her grave. Not until a couple of weeks ago.'

Cassandra thought back to where he would have been.

'Was that after you left Cornwall?'

He nodded. 'I was on my way back here. It was our meeting in the churchyard that prompted me. I've arranged for her grave to be properly tended now.'

Cassandra wanted to put her arms around him to comfort him, but she stayed wrapped in the towel a safe distance away.

'That is such an important and special thing to have done,' she whispered. 'You must feel good about it.'

'Yes, surprisingly, I do. Would you... I thought about doing the same for your parents, but I knew I should ask you first, if I saw you again.'

There was a long silence while Cassandra considered his offer; thought about the kindness behind the suggestion. Then she shook her head.

'That is one of the kindest offers I've had for a long time, but at the moment... I'll need to think about it for a bit. With our history...it might feel inappropriate.'

'Of course. I understand. But if you should change your mind, let me know.' He stood up in a supple movement, holding out a hand towards her. 'We should be getting back. We'll catch the last of the sunset from the water if we hurry.'

Cassandra accepted his hand and he pulled her to her feet.

Their shoulders collided and he moved away but kept her hand gripped in his.

'Come on. I'll take you to the boat. We don't want you falling over in the sea.'

Matheo leaned against the balustrade, swirling amber whisky in a heavy glass tumbler. He'd been for a run, trying in vain to dispel some of his pent-up frustration. A cold shower afterwards hadn't helped, either. His board shorts and T-shirt clung to his damp skin because he'd been too agitated to dry himself properly. He'd resorted to a bottle of his favourite malt, hoping a measure of the smoky spirit would calm him.

Images of Cassandra were running on a loop in his brain and it was driving him insane.

He'd come close, so terrifyingly close, to cracking and telling her what his father had done. Just thinking about it made him feel vulnerable and small. He'd never talk about it. He'd made that decision two years ago. If he did, he'd hand the control of it to someone else. As long as he kept it screwed down tight, he'd have it under control himself.

Cassandra made him softer. He could feel some of the tension he held in his body melt away every time he came close to her. It wasn't just her calming scent; that was tantalising enough. It was her aura of kindness and concern for others, her sympathetic, deep blue eyes, her sparkling enthusiasm for the work she did which entranced him. She should hate him, but she'd been able to turn those negative emotions into a positive vision for the future. She should resent her father and the failing business he'd bequeathed her, but she didn't, making allowances for him instead, and spending her trust fund on paying the staff. He wished he could allow himself to absorb just a fraction of her open-hearted, warm spirit.

Surely he'd feel less bitter if he could. But what if that bitterness had become so much a part of him that he could never shake it off? Buying the Hideaway had not given him the resolution he'd expected. What if he always felt there was another score to settle with his father?

It was a bleak thought.

He pushed himself upright and turned, intending to top up his drink, but a movement on the beach caught his eye. He looked again. Cassandra was walking across the sand towards the seashore. Under the moon, the scene was a monochrome study in silver and black, and her limbs glowed pale in the un-earthly light. She'd released her hair to let it flow around her face and down her back in a shimmering black mass, and she'd replaced the linen dress with the silk top she'd worn last night. It blew softly around her thighs, catching points of moonshine as she moved. She was gaining speed with every step.

Matheo watched, fascinated, memory tugging at his consciousness. As she reached the point where the ripples of water spent themselves into nothing on the sand, she pulled the top over her head. He thought she was wearing a bikini but it might have been underwear. She spread her arms wide and turned in a circle and threw back her head. Then she began to dance in and out of the shallow water, her feet skipping over the little foam-crested waves, twirling and dipping in a rhythm of her own making. He'd defy anyone who didn't know better not to believe they were seeing some ethereal sea nymph emerging from the water to dance for the sea gods.

And then the jagged pieces of memory that were rattling around in his brain started to fall, one at a time, into place. He was twenty-five again and back on a beach in Cornwall. He'd walked away from the furious argument raging between his father and Joe Greenwood and found his way to the beach. He was supposed to be backing his father up, providing the supporting arguments to his bid for the hotel, but he'd had no stomach for it.

Raw grief had permeated every corner of the place, and a kind of desperation informed every word Joe spoke—or, rather, shouted. Matheo had been stopped in his tracks by the sheer, unfathomable depth of sorrow that gaped in front of him whichever way he turned. He'd wondered how the loss of a single life could cause such an explosion of despair. He'd tried in vain to persuade his father to give up, go away, and leave these people to their overwhelming sadness.

The girl, who'd been a footnote to the few days they'd spent there, was on the beach.

He'd struck up a tenuous connection with her, once she'd realised he meant no harm and did not want to talk about the Hideaway. He'd had the feeling she hadn't talked to anyone else for weeks. She embodied his idea of a sprite, quick and elusive, disappearing among the rocks if he asked the wrong question or got too close.

He'd stood very still and watched as she danced in and out of the waves, lifting her skirt clear of the water, her long bare legs flashing in the low afternoon sun. Her hair blew out behind her in a tangled mass of curls, which looked as if they hadn't seen a brush or comb for weeks. For the first time in days, Matheo had felt a lifting of the gloom that sat, heavy as a storm cloud, over the hunched old building on the hill above them. He'd stepped forward and called her name.

She'd stopped, head turned towards him, standing stock still, and he remembered, suddenly and vividly, how the next wave had washed around her calves, catching the drooping hem of her skirt. And then she'd gathered it and taken to her heels, running like a deer through the shallow water towards the rocks at the far end of the beach. But the wet fabric had tangled around her legs, and she'd tripped...

By the time he'd reached her she was stumbling to her knees, pushing her hair out of her eyes.

'Let me help you… I'm sorry I surprised you. You don't need to be afraid.' He'd lifted her out of the shallow water, his hands around her upper arms, holding her as gently as he could. 'It's okay. I won't hurt you.' Instinctively, he'd spoken softly, anxious not to scare her.

She'd swayed towards him as she tried to regain her balance and looked up at him. He was captivated by her eyes, fringed with thick dark lashes, and her full lower lip, and for a fleeting second he'd thought he was going to kiss her. He'd dropped his head and slid one hand to the small of her back, knowing it was wrong but not knowing if he could resist her. He'd felt her stiffen and then she broke away from him and ran.

'No! Wait!' he'd called, but he might as well have been calling the wind. She'd reached the end of the beach and scrambled over the rocks, which the cliff had scattered into the sea, and by the time he got to them there was no trace of her. She'd vanished into thin air.

And then, just a few weeks ago, she'd slithered down that stepladder, into his arms. But he'd known all along that beneath the business reasons for his visit to the Hideaway had been the hope that she'd be there.

Now here she was, dancing on *his* beach this time. She was grown up, successful and self-confident but still wild when she allowed herself to be. He was through the door and halfway down the stairs before he realised what he was doing.

Cass shivered as the water swirled around her ankles, but she soon forgot its chill as sheer exhilaration seized her. How long was it since she'd danced on the beach? She couldn't remember, but the release it brought her was as clear in her mind as if it were yesterday. It had started when she was a baby. Her mother had danced in and out of the waves with Cass in her arms, and it had continued ever since. It was the best stress-buster she knew, and the best way to forget the bad times and revel in the good ones, however meagre they seemed.

She lost all track of time but eventually she paused, breathless, with the waves washing around her knees, and then she sank down into the silky water. She rolled onto her back and gazed up at the night sky.

She'd needed this, to break the tension that had thrummed through her ever since Matheo had taken her hand on the beach. The desire to turn into him, against his wide chest, to wrap them both in the towel he'd given her and just be with him, skin to skin, for a few seconds had been powerful. Resisting it had taken huge determination and she'd had to find a way to reset herself.

The sea had always been her place of solace and it had done its work.

She felt cleansed and refreshed as she picked her way back across the beach. The night breeze raised goose-bumps on her wet skin as she mounted the shallow steps onto the terrace.

A shadow detached itself from the darkness by the wall. She stopped, panting slightly, an arm's length from where Matheo stood. She was ready for anything.

Anything but this.

Silence, taut as a bowstring, stretched between them. He broke it first. 'Are you alright?'

'I'm fine. Thank you.'

It sounded abrupt but it was the truth.

'You must be a little cold. I brought a towel.'

He stepped forward and dropped a warm towel around her shoulders.

'Have you been watching me?'

'I have.'

'Why?'

She clutched the towel at her neck, wanting very much to get past him.

'I saw you from the terrace. It reminded me of seeing you dance on the beach in Cornwall.'

'Really?' She laughed. 'That's a bit unlikely.'

'Not recently. Years ago. When my father and I were there.'

Cass stiffened.

The memory, which had been flitting in and out of her brain for the past few weeks, suddenly became more tangible. Running down the beach, away from him. Tripping in the water. The feel of his hands on her arms, and that overwhelming desire to sink against him. To let him carry her burdens. Hearing her name called on the wind, but keeping on running...

'Oh!' she exclaimed, exhaling sharply. '*That* time.'

He moved aside so she could cross the threshold and followed her, putting his hand out to flick the light switch.

'I'm going to have a shower. I need to warm up. You can go, now you know I'm okay.'

Her throat felt tight and narrow and forming the words was a strain.

'I'll wait.'

'What for?'

She was avoiding his eyes, but that meant she was looking at the rest of him, and not finding any bit of him wanting. The neck of his T-shirt revealed tanned skin stretching over the tips of his collarbones, and she wanted, urgently, to bury her face there and breathe him in.

Finally, unavoidably, their eyes collided and the shock of what she saw in his made her try to step back. He felt the chemistry fizzing between them. He knew she felt it too and he was as out of control of it as she was. She swayed slightly, off balance, and felt his hand on her shoulder, steadying her.

'I need to apologise. I spoke harshly earlier.'

'What?' Her voice caught in her impeded throat, surprise blurring her reason. 'I thought you never made mistakes.'

'I don't know where you got that idea. I've made plenty, and at least one of them has been...catastrophic.'

'Matheo, I'm not comfortable with this.'

'Let me help you, then.'

'I didn't mean the towel.'

But his other hand had come up to where she was clutching the towel and was peeling her fingers away from it. It slipped to the floor, leaving her in the soaked bikini, which stuck to her body in dark wetness. She shivered as he slid a hand around the back of her head, tangling his fingers in her hair and pulling her towards him.

She knew she shouldn't, but she wanted this, more than she ever remembered wanting anything. She was drowning in the black depths of his eyes, losing all sense of time and space as his other hand came up to trap hers against him.

'I shouldn't want this...'

'Why not?'

'Do we even *like* each other?'

The first light, sure touch of his lips silenced her. Then he lifted his head and pulled her in, running his hands down her back, over her bottom. He pressed her pliancy against the rigidity of his body, bracing her against his rock-hard thighs and easing her head back to expose her throat. She felt his cool, dry lips touch the place there where her pulse beat, and then trace a path upwards to claim her mouth again.

This time there was no question of holding back. As his tongue parted the seam of her lips and invaded her mouth any resistance melted into a pool of pure, unfamiliar desire. Her arms went around his neck, pulling him down to deepen the kiss, kissing him back with a desperation bordering on insanity. Her body leapt in response as his hands travelled over her, and she pushed her own hands beneath his shirt, revelling in the feel of the hot silk of his skin shivering under her touch.

He was demolishing her defences and she was letting him do it, telling herself it was just this once. He made her body sing and her mind reel but tomorrow she'd leave and return to real life, where billionaire clients did not desire women like her, with control hang-ups and wild urges to dance in the sea.

She took a ragged breath as he gently nipped her bottom lip and then ran his tongue down her neck to the acutely sensitive hollow of her shoulder, and then she groaned in protest as he raised his head and rested his cheek against her hair, trapping her hands in his to stop their exquisite exploration of his body.

'I'm sorry. I didn't mean this to happen.'

Finally, her breathing quick and shallow, she got to bury her face in his chest and absorb the scent of him. She filled her lungs with it, concentrating hard, determined to remember it, because she knew this was never going to happen again. She felt his strong, capable hands smoothing her hair, caressing her back, and thought shakily that he didn't need to apologise for making her feel so amazing.

'Two apologies, Matheo, in quick succession,' she heard herself saying. 'But it's all right. I'm okay. I wanted this, very much.'

She was far from okay, because she wanted to stay here, in the circle of his arms, for ever, to kiss him again and to see what would happen after that. If he would hold her and help to satisfy the ache of longing which had started up in her heart, nothing else mattered. She shook her head against him, her lips brushing his skin, and she felt his abrupt intake of breath. Then he put firm hands on her shoulders and forced a small gap between them. 'Your shirt's wet,' she said shakily, glancing down.

'Small price.'

He wrapped his arms around her again and touched his forehead to hers.

'Cassandra?'

'Mmm...?'

'Stay.'

Her eyes, which had drifted closed, flew open.

'What?'

'Stay. Here with me, on St Celeste. We work well together, and we could explore...this thing between us. I think you've known for as long as I have that it exists.'

She nodded slowly, her eyes fixed on his.

'Yes. It exists. But we don't have to give in to it. It—this—feels amazing, but... I can't stay, Matheo.' She dropped her head onto his shoulder, inhaling his clean, soapy scent. 'I was going to tell you I wanted to leave this afternoon, but then you'd organised the picnic. I needed to go, to protect myself, and now I think I should have. But I wanted to be with you too.'

He shifted his stance, pulling her closer.

'Protect yourself from me? Cassandra, I'd never hurt you, or make you do anything you don't want.'

'Mostly from myself. Because I want you but I have to go back to London soon. And what would happen then? Perhaps you'd be okay with a no-strings fling, but I can't do that. I've worked hard to make myself strong, and I can't risk it.'

'Do you think you'll ever feel strong enough?'

'I don't think I'll know unless I meet someone who makes me feel...safe, through trust.'

'How do I make you feel?'

'Excited, crazy...impulsive, inspired. All dangerous.'

He put his hands on her shoulders and eased her further away from him.

'I'm glad you didn't leave this afternoon because then we

wouldn't have had this.' He dropped a kiss on her hair. 'You're right about me. I'm not the person you should trust with your emotions. But I think spending time with you has made me a better person. Less bad, anyway.'

Cassandra shook her head. 'No, Matheo. You're not bad. Don't think that of yourself. You had a traumatic childhood and something terrible has happened between you and your father...'

'Not that different from you, but you're positive, caring and warm. Everyone loves you.'

He turned her towards the bathroom door.

'You're shivering. Go and get warmed up.'

Cassandra stripped off her bikini and stood under the shower, turning the heat up as high as she could bear and staying until her teeth stopped chattering and she'd stopped shivering.

He was gone when she came out of the bathroom. She dried her hair roughly and climbed into bed, but she knew she could give up on sleep before she'd even tried. She was wired up and stressed and her body was in crazy overdrive, demanding something which she couldn't deliver. If this was desire, it was dangerous as hell. No wonder lust was a deadly sin.

CHAPTER THIRTEEN

'I DON'T AGREE with you, Nick.' Cassandra watched Nick twirl a pencil through his fingers in a complicated series of moves. 'And is that pencil actually an extension of your hand?'

Nick smiled. 'Don't change the subject. It won't work with me. It's rare that we don't agree on something, but this time I'm going to insist that I'm right.'

'But I got the trip to St Celeste. I lived in a bubble of luxury for five days—a whole working week. It's your turn. You should be the one to go to the conference.'

'Yes, a whole working week, and judging by the times at which some of your emails dropped into my inbox, you worked many more hours than in a normal week.'

Cass flicked her gaze away from his. 'Yes, we... I...did. But it didn't feel like work, in such a beautiful place, and Matheo and I...'

Nick waited. She wished she hadn't mentioned Matheo by name. She'd been careful to do that as little as possible, referring to him as 'Mr Chevalier' or 'the client'. Nick would have noticed that. And now he'd notice the silence. She rushed to fill it.

'We connected, on a professional level. It was easier than I thought it would be.'

'Good, because I did worry about you travelling out there on your own, to deal with such an established adversary. It's good you managed to put your differences aside and make progress on the project.' He tapped the end of the pencil on the table. 'The groundwork you did has been invaluable. Even if it apparently exhausted you.'

Cassandra opened her mouth to protest, but he held up a hand.

'You've looked tired and stressed ever since you returned… how many weeks ago? And you've lost weight.'

'That's from all the manual labour I did at the Hideaway. Who knew polishing floors and nailing slates onto a roof in a force-eight gale was such good exercise?'

'So I think you deserve a break. The conference in Dubai will be a blast. Have you been there?'

'No, but…'

'Well, then, that's decided. You need to see some of the incredible architecture, and there are interiors which defy description. You have to be there.'

'The Hideaway project—'

'Is going well. We're on schedule and there's no reason why you can't be away for a few days. You'll need to promote the company, at the exhibition, using the Sandpiper as an example of our latest success. And there's a gala reception, which will be a brilliant opportunity to meet people from across the globe and spread the message about FuturePlan.' He sent her a 'no arguments' look. 'And have some fun while you're there. Play the tourist. There's loads to see.'

Cassandra stood at the floor-to-ceiling window of her luxury room in one of the tallest hotels in the world and snapped a picture of the view on her phone. She sent it to Nick and added 'Thank you!' She knew he'd get the message she was trying to send.

She felt truly grateful to him for insisting she take this opportunity. The vibrancy and colour of the city and culture were so utterly different from Cornwall, London and, she dared herself to think, St Celeste that she'd been shaken out of herself by a host of new experiences. In between the morning and evening sessions at the exhibition centre, she'd braved the heat, still intense in September, and followed Nick's advice, and the previous two days had passed in a blur.

She'd been on a helicopter tour of the city and ridden a camel in the desert. She'd eaten dates and drunk thick, sweet coffee in a cavernous traditional tent, and raced over dunes and through wadis in a convoy of rugged four-by-four vehicles.

She'd chugged across the creek on an *abbra*, a traditional water taxi, past wharfs lined with dhows being loaded in preparation for voyages across the Arabian Sea. The labyrinth of lamplit alleys, which made up the old souk, had drawn her in with its scuffing of sandalled feet, and glimpses of bright silks worn by the women beneath their traditional black abayas.

The aroma of every spice in the world rose tantalisingly from the bags of vibrant powders and bunches of dried leaves and flowers, bringing to her a sudden sharp longing for India. The gold souk, with its wall-to-wall displays of intricate, bright jewellery and ropes of gleaming pearls, had left her speechless.

The heady scents of frankincense and myrrh still seemed to swirl about her as she tried to pull her attention back to where she stood.

She felt alive and carefree, for the first time for as long as she could remember, and she was looking forward to the gala reception in a few hours' time.

Nick pinged back a smiley face and a thumbs-up and she retreated to the bathroom to get ready.

The dress had been a perfect fit when she'd fallen in love with the lilacshot-silk fabric and bought it to wear to a charity ball a couple of years before. It was a little loose now, she thought, admitting that Nick was right about her weight loss. But the sculpted bodice still shaped her curves as the skirt flared over her hips and down to the floor in a shimmering sweep. She twisted to see the back and suddenly hoped it wasn't too daringly low.

'Too late,' she muttered. She had nothing else suitable. She clipped her amethyst pendant, inherited from her grandmother, around her neck and made sure the little sparkly clips that held her hair in place were secure. Then she threw an intricately embroidered shawl, which she'd bought in the souk, around her shoulders.

Outside her room, the passage curved towards the bank of lifts, the view down into the vast atrium unfolding as she walked. She was looking down at the throng of glamorous guests parading across the marble floor, far below, when the lift pinged behind her.

'Mon Dieu!'

She swung round, startled eyes flying wide at the achingly familiar, deep voice.

'Matheo…?' His name came out in a whisper, forcing itself past her constricted throat, shock and panic instantly racing through her, pumping adrenaline into her veins. She stood, frozen, unmoving, transfixed by his deep eyes, grey as a stormy sea.

The lift doors began to slide but he put out a hand to keep them open. Then, with the other hand, he reached for her, cupped her elbow, and drew her into the space beside him.

The doors closed on a soft, vacuum sigh.

Matheo seemed to fill the space. His dinner jacket fitted so well, so *perfectly*, across those powerful shoulders and biceps. A black silk bow tie contrasted with the dazzling white of his cotton shirtfront, and a black satin cummerbund defined rather than disguised a washboard abdomen. She stared at him, her brain frozen, as the lift began its descent.

* * *

Matheo dropped his hand and stepped back. Shock made him doubt he was seeing correctly. Had his incessant thoughts of Cassandra finally tricked his mind into conjuring her up in front of him? When the doors opened and he stepped out into the ballroom, would she fade away into the ether, leaving her tantalising scent lingering on the warm air?

But she was breathing, quick and shallow, as colour suffused cheeks which at first had faded to a deathly pale.

He kept his distance. He couldn't trust himself to touch her again, even though he wanted to make sure she was not a figment of his overactive imagination. He looked past her, only to be met with the dozens of images of her cool radiance reflected in the mirrored walls. He cursed inwardly. Whose appalling idea had it been to fit lifts with mirrors?

'Cassandra?' He had barely allowed himself to think her name, let alone say it out loud, since he'd guided her, shivering in her wet bikini, into the bathroom on St Celeste and closed the door behind her. The word sounded alien to him. 'Cass? How…? What are you doing here?'

'I…'

Her throat moved convulsively as she tried to speak and he saw the sparkle of an amethyst lying against her alabaster skin.

'Of course,' he said, 'an amethyst is the perfect jewel for you.'

'Thank you.' She nodded. 'I'm promoting the Sandpiper.'

What banal conversation, he thought, aware that the lift was sinking steadily, the numbers above the door counting down. He wanted it to stop. He had the insane thought that there might be a 'pause' button he could press, so he could be with her, alone, long enough to say something meaningful rather than comment stupidly on her jewellery.

But he remembered how she might react to that. She might

panic, feel trapped in a situation over which she had no control. He'd never do that to her. He wanted her to trust him.

'I arrived a few hours ago,' he said. 'It's the one conference I force myself to attend. I come for the networking at the gala and meetings over the next few days.'

She nodded, adjusting the shawl she had wrapped around her shoulders. He longed to see beyond it. Did her gown cover her shoulders? She looked thinner. He could see a more pronounced hollow than he remembered where her skin stretched over her delicate collarbones.

'How…how have you been?' He meant so much more than that. Did she think of him the way he thought of her? In other words, most of the time? Had she missed their easy exchange of ideas about buildings, interiors and every other subject under the Mediterranean sun? Had she been back to Cornwall, stood ankle-deep in the freezing sea and wondered where he was; what he was doing?

'Okay, thank you. The Hideaway project is going very well. It should open in time for Christmas.'

He didn't need to be told about the Hideaway. He kept track of that, minutely following every detail of the development, looking for signs of Cassandra, of her name, anywhere, of hints of things they'd discussed, decided, on St Celeste.

'Good,' was all he could conjure up as the lift came quietly to a stop and the doors opened.

Matheo stepped out and into a surging press of the global hotel trade's most glamorous and wealthy operators. This was why, he thought, he hated these occasions, but this time he had one good reason to be here. He paused to cast a glance over the glittering crowd surging through the marble and gold ballroom.

A step behind him he felt Cassandra hesitate.

She wouldn't like this, he realised. The noise, the hard, reflective surfaces, the lights, all contributed to an atmosphere that felt as if it teetered on the brink of chaos. He couldn't imagine anything further from the kind of ambience he knew she favoured. From working with her he'd learned to appreciate her love of deep, luxurious fabrics and rugs, the arrangement of furniture and placement of objects, which all contributed to the establishment of a calm, relaxed vibe, whether it was in a private study or a public reception room.

He glanced over his shoulder and saw her stop, her eyes wide and anxious, her hands tightening on the edges of her shawl. He took half a step back and turned slightly towards her.

'Will you be alright? If we move through this crowd there'll be more space, and I'll ask for the doors to the terrace to be opened if you like. You might be more comfortable out there.'

She nodded, her teeth nipping her bottom lip, but she didn't move. A few curious glances came their way. A photographer, obviously employed to document the event, snapped their picture. Matheo thought Cassandra was seconds from turning and fleeing back into the lift and he didn't want that. He wanted her by his side.

Trying to make the gesture as natural and casual as possible, he slipped an arm around her waist and gently urged her closer to him.

He couldn't have predicted that beneath the silky fall of the embroidered shawl he would find the naked skin of her back. His heart missed a beat.

Satiny skin shivered under the tips of his fingers. Just how low was the cut of her gown? he wondered, but he didn't explore to find out. He tried to control the hot spike of desire, which threatened to make him do or say something unacceptable. Her anxiety levels were already sky-high. A wrong move from him would definitely send her into retreat. He tightened his arm and bent to reassure her, desperate to keep her with him.

'You can do this, Cassandra. I promise I'll take care of you.'

She looked up at him and the anxiety faded from her ink-blue eyes. She nodded.

'I'm sorry. This crowd took me by surprise. I'll be okay now.'

As Matheo reluctantly dropped his hand from her back, she linked her fingers through his and they moved forward.

He felt her relax a little as they wove their way through the press of guests to a less crowded part of the vast room. Her grip on his fingers loosened and she slowed her pace, glancing round instead of keeping her gaze fixed on the floor. He was glad she'd regained her equilibrium. With a quick, light pressure on her fingers, he eased his hand from hers. He smiled down at her. 'Feeling better?' he murmured.

She gave a nod as he took two glasses of champagne from a passing waiter.

'Here's to our chance meeting.' He clinked his glass against hers and their eyes locked.

'Thank you for rescuing me, Matheo. I could have easily backed out and returned to my room.'

He inclined his head towards her.

'I could feel that, but it would be a pity to miss out on this gathering. If you want…'

He saw her face light up with the smile he wished was reserved only for him and she put her fingers on his jacket sleeve.

'Excuse me, Matheo. I've just spotted an acquaintance. I must say hello.'

She turned with a swish of silk and he watched her thread her way through the crowd. Groups of people had spilled out onto the terrace, enjoying the warm evening, but the level of noise hadn't lessened. Keeping his back to the wall, he tried to keep an eye on Cassandra.

Time dragged. Matheo made small talk with a few people he knew and many he didn't. Glancing at his watch, he wondered how soon he could leave without appearing rude. His eyes roved over the assembled glitterati. Cassandra was unknown in this crowd, and he saw the curiosity that her unselfconscious beauty provoked in both men and women. She was engaged in animated conversation with a world-renowned hotelier. The man was a notorious womaniser and Matheo's fingers tightened around the stem of his champagne flute. If he so much as touched her...

'Matheo. What a surprise! We weren't expecting to see you here.'

The huskiness of the voice had the cultivated falseness he remembered. He raised his head and met the appraising stare of his stepmother. It was difficult to think of her in those terms. She was the same age as him, for God's sake. The advantage of surprise brought a glitter of triumph to her eyes as her fingers closed around his forearm. He took in her tanned face and ice-blonde hair and her thin frame. Then he looked beyond her, searching for his father.

'Charles is somewhere here,' she said, with a flick of her head. 'Talking business, as usual.'

'Claudia.' To his surprise his voice sounded perfectly normal. 'That is to be expected at an industry event.' He wished she'd remove her hand from his arm. He felt a pressing need to shake her off.

'You're looking good, Matheo. We hear your new company is doing well.'

Her heavily made-up eyes swept over him. Was that an undercurrent of wistfulness? *Envy?*

'I'm very well. Hard work suits me.'

'Evidently. Your father will be surprised to see you. We hear you don't like leaving St Celeste these days.'

He flexed his shoulders. 'It's possible to work remotely. I have all the resources I need to run the business from there.'

She ran a pointed nail down his sleeve, slanting a look up at him.

'But surely it must be lonely?'

So that was where this was going. She was digging.

He glanced towards Cassandra. Her head was thrown back as she laughed at some comment her companion had made. The flawless amethyst glittered against her equally flawless skin as she put a long-fingered hand on the man's arm and turned towards Matheo.

A few strides would bring him to her side, but he held back, keeping his cool. She came towards him, lilac silk swishing softly around her hips, her eyes sparkling with amusement.

'Matheo, I must introduce you…'

The words died on her lips. Confusion flashed in her eyes as she saw Claudia. For a second her step faltered. He was sure he only noticed because he was so absolutely attuned to her every movement. Her eyes engaged with his and he read a question in their depths.

Who is this?

There was a subtle change in her demeanour. Her smile became formal, her eyes watchful.

'Matt, let me introduce you to Kristof.'

Matt. The intimacy of the abbreviation of his name slammed into his chest, almost robbing him of the ability to breathe. He put out his hand to greet the older man, shooting him a direct look.

Hands off.

'Kristof. It's been a while.' His gaze shifted back to Cassandra. 'We've known each other a long time. Watch him. He's a devil with women.'

Kristof threw back his head and laughed. 'A reputation I'm proud of, Matheo. But I've heard it said of you…'

'Forget what you've heard. I see you've met Cassandra.'

Kristof levelled a look at him.

'Yes. And *I* see you've thrown an exclusion zone all around her. I don't envy you trying to enforce it, my friend.'

He turned his full attention back to Cassandra, taking her hand in his and bowing low. His lips brushed her fingers.

'It has been a pleasure, *mademoiselle*, but I will leave you with Matheo. He's a tough guy to do business with. I wouldn't want to tangle with him on a personal level.'

He disappeared into the crowd.

'You could have introduced me, Matheo.' Claudia's voice was shrill, any sexy huskiness forgotten.

He turned to look at her, longing to slip an arm around Cassandra's waist. 'Ask your husband to introduce you. They're old friends.'

Claudia's eyes slid to Cassandra. 'Who's this? I thought you were alone…'

'Why would you think that? This is Cassandra.' He saw her chin lift a fraction and her jaw tighten and then she extended her right hand.

Claudia's narrowed gaze swept over her as she offered a perfunctory handshake. 'Nice necklace,' she said.

'Thank you.' Cassandra's response was cool. 'It's a family heirloom.'

'Your family? Or his?' She darted a look at Matheo.

Cassandra smiled. 'Mine, of course.'

Matheo saw her words find their mark as Claudia's light blue eyes registered satisfaction. *He hadn't bought it for her.* Maybe not, but he wished he had.

His attention was drawn to a movement behind Claudia, and he fielded a powerful kick of apprehension to the stomach as he saw his father approaching through the collection of everyone who was anyone in the hotel business. He lost the battle with his better self and slid his arm around Cassandra's waist.

* * *

Cassandra's pulse rate accelerated. Her heart began to thump against her ribcage. She breathed in, trying to concentrate on the flow of air deep into her lungs. It should have had a calming effect. But the exquisite touch of Matheo's hand on her naked back was the ultimate test. She'd have to work on refining her breathing technique. A frisson of sensation shivered through her as his hand slid around her waist, coming to rest on her hip.

She leaned into him and glanced up, seeing his gaze fixed on an approaching older man, and suddenly she understood. He was grey-haired and the hard planes of his once-handsome face had blurred with age, but she had not forgotten him. She slipped her hand over Matheo's.

'Matheo.' The accented voice was gravelly, accusing. 'We heard you weren't coming.'

'Never believe everything you hear.'

The man's gaze shifted to Cassandra, and his eyes narrowed. He raised his eyebrows in an unspoken question.

Cassandra put out her hand. 'How do you do? Cassandra Greenwood.'

There was a beat of silence.

'Joe Greenwood's daughter?' He swung round to face Matheo, anger twisting his features. 'What the hell are you doing with her?'

'We're working together on the Hideaway project,' he said calmly. 'Not that it has anything to do with you.'

Cassandra felt the heat of anger radiating from him and she squeezed his fingers where they rested on her hip. Lines of fury deepened beside his mouth, and the urge to reach up and stroke them away was powerful. But she stood rigid in the iron-hard circle of his arm, pressing her hand over his.

'Not content with snatching the hotel from under my nose,

you've taken possession of the contents as well,' Charles Chevalier sneered, his eyes raking over Cassandra, insultingly familiar. 'I suppose I should be proud of you, closing the deal *and* getting the girl thrown in. Did you, by any chance, get the family jewels too?' He laughed, but his eyes were narrowed.

Next to her, Cassandra felt a response to the jibe ripple through Matheo. The biceps of his arm pressing into her back bulged with tension and she was willing to bet his free hand was bunched into a fist. She had to stop him from using it.

The situation had to be defused somehow. She was almost sure Matheo would not hit his father, but he might say something that he'd regret, and which would damage his own reputation. She willed him to ignore his father's goading and walk away, but he stood still, his jaw clenched, his lips pressed together. Dark fire flashed in his eyes.

Cassandra turned towards him, dropping her eyelids, and then she stretched up on tiptoe and brushed her lips against his pale cheek, whispering in his ear. His arm around her flexed, then tightened, and surprise flickered across his face.

'Good evening.' He nodded curtly to his father and Claudia and began to steer Cassandra across the room towards the lifts.

She gripped his hand as if her life depended on it. If the look Claudia had given her was anything to go by, it probably did. As they made their way through the packed ballroom, Cassandra's only objective was to look like a couple whose sole intention was to get somewhere private as quickly as possible and tear each other's clothes off.

He punched the lift button. When the doors opened he drew her into the mirrored interior, keeping her clamped to his side.

Cassandra finally breathed out and turned to him, dropping her guard. 'They were surprised to see you. Did you know they'd be here?'

'He insulted you. He talked as if you were some asset that

was thrown into the hotel sale. I wanted to punch him,' Matheo ground out the words furiously, pushing the fingers of his free hand through his hair, 'and I'm not a violent man.'

'I know you're not,' she responded softly, 'and anyway, how would that have helped?'

'It might have made me feel a hell of a lot better.'

'Maybe, but not for long. And then it would just have been fuel for the gossip columns. Can you imagine the headlines?'

She tried to disengage herself from Matheo's arm, but he tightened his hold, keeping her close. She felt a fierce strength in him, as if he was putting every ounce of his energy into holding himself together, and the reality of how difficult the past few hours had been for him hit her. She put her fingers to his cheek and felt him flinch. 'You can relax now. It's over,' she said, dropping her voice. 'I can go back to my room, and you can raid the minibar in your penthouse suite, if that's where you are.'

'I'm sorry your evening has ended so abruptly. You were enjoying yourself, before…'

'Yes, I was, but I was growing tired of chatting and fending off the odd bit of unwanted attention.'

'Thank you for coming to my rescue.'

'If *you* hadn't helped *me* earlier, I'd have fled back to my room, and *my* minibar would now be empty.'

'Does that make us equal, then?'

Cassandra smiled. 'Hardly.'

They may be cocooned together in this lift, but a chasm separated them. She looked up and their eyes collided, and locked, and the foundations of her belief in their differences shook. The thread that pulled them towards each other was stronger than all of their differences.

And that was the problem.

She was hyped up after the encounter in the ballroom far

below, and she felt she was on the edge of giving in to a madness which, once tasted, would hold her in its grip for ever.

The rift between Matheo and his father was as wide and bitter as ever. Had his purchase of the Hideaway, which was meant to satisfy his need for revenge, been a waste of his money and time? And if that was true, would he remain embittered all of his life, allowing the corroding effects of his anger to destroy him? Her fragile sense of self-worth, so carefully built up, couldn't withstand such a negative force. It would destroy them both.

The lift glided to a stop and the doors opened, interrupting her racing thoughts, and Matheo stepped out with her.

'I'll…be fine, Matheo. Thank you for your support this evening…'

He shook his head.

'It is I who owe thanks. At least allow me to see you to your room.'

Cassandra dug in her clutch bag for her key card and Matheo took it from her fingers, swiping it so that the lock clicked open. She turned, feeling her smile wobble a little.

'Thank you.'

'So,' he said, running a finger along her jaw, 'when you said you needed to get back to your room, you didn't mean for me to accompany you?'

There was a teasing edge to his voice, but anger still burned in his eyes, and his mouth was stiff. She wondered, with a sudden swoop of her tummy, if he planned to return to the reception and continue the argument with his father. Surely he could see what a terrible idea that would be; the damage it would do. Perhaps, though, that was what his father wanted. Perhaps he was waiting for him to storm back into the ballroom and have a furious argument, or worse, in front of all those people and all those cameras. Any satisfaction Matheo had gained from buying the Hideaway would be turned to bitter shame and embarrassment. She needed to stop that from happening.

'If it will help you to relax, Matheo, I noticed a single malt in the minibar. Would you like to try it?'

He followed her into the room and the door clicked shut behind them. The curtains had been drawn across the wide windows, blocking out the deep sky, and the room was warm and dim, with just a pool of light coming from the bedside lamps.

Cassandra pointed towards the minibar.

'Please, help yourself. And I'll have a bottle of sparkling water.'

She perched on the edge of the small sofa. Matheo had poured the water into a glass for her, and she raised it to him.

'Here's to deciding not to punch your father, Matheo. Good decision.'

He sat on the chair at the desk and leaned forward, resting his elbows on his knees, one hand cradling his glass.

'I think you made the decision for me, Cassandra. Thank you.' He glanced across at her. 'And thank you for this. Otherwise by now I might have been back in the ballroom.'

'Mmm. That's what worried me. I assume Claudia is your father's partner.'

'Yes.' His eyes were fixed on the glass in his hand. Crystal facets sparkled with amber.

'And you don't like her.'

He sipped at his drink, then paused.

'No,' he finally said. 'I don't.'

'Have they been together a long time? She looks rather young.'

Matheo downed the inch of whisky in two swallows and placed the glass on the desk at his elbow.

'My father has had a string of women since my mother died. Claudia is the only one he has married.'

Cassandra thought about the loving, stable childhood she'd taken for granted until her mother had fallen ill, and her heart ached for Matheo and the insecure life he'd lived.

'I'm sorry, Matheo. So much of your childhood must have been confused and lonely.'

He laughed, without humour, the movement of his throat making Cassandra want to reach out and stroke away the tension.

'Yes. He sold the family home and after that I seemed to be sent to a different hotel, where he had a different woman on his arm, almost every school holiday. It was definitely confusing.'

'Perhaps he's settled down, now that he's found someone he wanted to marry. He might be angry about the Hideaway but maybe he'll let the old rivalries go if he's happy. You've done what you set out to do. Can you relax and let them go too?'

Cassandra held her breath. She longed for him to agree with her. She wanted to know that he could put his anger and desire for retribution behind him and move on. She'd seen the creative side of him, experienced his kindness and passion. He was so much more than simply a man retreating to his private island, being eaten up by anger and a need for revenge.

She watched as he scrubbed his hands over his face, dragged his fingers through his hair. His eyes were unfathomable when he stared at her again.

'Yes,' he muttered finally. 'Maybe. When I'm with you I feel different. Softer, somehow. More accepting of everything. I missed you, so much, when you left St Celeste. Your presence made everything better. I felt as if I could trust you, on every level. But I know trust is hard for you.' He shook his head and stood up. 'I should go. I've already said too much.' He sent her a half-smile. 'I'll send you into a panic and you'll run away, only we're already in your room...'

Cassandra's heart seemed to pause before launching into

a drumbeat, which she was sure he must be able to hear. In the dim lighting of the room the planes of his face were shadowed and sombre, his eyes unreadable. He took a step towards the door.

She stood.

'Don't go, Matheo.' Emotion made her voice husky. 'Stay with me.' She reached him and placed the palms of her hands on his chest, feeling the beat of his heart through the crisp white cotton of his dress shirt. 'I've missed you too. I've thought about our kiss a million times, and I want you to kiss me again. If you think you can trust me, then I think I can trust you too. Only I can't trust you to go back to your penthouse and not be angry and sad, so stay with me.'

The shawl slipped from her shoulders, revealing the shoestring straps of her dress for the first time. He tried to control his jagged intake of breath, placing his hands over hers, trapping them against his chest.

'How can I relax when I'm alone with you? When your beauty and kindness steal my breath?' He brushed his lips across her forehead. 'But I don't want to stay—' he lifted his head and rested his cheek on her hair '—if this is simply a tactic to stop me from meeting my father and Claudia again. I'll only stay if you want me…if you *need* me…to be with you.'

He heard her breath hitch and she entwined her fingers through his.

'I want you to stay because I can't bear for you to go.'

He shrugged off his jacket and tossed it away, then allowed his hands to rest on the smooth, cool skin of her shoulders. Her breath quickened and the pulse at her neck fluttered beneath his fingers as he stroked his thumbs across her collarbones. The urge to crush her against him was overwhelmingly powerful but he fought against it, feeling the need to hold back, to treat her gently and with infinite care. The most precious thing in the world was held in his hands and he was so afraid of breaking it.

So he kissed her with restraint, trying to control the urgency that surged through his body, and then he dragged his mouth away from hers, breathing deeply.

'Cassandra,' he muttered, 'are you sure?'

'Matt.' Her answer was a sigh on an exhaled breath. 'Yes.' She lifted her hands and locked her fingers behind his head, pulling his mouth down and giving him full access to her own. He wrapped his arms around her, then hauled her against him, feeling her softness against his hard strength, tracing his fingers down her spine, eliciting little heated gasps of pleasure.

His big hands flattened against her shoulder blades, feeling them pull down as her body arched towards him. When he circled his fingers on a spot below her ribs, her head fell back and he moved one hand up to support it, sliding his fingers into her hair. As his control began to slip, he brought his mouth down hard, onto hers.

Then his fingers slid to the silk straps of her dress and eased them off her shoulders.

Her gown shimmered to the floor in a lustrous pool of silk. His hands spanned her narrow hips as his eyes travelled over her neat, rose-tipped breasts, the half-moon indent of her navel and the long, long length of her legs. Then he put an arm behind her knees and the other around her shoulders and swept her feet from the floor. Her face dropped to his neck as he carried her to the bed.

CHAPTER FOURTEEN

FOR THE THIRD morning in a row Cassandra woke from what felt like a drugged sleep, her consciousness surfacing with reluctance through layers of satiated overindulgence. Parts of her ached with an unfamiliar but pleasurable hurt and a sensitised tenderness, but, as her mind began to catch up with her body and her eyes adjusted to the dim light, the ache in her chest swelled, overwhelming all the others.

It was the best feeling in the world.

She'd had three wild, uninhibited nights with a man she was supposed to detest, and who was meant to feel the same way about her. They'd discovered they were both wrong.

She turned her head. He lay on his back, his body totally relaxed in sleep. She reached out and ran her fingers along his shadowed jaw, down the strong column of his throat. Then she rolled over and curled into his side, resting her hand on the sprinkling of dark hair across his chest and feeling the steady, reassuring rhythm of his heart. Already she wanted it all again, more slowly, so she could savour every second, store it away somewhere safe, to be remembered over and over in the future.

His thick, dark hair flopped over his forehead, and she brushed it away with a stroke of her fingers and dropped a kiss onto his temple.

In his arms she felt utterly safe, secure. She'd surrendered her trust to him and let him take care of her, just as she'd wanted him to, all those years ago.

Spending time with him on St Celeste had enabled her to get past his guard a little. She'd come to enjoy his flashes of humour and admire his fierce intelligence and his belief in what was right.

In his arms she'd bared her soul to him; allowed him to see her at her most vulnerable and open, stripped of all restraint or reserve. He'd repaid her trust with infinite tenderness and gentle consideration, putting her needs before his own but allowing her to push him beyond the barriers of his self-control before they fell asleep in each other's arms.

The depth of trust, of emotion, had transcended anything Cassandra had ever experienced. The tight ball of anxiety and grief, which had become a permanent part of her, had dissolved under Matheo's hands and the sweet words he'd whispered to her as she'd unravelled in his arms.

This, she thought, is how it is supposed to be.

'Hey.' She propped her head in a hand and ran a finger across his lips.

'Hey back.' His eyes, heavy-lidded, opened, revealing smoky desire in their depths.

'I'm going for a swim. When I come back, we can...'

'We can what?' His voice was gravelly with sleep.

'Make love again? Maybe?'

'Mmm. Maybe? Why not now?'

He reached for her but she moved away, sliding out of the wide bed.

'Because now I'm going for a swim. But when I come back...'

'I'll order breakfast for when you come back, on my terrace. I need to replenish my energy.'

Cassandra bent over him and dropped a kiss onto his mouth,

deftly dodging the arm that tried to capture her to pull her back into bed.

'Have another half an hour of sleep, Matt.'

'Mmm. You've worn me out.'

She slipped into the ensuite and pulled on her bikini and a beach wrap and left the room, closing the door quietly behind her.

The infinity pool was almost deserted at such an early hour. On the far side, one swimmer ploughed up and down, getting in his daily exercise. The rays of the low sun were already warm on her back as she slid into the cool water and felt the instant joy of being immersed in it. She swam, unaware of the time or distance, until her muscles ached slightly and she'd become out of breath.

Then she stretched out on a sunbed to dry off and recover her breath, closing her eyes against the sun.

She felt rather than saw someone near her. Her heart gave a bump at the thought it might be Matheo, but when she raised her lids she saw brightly painted toenails on tanned feet next to her sunbed. Throwing her arm across her face to shield her eyes from the sun, she sat up.

Claudia, in a gold bikini and oversized sunglasses, gazed down at her.

'Swimming on your own? Where's Matheo?'

Cassandra's brain, still engaged in her swim, struggled to change speed. But she thought quickly enough to decide that Claudia did not need to know precisely where Matheo was.

'I imagine he's asleep,' she said, lifting her hair and twisting it in her hands to squeeze the excess water from it.

'He didn't introduce us properly the other night.' Claudia hitched up the straps of her bikini top. 'He should have shown more respect for his stepmother.' She pushed her sunglasses onto the top of her head, revealing her light blue eyes, locked onto Cassandra's face. 'Especially since, until two years ago, I was *his* wife.'

A dull roar in Cassandra's brain eclipsed the morning sounds of the hotel. She shook her head, trying to clear it, and finally found her voice. *'What?'* But the single word came out as a rasping whisper. She felt her heart begin to race as adrenaline poured into her bloodstream. She struggled to stand up, scrabbling for her beach wrap with hands that shook. She clutched it around her shoulders, suddenly feeling terribly cold. 'I don't... No, I don't believe you,' she stammered. 'You're just trying to cause trouble. That's a...wicked...thing to say.'

'Oops.' Claudia clapped a theatrical hand to her mouth. 'So sorry. It's true, though. Ask Matheo. Or should I say Matt? He won't deny it, since he's so picky about honesty. Strange that he's never told you.'

Nausea rose into Cassandra's throat, and she was suddenly desperately afraid she'd be sick in front of this woman. She pressed a fist against her mouth and stumbled away, not sure how she'd find her way back to her room through the blinding tears which had begun to spill down her cheeks.

She slammed her room door and leaned against it, palms flat on the hard surface. Then she sprinted for the bathroom.

Long minutes later, she rinsed her mouth and splashed her face with cold water. Her eyes were swollen and red, her lips puffy. The pain that clutched at her heart was almost unbearable, but she knew she had to find the strength, somewhere, to get away, before Matheo came searching for her.

The thought of ever facing him again felt impossible.

Shame spiked through her at the way she'd betrayed the memories of her parents and of the long line of ancestors who had hung on to the Hideaway, through good times and bad. Not only had she let their most bitter enemy get possession of it, but she'd also...*trusted*...him.

Something inside her had changed and it could never be changed back. She'd glimpsed a side to Matheo she wouldn't have believed existed: thoughtful, intelligent and...*gentle*. Away from the cut-throat world of mega-deals and takeovers, where he came across as remote and ruthless, he was a different person. Her opinion of him had changed, and feelings for him which she'd have believed impossible a few weeks ago had slid quietly into her heart.

He'd held her in his arms as if she was the most precious thing in the world to him, whispering words that made her blush as she remembered them. He'd been gentle, at least at first... But he'd responded unfailingly to her needs and desires, which, she thought, the heat in her face intensifying, she'd made very, very clear.

But it had all been a lie. He'd let her trust him with her deepest, most fragile emotions. She'd bared her soul to him, but he'd kept a shocking secret from her.

It didn't take long to pack. Anything in Matheo's penthouse suite could stay there. She'd never wear any of these clothes again. The memories and hurt they would carry would be too painful to bear.

Then she saw her key card to Matheo's door lying on the console table. Sliding it into her pocket alongside her own, she put down her bag and changed her mind.

From where she stood in the hallway of the penthouse, she could see him. He'd put on board shorts and followed through on his promise of breakfast. The table where he sat on the terrace held an array of covered dishes and a silver coffee pot. His stern profile was etched against the deep blue of the sky, his thick hair lifted from his forehead by the slight breeze, ever-present at this height above the sea.

Pain wrenched at her, and she had to resist the need to double over to ease it. The thought that she could pretend she didn't know occurred to her, but she dismissed it before it could even form properly. She knew she could never be that dishonest. One look at her and he'd know, anyway.

She had to confront him; let him know what she thought of him. Then she had to get as far away from him as possible in the shortest possible time. It would have been easier to simply disappear and let him work out what had happened for himself, but she'd made a split-second decision to face him, and she knew it was the right one.

As she watched, Matheo stretched his arms above his head, ran a hand through his hair and glanced down at his watch, brows drawing together. He must be wondering where she was. Taking a huge breath, she walked through the open-plan living space and stepped out onto the terrace.

Matheo looked up, his rare, heartbreaking smile lighting his face. Cassandra wanted to run to him, to wrap her arms around him, bury her face in his neck, breathe in his scent and let him tell her it wasn't true. But as he rose from his chair, his smile fading, her last shred of hope disintegrated. She could see, in those few seconds, that he understood what had happened.

'What's wrong, Cass?'

He moved towards her, but she put out a hand and he stopped.

'I saw Claudia by the pool. I think you know what's happened.'

His eyes, dark with anger, burned in a face from which all colour had drained. His chest rose on an unsteady breath and he put a hand on the table at his hip.

'I'm sorry, Cass.' He pulled his other hand down over his face, shaking his head. 'I was going to tell you, but... I thought they'd left.'

A hot tide of anger swept through her and she did not try to curb it. Her hurt and shock would come back later, she knew, but right now, to do what she had to do, she needed to be furious. She folded her arms across her chest and stared at him.

'Exactly when? *When* did you plan to tell me, Matheo? Because I think you've had loads of opportunities. So many that not using one of them looks suspiciously deliberate to me. And when you thought they'd left, did that mean you also thought you were out of danger? That I wouldn't find out, so that made it okay?'

'I… We were… I was afraid…' He dropped his head.

'Afraid of what? That I'd be shocked? You're right about that. I am shocked. But what shocks me most is that I let you deceive me. You're a Chevalier, after all. I should never have believed anything you said.' She sucked in a breath, trying to steady herself but feeling the iron grip she'd tried to impose on her emotions beginning to slip. 'I *trusted* you. And you let me, but it was all a lie. I tried to help you overcome your anger at your father and Claudia and you…let me. You…made love to me. Was it to block out memories of…*her*? Is that all it was? All it's been, these last three days? Has it even *worked*?'

His face, when he raised his head, was ashen.

'No, Cass. Believe me. It wasn't…it isn't…like that.'

'Like what, Matheo? Because I can't see what else it can be like. You said she was your *stepmother*…you said you didn't *like* her…'

'I don't.'

'But you did once. Enough to marry her.'

'No. Yes, I mean, yes, I did marry her. But it wasn't that kind of marriage.'

'Just how many different kinds of marriage are there, Matheo?'

'It was…two powerful families. Money played a part… I never wanted to be married. God knows, the example of my parents' marriage was hardly a recommendation. But it was convenient, and our families had been hoping it would happen since we were children. At first it was okay. Even good. But then...'

'This is the twenty-first century, not the Middle Ages. I'm afraid I just don't believe you. But if what you say is true, I understand why your father behaved as if I was some sort of bonus thrown into the sale of the Hideaway to sweeten the buyer. You pretended to be up-to-date outraged, but it's just the medieval way your family has always behaved.'

'No, I don't suppose you do believe me, and that's not surprising. But,' he said, his eyes capturing hers and holding her gaze, 'the only thing I do want you to believe is that I never intended to hurt you. I would have told you. I just needed...'

'The time to have told me, Matheo, was when I invited you into my room after I'd met your father and your...stepmother... at the gala reception. Yes, I would have been shocked. I mean, how the hell did something like that happen? But I would have listened, and I would have cared about how you felt.' Her voice cracked on a half-sob, and she swallowed, swiping the back of her hand across her cheeks. 'But deliberately deceiving me was unforgiveable. Pretending you cared for me...'

'I wasn't pretending.'

'But you let me give all of myself to you while you withheld something from me. You said you trusted me and that helped me to trust you. But you didn't trust me enough to share something so important with me. My trust has been wasted, shattered. You were just another man, telling me what he wanted me to hear to get what he wanted.'

Cassandra spun round, bunching her fists, and began to walk away. Matheo lunged after her, grabbing her by the arm.

'Cassandra, please, wait. I can explain...'

She shook his hand off. 'There's nothing left to explain, Matheo. I'm leaving now. Please don't follow me and please don't try to contact me, ever. I'll complete the Hideaway project, but I refuse to interact with you, on any level. I cannot work with someone who is so utterly selfish.' She walked across the marble floor to the door, sheer willpower keeping her upright.

'Cassandra…' She heard his voice crack, and her heart cracked with it, but she kept going. 'At least,' he shouted, sounding like a drowning man calling for help, one last time, 'now you know why the…*rift*…can never, ever be mended.'

That stopped her. She turned and stared at him across the space.

'Un-mended, the rift between you and your father will ensure that you remain a bitter, lonely and solitary man, so I suggest you find a way to repair it.' Her hand fluttered to cover her heart. '*This* rift…the one between us…*this* is the one which will never, ever heal.'

She wrapped both her shaking hands around the gold doorknob and yanked the heavy door open. It closed behind her with a muted click. There was no going back. She'd left the key card inside.

The tight band of pain around Matheo's chest tugged even tighter. He tried to slow down his breathing, to control the shake in his hands, but nothing seemed to work. He stared through the penthouse suite towards the door, hoping…hoping for what? That she'd come back? That was never going to happen. She'd said, quite clearly, that she wanted nothing to do with him, ever again. And why would she? Why would any woman?

What woman would want a man whose wife had left him for his father, thirty years his senior? What did that say about him? Did Cassandra think he'd wanted her not only to blot out the appalling fact of Claudia and his father being together, but also to repair the shattering blow he'd suffered to his masculinity? If so, she'd feel doubly used.

He felt physically sick at the thought of what he'd lost through his own stupidity, his lack of courage. He'd been desperate to tell her the truth. But every time he thought he could, he'd failed. Because the hurt and anger that slammed into him, when he had to acknowledge, to himself or to others, what had happened to him, terrified him with its destructive power. He couldn't bear the thought of how she'd react: the look of shock, her quick withdrawal, her retreat from him. Worst of all, the *pity*.

Anger kept him going, drove him to greater financial achievements, kept the reality of who he truly was at bay. Without it he'd crumble, have to face himself, admit he was an emotional failure and not worth anyone's love.

It had been a brutally painful experience. The betrayal of his wife had been compounded many times over by the complicit betrayal of his father. The pain he'd come to know—the twisting knife—flashed into his gut again. It was a match made in heaven, his father had stated, and, moreover, it was what his mother had said she wanted. He'd hoped they'd grow to love each other, that it would be all right, but he'd been wrong. Claudia had been in love with what she thought he could do for her, and when she saw his father could do more she'd easily made the switch.

His father had been delighted. He'd never been able to stop competing with the son who had stolen his wife's attention and love from the minute he was born.

Matheo turned away and walked to the edge of the terrace. The view, which he'd been looking forward to sharing with Cassandra over breakfast, was blighted. He resented the sun for continuing to shine in the cloudless, cerulean sky, the sailing boat skimming over the sparkling sea far below. He buried his face in his hands, trying to obliterate the image of Cassandra's tear-stained devastation.

He wanted to take her face between his hands and kiss away her sadness; tell her she was wrong about him. He was nothing like his father. The need to hold her, to keep her with him, was overwhelming. Without her he would simply cease to function.

He had to stop her from leaving. It would take her time to pack, to get a taxi. There might still be time.

He dragged on a shirt, raked his fingers through his hair and sprinted for the lifts.

Reaching Cassandra's floor, he looked up and down the empty corridor, then jogged towards her room. The floor concierge stepped out of his discreetly hidden office and Matheo stopped in front of him. He raised his hands, wanting to seize him by the lapels in his desperation for information, but politeness got the better of him and he dropped them to his sides, clenching his fists. The man's expression quickly changed from startled to polite helpfulness.

'Have you seen Mademoiselle Greenwood this morning?'

The man nodded and looked at his watch.

'Yes, sir, I have. She asked me to call a taxi to the airport for her.'

Matheo pinched the bridge of his nose between his thumb and forefinger, breathing and praying for patience. 'When was this?'

'Fifteen minutes ago, sir.' The man glanced down into the atrium. 'She seemed to be pressed for time. She'll be on her way by now.'

Matheo's heart plummeted. She'd either been ready to leave before she'd confronted him, or she'd left without any of her possessions.

'Did she say where to? Did she have luggage?'

He shook his head. 'Just the airport, sir, with her luggage. I assumed she was late for a flight.'

Matheo rested his hands on his hips. He dipped his head,

looking at the floor, and realised he hadn't put on any shoes. Dubai was an international hub. Hundreds of flights departed its airport for destinations around the world every day. Cassandra could be on her way to anywhere in the world.

'If there is anything more I can do for *monsieur*...?'

He shook his head.

'No, thank you. There's nothing anyone can do. I've screwed up. Big-time.'

He walked blindly back to the lifts and punched the button. Thin, silver-tipped fingers grasped his sleeve.

Turning his head, he looked down into Claudia's cold-as-ice eyes.

'Matt,' she purred. 'Is everything all right?'

'Don't call me Matt,' he snapped. 'And what does it look like?'

'Oh, dear. Sorry! I thought that was the endearment *du jour*. What's happened to the poor girl made good?'

'I don't think you need to ask me that question.'

'Ah. Trouble in paradise. Well, if you need a shoulder...'

'I'll never need a shoulder badly enough to need yours, Claudia.'

He stepped into the lift, closing the doors on whatever she was going to say next, and returned to the echoing emptiness of the penthouse. Grabbing his phone, he swore as his shaking fingers stumbled over the screen. But then he found her name and made the call. It went straight to voicemail. He clicked it off without leaving a message and tossed the phone aside. She was gone.

Panic clawed at him, stealing his breath and bringing him out in a cold sweat. He couldn't bear the thought that she'd gone for good. He'd held her, kissed her, stroked her, cradled her and soothed her when she'd cried out his name, over and over.

Matt, Matt, please...

He shook his head violently, trying to dispel the memory of her voice, her willing, supple body, her generosity. How was he ever going to get through the next hour, the next day, never mind the rest of his life, without her? No one else had ever called him Matt. Now no one ever could.

He sat on the end of the bed and pressed his fingers into his temples. He couldn't believe she could walk away from what they had; what they'd shared. He'd got to know her; experienced her kindness, her concern for others. He'd never meet anyone else who would spend their trust fund on paying the employees of a doomed hotel.

Then he thought about what he hadn't told her, and he could easily believe she could abandon it all.

He'd let her trust him, but the fear of revealing his true self had meant he'd been unable to be honest with her in return. She was justified in feeling betrayed.

He needed to find her to say sorry. To promise it could be different; that she'd never need to doubt him, ever again.

But then he remembered her parting words. She wouldn't listen to him or speak to him. And he couldn't blame her.

He needed her back, to tell her that what they had shared was fragile and irreplaceable. To tell her he'd wanted her, and her alone, and that the thought of how he'd hurt her was intolerable. He needed to tell her they'd stopped the clocks, changed the projected course of their histories. Together, the two of them could end the feud that had ripped their families apart for a century.

But he knew she never wanted to hear what he needed to say.

The vast marble halls of the airport hummed with life, and Cassandra plunged into the crowds, no longer looking over her shoulder, wondering if he'd come after her. She bit down on her bottom lip, walking fast to the departure gate, praying the flight wouldn't be delayed, keeping going until she was settled in her seat.

The big aircraft lifted into the warm air, banking over the sea. She leaned her forehead against the cool window glass and watched as the massive structure of the hotel came into view below them, standing tall on its own island, glinting gold and white in the bright sunlight.

She felt she had to press her hands over her heart to keep it from shattering. This couldn't be—she couldn't let three days define her life from now on. She thought she'd learned from Jason never to trust a man again. Her faith in her own judgement had been strong, but Matheo had slipped past her defences. She'd have to rebuild them, stronger than before. But as the hotel disappeared from view and all she could see was the shadow of the plane skittering over the waves far below, she knew she was leaving a part of her behind that she could never hope to get back.

Looking back was useless, she told herself. Yesterday was over and each new day meant she had the rest of her life ahead of her. But whatever all the tomorrows might bring, none of them would ever match up to the yesterdays with Matheo.

CHAPTER FIFTEEN

THE FIRST CLEARANCE his pilot had been able to get was in the early hours of the morning and now the journey, which Matheo usually enjoyed, seemed interminable. He downed the couple of inches of whisky that remained in the tumbler at his elbow and swore under his breath. He knew he shouldn't be drinking at this time of the day. His hand scraped over his unshaven jaw.

He'd tried to feel angry with her. When Claudia had left him for his father, he'd been almost blind with rage. An all-consuming need for revenge had followed soon afterwards.

He'd never felt like this. This sense of loss was unfathomable, and it had not lessened over the past two months. He refused to admit the thought that Cassandra might have gone for ever.

He'd left Dubai and withdrawn to St Celeste. He'd spoken to Nick, giving him free rein to carry on with the Hideaway project, but asking for regular, detailed updates on progress.

He hadn't mentioned Cassandra, but, towards the end of their conversation, Nick had.

'Cassandra,' he'd said, 'is prepared to complete her role in the project, providing she has no direct contact with you. Are you on board with that?'

'Yes,' had been his curt reply, forestalling any further discussion on the matter.

It didn't stop him thinking about her. He imagined he saw her footprints in the sand on the beach. One night, a trick of the light convinced him she was dancing at the water's edge. His chef requested a few days' holiday as the food he prepared was going to waste.

The project would be completed in December and after that there'd be no way to know where she was or what she was doing. The thought was unbearable. He had promised not to contact her, but he had to at least try to speak to her. There were things that had to be said and only he could say them. He'd made a decision and he wanted her to know.

At Heathrow he strode off the jet with the briefest nod to his pilot and crew. The doorman of the Mayfair hotel where he kept a suite received the same minimal acknowledgement. He resented the minutes it took for him to shower and change, and then he took the lift to the basement car park and slid behind the wheel of his sleek convertible. The engine purred into life and the wheels squealed on the concrete as he headed out into the London traffic. He had the FuturePlan office in his sights.

The receptionist looked up from her keyboard with a practised smile as he pushed through the glass doors.

'Good morning. How can I help you?'

'I need to see Miss Greenwood. Urgently.' He dragged a hand over the back of his neck. His hair still felt damp. 'Please,' he added, as an afterthought. Now that he was here, he was desperate to get this done.

'I'm sorry,' she said, 'Miss Greenwood isn't in today. But Nick Jones is in his office…'

'Then I'd like to see him, please.'

The girl nodded and lifted her phone. 'Your name, sir?'

'Matheo Chevalier,' he said over his shoulder as he headed towards the lift.

'Top floor, turn left out of the lift, sir.'

* * *

Nick Jones stood with his back to the panoramic view, evidently forewarned by the receptionist.

'Nick.' Matheo extended a hand.

Nick shook it. 'I wasn't expecting you…'

'No, and I apologise for intruding without notice. I need to see Miss Greenwood. Where is she?'

'She's on a routine site visit to the Hideaway. That fact is in the progress report I emailed you this morning.'

Matheo's shoulders dropped. He'd worked himself up to this, not giving himself time to think about how Cassandra would react to seeing him. It had never occurred to him that she might not even be here.

'I flew in early this morning.' He pulled a hand over his face, realising he'd forgotten to shave. Again. 'I haven't checked my emails.'

'Well,' said Nick, calmly, 'it's perhaps just as well she isn't here since she doesn't want to interact with you. Coffee?'

'Please.' Matheo threw himself into the chair Nick indicated. 'I'm aware of that, of course. But I need to talk to her. Just for a few minutes.'

'You could call her.' Nick moved to the coffee machine in the corner and then carried a cup over to Matheo, who took it and shook his head.

'She wouldn't pick up. I know that without even trying.'

Nick put his own coffee cup on his desk and sat down. 'She's returning tomorrow afternoon if you want to come back. But I will feel duty-bound to let her know to expect you.'

Matheo downed his coffee and replaced the cup on the saucer. It rattled slightly.

'How long,' he asked, 'will it take me to drive down there?'

Nick shrugged. 'Five hours?'

From the door, Matheo looked back.

'Please, Nick, give me a head start? Make up an excuse. Say something came up and you forgot. Just please don't warn her that I'm coming. I mean her no harm. I just have to talk to her and if she knows I'm coming, she might...' He shrugged. 'She'll probably leave.'

The look Nick returned was steady.

'Okay. It seems to me you've screwed this up once already and perhaps you deserve another chance. Just don't screw it up again.'

Autumn had made landfall in Cornwall. Golden leaves fluttered from the trees in a cool, brisk breeze, which ruffled the surface of the sea. The call of seagulls wheeling over the bay blended into the steady background track of the surf rolling into the cove. The waves had cast off their summer gentleness and rose and crashed onto the sand with purpose.

Cassandra picked her way over the rocks at the end of the beach until she reached her favourite one to sit on. She pulled up her legs and rested her chin on her knees. She could sit here for hours, listening to the hypnotic thrust and wash of the sea against the rocks. Behind her, the Hideaway crouched on the cliff, its windows blank and sightless without the softening frame of curtains or blinds. The sound of sporadic hammering drifted down towards her. The last few slates of the renewed roof were being fixed in position, making the ancient building weather-tight once more. She could almost feel nostalgic about her leaky attic bedroom, now that the rain could no longer find its way in.

The building works were almost complete and the interior decorators had swept in, working quickly against the deadline of early December. It would be finished on time, and in time for the grand opening, which the PR team for Marine Developments had planned.

Cassandra still felt conflicted about the role she had played in the transformation of her home. She supposed a part of her would always long for its old, worn comfort, the familiarity of things never changing. But the new version of the Hide-away was stunning. The early ideas that she and Matheo had discussed on St Celeste had mostly been incorporated, with huge success. They had given the hotel a brand-new lease of life, which would carry it through the decades to come.

She could *think* of Matheo's name now, although she'd never spoken it again. Saying it out loud might shatter the brittle shell she'd constructed around herself over the past months, and if that cracked, all of her pain would spill out, beyond her control, for the world to see.

After her site visit, on her way through the gardens, she'd stopped to talk to George. The old walled garden had been restored and planted with fruit and vegetables, protected from the salt-laden wind by the high stone walls, and he was puffed up with pride.

'It's what I always wanted to do, Cassandra,' he said, his arm sweeping out in a gesture that encompassed neat rows of sprouting winter vegetables, espaliered fruit and a long glass-house, built against the south-facing wall. 'Mr Chevalier has given me a most generous budget. Most generous.' His kind eyes studied her and she glanced away, afraid of what he might see in her face. 'Now, I know there's been bad feeling between your two families, but it seems to me he's a good man. Been good to the staff, too.'

She was pleased to hear he'd kept his side of the deal.

On her return to London she'd explained to Nick that they'd had a 'disagreement' and that she wanted no direct contact with him. Nick had listened, and not asked any awkward questions.

It had proved to be surprisingly easy to avoid him. He'd said he was happy for the project to progress and would be available for any urgent discussions or decisions. And then he'd allowed FuturePlan to get on with it.

There would be a couple more site visits she'd need to make and then there'd be the grand opening. In January she would start work on a new project and put the whole of her past behind her.

Waves splashed noisily onto the rocks near her feet, so she didn't hear his approach. She whipped her head round as a dislodged pebble plopped into a tidal pool. She scrambled to her feet, her back to the sea, narrowing her eyes against the low sun.

He hadn't shaved lately. His dark hair was rumpled and lifted from his forehead in the wind. Adrenaline set her heart banging against her ribs. Every muscle in her body tensed, ready to flee, but there was nowhere to go, unless she retreated into the icy sea.

He stepped over the rocks, keeping his eyes on her face, and stopped in front of her. A movement made her look down and she saw his hands clenching and unclenching at his sides. The look in his eyes said she wasn't going anywhere.

'Let me past, please.'

His eyes moved over her, as if he was intent on devouring every detail of her face and body. He shook his head.

'No. Not until you've listened to what I have to say.'

'Nothing you can say will interest me at all.' The wobble in her voice annoyed her, as did the shiver which raced over her skin, beneath the fleece she wore.

He nodded. 'Maybe. But I'm not asking you to be interested. I'm only asking you to listen.'

A strand of her hair blew across her face. She flicked it away. 'No...'

He crossed his arms over his chest, his knuckles white under the tanned skin of his hands.

'I've come a long way to speak to you, Cassandra. Please give me five minutes of your time. Then, if it's what you want, I'll leave and never bother you again.'

Cassandra stared at him and he dropped his eyes, but not before she'd seen the anguish burning in their obsidian depths. Against her will, it tugged at something deep inside her. He was hurting and he needed to talk to someone.

That feeling had been familiar to her since she was sixteen.

Short of pushing past him, there was no escape. She gave a quick nod and lifted her chin.

Relief flickered briefly across his face. The faint lines between his brows were more pronounced than she remembered. There was no sign of the almost-dimple.

He shoved a hand through his hair.

'I'm sorry.'

'No doubt you are.' Her voice was cool. 'Did you hope I'd never find out? That whatever it was you had with me would finish when we left Dubai and you'd never have to tell me? And if I'd found out later, from someone else, it wouldn't matter, because you'd have moved on?'

'No. That's not how it was. I wanted to tell you, that first night in your room. I knew I needed to, but...'

'But that would have ruined the atmosphere? I would have asked you to leave, instead of asking you to share my bed?'

'No,' he repeated. 'I knew I needed to, but I was too afraid.'

'Afraid I'd be...shocked?'

'I knew you'd be shocked. That was a given.' He sucked in an impeded breath and she saw how difficult this was for him. 'No, I was too afraid to show you who I really am. The man whose wife preferred his father. The man whose father thought it was okay to marry her. The man who couldn't talk about it because the depth of his anger and shame scares him.'

'I held nothing back from you. I was no threat. Yet you thought it was fine to take all I gave but not truly give yourself back. You said I could trust you, knowing exactly how difficult that was for me, but you weren't prepared to trust me in return.'

'I'm deeply sorry, Cassandra, for the terrible hurt I caused you. I betrayed your trust and I'll never forgive myself for that.'

'You speak as if it were all in the past. That kind of hurt might never heal.'

She bit her lip, trying to stop it from trembling.

'I'm appalled by what I did; by the damage I caused. When I held you, it felt as if I'd won the lottery and been able to choose the most precious thing in the world, and I chose you. How could I have destroyed that? I would give anything to be able to mend it, but I'll understand if you feel that's impossible.'

Cassandra glanced around at the beach where they'd stood in the freezing water, almost kissing; at the hotel on the cliffs above, which had been the cause of all this; at the squat tower of the little stone church on the headland, where her parents lay, and felt sorrow wrap around her like a heavy cloak.

'I don't think it can be mended. The cracks would always show, and they'd break apart eventually. The pressure of your toxic relationship with your father would be too much. You'd still be an angry, vengeful man and I'd be the person trying to smooth it over, make you feel better, compromising myself. I'm sorry, too. But I just can't do that.'

A muscle in his jaw ticked, and he frowned.

'I know now how it feels to be different. With you, the anger loosens inside me. Your kindness and generosity are contagious. You make me a better, nicer person, the person I want to be.'

'I can't be that mirror, reflecting the person you'd like to be. You'll have to find a way to become that, from within yourself.'

He nodded. 'I understand I can't ask that of you. So I've found another way. I'm going to start with forgiving my father.'

Cassandra watched him turn and stride away over the rocks, then leap down onto the sand and make his way to the foot of the cliff path. The stiff set of his broad shoulders radiated determination as he began to climb towards the skyline.

CHAPTER SIXTEEN

THE MARINE DEVELOPMENTS PR team had arrived at the Hideaway like a whirlwind. All the public rooms had been decorated for Christmas and the scent of cinnamon, citrus and pine hung in the air.

Three decorated Christmas trees, the golden angels on their tops brushing the newly painted ceilings, graced the hall, the drawing room and the dining room. The bannisters of the staircases sported garlands of ivy, interwoven with tiny lights, and arrangements of creamy, scented narcissi, red holly berries, bay leaves and spruce stood on tables. Candles were grouped on every surface.

Producing the celebration buffet in the dining room had been a valuable test for the new kitchen team and serving it had stretched the just-trained waiting staff to the limit, but there'd been no disasters.

At least, none that Cassandra had seen.

Puddings wreathed in blue flames had been carried in, accompanied by cheers and applause, and the whole event had finished with the pop of Christmas crackers.

The guests, many of whom had booked to stay for the weekend, drifted away to enjoy tea in the drawing room.

Cassandra slipped away from the festivities. She'd debated whether to come but, in the end, felt she owed it to the staff, especially Tess, to be there, and the temptation to experience the Hideaway decorated for Christmas and filled with people enjoying themselves was too strong to resist. This was how she'd be able to remember it, and she felt grateful for that.

She'd dressed up for the occasion in a green velvet dress embellished with delicate gold embroidery. The fabric swirled softly in a full skirt from a pointed dropped waist. It made her feel ethereal and medieval, as if she came from an earlier incarnation of the Hideaway.

The study remained her favourite room. The stonework of the ancient fireplace had been cleaned and repaired and a warm fire flickered in the grate. Around it the oak panelling had survived, stripped of centuries of dirt and smoke and polished to a deep shine. The once grimy walls had been painted in a soft shade of grey. The wide floorboards gleamed, a perfect foil for the intricate pattern of a Persian rug of ruby, sapphire and pearl wool.

The mullioned panes in the deep bay where she stood were softened by heavy linen curtains in a shade of rich cream. Her old desk faced the view and a lit lamp cast a soft glow on its oak surface. Some of her favourite pictures hung on the walls.

The pale light was fading fast over the cove, transforming the sea from winter blue to deep indigo. She'd wait for full darkness to fall, and then she'd leave.

To her intense relief, Matheo had not come to the party.

Two weeks after their last meeting, she'd had a message from him.

It's done.

It had been two days before she could make herself reply.

What happened?

You don't need to know, but it feels good.

I'm glad.

Then, two days later, when she'd had time to think it through, she'd sent:

Do you need to talk?

No, thank you.

That had been his reply. She'd heard no more from him. It was over.

'Will it rain tonight, do you think?'

Cassandra stiffened and a frisson of sensation prickled across her scalp and down her spine. The atmosphere in the room shifted subtly and she wondered, briefly, if she'd conjured up a ghost. His voice was dark, and very familiar.

'The wind has changed direction,' she said, 'and there's a weather front on the horizon. We won't see the sun again until tomorrow.'

'How do you know what the sun will do?'

He was behind her now. If she turned, would he disappear? Her breath moved to her throat, and her pulse quickened.

'You said you didn't want to talk.'

'I didn't. I wanted to see you.'

Cassandra turned. He took up more space in the low-ceilinged room than she remembered. Slim black jeans and a soft black V-necked sweater defined his powerful thighs and wide shoulders.

'You're not dressed for a party.'

'I haven't come for the party. And anyway, you make up for it. You look…you are…beautiful.'

'Thank you. The hotel looks amazing, don't you think?'

'I haven't looked. I'm here to see you.' He moved to stand next to her. 'I want to tell you about my father.'

Cassandra nodded. 'Okay. Do you still feel good?'

'Yes. Better each day. I went to see him after we spoke.' He glanced towards the beach. 'It wasn't…easy. We both shouted.'

'Nothing too horrible, I hope.'

One corner of his stern mouth lifted. 'No. I accused him of never stopping competing with me. Of neglecting my mother. Of being overbearing and a bully. Of betrayal.'

'All true, I think.'

He nodded. 'Yes. But he pointed out that, from the minute I was born, my mother's attention…and *love*…was focused on me. He felt excluded. The only way he could attract her notice was by behaving badly. I'd never seen it from that perspective.'

'That doesn't excuse his behaviour towards you and your… wife.'

'Ex-wife. He accepts that. He said he knew his actions were unforgiveable. But I said I want to move on, that I'm done with arguing. We shook hands and I left.'

'It must have been difficult.'

'Of course; it wasn't as easy as it sounds. But I'm trying to find it in myself to forgive him, and I'm making progress.' His face was sombre in the soft light. 'The man I was with you is the one I want to be all the time. I don't expect you to want to be with me. As you said, the pressure on you would be intolerable. But I want you to know that I am trying to be that person. It was you who showed me how I could be, by believing me and trusting me, even though I didn't deserve it. I'd like to think that one day I might become the sort of man who could earn your trust, and your love.'

'Matt.' It was so long since she'd allowed his name to cross her lips that it felt odd. She put out a hand and rested it on the soft jumper, feeling his racing heart and knowing how hard this must be for him. He'd learned from childhood to keep his feelings hidden, his emotions in check. He'd suffered loss, he'd feared and then despised his own father, been betrayed by him and his wife. And yet he was willing to try to change, for her sake. 'Matt,' she said, again, 'you're incredibly brave. I know how afraid you are of trusting anyone. This must be terrifying for you.'

'Yes.' He nodded. 'It is. But I can do it if I think of how you trusted me, when I know how frightening that was for you too.'

A shiver of emotion shook Cassandra. Matheo put his hands on her shoulders.

'You're cold.'

She shook her head, breathing in deep, shaky gulps.

'It's not cold.' Her teeth chattered. 'The new eco-friendly heating works beautifully.' She gave him a shaky smile. 'It's… emotion. I wasn't prepared for this, but… I regretted the things I said to you when I left you. I was so shaken, so broken, but I should have let you speak. I was terrified you'd persuade me to stay, because I wanted you so much, but I knew I had to go if I was to have a chance of surviving as myself.'

He slid his hands down her arms and linked his hands with hers, pulling her towards him.

'If it's what you want, Cass, I will *never* let you go again. Not ever.'

He loosened his grip on her hands and smoothed a stray strand of hair off her cheek, pressing his lips to her forehead.

'Oh, Matt, it's what I want, but I'm so afraid of it.'

'Let me help you to build your trust in me. Allowing me to love and trust you is a way of allowing yourself to love and trust me.'

He wrapped his arms around her and she buried her face in his chest, inhaling his familiar scent, absorbing his strength, and feeling that need to allow him to shoulder her cares, to look after her.

His lips hovered close to hers. As if in anticipation, the tip of her tongue touched her top lip. She felt his chest rise sharply, pressing against hers. Her eyelids fluttered up and the grey depths of his eyes swamped her. His fingers speared into her hair, and he cupped her head in his hands.

'There is a culture,' she said softly, 'with a tradition of mending broken porcelain with molten gold, rather than trying to hide the cracks. The repaired object is regarded as more beautiful than the original, and much stronger, too.' She took a quick breath, seeing the silver flames which ignited in his eyes. 'If we can mend each other so that our relationship is shot through with gold, we'll be strong enough to face anything together.'

His deep, slow kiss was what she'd been longing for. He cupped her face and angled her head to ease her lips apart under his. Her hands moved from his shoulders, and she tangled her fingers in his hair, pulling him down to her, revelling in the feel of his hard body. She surrendered to the erotic slide of his tongue against hers, and to the deep sound of desire that came from his throat. His hands left her face and drifted down, leaving a burning trail of need in their wake.

When they broke the kiss, to drag air into their lungs, Cassandra ran her hands over his broad chest.

'Have you seen the rest of the hotel?' she murmured. 'I'd like to show you around.'

'Mmm. Yes. But there's something I want to show you here first.'

He placed his hand on her back and urged her towards the fireplace. On the hearth stood an ancient wooden chest, bound in rusted iron.

'I've never seen this before. What's it doing here?'

'I had it brought from its temporary home in a bank vault. At some point I thought I'd find you in this room, and I wanted you to see it.'

'But what *is* it?' Her eyes flew wide.

'The builders working on repairing the chimney caused part of it to collapse. They found this in the rubble. It had been built into a cavity in the brickwork. Are you going to open it?'

Cassandra knelt and gripped the iron hasp between her fingers. The rusty hinges creaked as she raised the lid, releasing the faint scent of sandalwood.

The glitter of gold, threaded through with rubies, sapphires and emeralds, gleamed against the dark wood. Ropes of lustrous pearls lay in thick coils among the jewels. A coronet of diamonds rested on a velvet cushion.

'This is what my father and grandfather *really* wanted. They had scant interest in a failing hotel, but a lot of interest in the rumour, which persisted down the centuries, of the Chevalier treasure my escaping ancestors had brought with them from France in 1789.' He shook his head. 'Generations of people have searched for it. Most people had discounted it as a legend, as I think you had. At auction, the contents of this old chest will more than replenish your trust fund. You'll be free to do exactly as you please.'

'Dance in the sea...?'

He nodded.

'Fasten my hair with a pencil?'

'Of course.' His voice was quiet. 'If that's what you want.'

'But, Matt, there's only one thing I want.'

He raised an eyebrow at her. 'Which is?'

'I want to be with you,' she said. 'I want to be able to love you without restraint, and I want you to love me back.'

He knelt beside her and pulled her close, flattening his

hands over her shoulder blades, smoothing his palms down her back.

'That's what I want, too,' he said, his voice muffled against her hair. 'But there's one thing in there that I'd like you to keep.' His tone became grave. 'If you want it.'

He closed his fingers around something in the box and then opened his hand. The amethyst in the ring that lay in his palm sparkled with gentian fire. Diamonds surrounded the purple gem, creating a rainbow halo of light.

She drew in a long, long breath. 'It's the most exquisite, beautiful thing. It's so delicate yet its light shines so brightly.'

'It reminds me of you,' he murmured. 'Delicate, yet your light shines strong and true. And you're the most beautiful thing I've ever seen.' He dipped his head to rest his forehead against hers. 'You've shown me the importance of honesty and trust and that I'm capable of loving you so deeply that I know I'll never, ever stop.' She turned her head and rested a cheek against his chest. His heartbeat was as steadfast as his embrace. 'We'll be together, whatever the future holds,' he said, 'starting tonight.'

'Oh, Matt. I'm afraid I have to leave. I'm getting the train back to London. All the rooms here are booked for tonight.'

He nodded. 'Yes,' he said, 'they are. And one of the master suites happens to be in my name.' He gripped her hand in his. 'Let me show you.'

* * * * *

COMING SOON!

We really hope you enjoyed reading this book. If you're looking for more romance be sure to head to the shops when new books are available on

Thursday 11th May

MILLS & BOON

MILLS & BOON®

Coming next month

SECOND CHANCE HAWAIIAN HONEYMOON
Cara Colter

It was full seconds since she had spoken, but suddenly he registered her voice.

Something clicked.

No.

It. Was. Not. Possible.

It was just because he had been thinking about her when all this happened. It was just because it should have been him and her, Mr. and Mrs. Blackwell, coming through that door. Would he have carried her?

Thank goodness she wasn't here. What a terrible start to a honeymoon this would have made! To be carrying her over the threshold when a stranger came at them out of the dark.

Still, with mind both roaming and focused, Joe contemplated the ancient role of warrior protector, as that scent tickled his nose again.

He knew only one person whose hair had the exotic and unusual combination of lavender and lemongrass. He opened his eyes. He let go of one wrist, flicked the brim of the cap, and her face came out of the shadow.

She managed to stop her momentum midswing, which was good because she obviously fully intended to hit him with that freed hand.

They stared at each other, completely shocked.

Completely frozen.

"Blossom."

Really? A man should not say a woman's name like that. Especially a woman who had just attacked him. Especially a woman who had basically left him at the altar. Especially a woman who had challenged every single thing he thought he knew about love.

A man should not say her name as if it was a blessing that had been bestowed upon him, a blessing that turned a world black-and-white back to color.

"Joe."

A man had to remember who had turned that world black-and-white in the first place.

So he stripped the tenderness from his voice, hoping in her shock, with her adrenaline running on high, that she had not heard what he so did not want her to hear.

"What the hell are you doing here?" he growled, letting go of her wrists.

She scrambled off him, stood up and took off her baseball cap. Her hair, which she had rarely worn loose in the course of their relationship, cascaded over slender shoulders in a luxurious, shiny dark wave.

Joe extinguished the unexpected longing of having her familiar curves pressed against him, that the simple cascade of her hair falling over her shoulder caused in him. Too easy to imagine his fingers combing through it.

Slowly, he found his feet and stood glaring down at his ex-fiancé, Blossom DuPont.

"What are you doing here?" she shot back at him.

Continue reading
SECOND CHANCE HAWAIIAN HONEYMOON
Cara Colter

Available next month
www.millsandboon.co.uk

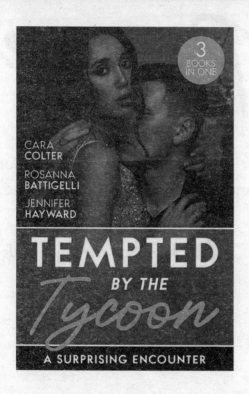

MILLS & BOON

THE HEART OF ROMANCE

A ROMANCE FOR EVERY READER

MODERN
Prepare to be swept off your feet by sophisticated, sexy and seductive heroes, in some of the world's most glamourous and romantic locations, where power and passion collide.

HISTORICAL
Escape with historical heroes from time gone by. Whether your passion is for wicked Regency Rakes, muscled Vikings or rugged Highlanders, awaken the romance of the past.

MEDICAL
Set your pulse racing with dedicated, delectable doctors in the high-pressure world of medicine, where emotions run high and passion, comfort and love are the best medicine.

True Love
Celebrate true love with tender stories of heartfelt romance, from the rush of falling in love to the joy a new baby can bring, and a focus on the emotional heart of a relationship.

Desire
Indulge in secrets and scandal, intense drama and sizzling hot action with heroes who have it all: wealth, status, good looks…everything but the right woman.

HEROES
The excitement of a gripping thriller, with intense romance at its heart. Resourceful, true-to-life women and strong, fearless men face danger and desire - a killer combination!

To see which titles are coming soon, please visit

millsandboon.co.uk/nextmonth

GET YOUR ROMANCE FIX!

Get the latest romance news, exclusive author interviews, story extracts and much more!